I0661791

DEADLY GAMES

TOM BALE

Boldwood

First published in Great Britain in 2025 by Boldwood Books Ltd.

Copyright © Tom Bale, 2025

Cover Design by Tom Sanderson

Cover Images: Shutterstock

The moral right of Tom Bale to be identified as the author of this work has been asserted in accordance with the Copyright, Designs and Patents Act 1988.

All rights reserved. No part of this book may be reproduced in any form or by any electronic or mechanical means, including information storage and retrieval systems, without written permission from the author, except for the use of brief quotations in a book review. This book is a work of fiction and, except in the case of historical fact, any resemblance to actual persons, living or dead, is purely coincidental.

Every effort has been made to obtain the necessary permissions with reference to copyright material, both illustrative and quoted. We apologise for any omissions in this respect and will be pleased to make the appropriate acknowledgements in any future edition.

A CIP catalogue record for this book is available from the British Library.

Paperback ISBN 978-1-80656-078-3

Large Print ISBN 978-1-80656-074-5

Hardback ISBN 978-1-80656-068-4

Trade Paperback ISBN 978-1-80656-069-1

Ebook ISBN 978-1-80656-075-2

Kindle ISBN 978-1-80656-073-8

Audio CD ISBN 978-1-80656-070-7

MP3 CD ISBN 978-1-80656-072-1

Digital audio download ISBN 978-1-80656-071-4

This book is printed on certified sustainable paper. Boldwood Books is dedicated to putting sustainability at the heart of our business. For more information please visit https://www.boldwoodbooks.com/about-us/sustainability/

Boldwood Books Ltd, 23 Bowerdean Street, London, SW6 3TN

www.boldwoodbooks.com

To my mum, Ann Harrison, and in memory of my dad, John Harrison, 1938–2023

1

An inquest is nothing like a trial.

I had imagined it as a hallowed occasion. Not everyone would care, of course, but there should have been a common interest in learning the truth about how and why he was taken from us.

The setting was a modern municipal building. There were people I couldn't identify – reporters, probably, and perhaps a few stray members of the public with nowhere better to be. The whole thing took less than two hours, and for most of that time I could hear a bluebottle buzzing furiously inside one of the light fittings. Its frustration had nothing on mine.

There was deference to the coroner, but not to the extent that would be afforded to a judge. Attend a court hearing and you sense witnesses and lawyers walking on coals, whereas these proceedings had a relaxed, unceremonious air that I might have appreciated, had I attended in any other capacity than that of a grieving father.

The statements from the police officers and the doctor went unopposed. We had instructed a solicitor to question the vital witnesses, Nathan Webb and three of his young friends, but they would not deviate from a word of their hazy, intoxicated (and yet extraordinarily similar) recollection of the events of that night.

I was sitting slightly adjacent to Webb, ten or eleven feet away. Close enough to lunge and strike before anyone could stop me. Close enough to spot the smirk that adorned his face when our solicitor threw in the towel. After that it was a swift downhill run to the verdict, as unstoppable by that stage as an avalanche.

Misadventure, the coroner solemnly declared.

Misadventure, she regretfully intoned.

Misadventure, by fair means or foul. Misadventure, I do declare!

Possibly my sanity went for a stroll around the block, because I came perilously close to an eruption of manic laughter. The room filled with white noise while in my head I could hear that word – that verdict – in all manner of shades and tones and contexts, but none that made sense of its essential meaning. The bluebottle probably understood it better.

The coroner concluded by extending her deepest condolences to Freddie's family and friends. 'I do appreciate how incredibly painful this is. I'd like to express my admiration for your courage and forbearance throughout this process.'

Perhaps she delivered a version of the same message to all the poor souls who came to sit red-eyed and broken-hearted before her, but nevertheless I had no doubt it was meant sincerely. I smiled in acknowledgement of the comfort she intended to convey, then I checked on Nathan Webb's smirk and it was absent. Even a man like that knew when to idle in neutral.

Today was my first proper look at him. I'd waited, raging impotently, for hours outside the police station while he was being questioned, but caught only a single glimpse. He was a tall, slender man who exuded an air of physicality as well as psychological strength. He was forty, I knew that from the newspaper reports, but he could have passed for five years younger. He had luxurious brown hair, naturally tanned skin, dark eyes, good teeth. He wore a flashy watch with a platinum dial, and a thick platinum band on his wedding finger.

He was smartly dressed, though I didn't care for the white sneakers with his navy blue suit. For most of the inquest he had assumed a posture that was, to my mind, inappropriately languid. In a Crown Court, I told myself, he would have felt overawed by the occasion. Pressured by the great weight of justice to tell the whole truth, and nothing but. Whereas this dusty shrine to small town bureaucracy felt more suited to the awarding of a catering contract, the approval of a new dropped kerb. A place of *motions for the going through, Madam Chair*, not a diamond hard study of the violent death of a teenager who should have had a whole life still to be lived and cherished and shared by all who loved him.

By us.

Did we get the truth? Not even close, in my view. But I learned something important, just the same. I discovered that I had it in me to wish death on another human being.

And I vowed to myself that I would kill Nathan Webb.

* * *

Once it was over, Webb couldn't wait to leave and neither could we. It wasn't like the funeral, after which there had been a wonderful gathering (at least we had striven to take only the wonderful from it) where many of his friends from sixth form college had come together to celebrate Freddie's life.

Throughout that afternoon I had been energised, comforted, even inspired by the warmth and generosity of the young people who were proud to have called my son a friend. But I remember how, upon waking the next morning, the enormity of his loss felt yet more achingly profound, inarguable, *unbearable* than ever.

Because Freddie was gone, and now that we had said goodbye there was nothing else. Nothing except to find out *why* this tragedy had occurred – and after today's ritual nonsense, we had been denied even that small solace. I could tell as much from the slightly evasive manner of our solicitor, who would no doubt chalk this up as a somewhat unsatisfactory outcome, albeit one where his fee would be paid on time and in full.

Prior to the inquest, we'd been told that as 'interested persons' – i.e. parents – Anita and I would have the right to question the witnesses ourselves, if we wished. After long deliberation, we had elected to instruct a solicitor to act on our behalf. We both feared becoming too emotional in the heat of the moment, when getting to the truth surely called for a cool, dispassionate approach.

Now I had to wonder if that had been an error. Perhaps I could have riled one of the young people into an admission that this hadn't been mere 'high spirits', or 'the kind of stuff you do when you're drunk'.

But I would probably never know. The official process was complete. Error or not, Anita and I had to live with our decision.

As we filed out of the building I noticed a pale grey Jaguar gliding to the kerb where Nathan Webb was standing. The driver was female but I couldn't see much more than a sweep of golden hair: his wife, presumably. Webb slipped inside and the car was drawing away before he had closed the door. He didn't look back.

On the pavement we formed an awkward huddle. The whole painful performance – but especially the verdict – hung heavy on us all. Office workers anxious to make the most of their lunch breaks huffed and glared as they negotiated the cluster of milling, useless bodies; on any other day I might have been one of them.

Our daughter Jody was first to leave. She'd come alone because her boyfriend Luke had a lot of work on at the moment, and he was also worried about leaving Trill, their Yorkshire terrier. 'Two excuses for the price of one,' her older brother Adam had murmured when we converged in the car park this morning.

Now he shook his head at her departing form, his eyes glistening as he made an attempt at humour: 'All that fussing over a small dog. Who's the gay couple around here?'

'Cultural appropriation,' added his husband, Jay, but the words came out thick with emotion.

'We each deal with this in our own way,' I reminded Adam. 'And to be fair to your sister, it's a long drive to Devizes.'

'It's quite a long drive to Borehamwood,' he countered, 'and far worse traffic.'

Anita clicked her tongue, while handing our eldest son a tissue. As he wiped his eyes, she said, 'Don't make everything a competition. We're grateful you came. All of you.'

I echoed her sentiments, and tried not to dwell on the fact that both Adam and Jody had preferred Freddie to one another. He had been the cartilage between two bones which now would scrape painfully together.

We hugged the boys at their car and then walked to our own. Anita got into the passenger seat but I lingered a moment, absorbing the simple fact that the world hadn't stopped in its tracks. The sun still shone. The dratted seagulls still dived and screeched. Trucks and vans still rumbled past, belching poison in the name of commerce.

And our son, our precious youngest child was still dead, taken from us, and this morning had provided the official confirmation that nobody would pay.

It was up to me now.

I climbed in, and we were halfway home when it struck me that Anita hadn't tried to persuade anyone to come back for refreshments.

I suspected this didn't bode well, and I was right.

2

_____

'I think it's time we made the break.'

'*Now*?'

'It's doing us no good, Harry, stumbling along. And we did say, once this was over...'

'But where would you go? Is Gareth...?'

'He said I can move in any time.'

'I see. Well, that's... decent of him.'

This was a shock, I couldn't deny it. Even the things you fully expect can come as a shock when they finally happen. Perhaps the main difficulty I had was in her suggestion that this – the search for the truth about Freddie's death – was over.

I placed my palms against my cheeks and pressed hard, not caring if it caused my lips to bulge into a grotesque pout. I'd made all my children laugh helplessly with this face, back in the days when helpless laughter could be achieved by no more than gurning, or some spluttering fart noises.

Anita was resting against the kitchen worktop. Although the kettle had boiled, neither of us made any move to pour hot water into the waiting mugs.

'I don't suppose it's worth asking if that's what you really want?' I said.

She shook her head, as if trying to dislodge the pity that was evident in her expression. 'It definitely is.'

In a bid to be equally decisive, I moved towards the kettle. Anita shifted to make room, and said, 'You're just not here for me, Harry. Not in the way I need.'

'But Gareth works longer hours than I do. He lives and breathes the business.'

'Yes. And I daresay that's something I'll have to adjust to. But at least, when he's with me, he'll be *truly* with me. You're not.'

I added an unhealthy dose of sugar to my tea, and tapped the spoon twice on the rim of the mug. 'Then where am I?'

She answered with a sad sigh. 'I don't know, Harry. Where are you?'

I suppose she had a valid point. My dad used to say it to my mum all the time: 'Lives in his own head, that's what's wrong with Harry.' It was somewhat hurtful, particularly as Mum might only have grumbled about some minor task that I'd neglected to complete. She hadn't actually posed the question: *What is wrong with our son?*

My kids had said it, too, commiserating with their mother when someone mentioned an upcoming event of which I claimed no knowledge. I became accustomed to responses along the lines of:

'Oh God, Dad, you've known about this for, like, *ages*.'

'You asked who else was going, remember?'

'You literally promised to be there, Dad.'

I would always apologise, and I think the family understood my failings were never malicious, or intentionally disrespectful – and thankfully I was still young enough that nobody suspected some form of creeping dementia. Anita knew I'd been like it even when we started going out, when I was just nineteen and she was twenty. I'd once heard her explaining it to our youngest child: 'You have to understand, Daddy's often in a world of his own.'

'Can I go with him?' the toddler Freddie had asked.

'Not really. It's in here.' Anita had tapped her forefinger against my temple. 'A world of his imagination.'

'I still want to go,' Freddie said, and then I had stepped in.

'You can do that any time. It's all about pretending. Make-believe.'

Flashback: walking Freddie home from infant school when he declared his intention to fly. 'I'll be Superman, you can be Batman. Can he fly?'

'Er... no. He tends to swing on ropes, or wires.'

'Like Spiderman, with his web?'

'That's right.'

'Okay. Let's both be Superman and fly.'

So we did: running zooming swooping giddily along the street, each of us with one clenched fist thrust out in the classic pose, our coats flapping like cumbersome pocket-laden capes, other parents sidestepping our flight paths with indulgent smiles.

A vivid mindset is nothing unusual in a child, but I suppose mine was particularly well developed. Even as an adolescent I would routinely picture the effects of a thousand-foot tsunami as I stood on the cliffs above my home town, or reel back from a mighty pterodactyl, battling with a squadron of World War Two Spitfires in the skies overhead. On a walk along the high street I could turn and grin at how deftly a mischievous baby dragon darted out of sight, or pay wary respect to the blank-faced robot armies who posed so convincingly as shop mannequins.

Gradually I became aware that most people grew out of such fantastical behaviour, their inner vision 'corrected' to see only what was expected to be there. But I couldn't stop it if I wanted to, and after graduating with a 2:1 in Art and Design from Goldsmiths, I managed to get a job with a West End theatre company as a props assistant. Every day I worked among – and constructed – buildings and vehicles and landscapes that weren't actually there.

A couple of years later I progressed to a set builders based in London, but with lots of travel to studios and location shoots. It was an exciting, rewarding role, though never remotely glamorous in the way many people imagine – and it certainly wasn't a suitable lifestyle for the father of a young family. When Adam was two and Anita was pregnant with Jody, we decided to move back to the South Coast. There I joined Gareth Walcott and his wife Melanie at their new company, Melgar Creations, and I'd been there ever since. Twenty-five years and counting.

Melgar made props, models, masks and costumes, as well as large scale sets and art installations. In recent years we'd worked with museums and heritage organisations to produce replica artworks for special displays or marketing events. And we had a side-line in giftware for the tourist industry. Ever dragged the kids to a stately home or castle and tried to pacify them with a treat from the gift shop? Well, Melgar might have designed the little knight in armour, or the Saxon-style wooden sword.

For decades my propensity for daydreaming helped put bread on the table, but it had come at a cost I'd failed to appreciate in time. Unlike Gareth, I hadn't been as adept at leaving my imagination at the door when I got home from work.

Now, I decided, things would have to change. Time to snap out of the old habits and form a sharper, more dynamic persona. Not in the hope of getting Anita back: that would be a futile pursuit, as she had made clear. This was purely about myself.

I had to be sharper and more dynamic if I was to get away with murder.

3

The premises of Melgar Creations were a pleasant fifteen-minute walk from my home. The building was one of five nondescript cubes on a 1980s industrial park, constructed on the playing fields of what had once been a private school of modest reputation. The school buildings had long been supplanted by countless boxy homes with postage stamp gardens and inadequate parking. A new road meandered through the estate, pausing at a mini-roundabout which fed into our little hive of modern industry before descending through a mix of residential and retail until it met the seafront.

Traversing the plateau where the offspring of respectable Edwardian merchants had once run the hundred-yard dash, I was afforded regular glimpses of the sea between the apartment blocks that flanked the coast road. Today the sun was sparkling on a body of water as still and shiny as resin. Far out at sea, a congregation of gulls threw back their plaintive cries, a single echoing note that was somewhat more palatable than the rooftop cacophony that woke me repeatedly between sunrise and the bleep of my alarm.

We had risen together this morning, Anita and I, for the last time. We had breakfasted together, almost shyly, at the small kitchen table. After donating a surplus segment of her toast, my ex-wife-to-be brushed a crumb from the corner of my mouth and said, with a smile, 'Marmalade.'

'Marmalade to you, too.'

Yesterday afternoon I had helped her to pack, and we'd had the rather trying experience of informing our children. At one stage Anita had slipped away to speak to Gareth on the phone, returning with the news that she would be moving out tomorrow rather than immediately. I didn't ask whether that was her idea or Gareth's; I suspected the latter, and for my sake rather than his. Of course I couldn't rule out that Gareth wished to savour one more evening as a bachelor, though it would have been impolite to ask.

As for our final night together (neither of us quipped about a 'last supper') Anita and I had a pleasant but unexciting risotto. There had been talk of a takeaway, but after the twin traumas of the inquest and our attempts to talk to Adam and Jody about the separation, neither of us had much of an appetite.

We had hardly discussed the verdict. 'What is there to say?' Anita had asked, and of course in a sense she was right. *Nothing*, I wanted to reply. Nothing, and yet everything.

I had also attempted to probe the source of her dissatisfaction with her life. Notwithstanding her undoubted feelings for Gareth, was there anything else, aside from my introspection?

'This place doesn't help.' A disparaging gesture at the four walls around us. 'I'm too young for a bungalow.'

I found this confusing. When we had downsized five years ago, it was because only Freddie was still living with us, and our older children were keen to get on the property ladder. The appeal of the bungalow was its proximity to the coast, and the sale of our larger home left excess capital that we could divide between our children to go towards the deposits for places of their own. The fear of being unable to negotiate the stairs in our dotage had never been a factor.

'It's like a constant reminder of what's to come,' Anita said when I made that point. 'Do you realise that if either of us needed a Zimmer frame, we wouldn't have to make a single modification to this place? I could be a little old lady, shuffling from the bedroom to the kitchen?'

'But we don't need Zimmer frames, and you're not a little old lady. You look incredible for your age – everyone says so.'

The compliment, by no means an afterthought, was dismissed as irrelevant to her inner conviction. What Anita meant was that, at fifty-three, she feared the creeping advance of age, and since I was only a year behind her, I knew exactly how unnerving it could be.

In any case, she had made her choice, and in some ways I couldn't fault her preference. Anita had once summed up our friend's appearance by saying, 'Gareth's like a more rugged version of you.'

It wasn't intended to hurt me in any way. She was a plain-speaking woman, and had always possessed a clear, perceptive eye. Both were qualities I appreciated.

* * *

I couldn't deny a certain apprehension as I entered the building this morning. As usual, I stuck my head into the workshop and raised a hand in greeting to my colleagues, then opened the second door to my right and entered the office. Gareth was in his customary position, hunched over and stabbing at his computer keyboard, all but hidden by the two giant Dell 4K monitors that he used for high-end design work.

Gareth's desk was the largest of four in a room that had grown ever more cluttered over the years. My desk faced his, diagonally; the one opposite mine had once been Mel's but now belonged to Robyn, who was responsible for administrative and HR issues. She was employed part-time, and as a mother of three and a put-upon carer for an elderly parent, she increasingly worked from home.

The desk opposite Gareth's was home to piles of paper – memos, reports, journals, schematics – as well as all manner of junk which we regarded as viable spare parts or incomplete prototypes. Neither of us was very good at throwing anything away, which was a perfectly logical approach in an industry where some of the most effective props were constructed from everyday materials, waste products, detritus.

This was another of my tendencies that could drive Anita to distraction. Fortunately, in stark contrast to his office, Gareth maintained a scrupulously tidy home, and since the death of his wife a little over three years ago, his taste in decor had become increasingly minimalist.

Was it my imagination, or did I sense a measure of reluctance to look up and greet me? I was mindful of the potential for the new living arrangement to place a strain on our working relationship, and I was committed to doing whatever was necessary to avoid that.

It wasn't that I didn't love Anita, and I certainly regretted her departure. But having been blessed with a (mostly) rational temperament, I had a tendency to appreciate both sides of an argument, and I had never believed in adopting a position simply because it was the one most people expected.

To put it even more simply, I loved my job. I loved Gareth like a brother. Most of all, after losing Freddie so senselessly, I wanted to see happiness flourish wherever it could.

'Morning!'

Gareth's nod in response had a decidedly sheepish air. His gaze was loaded with sorrow when I asked how yesterday had gone. Both Anita and I had insisted that he hadn't needed to attend the inquest, especially as he'd been scheduled to meet an influential producer in Soho, with a significant contract at stake.

'Cancelled at the last minute,' Gareth reported. 'Though he insists we're still good for the contract. Anyway, that's irrelevant compared to... what you guys had to do.'

Suddenly I found it impossible to speak. I sat down and brought my own computer to life with a waggle of the mouse.

Resurrection, I thought. As simple as that.

Gareth abruptly said, 'Misadventure – what does that even mean?'

Taking it as a rhetorical question, I sat back in my chair, then realised I was holding my breath. I released it as though freeing a hostage in fragile health.

'Anything else was always a long shot,' I said. 'Our solicitor did warn us.'

'Even so.' Gareth thrust himself to his feet and asked if I wanted coffee. I didn't, but nodded anyway.

He moved to the corner of the room. We had our own filter coffee machine, a needless luxury given that there was a rest room with a kitchenette right next door. But Gareth, even at the age of fifty-eight, was still inclined to work the occasional all-nighter, sustained by jug after jug of blended Arabica.

Gareth was mixed race, the son of a Caribbean-born welder and a Brummie nurse. At six one he was a couple of inches taller than me, as well as broader and thicker, not just in the torso but in his arms, his legs. He had a rugby player's physique – an ex-rugby player, anyway – while I was more of an ex-footballer. His hair was a darker shade of brown than my own, and close cropped whereas mine was almost long enough to be described as 'tousled'. We both took an immature pride in the relative lack of grey that had so far appeared.

His features were slightly bolder, I would have said, and his eyes a rich dark brown, while mine were almost hazel. His stubble grew so rapidly that he almost always had the beginnings of a beard. Anita thought his five o'clock shadow was irresistibly sexy, whereas mine just looked scruffy. He was Denzel, I was a hobo.

I thanked him for the coffee, and when he perched on the corner of the vacant desk I knew I wouldn't be getting straight down to work.

'We all okay, about... Neet's decision?'

'Of course.'

'Took me by surprise, I gotta say.'

'You hadn't discussed it?'

He squirmed a little. 'Well, yeah. As a possibility.' Gareth took a rapid slurp of coffee and dripped some on his shirt. 'Don't know if it's the best timing, though.'

'For you?'

'Christ, no. I'd have been happy whenever, depending on you two...'

'No point delaying the inevitable.'

'Fair enough. I just... I really appreciate the stance you've taken, Harry. Especially at a time like this.'

'It's fine. I wouldn't want anything to change how we work.'

'Me neither, bloody hell!'

Gareth returned to his desk, content to leave it there, which was what I thought I wanted. And yet, as he sat down, I heard myself saying, 'I saw Nathan Webb, of course.'

'That scumbag.' Gareth's hostility was genuine: he'd dearly loved Freddie – he loved all the children – and had long been regarded as one of the family.

'It was how confident he looked, how smug. Breezing out of the room without a care in the world. I felt like... like I could kill him with my bare hands.'

'It's what he deserves.'

'And it hasn't gone away. I woke up this morning every bit as determined.'

Gareth nodded. 'Don't blame you, bro.'

Encouraged, I held his gaze. 'So I might have to do it.'

The nodding ceased. 'Do what?'

'Kill him.'

'But...' Gareth's brow creased. 'You can't.'

'You just said it's what he deserves.'

'Yeah, because I thought you meant figuratively. But, you know, we're a country of laws. Due process.'

'Except the law failed. "Misadventure". Nathan walked free – never even got charged with anything.'

'I know, mate. It's a bloody disgrace. But taking it into your own hands, that's more what you'd expect in... well, Sicily or somewhere. Blood feuds. It doesn't happen here.'

For discretion's sake, I fixed an expression that mirrored my friend's wry amusement. But inside I was thinking: *Well maybe it should.*

4

I left work at about ten to six. It was a marvellously warm evening, and since I knew I would be returning to an empty home, it was my intention to dawdle rather than sprint. But I hadn't reckoned with my overactive imagination.

It was a peculiar moment, because I didn't set out to create a fantasy. It was more that I happened to glance down and somehow he was there beside me: five-year-old Freddie, resuming the conversation from that walk home, all those years ago.

'Why can Superman fly, but not Batman or Spiderman?'

'It's, um... they have different abilities. Different super powers.'

'Will I be able to fly, when I'm older?'

'Mmm... not really. I'm afraid Superman, and the other superheroes, aren't... well, it's only in stories that people can fly.'

'Oh.'

'Sorry, Fred.'

'But we can still try, can't we?'

'Yes. I suppose we can.'

And so it was that I ran and dived and swooped along the pavement for about fifty yards, one arm thrust forward in the classic pose, in the course of which I was passed by a number of motorists and several pedestrians, including a man of my own age who stared at me with undisguised horror.

I knew Freddie wasn't *actually* beside me. I knew I was only imagining it, but that was okay. It just felt so good to hear his gasps of laughter as we ran. He didn't have a care in the world, and for those few seconds neither did I.

It meant I was agreeably short of breath when I unlocked the front door. The house was tremendously still, but I had prepared for this moment and quickly unfurled a metaphorical umbrella against any sudden deluge of self-pity.

Anita had moved out, though at this stage she'd only been able to take what she would need in the immediate future. Consequently the place looked partially ransacked, as if by a fair-minded burglar who'd made sure to leave a little of everything.

Rather than succumbing to alcohol, I made a pot of tea, then settled for a tuna sandwich instead of cooking for myself. I vowed that this wouldn't become a habit; I wasn't a bad cook, although my tendency to get distracted meant it was safer to have somebody else present while things boiled, baked or grilled.

This evening I was still preoccupied with Freddie's sudden appearance at my side. Every time I thought of him, it was like firing a pinball that proceeded to ricochet from memory to memory before settling into a slot marked Grief, Pain, or Loss.

There was just no way to recall him without also confronting the dreadful reality that he was gone.

* * *

Nathan Webb's residence was located to the north west of the town centre, at an elevation that offered spectacular sea views as well as looking west towards the majestic South Downs. By car it was about ten minutes away, though I didn't actually have a car. We'd agreed that Anita would take our Mazda CX-5, since her work as a self-employed accountant required her to visit clients all over Kent and East Sussex.

The walk entailed a steep uphill climb. In deference to the warm weather I dressed in shorts and a T-shirt, and for the added health benefits I route marched most of the way. I kept reminding myself of the need to take the utmost care. This could not be anything more than a swift reconnaissance mission.

I'd already done some homework, courtesy of Google Maps. Webb's home was a vast modern property in an architectural style that might be termed 'Grand Designs Predictable': a two-storey flat-roofed cube with white rendered walls and acres of glass. Featureless on the outside, but no doubt boasting a magnificent open-plan interior.

By the time I reached Gimlet Lane, my shins and calves were protesting and I could feel sweat trickling down my spine. The hiss of sprinklers was a cruel reminder that I'd failed to bring any water. I stopped to rest, lifting the front of my T-shirt to mop my face. As I lowered it, I noticed an elderly couple sitting in the garden of the corner property, champagne glasses in hand, who studied me with a genteel hostility until I resumed my walk.

I was only seconds from Webb's home when a Mercedes glided past and swung into a driveway next door to my target's address. A man in his thirties hopped out, glanced in my direction and said, 'Evening?' in a tone so surly that he was really saying: *Belong here, do you?*

'Evening!' I responded cheerfully, as if to reply: *Yes I do, thanks!*

Then I reached Webb's perimeter wall. Either I hadn't noticed it properly on Street View, or else the camera's perspective had made it appear lower than it was. I wouldn't be able to see anything on this side of the street, but feared that abruptly crossing the road might attract attention.

I tried my best to saunter, still immersed in method acting: *I live locally, I'm taking a perfectly legitimate stroll on a fine summer's evening.* The outside wall was interrupted by a set of timber gates; through the bars I glimpsed a wide driveway that curved towards an integrated triple garage. Above that, several windows were ablaze with the reflection of the setting sun, though in one of them a woman stood close to the glass, gazing out to sea. From the golden tresses, I concluded it was the same individual who had collected him from the inquest.

I knew almost nothing about Webb's private life. Even the media, when they reported on the investigation into Freddie's death, had produced very little information. I'd seen one or two snatched photographs of Webb himself, but none of his wife or any other family he might have had.

Once I was past the house I pulled out my phone and pretended to be reading as I ambled across the road, before casually turning to look back.

The woman, perfectly framed in the window, was a portrait of sadness in charcoal shading, her hair the only vivid colour. There was some sort of braiding in amongst the loose strands, and the combination of that style and her ethereal grace put me in mind of a fairy-tale princess, imprisoned in a tower.

She must have sensed my gaze, for she turned to stare in my direction as I spun, somewhat clumsily, and marched away.

What an excellent start! I thought sarcastically. Perhaps next time I should go one step further and put a threatening note through their letterbox, complete with my name and address.

5

On Saturday morning I woke to a text from Anita, inviting me to join them for dinner at Gareth's apartment this evening.

It prompted an image of my wife and my boss – I chose to visualise them at breakfast, rather than entwined in a post-coital glow – debating what to do about me:

'It's his first weekend on his own.'

'Yes. And it's our first weekend together.'

'So we should be magnanimous, and ask him to join us.'

'He probably won't want to. He'll be fine.'

'I don't like to think of him alone. He's not much of a chef.'

'There's takeaways galore, practically on his doorstep.'

'But he's dealt with this so maturely. Let's make sure we maintain the goodwill.'

'Oh, all right. Will you text him, or shall I do it?'

I toyed with different permutations of this exchange and realised I couldn't decide which of them was saying what. But I decided it would be churlish to decline, so I messaged back:

Sounds great!

As I got up, I heard the familiar clump of a seagull marching across the roof. I imagined its displeasure at having failed to prevent my lie-in, though of course I had lain awake for nearly an hour around dawn, wishing I had a shotgun to put a stop to the racket.

Wishing I had a shotgun for other purposes, too. In the small hours it was easy to indulge my fantasies of violent retribution against Nathan Webb. A Tarantino-style showdown incorporating blistering truths and noisy blood-shed, then satisfying closure.

*　　*　　*

The reality would be starkly different. I had to keep that in mind and proceed with the utmost care. I had read of trials where the accused's search history had condemned them to a life sentence: What's the best method for killing someone? How do I get away with murder?

Cover your tracks from the start, that would be the best advice – notwithstanding that I had used Google Maps to examine Nathan Webb's property. And after Gareth's reaction on Thursday, I decided to say nothing more about my desire for revenge – to him or anyone else. But I did intend to conduct another reconnaissance mission.

The weather was still blisteringly hot. This time I prepared a backpack with a bottle of water, a spare T-shirt and some sun cream. I also packed a towel and swimming shorts, intending to hit the beach afterwards. I walked a little more slowly this morning, and as a consequence I almost missed him.

I was climbing the final ascent to Gimlet Lane when I saw the grey Jaguar coming my way. I froze in shock but fortunately the car took a right turn, Nathan Webb briefly visible at the wheel. I quickly backtracked to the junction I'd just crossed. As I trotted downhill the Jaguar passed me, a couple of hundred yards away. His destination had to be either the seafront or the central shopping area.

I decided to follow in the hope of spotting his car once he'd parked. Establishing Webb's routine could be of real value to me.

It took me ten minutes to reach the outskirts of the main retail district. The Jaguar had long been lost from sight. I was more or less resolved to having a swim, and perhaps a wander back to Gimlet Lane this afternoon.

Then I reached the corner of Barkers Way, a long crescent-shaped street that sat one tier up from the high street and was home to several of the town's most historic buildings. It was a street I had taken pains to avoid in recent months. I cursed myself for not having thought of it sooner.

* * *

Aside from the day we learned of Freddie's death, perhaps the worst moment came some eight weeks later, when the detective leading the investigation sat down with Anita and me, and gravely informed us that he – and more crucially, the Crown Prosecution Service – saw no realistic prospect of bringing charges against Nathan Webb or anyone else who was present when Freddie died.

We pressed him on that decision – quite forcefully in my case. I suppose it reflected poorly on me that I lost my temper. I would maintain that it was an understandable reaction in the circumstances, and Detective Inspector Dan Hawkins, a pale, red-haired man with the demeanour of an IT developer, graciously said as much once Anita had calmed me down.

The circumstances were murky, I accepted that. Freddie had died in the Tannery, a once grand Victorian construction at the eastern end of Barkers Way. Built of red brick, it was four storeys high and had been in a dilapidated state for decades. It sat on a large patch of waste ground, the two adjacent buildings having been demolished after a fire in 2001.

The entire site was owned by Nathan Webb, which meant he and the other participants couldn't even be accused of trespassing. The building had once been a magnet for down-and-outs, but after two homeless men were found dead from a heroin overdose Webb had taken steps to improve security, pending the success of his application for redevelopment.

What the police discovered was that the building had become a favourite haunt for local youths, who gathered most weekends to drink and dance and take drugs. It transpired that Nathan Webb often joined them, though he strenuously denied any knowledge of drug-taking.

On the face of it, there was no overt criminality that night. The youths were eighteen or older. No drugs were found on the scene when the police arrived, although everyone was apparently drunk or high or both. This was at four in the morning, and of course nobody was particularly coherent. Mobile phones were surrendered, but although there was footage from earlier in the evening – which supported the witness accounts of a raucous but essentially peaceful celebration – there was nothing that could assist in explaining what had happened to Freddie.

He had fallen, or so we were told at first. The additional details took several weeks to emerge, and even then the account was far from complete.

It was regarded as a failure on the part of the constabulary's intelligence unit that they had no prior awareness of these gatherings, especially as there were long-standing suspicions that Nathan Webb was a key figure in the local drug trade. His late father had been an entrepreneur whose assets were out of all proportion to the profits generated by his legitimate business, and Nathan seemed to be following in his footsteps.

Webb senior had died some years before, in a car accident on the Costa del Sol, and as far as I could tell he had never served a day in prison in his life. Whatever crimes he might have committed, he'd got clean away with them.

I was determined his son wouldn't do the same.

* * *

Webb's Jaguar was parked with two wheels up on the pavement, next to a gate set into the high timber hoarding that protected the site. The gate was ajar, and for one heart-stopping moment I was minded to rush through it and confront Webb right there on his own territory. At the scene of the crime.

To my relief, sanity prevailed when I was just yards from the entrance. I veered away and hurried across the road, to where a line of parked cars would afford me some cover while I observed the building. As my right foot landed on the pavement, I glanced round and saw Nathan Webb striding out through the gate.

My only guiding instinct was, *He must not see me.* Dropping beside a Ford Focus, I smacked my knee against the ground and almost cried out. An agonising few seconds passed while I crouched like a sprinter on the blocks – until finally I heard the clunk of a car door, and the Jaguar roared away.

I rose, brushing gravel and a cigarette butt from my knee, and vowed to improve my surveillance techniques in future. But right now I needed a swim.

6

Ever since childhood the sea had felt like my natural home. When I swam, my movements were smooth and graceful. I never tripped or stumbled, I couldn't fidget. On land I sometimes resembled a new-born foal; in the water I was a ballet dancer – or so it seemed to me.

This season I'd been swimming for the past two months. The temperature had progressed from bearable to pleasant, and I could comfortably endure about twenty minutes before my extremities started to protest. More than enough time for my now inevitable routine: relax, reflect, sob my heart out, then swim underwater until I was so exhausted that I became incapable of further thought.

Today I went through that cycle twice, with half an hour lying on the beach in between. Then I plodded home, rejecting any thought of cruising Webb's neighbourhood.

After a quiet afternoon of chores, I showered and shaved for tonight's dinner. The incongruity of my preparation struck me as I deliberated over a selection of formal shirts. I could have been dressing for a date, though tonight's gathering was the very antithesis of that.

In truth I felt slightly apprehensive, uncertain about the kind of gathering that lay ahead. But I had to remind myself that the offer of good food was always to be welcomed, and my company for the evening remained – despite the unorthodox circumstances – my two closest friends in the world.

* * *

Gareth lived in the same general direction as Nathan Webb, west of the town centre. A year after Melanie's death he had sold their home in the town of Battle and bought a smart new duplex apartment in an area that until recently had been regarded as undesirable. Gareth had cheerfully shrugged off the risks of car thefts and muggings; a price worth paying, he said, for views of the pier and a choice of eleven pubs within a half-mile radius.

I walked slowly, so as not to perspire beneath my floral print shirt and linen blazer. I was buzzed into their building and met at the door by Anita, who already looked transformed by her decision to leave. There was a vitality about her, a spark that, I realised now, had been missing since long before Freddie's death. I felt somewhat ashamed that I was more aware of its return than its absence.

'Have you had your hair coloured?' I asked, once we'd embraced.

'Just a small enhancement,' she admitted coyly.

Gareth, drifting into the hall, heard that last word and said, 'Don't be getting plastic surgery on my behalf. I like it all real.'

Anita's frown couldn't survive Gareth's ebullient laughter, or the way he trailed his fingers across the small of her back as he moved past to greet me.

After pumping my hand as if we hadn't seen each other for weeks, he fetched me an ice cold Moretti, then made himself scarce to put the finishing touches to the meal. It seemed more like a diplomatic retreat, allowing Anita and me an opportunity to gauge how we felt about spending the evening together, particularly as I'd been shown into the smaller, second lounge. The main living space was an open-plan affair with sofas, a dining table and an integral kitchen.

'Have you been well?' Anita enquired. Again I wondered if I'd blacked out and several weeks had passed.

'Yes, thanks. Lovely swim today. You?'

'Oh, it's far too cold for me.'

'No, I mean, are you settling in?'

'Of course.' She was tense, understandably. After a sip of wine, she asked if I had any time free on Monday. 'Perhaps mid-morning?'

'I can take an early lunch. Why?'

'Now the inquest's done, we need to register the death. And I thought we should both go, don't you?'

I felt stunned. We'd discussed it briefly on Wednesday, but then I had put it out of my mind. And there was something else, which I hadn't yet decided how to broach.

'Actually, I've been looking online to see if there's scope for an appeal.'

'Appeal?'

'Against the verdict. I don't think—'

'We are *not* going to challenge the verdict, Harry. You're just...' She swallowed. 'You're making the whole thing so much more painful. We have to move on with our lives, that's what he would have wanted—'

'Freddie. It's what *Freddie* would have wanted.'

'Yes.'

'But you didn't say his name. It's like you'd prefer to forget him.'

'How dare you!' she cried. 'The *last* thing I want to do is forget him – as you're about to find out.'

I flinched at the pain in her voice, and immediately apologised. But I didn't get a chance to ask what she meant, because Gareth materialised to announce that the food was ready. If he was alert to the tension in the room, he hid it very well, though I couldn't help thinking back to the conversation I'd imagined this morning, and wondered which of them now regretted having got their way.

* * *

After this slightly rocky start, the evening rapidly improved. Gareth had cooked one of his phenomenal curries, and of course booze played its part – bottle after bottle of Rioja seemed to vanish as swiftly as it was uncorked. Our conversation ranged from Melgar projects past and future, to Anita's motley collection of clients, to the horrors of summer crowds and traffic – and finally, when we were at once safely drunk and dangerously maudlin, to the subject of Freddie.

It was past midnight. I'd reached the stage of needing to pee every ten minutes and was finding it increasingly difficult to walk straight – or, indeed, to pee straight. Out of respect for my friend's bathroom floor, I sat down on the toilet and pondered what I had just learned.

'We need to commemorate his life,' Anita had told me. 'With something lasting. Something beautiful, but also practical.'

Gareth, nodding enthusiastically, said, 'I want to contribute too, if that's all right?'

'Of course. But how?' My imagination must have been blunted by drink, because all I could picture was a bench with a plaque: a common feature on the seafront. It didn't seem an appropriate memorial for a lively teenage boy.

'That part isn't nailed down,' Gareth said. 'It's important you're in on this from the start.'

Anita gave him a half glance that I couldn't quite read. 'We've been mulling over an endowment, or scholarship. Maybe financial support for a pupil at Freddie's school to go into higher education.'

I reflected on it while I washed my hands, and returned to the living room to tell them: 'I think that's a fantastic idea. Very worthwhile.'

Perhaps Anita hadn't expected me to go along with it, for she jumped up and hugged me. 'Thanks, Harry. You do see that we can't respect Freddie's memory with negativity? It has to be positive. Future facing.'

'Absolutely. Yes.'

As we broke apart I saw Gareth looking amused. 'Good to hear it, bro. You had me worried the other day, all that stuff about murdering Nathan Webb.'

'What?' Anita turned to stare at me. 'You *were* joking?'

'Well...'

I suppose I should have been grateful when Anita dropped the horrified expression and burst out laughing. 'Kill someone? You wouldn't hurt a fly!'

I felt perversely aggrieved by her scorn. 'I've swatted flies before.'

'Spiders, then. I've seen you waste five minutes trying to trap a spider with a cup and put it outside.'

'Only because I don't like the idea of squashing them.'

Now it was Gareth's turn to honk with laughter. 'Harry Manning: arachnid liberator by day, bloodthirsty crusader by night!'

My smile was one of capitulation, but I reminded myself that this was good news. If even my wife and best friend didn't suspect I was capable of murder, I surely stood more chance of getting away with it.

I was perhaps too drunk to appreciate the downside, which wouldn't occur to me until I walked home, about twenty minutes later.

We parted on good terms. Gareth insisted I take some leftover curry: three portions in individual containers, bumping together in a Sainsbury's carrier bag. Evidently they feared that I was incapable of feeding myself.

I made for the seafront, passing one or two clusters of late-night revellers, and caught laughter and the splash of water from the beaches closest to the town centre. The idea of young people spilling out of the pubs to go skinny dipping gave me a thrill of nostalgia for my own youth. Few things can make you feel more gloriously alive and in touch with the universe than swimming at night.

I started humming the REM song on that subject as I walked or, more accurately, staggered along the promenade. I was approaching a quieter section of the seafront, the slightly shabby, tourist-focused facsimile of what had once been the town's thriving harbour, when I realised what I should have said in reply to Anita.

I'd struggle to kill a spider because I bore it no malice. What had it ever done to me?

Nathan Webb, on the other hand, had taken my son's life. You couldn't think of a better justification for violence.

At the same time, I had to accept that Anita and Gareth knew me very well. If they felt I was incapable of harming another human being, who was to say they weren't correct? Imagine if I worked myself into a position to kill Webb, only to find I was unable to go through with it?

Ideally, I needed to put myself to the test with a non-human victim. Find a way of unleashing the bloodthirsty side of my nature.

But with what?

I was still walking along the promenade when it occurred to me, the answer so obvious that I actually slapped my palm against my forehead. *D'oh!*

The ideal victim was right on my doorstep.

7

Or not doorstep, exactly. To be precise, it was my roof.

I would kill one of the damn seagulls that stamped and squawked me out of sleep every morning.

My first instinct was to build some form of trap, using spare materials from the Melgar workshop. I could even pop in and do it tomorrow – or, rather, later today.

I'd reached the point where I needed to cross the road and head uphill to my home. It was also the point where I realised that I was in desperate need of yet another piss. Grabbing the handrail, I swung myself clumsily down the steps on to the beach, the carrier bag bumping against my legs.

In the shadow of the sea wall I fumbled to unzip my jeans and enjoyed a heavenly relief, marred only by the unending nature of what poured forth. If it didn't stop soon, someone was going to find me here and I'd get arrested. I already felt as though I was being watched, though that was no doubt just my imagination—

A flash of white caught my eye, forty or fifty feet away. I had the impression of stealthy movement on the beach.

Finished at last, I zipped up and took a couple of deep breaths in the hope that it would help me feel slightly less intoxicated, just in case I was about to be robbed or threatened in some way.

Then I saw what awaited me, and I could have danced a jig. This was perfect!

* * *

Despite my excitement, I advanced carefully over the shingle. I could see the bird was nosing at something caught amid the stones. Setting the carrier bag down made a tiny rustling noise which caused the gull to turn in my direction. It seemed to examine me with hateful eyes. Perhaps it was the effect of the booze, but I felt I recognised this particular bird.

It was my winged tormentor. My roof-stomping, sleep-denying nemesis.

I took another step. A dim memory surfaced, of stories in the local paper about the legal protection afforded to seagulls. They might be commonly regarded as vermin, but it was illegal to harm them. If I went through with this, I'd be breaking the law...

And killing Nathan Webb isn't *illegal? Get on with it, pillock!*

I planted my feet and prepared to attack – only for the wretched creature to flap its wings and come straight at me. Completely unprovoked, I thought indignantly, as I felt its beak jabbing against my calf. I stumbled and fell, landing heavily on my backside, then felt another vicious bite on my leg and heard a noisy disturbance in the air above me.

More of them were swooping down – five, six, seven? – all screeching and screaming, huge wings beating the air with a force that brought to mind a helicopter's downdraft. I glimpsed one of them tearing at the carrier bag, the plastic tubs of curry spilling out, but the rest were diving straight for me. I held my hands in front of my face for protection and tried to roll over so I could climb to my feet.

The birds were in a frenzy; I felt the solid but silky texture of a wing as it brushed against my forehead; others were plucking at my jacket, biting my arms and legs. So much for a dry run. I could almost hear Anita roaring with laughter at my inability to threaten even a single seabird...

And suddenly I wasn't just drunk, or scared, or humiliated. I was *furious*. I forced myself up and lurched in a shambolic circle, thrashing my arms and occasionally striking my attackers. A particularly lucky punch drove one of the gulls on to the beach; I heard the impact as it hit the stones and then, quite suddenly, the air around me was clear.

Had I frightened them away?

In my confusion I turned and found I was now about twenty feet from the carrier bag. The cartons had burst open and the gulls were scrambling for the food – all except the bird I'd hit, which lay unmoving. Feathers were scattered over the stones, like splatters of white paint in the darkness.

The irony wasn't lost on me: I had Gareth's leftovers to thank for saving me from a bunch of bloody seagulls.

Christ Almighty. I would have to do better than this.

8

I woke at six and immediately pictured the carnage on the beach, although I couldn't recall how I had got back home or put myself to bed. But evidently I had, and I'd even taken the trouble to hang my jacket up on the door, without noticing that one of the sleeves was torn.

I felt weak, nauseous, lethargic. Creeping to the bathroom, I had to shield my eyes from the ferocious light streaming through the hall window.

I showered and brushed my teeth; these were the first of my tried and tested responses to a hangover. It would be a couple of hours before I could contemplate food, but perhaps a cup of tea and then back to bed?

I inspected my wounds and found half a dozen welts on my arms and legs from where the gulls had tried to bite me through my clothes. My torso was covered in bruises, causing me to wonder if the tussle on the beach had been more violent than I remembered it. Hadn't I killed one of the gulls?

An image of the food cartons provoked another twinge of guilt. Few things enraged me as much as seeing litter discarded on a beach, so after dressing in shorts and a T-shirt, I took some painkillers and gulped down a glass of cranberry juice. The tea would have to wait.

I found a bin bag in one of the kitchen drawers, fetched gardening gloves and a trowel from the shed, and to be on the safe side I decided to take detergent spray and some paper towels. I put everything in my backpack, then added my swimming gear and the obligatory bottle of water.

It was a morning of fresh and sparkling perfection, and as usual my heart went through some painful contortions as I wrestled with the difficulty of trying to savour the simple pleasures of life – *needing* to savour them, in the way Freddie would have wanted – while simultaneously raging at the fact that my son was no longer present to savour them himself.

I walked slowly, my head gently throbbing to the rhythm of my footsteps, my eyes narrowed against a glare that my sunglasses couldn't adequately reduce. I was at the harbourside by twenty to seven, and aside from a couple of runners in the distance there was nobody in sight...

Except for Len Bowden. He'd been hidden by the high wall that ran down the centre of the breakwater on the western flank of the harbour; to each side there was a walkway with a protective railing that offered a handy platform for anglers, seven or eight feet above the waterline.

'You're up late,' he said drily. Len was tall and wiry, with a ruddy, wind-and-sun-blasted complexion. He wore his customary wardrobe of black boots and combats, a grey hoodie and porkpie hat, and he was carrying his tackle box and rod. He possessed an inscrutable long-distance gaze and only ever spoke from the corner of his mouth, as if to open it fully was a needless extravagance.

'What time were you out there?' I asked him.

'About half four. I'm off for a full English at BB's.'

'Fantastic. Well-deserved, I'm sure.'

Perhaps I looked queasy, for he studied my face and said, 'Hungover?'

'Slightly.'

His gaze switched to my backpack. 'Swimming to clear your head?'

'Yep.'

'Madness. You need raw eggs, and a few more hours in bed.'

'I'll try that next time.'

When we first got chatting, several years ago, I had been guilty of making all kinds of assumptions based on his appearance and manner. I turned out to be completely wrong on just about every count. Len was in his late seventies but looked a decade younger. He had been a bricklayer, a college lecturer and had managed a hotel in the Philippines. He'd been married three times but was now widowed, and had five children and more than a dozen grandchildren. And despite all the hours he spent motionless at the end of the breakwater, he claimed he wasn't all that keen on fishing.

'It's just where I come to think,' he told me once. 'Or perhaps that's how I justify not catching many fish.'

As we parted, Len gestured towards the beach next to the breakwater. 'Give that one a wide margin. Someone's been scrapping with the wildlife.'

'Sounds nasty!' To my ears it was an unconvincing response, and the look he gave me only confirmed that.

Now I had to slow my pace until he was out of sight, or else it would appear that I'd refused to heed his warning. I'd always had an excessive aversion to offending people, and I realised that this was another aspect of my personality that was incompatible with my new, hard-edged character.

I'm going to kill you, Nathan Webb.

'I'd rather you didn't,' Nathan protests.

No, of course not. Perish the thought, my dear man.

* * *

The beach was a mess, Len wasn't wrong about that. The only saving grace was that there was no sign of the seagull I'd left for dead. Either it had just been stunned and later recovered, or else some other scavenger had dragged it away.

But the curry evidently hadn't been a hit with the gulls. There were great dollops of it spread over a wide area, some of it looking as though it had been consumed and then regurgitated. I could feel my gorge rising as I traipsed over the stones.

I donned my gloves and got to work. There was so little breeze that even the carrier bag still lay on the beach, albeit some distance away. I collected that first, then gathered up the plastic containers before stopping to rest and take some deep breaths. Bending over was making me light-headed, but worse than that, my frailty made me feel old and decrepit. Perhaps the days of Zimmer frames were closer than I thought.

I could hear the occasional car passing along the front, but no one had yet ventured on to the beach. The sea was flat as a pond and a perfect shade of pale blue. I was already sweating profusely and couldn't wait to swim.

I gathered up most of the feathers. A couple had what looked like blood on them, and again I wondered if I'd been more violent than I remembered. Finally I used the paper towels to mop up the largest patches of regurgitated curry. Good enough, I thought, as I trudged back to the steps with the black bag. Nobody coming here now would guess at what had gone on.

There was a bin on the promenade, not too far away. It was only when I'd climbed the steps that I saw I hadn't gone unobserved. A young woman was sitting on a bench that overlooked the beach, and although we weren't acquainted, I recognised her at once.

That long blonde hair, fashioned in a braid, was quite unmistakable.

9

I must have looked startled that it was her. But given what I'd been doing, and the fact that the seafront was virtually deserted, I hoped she wouldn't interpret it in that way.

'Sorry!' I gasped. 'Made me jump.'

'Then shouldn't I be the one to apologise?'

I grinned, and possibly went a little red. 'I suppose.'

I skirted round the bench, moving behind her. The woman was resting back, one leg crossed over the other, her hands cupped in her lap. She wore jeans and a lemon-coloured top. Her hair was a beguiling mix of shades, what I could imagine a stylist describing as honey and gold and ash. Her skin, unblemished and free of make-up, was evenly tanned.

After depositing the bag in the bin, I turned to find her regarding me with a smile. 'You shouldn't look guilty, you know.'

I tensed, only for her to indicate the beach. 'What you're doing is really public spirited. Was it a dead seagull?'

With a grateful sigh, I said, 'Just feathers and a lot of mess. I didn't want families coming down here and finding it.'

'Yeah, that would be nasty.' She turned to gaze at the sea. In profile, her features were perfectly proportioned. 'Do you like seagulls?'

'Well, I couldn't eat a whole one.'

She smiled politely, but I felt mortified. A *dad* joke? Good grief.

'I find them quite irritating,' she admitted. 'So screechy in the mornings.'

'Like a rogue alarm clock you can't shut off.'

She chuckled. 'Now that's an image. Half a dozen winged alarm clocks circling over my house.'

'A Dali painting,' I said, and while nodding, she abruptly turned serious.

'I've seen you up there, haven't I?'

I gulped – a clumsy, cartoon-like reaction.

'Sorry?' I said. 'Up where?'

'Gimlet Lane, the other evening.'

'Gimlet...' I frowned, as if searching a vast internal directory.

'Near Victoria Park. Perhaps you live over that way?'

It felt as though she was deliberately letting me off the hook. 'I do go for some long walks,' I said, 'and I'm hopeless with street names.'

Rather than challenge this weak excuse, she nodded approvingly. 'That means you're a local. I read somewhere that locals navigate by landmarks. They don't need to know the street names so they never learn them.'

'Might be something in that. I've lived here twenty-five years. How about you?'

'Only seven or eight – still a newcomer, really.' Her eyes seemed to glitter with humour. They were a delicate shade of pale blue, as pure and inviting as the sea itself. 'Before that I lived in Seaford.'

'Really? I grew up in Seaford!'

'No way!' We both seemed ridiculously excited by the coincidence, despite the fact that Seaford was barely thirty miles from here. 'How old are you?' she asked.

'Fifty-two.'

'Oh. You look younger than that.'

'Thank you. What are you – about twenty-five?'

She rolled her eyes. 'I'm thirty-six.'

I did the calculations, and chuckled. 'We weren't at school together, then.'

'Maybe I saw you walking past, while I was clinging to the fence and wishing I was anywhere else.' Her eyes darted away from me, and I had a feeling that she'd revealed too much.

'Not the best days of your life?'

She went to reply, only to hesitate, and then sigh. 'Actually, they might have been.'

I wanted to ask more, but the entire conversation was already fraught with danger, so I nodded and said, 'Well, I'd better be going for that swim.'

She made an exaggerated shivering motion. 'Bit too early for me.'

'Mid-July?'

'The time. Maybe this afternoon, when the sun's higher.'

For a moment I pictured myself cheekily asking what time I'd be seeing her, but was sure I'd look like a fool. I did manage to say, 'I'm Harry, by the way.'

'Erin. Pleased to meet you, Harry. Enjoy your swim.'

With a farewell smile, I trotted down the steps – almost tripping, because I seemed to have forgotten how to coordinate my limbs – grabbed my rucksack and walked towards the shore. I tried to look relaxed, but my mind was in turmoil. It hadn't felt at all like I'd been talking to the wife of Nathan Webb.

I despised Nathan Webb. I wanted – *intended* – to kill him. Surely I should feel almost as hostile towards the woman who had chosen to spend her life with him?

And yet, quite evidently, I didn't. Possibly because the whole encounter had been so unexpected, or that she had been friendly, likeable, normal…

Or, if I were brutally honest, wasn't it that her beauty had taken my breath away?

I strode purposefully to the shore and waded in up to my thighs before finally surrendering to the impulse to turn. Erin half rose from the bench to wave with what seemed like giddy enthusiasm. Giddy enthusiasm that caused a surge of adrenalin – I may have responded with a casual hand raise, but middle-aged male pride now demanded an Olympic-level performance.

I filled my lungs with air and dived beneath the surface, keeping my face submerged while I swam a fast powerful crawl, my arms scything through the water, my legs hardly needed; just an occasional flick of the feet as my upper body did most of the work.

I was keeping a rough tally of strokes, but the only measure that counted was the pressure in my chest; as I passed thirty I started to feel light-headed, and the booming pain of my hangover threatened to return. Like a pathetic fool I pressed on: three, four, five more strokes, then I burst up and flipped on to my back while sucking in gasp after gasp of oxygen.

My eyes were shut, and my head continued to pound even as my heart rate returned to normal. *Serves me right*, I thought, and actually it was a price my vanity was willing to pay – though when I finally opened my eyes and swivelled towards the beach, the disappointment I felt was as harsh as the slap of a seagull's wing.

Erin had gone, and with the promenade still deserted it was hard to believe she had ever been there at all.

10

Erin admires the way he carves through the water; it almost makes her wish she'd brought her swimsuit. But she decides not to stay; she knows what it's like to be observed when you're trying to relax. He probably came down here to be alone, just as she had.

Waking before six, she knew she wouldn't get back to sleep. Nathan stirred as she slipped out of bed so she told him she was hitting the gym. 'Nice one,' he said, and rolled over without another word.

The gym is in the basement of their lavish hilltop home. Erin frequently uses the treadmill and the punchbag, while Nathan favours the rower and weight bench. Today she ran for only five minutes before realising she needed space, fresh air, sunlight.

It was lazy to drive to the seafront, but she's glad now that she did. After starting the engine, unable to face going home, she decides to visit her sister instead. That creates a dilemma. Does she message Nathan now and risk disturbing him, or leave it until later and risk him waking to find her gone, with no explanation?

Risks, risks, risks from morning till night. *Tell him when I'm in Seaford*, she decides.

The journey doesn't take long at this time of the morning. It's still too early to message Nathan, and perhaps a bit early for an unscheduled appearance. But Milly is usually awake by seven, so her adoptive parents should be, too.

Gordon Ryan is as welcoming as ever. He adores Milly, so anything that Big Sis Erin wants is good with him. His wife Barbara is a harder sell, perhaps because life with Milly hasn't turned out as rosy as she once imagined. She rarely fails to get in a snide comment about money, as if Nathan's wealth belongs to Erin in any meaningful way.

But it's what they think. It's probably what everyone thinks.

All that matters is seeing Milly. If there's a happier, more life affirming human being on the planet, Erin would like to meet them. Ten minutes in Milly's presence and it's almost impossible not to make some glib comment about the positive side of disability, as if what she lacks has been replaced by this indefatigably sunny nature.

Erin doesn't believe it can be that simple. Even if it is, she's not sure she'd choose for Milly to be like this – or that she'd want to swap places with her. Carrying a mental age of three or four into adulthood doesn't guarantee to shield you from the horrors of life.

Sometimes it can do the opposite.

* * *

It's forecast to hit thirty degrees again today, but Milly insists on wearing the same heavy outfits as in winter. Erin has tried, over the years, to interest her little sister in dresses and skirts, in bright colours, but Milly won't have it. 'This pretty,' she'll say of her black leggings and baggy purple sweater. 'This pretty.'

'Fair enough, Milly. You're a Goth at heart.'

They take a slow wander into town, stopping at a cafe where Milly devours beans on toast and Erin sips a cappuccino. They don't catch up, exactly, because her sister has poor recollection and a hazy sense of time. Erin, if she wanted, could claim she saw Milly every day and her sister wouldn't dispute that.

As well as struggling with time, Milly doesn't really get the concept of death. It means they talk about their mum, Sonia, as if she's still alive. Erin finds that particularly hard, but for Milly's sake she can't ever let on.

It's gone nine when Erin realises she hasn't texted Nathan. He's likely to be awake by now but hasn't messaged. Quickly she takes a selfie with Milly, cheek to cheek and grinning inanely, the slightly shabby cafe visible in the background. She sends this on WhatsApp with a message:

Just with Milly, won't be late home xxx

Her sister, watching her tap anxiously on the iPhone, wants to know, 'Why a picture?'

'It's to prove I'm here, with you.' Erin shouldn't tell the truth, but she can count on Milly not to appreciate the significance of her reply. 'For Nathan.'

As ever, Milly wrinkles her nose. 'Don't like No-than.'

She's always struggled with his name, but Erin thinks *No-than* gets it about right.

'Nor do I, really,' she mutters.

* * *

From the cafe she intended on heading for the seafront, but Milly directs her to take a right turn off Broad Street and won't be diverted.

'Mum pub,' she says, so *Mum pub* it is. It's closed, of course, so Erin doesn't have to lead her in through one door and out through the other to prove Mum isn't there today.

But even the exterior brings back painful memories. Sonia Blake toiled at this pub through two bouts of cancer, and finally collapsed and died of heart failure just a couple of hours after finishing an extra shift. Erin is sure it was the stress of trying to provide for her daughters that caused her early death, aged just forty-eight. It's a cautionary tale that led Erin to make some disastrous choices of her own, though she would never, ever hold that against her mother.

Milly plants herself on the pavement next to the cellar hatch and heaves out a pantomime sigh. 'Shut now.'

'Shut,' Erin agrees.

'Mum here later?'

'Not today, honey. But you saw her before.'

'Want to see her.'

'I know – and one day you will.' Erin gives her a playful tickle and kisses her cheek. 'Until then, Barbara's your mummy, remember?'

Milly nods, but there's a slight downward twitch of her lips. Erin shouldn't, because her sister's health is a constant worry, but she promises an ice cream on the walk back. A 99 cone with a Flake.

Their route takes them past one of Erin's old schools, and she is reminded of what she told that man, Harry, this morning. Had they been the best days of her life? Right now, God forbid, it feels like they were.

By the time she's delivered Milly home, it's gone eleven. Still silence from Nathan. She considers phoning but decides on a text:

> Leaving now. See you soon hun xxx

She worries all the way back. The traffic is foul on the A259, but according to the radio it's equally foul on the A27. A baking hot Sunday in July, it's inevitable. Unless she can levitate, she won't be there any time soon.

Not until nearly half past twelve, in fact. She finds him on a stool at the kitchen island, a stack of newspapers piled on the granite worktop. He doesn't look up until she greets him, and even then he says nothing.

'I was just visiting Milly.'

No response.

'I sent you a pict—'

'I'm hearing it a lot lately, that word, "just".' He mocks her with a weedy high-pitched voice. '"I'm *just* doing this" and "I'm *just* going there". How about showing me some respect?'

'But I've—'

'Quiet! You show your respect, Erin, by asking me, "*Can* I do this, Nathan?" "Do you *mind* if I go there, *please Nathan*?" Not "just" doing whatever you fucking well feel like.'

Erin is well aware that when he manufactures a rant like this, trying to justify her position will only make it worse.

'I'm sorry,' she says. 'I'll ask next time.'

'Yes, you will. Now undress.'

She goes cold inside. *Mum slaved her arse off and died young. Milly is a thirty-year-old toddler. How can I be the worst off, here in this million-pound house?*

'Not upstairs?' she says. The very last thing she wants is sex, but that's irrelevant and they both know it. 'I could shower first, put on—'

'I told you to undress. Now do it.'

Because it isn't sex. It's punishment.

11

I had no sound reason to return to Gimlet Lane, but unfortunately that didn't stop me.

After this morning's encounter with Erin Webb, it was undoubtedly a foolish thing to do. She surely hadn't believed my nonsense about long walks, and yet I kept telling myself it wouldn't hurt to stroll past the house again.

What, exactly, was I trying to achieve? Meeting Erin had spurred me to re-examine my entire strategy. I'd thought about little else when I returned home – at least until I dozed off on the sofa. I'd woken at about half eleven, made a bacon sandwich for lunch and even went so far as to pick up a notepad and pencil.

But instead of devising an ingenious plan, I found myself idly sketching Erin's face in profile, her braided hair. I didn't reach any conclusions about Nathan Webb, or how my desire for revenge might be affected by the connection I'd made with his wife. I didn't fix on a purpose for going up there – or at least I didn't admit to one – though in fact it was glaringly obvious.

I was hoping to see her again.

This is ridiculous, I thought as I hauled myself up the hill in the sweltering afternoon heat. *I'm not some giddy adolescent. I'm a middle-aged man—*

Whose wife has just left you for your best friend, a blunt voice finished for me. And shallow as it was, maybe that explained it. A beautiful woman had shone her attention upon me, and consequently I was... what? Infatuated with her?

I could feel my self-disgust increasing as I turned into Gimlet Lane. The old couple weren't in their garden, but there were other people in sight: a man trimming a hedge, a woman unloading shopping from her car, a kid performing somersaults on a trampoline.

At Webb's there were two cars on the drive: the grey Jaguar and a Renault Clio. Some of the house's upper windows were open; in one, a curtain undulated in the breeze. I imagined Erin inside, lying on their emperor bed. Nathan would be downstairs, rustling up the martinis. They'd just made love, of course, and after that blissful release they would drink and talk, then perhaps spoon up and doze a while...

I naturally pictured them as joyously happy, for how could they be anything else? Both relatively young, in good health, physically attractive. No money worries, a sumptuous home. I'd have thought them a perfect match – if I hadn't known that Nathan was evil, while Erin had seemed so genuinely sweet and funny.

Unless I'd been taken in, blinded to her true nature by her appearance. It wouldn't be the first time. *Close your mouth*, Anita had murmured to me once at an awards show, when I'd been introduced to an actress who was considered one of the world's great beauties, but known throughout the industry as a vicious sociopath.

Or maybe my assessment was wrong in the opposite way, an idea that posed far more of a challenge. Perhaps Nathan Webb *wasn't* the monster I made him out to be. Perhaps he was truly deserving of a partner as lovely as Erin?

Either way, I had to consider the impact on Erin if I went through with it. I wouldn't just be murdering a man in cold blood, but visiting a tragedy upon his wife.

How could I do that and claim I was acting out of respect for my son's memory?

* * *

The coroner's office had helpfully informed us that 'interested persons' were entitled to sight of the witness statements and reports. Anita refused to look at any of them. She was furious when I told her I had read the post mortem report, as if my knowledge of its horrific contents would somehow transmit itself to her, as if by a form of osmosis.

I had to admit that in many ways I did regret reading it. I managed it only by performing a kind of disassociation: this wasn't my son under discussion, a once vibrant, beautiful human being. It was a grisly inanimate object, a laboratory specimen.

The witness statements were different. I'd pored over every word, obsessively hunting for anomalies, contradictions, evidence of a cover-up or conspiracy.

Nathan Webb's was the least informative, but the one I had studied the most. He claimed to have arrived at the Tannery around 2 a.m., by which time the party had been going for several hours. Some of the attendees had already left, and it was thought that only ten or fifteen remained – including Freddie.

Nathan had been asked why he permitted the parties, and also why these young people tolerated his presence. He said he remembered what it was like, having nowhere to hang out without being harassed by the cops or 'the miserable older generation'. By making them welcome at the Tannery, and occasionally treating them to a box of beer or a bottle of cheap voddy, he'd been accepted as 'one of the crowd'.

But hadn't he thought of the risks? He knew the Tannery was in a dangerous condition.

Nathan conceded that he did, and said he'd repeatedly warned the kids to take care. They tended to gravitate towards the top floor, because the other floors had piles of rusting junk and a lot of filth and debris left over from when the druggies had occupied the building. He encouraged them to party at the safer end, away from the holes in the floor, but there were also holes in the roof at the dangerous end, and on clear nights they liked to gaze up at the stars as they danced.

Sometime around 3 a.m., while Nathan claimed to be deep in conversation with a couple of girls, Freddie had apparently danced too close to one of the holes, which had wooden planks laid over it for safety. These planks had given way, and Freddie had fallen. A few of the others were dancing nearby, but they were admittedly 'off their heads' – as Nathan put it – and no one had actually noticed Freddie's disappearance for several minutes.

The interviewing officers had pressed Nathan on the issue of illegal substances. Did he take drugs? Did the young people? Did he supply them with drugs? Or was it sex? Did he sleep with any of these girls or boys who were young enough to be his children?

Nathan hadn't taken the bait. From reading the text, I sensed his tone was one of weary disbelief that they would waste his time with such lazy assumptions. And he never betrayed an iota of concern that his account would be contradicted. They had nothing on him: he knew it, and they knew it.

And so did I.

But that didn't stop me taking an impulsive detour along Barkers Way. If Nathan and his beautiful wife were at home right now, this was an ideal opportunity to take a closer look at the Tannery.

There was the usual line of parked cars on the other side of the road, and one or two people about. I strode up to the gate and noted a digital lock with a keypad. I tried the handle but the gate didn't budge.

I continued along the road and took the next left turn, passing a terrace of three-storey Edwardian homes. Beyond the terrace there was a small access road leading to a set of garages. The access road ended at the high perimeter fence, which on this side was chain link rather than an opaque hoarding. The derelict building and the weed-infested, rubble-strewn wasteland around it made for a grim perspective for the residents in the terrace.

I was peering through the fence when a figure ghosted into view from a shattered window on the top floor of the Tannery. It was a young man, tall and very thin, with a stark contrast between his black hair and his round, white face. My sense, from a distance, was of coal dark eyes and an intense, malevolent gaze.

He regarded me for a moment, before raising one arm to shoulder height, his hand palm out. A peculiar gesture, which confused me until I realised he might be holding a phone.

Was he filming me?

Fighting the urge to cover my face, I turned and hurried away, feeling unaccountably afraid as well as ashamed.

12

On Monday I met Anita at the town hall and we completed the formal process of registering Freddie's death. Afterwards we emerged into the sunshine, both blinking away tears and unsure what to say.

For some reason I had woken feeling even rougher this morning than I had yesterday. The moment she set eyes on me, Anita had exclaimed, 'You look dreadful. Are you ill?'

'Just hungover.'

'What, *again*?'

'From Saturday. Must be a delayed reaction.'

'I doubt it. Though you did get into a state.'

'We were all drinking, to be fair.'

'Not throwing it back like you were.' She clasped her hands together in a beseeching gesture. 'You won't go down that route, will you?'

'Become a hopeless alcoholic? Would it matter if I did?'

Anita's reaction took me by surprise. She stepped forward and put her arms around me. 'Of course it would matter. How could you say that?'

'Sorry,' I said, awkwardly. 'I wasn't being serious.'

She continued to grasp my arms as she examined me. 'Gareth warned me this might be too soon. I suppose my head was saying the same, but I went with my heart. And when you arrived on Saturday you seemed to have adjusted so well, I didn't think I'd have to worry...'

'You don't have to worry,' I insisted. *Not about me hitting the bottle, at least.*

'I hope not. I really do wish this hadn't happened, and sometimes I even—' She broke off, biting her lip.

'Yes?' I asked.

'I wish that every fibre of my being didn't... *yearn* to be with Gareth.' She let go of me and made an open-palmed gesture of helplessness. 'But it just does.'

* * *

Not much I could say to that. The decision was made, and here we were.

With our task complete, I was anticipating a hurried farewell. But Anita glanced at her watch and said, 'Do you want to grab a coffee?'

We found a cafe in one of the old Victorian arcades which had become home to a number of exclusive producers of cheese, pastries and other food-stuffs. As we passed a chalkboard sign for sourdough breads and air-dried charcuterie, I nudged Anita. 'You know that "artisan" is an old Latin word for "overpriced".'

'You've made that joke before,' she said, but also conceded a giggle. It was a sound I'd missed, these past few evenings alone in the house.

After ordering our coffees, we carried them to a table and sat down. By then I could sense Anita had a specific issue to discuss, and she wasted no time getting to it.

'Going back to Saturday's conversation, you like our suggestion of a bursary or endowment?'

'I think it's a lovely idea. Why?'

'I want to be sure you're not telling me what I want to hear, while actually thinking about something different.'

I affected bafflement. 'Such as?'

'Such as, this idea of...' She paused, eyes darting left and right, and hissed, 'Getting back at Nathan Webb.'

'I see.' My right leg had started juddering in the way it was wont to do; Anita noticed, and I forced it to stop. 'That was just a heat of the moment thing. Don't tell me you haven't wanted to lash out?'

'I suppose. But never seriously.' She sipped her coffee and kept the cup poised beneath her lips. 'Taking the life of another human being, no matter how despicable he might be, won't ease our pain one bit. And it certainly wouldn't honour Freddie's memory.'

Although I knew she was right, I said, 'I've been over the statements and it's all so convenient. Nobody else was near the hole. Nobody was dancing with Freddie. Nathan Webb was deep in conversation and didn't even *know* Freddie.' I threw up my hands. 'Do you really believe all that?'

'None of it is impossible. And even if some elements aren't true, it doesn't change the fundamental nature of the event. Nor does it prove that there's a... a nefarious conspiracy with Nathan Webb at its heart.'

'But it's his building. He knew it was unsafe.'

'He said he warned them. And he took steps to cover the holes with boards.'

'It's not enough.'

'We're bound to feel that way, aren't we? But the coroner considered it very carefully, and "misadventure" – as much as it breaks my heart – is probably the right conclusion. A momentary act of foolishness in the midst of a happy, drunken celebration.'

'He wasn't that drunk. The blood alcohol level—'

'Harry, please.' Her tone was weary, not cross. 'This is exactly what I meant. The inability to move on.'

I sighed, and we drank our coffees and let the tension disperse. But I couldn't quite leave the subject.

'There is a wider issue that's still relevant. Nathan Webb is almost certainly a drug dealer.'

Now Anita looked sympathetic. 'You're probably right. But that's a matter for the police. What you need to do, Harry, for your own sake, is let it go. Destroy all the statements, and those horrible reports.'

I went to speak, but our attention was diverted by a minor commotion at the door. Half a dozen youths had joined the queue at the counter, though there weren't enough seats available for them.

Anita said, 'Let's get going, free up a table.'

I nodded. It wasn't lost on either of us that they were about Freddie's age.

Outside, our farewell hug had less intensity than the one I'd received earlier; I hoped that meant I had alleviated some of her concerns. Anita made to turn away, then said, 'Oh, Gareth has a favour to ask.'

'What's that?'

'Sorry, gotta be in Dymchurch for two. He'll tell you.'

* * *

When I got back to work, my best friend had his sombre expression ready. 'How did it go?'

'It's done. I suppose that's all you can say about it.' I took my seat. 'Anita mentioned a favour?'

'Oh. I thought *she* was going to ask you.'

'She dipped out, so it must be bad!' I joked.

He shrugged. 'It's just, we've been talking about a weekend away, and it sort of escalated. What started as a city break in Europe is now looking like three weeks in Peru. Machu Picchu and all that.'

'I see.' I tried to keep my face neutral. For our entire marriage Machu Picchu had been our dream destination, the first place Anita and I would visit upon retirement.

'So, it's mainly that you'd be running the show here, if you're okay to step in?'

'Sure. When do you think you'll go?'

Gareth winced. 'Early next month, possibly.'

'Okay.' I was now so eager to end the conversation that I'd have agreed to just about anything. Gareth offered his effusive thanks, and we got to work.

But Anita's comments had provoked a nagging question. I waited a few minutes, then said, 'What we discussed last week... I suppose you thought I'd lost my mind?'

'The stuff about killing Webb? Gotta say I did, yeah.' Gareth's orthopaedic chair groaned as he sat back and laced his hands behind his head. 'Did you ever consider the practical difficulties? Like: how you'd do it, and the chances of everything going to plan?'

I could only smile, reflecting on how I'd been bested by a few seagulls. 'Never got that far.'

'I mean, guns are a nonstarter – unless you're mixing in different circles these days?' He sniggered. 'And an up-close attack is too risky. Go at him with a knife or a cricket bat and you could end up finding your own weapon being used against you. So what does that leave? A car bomb? Novichok on his door handle?'

'I know. It was a ridiculous idea.'

'But totally understandable – that's what I told Neet. She was seriously freaked out, bro. Made me promise to warn her if it ever looked like you might be planning something.'

Was this a signal that secretly Gareth approved, but required me not to confide in him? On balance it seemed unlikely.

'You can tell her not to worry. It was a temporary aberration.'

'That's a relief to us both.' Gareth went on nodding sagely. 'I know it's not my place to say this, but my advice would be to focus on something new. Maybe look at getting back into the dating game?'

I stared at him in disbelief. 'Dating?'

'Yeah. It's a totally new world since we were young.' He winked. 'Get yourself on Tinder and live a little. Best thing you could do after all the crap you've had to deal with.'

13

I didn't comment on Gareth's advice, let alone point out the rather glaring irony. If he hadn't just set up home with my wife, I'd have one less bit of 'crap' to deal with.

But such a response could sour the atmosphere at work – not a good idea when the two of us were together nine or ten hours a day.

It wasn't until that night, munching on a Greek salad in front of the TV, that I pondered the bleak reality. At fifty-two I might realistically have another three decades of life. If I didn't want to spend all that time alone, I would probably have to consider doing what Gareth suggested. Not necessarily signing up to some tawdry online cattle market – as I saw it – but putting myself out there. Being alive to the possibility of meeting someone.

Try as I might, I couldn't picture it happening any time soon. And yet, even as I dismissed the very concept, I found myself thinking of Erin Webb, and the way we'd chatted and laughed yesterday morning...

* * *

On Tuesday I woke to find the town blanketed by heavy cloud. A chilly wind accosted me on my walk to the office: a perfect accompaniment to the melancholy I felt, having finally convinced myself that Anita and Gareth were absolutely right.

I couldn't kill Nathan Webb. If I tried, I would undoubtedly make a hash of it. Better to forget all about him. Forget about him *and* his wife.

That resolve lasted approximately four hours, until I popped to a book-shop at lunchtime and emerged into the pedestrian precinct to find her walking towards me.

It was like a reversal of our encounter on Sunday; this time it was Erin who jumped when she saw me. I wondered if that meant she had subsequently learned who I was, and I braced myself for a difficult conversation.

'Nice to see you again,' I said.

Her smile looked slightly dutiful. 'Not swimming today?'

'Doubt it. I'm just on my lunch break. How about you?'

'Oh, I don't... I'm not...' She looked left and right, then indicated an alley between two of the shops. 'Do you mind if we go over there? We're a bit in the way here.'

I didn't see any harm in complying, though the precinct was about a hundred feet wide and the footfall today was far from excessive. There was zero chance of us causing an obstruction.

And I was confused by her body language; she didn't seem hostile towards me, and yet she was clearly agitated. As we moved to this more discreet location, she said, 'Are you married?'

'Separated. Very recently, in fact.'

'I'm sorry to hear that. It's just, when we were talking on Sunday, you seemed a bit nervous.'

'Did I?' *Not nervous so much as stunned by your beauty.*

For a single mortifying instant I thought I'd said it out loud. At the same time I had the peculiar sense that Erin had read my mind, and I caught a hint of disappointment in her eyes.

She said, 'Then I wondered if you were worried about being seen with me.'

'Not really. Why?'

'Do you know who my husband is? Nathan Webb?'

I had a microsecond in which to prepare a lie. It wasn't long enough. 'Yes.'

'And are you stalking me?'

'What? God, no! I wouldn't ever do that. I just went—'

'I believe you.' Her pale blue eyes took on a steely aspect. 'In that case, it must be about him – the way you were looking at the house?'

I stared at the ground for a moment, summoning a little extra strength before I faced her again.

'Actually, it's about my son.'

I expected her to know who I meant, but Erin looked blank. 'I don't understand.'

Now I found myself glancing around, as if infected by her unease. There were a few shoppers criss-crossing the precinct, a kid on a mountain bike weaving insolently between them.

'I ought to get back to work. But later, would you be willing to have a coffee, or—?'

'Not really. Why?'

'My son, uh... Freddie Manning.' I had to pause, gasping as if suddenly winded. 'He fell to his death in the Tannery.'

'Oh God! You're his dad? I thought your face was a bit familiar.'

'I was in a couple of the news reports, which you maybe saw...'

Erin cringed. 'It was so awful, I couldn't bear to hear about it. That's why I wasn't at the...'

'Inquest,' I finished for her.

She nodded. 'I really don't know anything about it.'

Her fearful tone made me feel wretched. 'Okay,' I said. 'But is there any chance I could talk to you properly?'

'Why?' she asked again. 'What would it achieve?'

I could only stammer: 'M-maybe nothing. It's just, on Sunday you seemed so friendly. So unlike the image I had of—'

I realised the mess I was making, and stopped there. Erin snorted.

'No promises, but give me your number.'

* * *

I returned to the office with low expectations. Erin's discomfort had been so apparent, I couldn't see her wanting anything more to do with me. And yet, a couple of hours later, while I was using the landline to speak to a subcontractor in Crawley who did our injection moulding, I saw an unfamiliar number pop up on my mobile, with a brief text message.

This is Erin. Can you make tomorrow at 8pm, at the Chrysalis?

Once I'd finished the call, I stared at the message for a full thirty seconds, trying to process a bewildering mix of emotions. Gareth stood up to make coffee and must have seen my expression.

'All right, bro? You're looking kind of dazed.'

'Oh... just pondering the mysteries of life.'

'That so?' He gave me a sly grin. 'I thought maybe you'd got your first Tinder date.'

14

Erin sends the message in a spirit of defiance. A second later panic seizes control of her system, shrieking: *Retract! Retract!* like an automated warning on a falling plane. It takes all her courage to shut off that alarm and stick to her course.

This isn't like sneaking away to visit Milly. If anything goes wrong, there will be terrible consequences.

Common sense says it's not a risk to be taking for a man she doesn't know. But then if she'd listened to common sense she would never have married Nathan. The signs were present from the beginning and she had ignored them, because the pot of gold Nathan offered wasn't at the end of the rainbow; it was right there in his wallet and on his wrist, in the cars he drove, the house he owned. Irresistible, at that point in her life.

So why compound the error? It must be something intrinsic to her nature. Her father, according to her mum, had been a hopeless gambler. Always persuading himself that this time would be different.

Fortunately there is one friend Erin can trust. She calls Stella before going home, and experiences only a brief instance of real fear – when she finds herself wondering if Nathan has bugged her phone.

Having listened to the request, Stella makes the obvious assumption. 'Unless he's Chris effing Hemsworth, you don't wanna be doing this, hun.'

'It's nothing like that,' Erin assures her, thinking: *Potentially it's worse.*

But Stella agrees to go along with it, and only at the end of the conversation says, 'You totally sure about this?'

Erin says she is, then works hard to banish it from her mind. If she hasn't spoken to Harry, then she isn't guilty of anything. If she isn't guilty, she won't arouse suspicion. If she doesn't arouse suspicion, she shouldn't – all being well, fingers crossed, etc. – suffer any punishment. The key is to *forget*, at will, and it isn't always easy.

When she gets home Nathan isn't there: *yippee!* He finally rolls in around eight, in an unusually chirpy mood. It turns out he's already eaten, so the meal she's cooking will go to waste.

'Stella's asked if I'm free to go out tomorrow night.' She shows Nathan the prearranged WhatsApp message from Stella, saying exactly that. 'Is it okay with you?'

After a protracted show of contemplation, he shrugs. 'I suppose. Got tonnes on this week.'

She is required to show her appreciation. It's only later, when he's idly scrolling through his phone, that his expression hardens slightly. 'What d'you get up to today?'

This spells danger: a risk of unforgetting, which might show in her voice.

'Did the gym here, then some housework. Popped into town for a bit of shopping.'

'Where in town?'

'Uh, the precinct. I needed a birthday card.'

He looks up from his phone. 'Kel saw you.'

'Okay.' Erin fears that she has gone pale. 'I went in Card Factory, and also a little independent place. The card's in the kitchen.' When he doesn't comment, she's forced to ask: 'Why?'

He glances at the phone again. 'No reason.'

* * *

On Tuesday I spent a quiet evening at home, and again reflected on the fact that there could be thousands of evenings like this ahead of me: blank, unvarying portions of time. I could see the danger of settling into an inflexible routine, how I might come to resent any variation, in the way my own father had been wont to do in the years after my mother's death.

But it was early days, I reminded myself, and tomorrow certainly wouldn't be lacking in variation.

I was going to have dinner with the wife of Nathan Webb.

I said nothing about that to Gareth, of course. Fortunately, Wednesday was a busy day, and the hours at work flew by. That evening I dressed in jeans, a black shirt and a slightly heavy grey jacket (my lighter jacket having been ruined in the seagull skirmish).

I left the house at seven forty and walked slowly down to the harbour. It had been another overcast day, though the air was warm and humid; on the horizon the falling sun had broken through to cast its golden light across the sea. I had to shield my eyes to make out the lonely figure seated at the end of the breakwater. I couldn't be sure it was Len Bowden until he seemed to twist in my direction, then languidly raised a hand.

I waved back, feeling like I needed some small gesture of encouragement from a father figure before I embarked on my mission, as utterly foolish as it was.

She's the wife of Nathan Webb, I had told myself repeatedly. Nothing less and nothing more. The wife of Nathan Webb.

* * *

Erin has planned the evening with military precision. Stella lives in a three-bedroom house on one of the town's northerly estates. According to Stella, her husband of twenty years is 'a miserable sod', but to Erin his habitual sullenness is rather endearing. He greets her at the door, and to his credit doesn't ask what the hell they're playing at.

It's seven-thirty and Stella is all set to go. Ten minutes later they're at a pub and have ordered two drinks each. They take a selection of photos, with different drinks at different levels; between drinks, Erin removes her cardigan and musses her hair slightly, as though by now she has sat for an hour or two, fiddling with it.

By five to eight Stella is back home and changing into her slob-out clothes, while Erin pushes the Clio towards the seafront. She selected the Chrysalis because, firstly, it's never been in favour with the town's 'in-crowd', which invariably includes everyone who might already know or want to ingratiate themselves with Nathan.

Secondly, when she and Nathan went there a couple of years ago, he fell out with the manager after demanding a discount and getting only half the figure he expected. As a result he vowed never to set foot in the place again, though the manager got off very lightly. Similar disputes have resulted in a 3 a.m. firebombing, weeks or months later.

After parking, she sends the first of the staged pictures to Nathan and watches the double ticks turn blue, though he doesn't respond.

She is greeted by one of the waiting staff, who informs her that 'your friend' is at the table. She threads her way through the crowded restaurant, glad that the table isn't anywhere close to the window, and then she sees him.

This is a moment Erin will remember for a long time. It's the look on Harry's face: initially anxious, expectant, a man keeping a lid on a complicated stew of emotions; then a sudden flare of pleasure when he spots her, rising to his feet with his hands outstretched in greeting.

It makes her heart quietly break for the life she might have had. The person she could have been.

15

My heart was trip hammering. I felt like I was fifteen again.

It was a crazy response. Completely inappropriate – and yet understandable, if the reaction of the other diners was anything to go by. It seemed like everyone in the room – male or female – was compelled to check her out, some of them blatantly turning to stare.

But Erin floated to my table as if divinely unaware of the effect she was having. Dressed simply, in black jeans and a shirt that looked like denim but probably wasn't – its pale blue a fair match for her eyes. Her hair was braided but also piled up in a more complicated and quite stunning arrangement.

She took my hand and her skin felt warm and soft. Her nails were short, with a shade of pink varnish which complemented her lipstick.

'Thank you for coming,' I said, which produced a wry smile.

'Did you think I wouldn't?'

'It had to be a possibility. I take it you haven't mentioned this to Nathan?'

Her shudder was all the answer I needed.

Tentatively, I asked, 'And if he were to find out?'

'Let's not go there.'

I knew I would have to respect her wishes, though this, to me, was another indication of Webb's barbaric nature.

The waiter brought menus and asked for our drinks order. I'd almost finished a beer, but when Erin said only water for her, I opted for the same. Important to maintain a clear head.

Over the next few minutes we chatted about the weather, swimming, exercise in general. Then she asked about my work, and she seemed astonished to learn that I made props for the entertainment industry.

'It might sound glamorous, but it really isn't.'

'Maybe not, but somehow you don't expect to find people creating something... *magical* in a town like this.'

'Well, here we are.' I launched into one of my few genuinely high-level anecdotes about helping fit a robotic suit to a Hollywood star, only to be interrupted by the waiter. I feared that my punchline – 'It turned out he was an A list actor, but not the Ryan I'd just been praising to the hilt!' – wouldn't have quite the same effect.

We ordered quickly – I went for grilled swordfish and Erin had the seafood linguine – and she seemed to take genuine pleasure from my story when it resumed.

'I think both those Ryans are pretty hot,' she admitted with a guilty smile, then added, 'Did you say you've just separated from your wife?'

'Last week. Though it had been on the cards for a long time.'

'I'm sorry to hear that. Was it by mutual agreement?'

'More or less. She's been in love with my best friend for a few years now.'

Perhaps it was a bit unfair to say it in such a matter-of-fact tone; I had to remind myself that most people were accustomed to a lot of heat and drama when relationships took that sort of turn. Erin certainly looked stunned.

'Your *best friend*? Oh my God! Was she cheating on you?'

'No. I knew about it from the start. I won't bore you with all the details, but his wife died, and in the aftermath of that, when we were both supporting him as much as we could, I saw them falling in love with each other.'

I paused, hoping not to let on how much I was struggling to maintain eye contact with her. I was simultaneously drinking in her gaze and yet intimidated by it, the intensity of her focus almost too much to bear.

'Neither of them wanted to act on it. For a long time we just sort of stumbled along, and they only saw each other as friends—'

'You know that for certain?' Erin cut in, then looked embarrassed. 'Sorry, I shouldn't...'

'It's fine. I suppose I'll never know for sure, but I believe they kept to their word.' I took a drink of water, needing a distraction because this was a slightly abridged – if not censored – version of the story. 'But then, after losing Freddie... I suppose that was the catalyst for all of us to reassess our circumstances. Anita felt her future should be with Gareth, and with the inquest complete, it seemed like the right time...'

I could feel myself becoming emotional. Partly it was the tenderness in Erin's response; I sensed she was fighting an urge to take my hand, and suddenly I craved even the most superficial form of physical contact. Even her foot nudging against mine would have been enough.

'What about this Gareth?' she asked. 'Will you ever be able to look him in the eye?'

'I don't have much choice. He owns Melgar Creations.'

'You're kidding?'

'Nope. We've worked together for a quarter of a century.'

'I don't know how you don't want to...' She shook her head, expressing not just disbelief but a degree of exasperation, it seemed.

'I'm sure some people would react with aggression. I'm not like that. And I know he and Anita never meant to hurt me – in fact, they went out of their way to avoid it.'

I paused for another sip of water, and wished I'd gone for beer after all. 'Perhaps I could have told Gareth to stay away from my wife, and ordered Anita never to speak to him again. But at what cost? Even if they went along with that, I'd have to live every day knowing my wife was unhappy, that she wanted to be with someone else. That's no life for any of us.'

Erin was silent for a moment, before saying, 'I don't think I've ever met anyone who took such a mature approach to something like this. But it also makes me wonder if you really loved your wife any more?'

Now it was my turn to look shocked. I hadn't completely shied away from this question, of course, but it was fair to say that I'd avoided any serious analysis.

'I suppose we'd reached the stage where we were great friends, confidants, companions, but mainly just parents. There wasn't a lot of passion, or *need* for each other. I take a lot of the responsibility for that.'

She was nodding sadly. 'I guess it's so difficult, after twenty or thirty years together, raising kids. Were you still... you know... *physical*?'

'Very occasionally.' I could feel myself reddening, and escaped into humour. 'I've heard my kids' generation talking about this thing, "friends with benefits", and it struck me that it's actually the perfect description for a lot of thirty-year marriages. Though the degree of friendship can vary a lot – as can the quality of the benefits.'

Her laughter was absurdly gratifying. Our food arrived, and we said little for a few minutes. But I thought that the candour with which I'd discussed my broken marriage entitled me to probe a little into her own relationship.

'How long have you been with Nathan? And how did you meet?'

'About eight years. I managed the office of a construction firm in Eastbourne. Nathan started using us to refurbish his properties, and over a few months we got talking more and more—'

'So the property empire is genuine?' It was rude to interrupt, but I couldn't stop myself. 'Not just a front for... uh, drug dealing, money laundering and so on.'

Erin stared at me for the longest three seconds I'd ever endured. It didn't seem impossible that she would get up and walk out.

Then she said, 'He has a large property portfolio. Some of it he inherited from his father, but mostly he's had a good eye for the market. He buys up rundown houses in the less appealing areas and converts them into student accommodation. He's also sitting on quite a lot of land, waiting for permission to develop.'

'Like the Tannery?'

She nodded, perhaps with a certain reluctance that the flow of the conversation had landed us here.

Or beached us, I thought.

16

Erin can tell that Harry is aware of her discomfort, but she doubts if he could guess the reason. He may put it down to guilt about her association with Nathan, when in fact it's the proximity to Harry's pain that she finds so difficult to bear.

For the past eight years she's been cocooned within her own misery. An item of property in Nathan's possession, forbidden to engage or empathise with anyone else. It comes as a jolt to be reminded that other people are suffering. And in this case, Harry's suffering has essentially the same root cause as her own – Nathan – though it would be the most reckless act of all to admit that to him.

Now the Tannery is the subject under discussion, Erin will have to tread as carefully as if she were negotiating the tumbledown building itself.

'It's the jewel in his crown,' she says. 'If and when it gets the go-ahead, it'll put him in a different league.'

Harry nods glumly, before veering away from the subject. Perhaps he's sensed her dread and doesn't want to feast on it, the way Nathan would.

'Do you still work for the building company?' he asks.

'I gave it up a few weeks into our relationship. Nathan wanted me to come and live over here, and I wasn't crazy about the commute to Eastbourne.'

That's not the real reason, of course, but Harry has no cause to dispute it.

He looks to be charmingly gullible, though his next question can't help but raise her hackles.

'I imagine you don't actually need to work, financially speaking?'

'No, I spend all day in the bath, sipping champagne and eating oysters...'

Once again his cheeks redden; she's never known a grown man to blush so often. 'Sorry, that was rude. Do you have any children?'

'We don't,' she says, in a tone that seals the subject in a bombproof chamber.

'And your family? Do they still live around here?'

'My dad walked out when I was seven. Mum died eleven years ago. I have a sister, Milly, who's thirty. But she was sort of adopted, as an adult, when Mum had cancer. She has special needs. Learning difficulties.'

Erin has become hesitant, partly because it's been so long since she had an opportunity to talk about her family. She hates the idea of Milly being categorised, because from that moment the person she's speaking to will see only the condition, not the person. They'll stare at her the way Harry is staring now, all earnest and sympathetic.

'How serious are the learning difficulties?'

'Quite serious. She's basically a three-year-old adult – though I don't think Milly should be defined by her mental capacity. I mean, I wouldn't say, "My alibi for tonight is my close friend Stella, who believes almost everything she reads in the *Daily Mail*." Or, with Nathan, I wouldn't focus on how little attention he paid at school, when he's easily the smartest, most cunning person I've ever met. My sister's key qualities are her affection, her devotion to people and animals, her readiness to laugh and get the best out of life. But if I say all that *without* mentioning the disability, it feels like I'm being dishonest.'

She registers that Harry is nodding with admiration. 'I can tell you're very proud of her. I'm sure she's lucky to have you as an older sister. Do you get to see her much?'

'She's in Seaford, so I visit when I can. It's not always easy.'

'I suppose life gets in the way?'

Now she feels humbled into the truth. 'Actually, it's because Nathan doesn't like me seeing her.'

'Why not? She's your sister!'

'Mm. Perhaps if she wasn't "special needs". If she made the grade, in his eyes, then it would be different.'

But even as the words leave her mouth, Erin realises this isn't true. A sister with a higher IQ would be doing her utmost to drag Erin free of him, and Nathan would never tolerate that.

* * *

The mention of Stella has reminded Erin about the pictures they took. Excusing herself, she retreats to the ladies, where she WhatsApps the second photograph to Nathan and promises not to be late home. Then she sits a moment, pondering the notion that this has been, despite the risks, a fascinating evening. Enjoyable, even.

The situation with Harry's wife and his best friend seems too fantastical to be true. Even if he had no love left for Anita, surely Harry couldn't accept this other man taking her from him?

The contrast with her own relationship is staggering. Nathan would kill her rather than lose her to someone else. That had been made clear by their fourth date, when she made the mistake of smiling in farewell to a barman who'd been friendly to them both. She was fairly certain the man was gay, but that hadn't stopped Nathan from pinning her against the car and warning that she had to choose, right now. Was she loyal to him, or was she not?

At the time she'd blamed herself, assuming she had given out the wrong signal without realising it; Nathan's aggression she attributed to the coke he'd done in the toilets and then denied, even when she could see traces of powder around his nostrils. *This is how passionately he loves you*, her brainwashed inner self had crowed. *Lots of women would envy you for having a man who cares so much.*

While washing her hands she checks herself in the mirror. She looks different, somehow, from the Erin who earlier posed for a photograph to represent this stage of the evening. *Gonna be a hell of a lot to forget before I see Nathan.*

Heading back, she notices that Harry, instead of fending off solitude with his mobile phone, is gazing towards the window, his eyes unfocused and a little misty. At the table beyond theirs, a man of about sixty with a bulbous nose scans Erin's body with practised skill – boobs-legs-boobs-face-boobs – then flicks a scornful glance at Harry, as if to protest: *How in God's name did you get so lucky?*

As she eases her way round the table, Erin is sorely tempted to give Harry a caress, perhaps run her fingers through his hair.

She shivers. *Careful, now.* Harry welcomes her back with a boyish grin, and asks if she could manage a dessert. She folds her napkin and says she ought to be leaving.

'Right now? It's only half nine.'

'Best not to push my luck. You do understand?'

He nods reluctantly. 'I don't suppose you'd like a walk on the front?'

'I can't. Nathan has his spies everywhere. The wasps, I call them.'

'Wasps?'

'Because of how they buzz around town on their e-scooters and bikes. As irritating and pointless as wasps.'

'These are Nathan's acolytes? The young people who attend the parties at the Tannery?' He sits upright, energised by the opportunity she's just presented. 'I can't understand why he hangs around with a bunch of teenagers. And what on earth do they see in him?'

'Some of them are his tenants,' she tells him. 'Providing you look after the place, and pay your rent on time, he's a decent landlord. He regards it as good business to get to know them, help them with advice when they need it. Doesn't take much to get them eating out of his hands.'

In fact, the phrase Nathan uses is a little more graphic: *They'd suck my dick if I wanted them to.* But Harry doesn't need to hear that.

'So their... adoration,' he says. 'Could it reach a point where they'd lie for him?'

'I don't know. Why?'

'The other witnesses at the party. They all gave these ridiculously vague, anodyne statements. And they were practically identical, as though Na— *someone* had dictated it to them.'

'That's quite a leap. Didn't it happen at, what, three or four in the morning? And they'd probably all been drinking, smoking weed—'

'Except no drugs were found at the scene. Quite convenient, wouldn't you say?'

Erin sighs. 'Do I have to express an opinion?'

'Not if you don't have one. But if you know anything at all, any tiny detail, please tell me.'

She sighs again. Harry is so gently persistent, offering almost nothing to fight back with, and yet he will succeed in extracting information from her. In its own way it's almost as effective as Nathan's methods. A pillow to muffle the punches. A cigarette lighter's shivering flame.

'All right,' she says. 'But not here.'

17

I understood what she meant; the waiter was hovering, perhaps alert to the tension and trying to listen in.

I signalled for the bill but of course he chose that moment to turn away. Erin spared my embarrassment by rolling her eyes. 'I hate it when they do that.'

There was an enjoyable tussle over payment – Erin produced a handful of twenties, and I realised she couldn't risk using a card – but I insisted on getting it. 'You didn't have to agree to this,' I reminded her.

'Why do I have a feeling I might still regret it?' she asked drily.

We stepped outside. The newly dark evening was warm and fragrant, and I found myself yearning for a way to prolong it: drinks, dancing, intense conversation... even though I understood that none of these things was possible, or appropriate.

She was Nathan Webb's wife.

That reminder loomed large as I saw her carefully scanning the street. When I suggested we find a quiet pub, she shook her head.

'A wasp in every one.' Instead, she indicated a nearby car park. 'I'll drive you home, providing you hunker down in the seat.'

I was happy to comply, though I felt guilty about the frisson I experienced as I climbed into her Renault Clio. The interior of a car can be a thrillingly intimate space.

I directed her to my street and we were there so swiftly that I regretted not sending her on a more convoluted route. As she cut the engine, I said, 'You're welcome to come in for a coffee.'

'Here will do.'

'There's no ulterior motive—'

'I know that.' Her smile was just the right side of a smirk. 'Ask your questions, Harry.'

I took a moment to compose myself, trying to breathe deeply. 'Have you ever heard anything... untoward about Freddie's death? Any whispers or stray comments that don't correspond to the official account?'

She shook her head. 'It doesn't come up in conversation.' Then I felt the weight of her hand on my forearm. 'I'm sorry. I'm not trying to minimise what you're going through.'

I nodded, but what with the subject matter, the close contact, the illicit nature of our being together, I could barely produce a coherent thought.

'I suppose it just goes to show that Nathan doesn't give a damn about my son.'

Was that overstepping the mark? The withdrawal of her hand suggested it was, but then she said, 'You have to understand, Nathan cares about nobody but himself. Well, his mum is still important to him. But that's all.'

Not you? I wanted to ask. Instead, I said, 'Then surely he's capable of threats, intimidation, violence?'

'I don't get what you...'

'The witness statements. Isn't it possible they were coerced into clearing him?'

Erin wriggled her shoulders. 'Like I say, I've only ever heard it described as an accident. The police investigated, and concluded that nobody had done anything wrong. If you want to dispute that, surely you accept that they'll need fresh evidence?'

'I do. It's why I'm here now, pleading for your help.'

'But I don't know anything. I really don't.' The way she looked at me, I almost reached out to her. 'Why do this to yourself, Harry? You must see it's only going to stir up a lot of trouble?'

'Anita's made the same point. I daresay you're both right. But I can't let it go.'

'You want someone to blame, that's natural. But are you ready for the consequences, if you make an enemy of a man like Nathan?'

I shrugged, partly to disguise a tremor of unease. 'Just how dangerous is that, exactly?'

'Nathan's a bully, I'm not going to lie to you. And he's...' Erin choked up, and brushed her nose with her hand. 'He is capable of things.'

'*Things*?'

'I don't want to go into detail.'

Her curt response only heightened my concern. 'Then help me, please. If you can find something, and we both go to the police...'

'Incriminate my husband?' She gave a derisive laugh. 'That won't happen, even if I wanted to.'

'Why not?'

'Because Nathan was brought up to believe he's special. To expect the world to bend to his will, the dice to land in his favour. And he does whatever's needed to ensure that happens.'

Her words chilled me, but also caused frustration. 'You're hinting at things here. But back in the restaurant, I got the impression you had something for me. Cold hard facts.'

'I do, but not about Freddie's death. The rumours about drugs? I don't have a lot of detail, but yes, he's heavily involved in the local trade. And before you ask, I won't go to the police. If you betray my confidence, I'll deny I ever said it – because I'll have to, you understand?'

I nodded forlornly. Her disclaimer had dampened my spirits, though I had to remind myself that this was still a major step forward. I found myself saying, 'It's none of my business, but do you love him?'

'I'm not sure how I feel any more.'

'Are you happy with him?'

'Not really.'

'Then why not leave?'

A sigh. 'Because I'm weak. Scared. Because I have no money, no resources of my own. No real family...'

'Except Milly.'

'She's the main reason I stay. If I ever walk out on him, Nathan will retaliate against her.'

'He really said that to you?'

She nodded. 'For Nathan, the key thing is to get leverage over someone. Find their weak spot. And in my case... it's Milly. He knows I'd do anything for her.'

I took her hand in both of mine and gazed into her eyes. The blue of her irises looked darker, flinty, even while they glistened with tears.

'I shouldn't tell you this, but last week, after the inquest, I seriously thought about killing him.'

There was a tiny gasp, before she said, 'You're a good man, Harry. Far too good to be committing murder.'

And before I could react, she leaned over and kissed me on the lips.

I think she wished me goodnight. Like a man in a trance, I nodded and got out of the car and watched her drive away. As I strode along the path to my front door, I was dimly aware of a faint sibilance from the road behind me, but I was far too preoccupied to give it any real consideration.

With a little more focus I might have identified it as the hiss of bicycle tyres, and perhaps even grasped the potential implications of that sound, for Erin and for me.

18

I woke to the patter of rain and a corresponding dampness on my cheeks. Had I left a window open? Was the roof leaking?

I felt the bed beside me: no Anita. Normally I would stir when she got up, though I knew I'd been caught inside a compelling dream: Freddie and I, zipping recklessly through the pedestrian precinct on our bikes. But even as he whooped with exhilaration I was yelling at him to slow down, and in fact I might have been in tears. But why—

Another millisecond for the circuits to reconnect, and then *BOOM*! My memory was fully – painfully – functional again.

Freddie was gone.

There would be no more bike rides. No more whoops of exhilaration.

And the bed was empty because Anita had moved out.

Only then did I remember last night's meal with Erin, and how giddily excited I'd been when I got home. Reflecting on it now, the kiss didn't seem particularly extraordinary. More a case of politeness, or perhaps a way to forestall another of my appeals for help.

The far more significant message was that Erin was scared of Nathan, and for my sake she was urging me to forget it and move on. Just as Anita had. And Gareth.

Who was I to say they were wrong?

I climbed out of bed, wiped away the tears and got ready for work. I was cheered by a text from Jody:

> Hi Pops, just wanted to see how you're doing? xx

Both she and Adam had messaged several times over the past week, a far greater frequency than normal. Last Wednesday, Anita had revealed that she'd drafted an email to them both, setting out the reasons for her decision to leave me for Gareth. Once it was sent, we had suggested a family conference call or video chat. But both Jody and Adam had replied to their mum with rather severe comments, while sending me much warmer messages of support.

I had urged them both not to think harshly of their mother, and assured them that I was completely behind her decision. *Let's stay friendly*, I said. *We all still love each other.*

Adam, perhaps influenced by Jay's slightly wiser perspective, phoned me the next day and said through gritted teeth that he would abide by my wishes. But Jody didn't respond, and when I called, she raged at me for 'taking it lying down'. She said I ought to 'fight' for my marriage.

This hadn't surprised me. I'd anticipated that many people were likely to find my reaction inexplicable, or even offensive to their sense of propriety. But I would simply have to learn to live with that – and so would they.

The split hadn't come as a total shock. Over the past few years the children had picked up on various hints that something was amiss. Freddie in particular had shown great maturity when he discussed it with me last year. He'd just been through a painful break-up with his first real girlfriend, and unlike many teenagers – certainly unlike me at that age – he had unashamedly admitted to the pain he was feeling.

He'd also been admirably direct. 'You and Mum aren't in love any more, are you?' he asked me on a rare boys' night in our favourite seafront pub, The Anchor. We were on our third pint of lager and our fourth game of pool.

'We're very fond of each other,' I said.

He chuckled. 'Sounds like a cop-out to me.'

'I suppose it does. But it's complicated – as you, I'm afraid, will continue to learn throughout your life.'

I was wrong on that point, of course. Tragically, hideously wrong.

'So what, then? You gonna split up? And she'll get together with Uncle Gareth or someone, and live happily ever after?'

'Who knows?' I said. 'Maybe one day.'

'But where would that leave you? What about *your* "happy ever after"?'

'Perhaps I won't get one. Not everybody can. But I hope Anita will always be my friend, and Gareth too. And as long as I have you guys, I'll be just fine.'

I could still picture him standing by the pool table, his cue held vertically like a spear, grinning at me with an expression that held shades of scepticism and disappointment, but mostly an abundance of concern for his daft old dad—

It was a cardinal error to sink so deeply into recollection. The grief came in like a tsunami, forcing me to drop and curl into a protective comma on the carpet, my heart and lungs and guts all squeezed as I surrendered yet again to the desperate, deluded appeal to God, to the universe, to Fate:

Restore my son to me, I beg you: give me one day, even just an hour. One last smile and a hug and a chance to say I love you...

It was about twenty minutes before I had recovered sufficiently to leave the house. The rain felt warm and gently reviving, and I needed the fresh air, I needed the chance to think – and, if nothing else, this was another opportunity to test my resolve in the face of a recurring compulsion to march down to the beach and wade fully clothed into the sea, let the waters close over my head and be with Freddie in the only way I could...

* * *

Erin is in the gym when Nathan joins her. He's put on one of his favourite suits: the pale blue Paul Smith. His manner is relaxed and cheerful but she can sense another mood, darker and meaner, below the surface.

Equally it could be a product of her own guilty imagination. She has a genuine fear that Nathan can look into her eyes and see the track of her thoughts as clearly as if they were being displayed in twenty-point type on a whiteboard.

On the journey home last night, the secret she carried was like another occupant in the car. Walking across the driveway, it seemed to be cavorting around her, practically daring Nathan to take notice.

She knew he'd seen the pictures she'd taken with Stella, though he made no comment on them. In fact, he didn't ask anything about her evening, which was highly unusual, and therefore unsettling.

He was in his office, papers spread across his desk, but it was clear from his heavy-lidded gaze that he was finished for the day. Within five minutes he had her on the bed, naked. He was far too aroused for her liking and went at her hard and forcefully. Which was unsettling, but not remotely unusual.

Now she stabs at the treadmill's controls, taking the speed down to a brisk walk, and uses her towel to hide her face under the pretext of wiping off sweat.

'You look smart,' she says. 'What's the occasion?'

'You'll see.' He's more interested in his phone. 'I'm off in a bit, not sure when I'll be back.'

'Have you had breakfast?'

'I'll get something in town.' He examines her more carefully. 'Sore head?'

'No. I drove, didn't I?' She smiles, but it's hard not to second guess herself. Does she sound convincing? 'I'll be doing the online shop later. Anything you know we need?'

'That's what I leave to you.' He checks his phone again. 'And be ready this afternoon. Smarten up.'

'What?'

'Hair. Make-up. Dress. I want you looking like sex on fucking legs.'

For a moment Erin can only stare at him. *This can't be the life I have now,* she thinks. *Not when it began with such promise, such breathless romance, and it's still the same two people in the same house with the same living arrangements. Surely I'm going to wake up from this at some point?*

'Can I ask where—?'

'You'll see,' he says again, then turns and walks out.

19

It was another busy morning at Melgar. At lunchtime I made a quick circuit of the precinct, ostensibly for exercise but actually in the hope of a chance encounter with Erin. Several times I rejected the idea of texting her.

On the way back I popped into the town's best bakery and collected sandwiches for us both. 'No doughnuts,' Gareth had instructed me sternly. 'We're too old to be eating that crap.'

I knew what he meant, but I still bought the doughnuts. Gareth issued a half-hearted protest before eating two and putting a third aside for later. With his feet up on the desk, his attention was on the wall-mounted TV, which we'd installed to review footage of our props in action, but more often used to keep up with test cricket, Wimbledon and other big sporting events.

As the picture swam into view, I first registered that it was a local news bulletin, then recognised our home town. A camera tracked along the promenade before cutting to a portrait of a familiar figure.

Nathan Webb.

I felt my stomach drop. My first, horrific assumption was that Erin was dead. Nathan had learned about last night and he had killed her.

Gareth increased the volume just as the bulletin cut to aerial footage of some waste ground: the Tannery site. I caught the words, 'major development' and then we were watching a press conference. Eight or nine people were assembled on a stage, some vaguely familiar as local politicians, including a rotund, curly-haired buffoon in a mayoral chain. Nathan Webb was speaking into the microphone, and we joined him at what must have been the closing passage of his speech:

'...a scar on the landscape. In its place we will create something *spectacular*. It's time to clean up this town, restore some local pride, and give everyone who comes to live at Tannery Heights a little bit of everyday joy!'

While a glossy CGI rendering of the proposed development played on screen, the voiceover described how Tannery Heights would provide a partial solution to the town's chronic housing shortage, encompassing a total of a hundred and forty homes, as well as several retail units and a coffee shop. Plenty of environmental bells and whistles were promised, along with the obligatory (and usually spurious) commitment to 'affordable housing'.

As the report ended, it was Gareth who growled, 'The bastard'll be raking it in.'

That was true – and it was sickening – but the real pain came from knowing that Nathan was still at liberty, absolved by that damn verdict.

'Still,' Gareth added, 'I won't be sorry to see that bloody building come down.'

I caught my breath. Of course: the Tannery would be demolished, and with its destruction would go any last hope of learning the truth.

I had to do something.

My sudden resolve must have shown in my face, because I caught Gareth giving me one of his looks. 'You're all right, aren't you, bro?'

'I'm fine,' I lied.

Then I picked up my phone and started to compose a text.

* * *

Erin sees the same broadcast. She isn't surprised that the development has got the green light. It's supposedly been imminent for months, though she wonders if the inquest into Harry's son's death contributed to the delay. She understands now why Nathan has been both preoccupied and uncharacteristically cheerful this week.

Then Harry texts:

> Do you know when they intend to demolish the
> Tannery?

She considers a bland response before giving him the truth.

> Soon as they can, I expect.

Then she waits for the inevitable. It doesn't take long.

> I hate to say this after what you told me, but is there
> any way you could get me into the building? I feel
> like, if I could have a look round inside, it might help
> me come to terms with Freddie's death.

It's pretty naked emotional blackmail. As sorry as Erin feels for him, this has made her cross. After several attempts at a reply, she simply opts to ignore him.

Which is ironic, because he's been on her mind a lot today. She is still marvelling at the situation with his wife and his boss. But perhaps she has put too much emphasis on this aspect of Harry's life, and not enough on the darker side of his nature. After all, he'd openly declared an intention to murder her husband, and these texts demonstrate that he isn't letting up in his quest for the truth.

She's been reflecting on what she'd told him, and what she had omitted. Naturally he regarded Nathan as a monster, and therefore couldn't comprehend why she was with him. Fair enough: Erin frequently wondered that herself. But it hadn't always been as complicated.

Initially, Nathan had swept her off her feet in an agreeably clichéd fashion. He was good-looking, charismatic, and loaded. For a time she had been lavished with jewellery and clothes, whisked off to Paris, New York, the Maldives; made to feel loved and cherished and most of all protected. And he had extended that protection, in his own idiosyncratic way, to the one other person Erin cared about.

Erin's father had done a runner once it became clear that Milly's problems were permanent. 'A bit touched', he used to say of his youngest daughter, then a happy, smiling toddler who idolised her father, regardless of his indifference towards her.

A few years later Stepdad Keith entered the scene. He was a regular drinker at her mum's pub, a thin man in early middle age with bad teeth, faded tattoos and no obvious source of income, despite a pocket full of crumpled banknotes. Then aged thirteen, it wasn't until adulthood that Erin realised Keith probably had his eye on the girls from the start.

Her own experience is not one she wants to dwell upon, but she first suspected Keith of abusing Milly shortly after her sister turned sixteen. By then Mum was seriously ill but still working, permanently exhausted and unaware of the scorn Keith displayed towards them in her absence. Erin was 'Mouthy Bitch' and 'Princess Prick Tease'. Milly was 'Cabbage' or 'the Mong'.

When Erin made sense of Milly's strange accounts of bedroom visitations, she decided to confront Keith about it before she went to her mother. Keith's denials quickly crumbled in the face of specific details, forcing him to change tack.

'So what if we had a bit of fun? She's sixteen.'

'That's not her mental age. She doesn't understand, so she can't consent.'

'Milly don't mind – she *likes* it. And she sure as hell ain't gonna be getting it anywhere else, is she? There'll be no boyfriends or sweethearts for her.'

By then Erin was twenty-two, and better able to withstand the rigours of a police interview, a court case. *Get out of our lives right now*, she told him, *or I'll tell the police what you did to* me.

The next day he vanished without a word to anyone, which meant Erin had the appalling task of explaining his departure to her mum. Sonia had been devastated, blaming herself for what Keith had done to them. It was an episode in their lives that Erin could not forget, and when she started dating Nathan, five or six years later, it felt important that he should know what had happened.

At that stage of their relationship Nathan was only too keen to demonstrate his powers. Within a couple of weeks, he affected less than convincing surprise when Erin relayed the news report of a fifty-seven-year-old man, discovered near Brighton racecourse with extensive injuries including fractures to all four limbs and a devastating wound to his groin.

'Burst his bollocks, I daresay,' Nathan said. 'Terrible the things that can happen when you least expect it.'

To a man as conventional as Harry, this might be yet more evidence of Nathan's reprehensible character. Why hadn't Erin run a mile from someone capable of such brutality? But at the time she was uniquely vulnerable: her mum had died, Milly had brand new parents, while Erin had no one. She already knew the world was a cold and hostile place. Better to have a man like Nathan at her side than be on her own.

She's still debating whether to call Harry when Nathan comes home. He's on a natural high from the press conference, but it's a high that has been chemically enhanced. His pupils are dilated and his energy is restless, uncoordinated, shot through with a sliver of violence.

'Big celebration tonight,' he tells her. A champagne reception for all the interested parties, and Nathan has very specific ideas about how Erin must look and behave.

20

Erin's failure to respond to my text was an answer of sorts, if I had the wisdom to accept it. But it meant that the next hour passed with an aching slowness.

Then Gareth received a distress call from a production company who'd given us a lot of work over the years. They had a sitcom due to begin filming in the next couple of weeks; its writer and star, a high-profile name in TV, had amended the script to incorporate a scene that spoofed 1970s sci-fi shows. Could we put together a flight deck for a spaceship, plus half a dozen ray guns and messaging devices, the cheesier looking the better?

Frankly, you couldn't ask for a more delightful brief. It took us back to our earliest days, improvising at great speed and low cost, and because the staff were committed to ongoing projects, the majority of the work would fall to Gareth and myself.

Half an hour later we were wandering the aisles of a DIY store like the proverbial kids in a sweetshop. The bathroom section was generally a gold-mine for futuristic designs: lots of ceramic and chrome in a variety of exotic shapes that could be made to look like almost anything.

Electrical, plumbing and lighting accessories provided the rest of the raw materials, all for less than three hundred quid. On the way back to the office we were discussing the designs, and how we'd clear the spare desk and create an impromptu workshop.

'You okay with a late shift?' Gareth asked.

'What else would I be doing?'

I'd aimed for levity, but it drew a wince from Gareth. 'The thing is, we're meant to be at a gig tonight. Neet booked the tickets last week.'

'That's fine. I can stay a few hours on my own.'

'Sure? I'll get in extra early tomorrow to do my bit.'

There was a slightly busy quality to the silence that followed. After we'd parked and were lifting our purchases from the boot of his Mercedes, Gareth nudged me.

'I've gotta say this, bro. There are times when I ask myself: if our positions were reversed – if you'd lost Anita, and then I'd seen that you and Mel had, you know... feelings for each other – would I be okay with that? And of course I wanna believe I would. But I just don't know.'

I could only shrug. 'Everyone's different.'

'Yeah, but it's like, how can you be this generous when I'm not?'

'You don't know that. I could never have predicted my reaction, before it happened.'

'I suppose we never know what we're capable of till the chips are down.' He gave me a rueful smile, and suddenly we had transitioned to a different subject altogether. 'This news about the Tannery, you're not gonna get any mad ideas, are you?'

'Mad ideas?'

'About revenge. I don't wanna be reporting back to Neet that you're buying a sniper rifle or something.'

'No need to worry on that score.' Even as I said it, I was able to step back and admire, with a certain degree of guilt, my newfound ability to lie so convincingly.

Then I forgot about it, mostly because the rest of that long working day was so deliciously intense. But my untruths returned to me when I left the office at ten o'clock that night and set off for home, only to end up outside the Tannery instead.

* * *

Nathan has planned it well, Erin has to give him that. And while the reality of the Tannery development can't be denied, it's still difficult to believe the entire evening hasn't been designed specifically to punish her.

First, there's her outfit. He insists on a miniscule black dress he bought her in Harrods a few weeks ago. It's a creation best suited to a flat-chested catwalk model; Erin can just about deal with what it shows of her legs – though sitting down is next to impossible – but the amount of cleavage on show is outrageous.

'You really want all those men leering at my tits?'

'Yeah. 'Cause when I'm watching them, it'll drive 'em crazy trying not to look.'

He directs the style of her hair – a half-up fishtail braid – and the tone of her make-up. Her shoes, naturally, have to be Louboutins with killer heels.

'Thanks to the Tannery I'm being crowned king of this town,' he declares. 'This is day one of my reign, and I want them fuckers to get that from the start.'

He encourages her to take a line or two before they leave. The cab's been waiting outside for twenty minutes at this point (not daring to run the clock) and Erin refuses, but she does gulp down a neat vodka to numb the embarrassment that lies ahead.

At the door, his hand cupping her bum as he ushers her past, Nathan whispers, 'Got a surprise for you later.'

'What?'

'It's a secret. I know how you love your secrets.'

* * *

The reception is in the ballroom of the town's 'best' hotel. Nearly two hundred guests, most of whom have something to gain from the development or something to offer Nathan – or both.

Just as he intended, the dress provokes hungry gazes, as well as varying degrees of contempt and disdain. Erin is led like a prisoner from VIP to VIP, two or three minutes for each session of glazed eyes and grating laughter; hot foul breath in her face, and pudgy fingers that squeeze hers in a slimy grip.

Nathan takes a particular delight in his joshing small talk with two of the county's most senior police officers, his eyes glittering a secret message to Erin. *See what I can get away with?*

There's one character who won't leave her alone. Trevor McPherson is short and overweight, a shiny-faced ex-boxer with capped teeth and a carefully reconstructed nose. He has a lot of influence on planning, specifically in relation to highways. Nathan has been fretting that the main road through the development is overly spacious; restrict it a little and you could squeeze in another dozen units.

'Trouble is,' Nathan explains when he takes her aside, sometime around ten o'clock, 'money's no leverage because he's already loaded. But I do know how he feels about you.'

As he sniggers, she notices a curly-haired clown waiting patiently for his audience. It's the mayor, Erin realises. She's in danger of throwing up at the feet of the town's mayor.

'So we'll see how it goes,' Nathan murmurs, 'but I might have to let Trevor fuck you. Under very specific conditions, of course.'

Erin spins away from him, a hand clamped over her mouth, but he grabs her arm and grazes her shoulder with his lips; it must look seductive, if the mayor's envious leer is any judge. Erin just about survives a glassy-eyed encounter with him before fleeing to the ladies, where she vomits within an instant of the cubicle door closing.

She cleans up and manages to escape outside. There are smokers on the pavement, puffed up men and women in dicky bows and fascinators. As one they turn and sneer like she's shit on their shoe; without thinking she glares back and mouths, '*Fuck off.*'

Then turns away and lifts her phone and of course there's another bloody text from Harry:

> I'm at the Tannery. Do you know the code for the gate?

* * *

21

The Tannery gate was locked, though by pressing on it I created a tiny gap between the door and the jamb, and glimpsed a security light illuminating the fractured concrete and clumps of weeds that surrounded the building. The night was calm and I couldn't hear any noise coming from the site.

After staring at the keypad for a few seconds, I pulled out my phone and texted Erin. I had no real expectation of a response, but to my delight my phone lit up with an incoming call.

'Erin, hi! I hope you didn't mind—'

'Texting isn't a good idea, Harry. Neither is trying to get into the Tannery.'

'Maybe not. But if Nathan's desperate to get it pulled down, that suggests there could be evidence the police missed—'

'I don't think he's the slightest bit worried about "evidence". He's on course to make over ten million in profit from this build.'

For a moment I couldn't speak. I thought back to Gareth's similar comment and there was the same corresponding tightness in my chest. How was that for a bonus after getting away with murder?

'Please, Erin. This is the last favour I'll ask.'

Now she was silent. From the background noise I had the impression she was outside somewhere.

'It's 7-1-7-2-7-3. I think.'

My gratitude wasn't without a clutch of fear. I had no idea what – or who –

might lie in wait for me inside the ruined structure, but after pestering Erin like this I could hardly back out.

I kept the phone at my ear as I punched in the number; about halfway through I sensed Erin moving and heard a sharp intake of breath. I hit the final digit and pushed at the gate, but it held firm.

'Not budging. Is this—?'

'I've gotta go. I can't help any more.'

'But Erin—'

She'd gone. I stared at the screen, then kicked the gate in a petulant outburst, though in truth I couldn't have said whether I was more relieved than frustrated.

* * *

The smokers notice him first. Erin is vaguely facing in their direction and sees how they react, but Harry is complaining that the code doesn't work; she has to end the call and forget the conversation ever happened, and her hand is trembling as she tries to slip the phone into her bag—

A hand grips her arm, and pulls her round to face him. 'Talking to someone?'

'Just Stella.'

'Bullshit.' Nathan snatches the phone from her hand, his body so close to hers that the smokers can't tell precisely what's going on – though surely they must pick up on the aggression in his stance, and the fear in hers? 'A few good-byes and we're out of here.'

He steers her back inside. For the next ten minutes she could be a puppet, an automaton, for all the awareness she has of who she is obliged to hug or kiss, whose hands or lips she must accept on her skin.

One moment of clarity: when Nathan abandons her to say his own lingering farewell to a tall, elegant woman in a stunning maroon ankle-length gown. Her hair is a dark, silky cascade, and Erin swears that Nathan brushes a lock of it from the woman's shoulder before placing a kiss on the side of her neck.

He struts back, beaming. 'That's Keira. Interior designer. Gonna brighten up the site to have her around. Make a change from all those builders' hairy arse cracks.'

In the taxi Erin reminds herself it wouldn't necessarily be a bad thing, if he's found someone else. The issue is more how he tends to treat any possession that's been superseded by a newer, sleeker model.

He slings it out, and doesn't do it gently.

In Gimlet Lane he exchanges banter with the driver, slips him an extra tenner and then appears to escort Erin through the gates with a chivalrous hand on her back. Only when the front door shuts behind them does the entire world shift on its axis.

Erin has removed one shoe and is stooping to prise off the other. Without warning he shoves her so hard that she hits the wall; on the rebound she takes a punch to the stomach and collapses. Nathan stands over her as he examines her phone. Harry is called 'Helen' in her contacts; she's been deleting his texts as soon as she receives them, but tonight she was going to do it after she'd called him.

'At the Tannery, eh? This'll be your mate, Harry.'

She can't disguise her shock. 'I'm not sleeping with—'

'Christ, you'd be fucking dead if you were.'

'He just wanted to t-talk to me. About h-his—'

'His sonny boy. Poor dead Fred.' Nathan sucks his teeth while he examines her. 'Did you give him the code?'

'I don't have it.'

'So what did you tell him? Why's he want to go in there?'

'I don't know. I-I told him it was an accident, I promise.'

'Then why doesn't he believe you?'

She can only shake her head. 'It w-was an accident, wasn't it?'

'Are you doubting my word?' He draws back a foot to kick her.

'No. But he seems to think—'

'That I killed Freddie. So I've gathered. But why?'

'He just feels there might have been more to it. Because of the drink. The drugs.'

'What proof does he have?'

'Nothing.'

'So that's why he approached you, is it? For help?'

'I don't... we d-didn't get that far—'

'You had a meal together. Plenty of time to talk.'

'That wasn't... we discussed oth-other things.'

'Oh, like a date? Whispering sweet nothings?'

'Definitely not.' It's important to be fierce about this.

'"Definitely not".' He mimics her angry growl. 'You'll swear on that, will you?'

'Yes.'

'Well, that's good. Wait there.'

He hurries out of the room. There's a vague notion that she could leap to her feet and run outside, or lock herself in a bathroom and call for help from the window, but it's only ever a theoretical proposition. Erin couldn't do those things, even if she desperately wanted to – nor could she explain why it feels so impossible.

When he marches back in, there's a large pair of scissors in his hand. He smiles as he displays them, snapping open the blades like hungry jaws.

'Lucky for you, babe, I believe what you've told me. But there still has to be a punishment.'

Erin has made it into a sitting position, and says, 'Nathan, please. This was your day to celebrate. Don't—'

'Shut up! You're fucking right it was my day, and you just spoilt it. Which is why this has to happen.'

She tries to ward him off but he swats her with a lazy backhand. Pain blooms along her jawbone, blood spraying from her mouth as she cries out. Nathan pins her face down on the hardwood floor and sits astride her. The scissors are in his right hand, and with his left he grabs as much of her hair as he can hold in his fist.

Then he gets to work.

22

I slept badly that night and woke on Friday feeling more tired than when I'd gone to bed. I knew I'd been plagued with dreams – some had featured Freddie, and some Erin – but I had no clear recollection of them beyond a vague sense of dread.

I'd walked home, fighting the urge to text Erin again. The same impulse returned to me now. I grabbed my phone as soon as I was awake, but the only new message was from Jody. Did I want to stay with them for the weekend?

It was a kind offer, so I shouldn't really have been gritting my teeth while I typed a reply:

> A bit too much on at work right now, but I'd love to come later in the summer xxx

Still nothing from Erin when I left the house. I thought back to our conversation in the car. *He is capable of things. I don't want to go into detail.* Was I letting her down by not racing over to Gimlet Lane to make sure she was all right?

Of course not. But after conducting an internal debate, I concluded that it wasn't unreasonable to send a message, asking if she was okay.

At Melgar I found Gareth in the workshop, naked to the waist as he sprayed a basecoat on the MDF panels that would be transformed into the spaceship's console. He was sweating profusely, and there were blobs of silver paint on his arms and chest. It turned out he'd been here since 5 a.m.

'Neet guilt-tripped me last night. Said it was unfair to leave you slaving away while I was out on the town.'

'Better than you missing the gig. Did you both enjoy it, though?'

'Bloody marvellous. And Neet would've been disappointed if we'd cancelled.'

I smiled. 'So all's well that ends well.'

That phrase left me feeling oddly disturbed. Before getting to work, I sent Erin a second message. That had to be it until lunchtime. By then she was bound to have got in touch, probably chiding me for worrying unnecessarily.

Thankfully the hours flew past. When Gareth and I took a break at midday, I found there was still no reply and allowed myself one last message, with a rather more urgent tone.

It was only after sending it that I realised none of the messages appeared to have been delivered. Was her phone dead? Or had she blocked my number? The latter seemed more likely, and I couldn't deny it came as a blow. Then another, far worse possibility occurred to me.

What if blocking my number hadn't been Erin's decision?

* * *

Erin spends the night in one of the spare rooms, and not through choice. 'I don't want you sleeping with me,' Nathan had snarled as he examined his handiwork. 'You're a fucking mess.'

For most of the night she lies awake, unable to settle or even to think straight. Her stomach aches, and there is a sharp, throbbing pain from where the scissors have gouged her scalp.

She tries both ibuprofen and paracetamol but neither seems to have much effect. Finally she succumbs to the temptation of zopiclone, which she was prescribed last year after convincing her GP that she suffered from insomnia. It wasn't a complete lie – it was insomnia combined with depression and suicidal thoughts, which she hadn't dared admit to. These pills were her escape plan: if life became utterly intolerable there was at least an exit to hand.

That concept is very much in her mind when she swallows them down. Succumb just a little bit more and get it over with. But she doesn't: the bond with Milly and a tiny, irrepressible hope for better times sees to that.

She writhes her way up from the cloying depths of unconsciousness to find it's almost three in the afternoon. There's no indication that the bedclothes have been disturbed by anyone else, though she can't rule out that Nathan did something to her while she was out cold. This is one of the reasons she's been reluctant to use sleeping pills before now.

To her enormous relief, the house is empty. Swathed in a towelling robe, she descends to the kitchen and finds that Nathan has left her phone on the worktop. It's undoubtedly a test. Erin has checked her phone for spyware in the past, and she does so again now.

Then she goes to her contacts. Harry's number has been blocked. When she unblocks it, several texts come tumbling in:

> Hey, it's me. Sorry about last night. Hope you're OK?

> Sorry to get in touch again. Just wondered how you are?

> I don't want to cause problems by messaging, but please let me know that you're all right.

She can picture him becoming increasingly frantic; to Nathan this would be incontrovertible proof that she and Harry are lovers. It isn't only this fear that dissuades her from replying, but the question of what she would say. She doesn't want to lie to Harry; nor can she risk telling him the truth.

She forces herself to chew and swallow a couple of dry crackers. She drinks fruit juice, a glass of water and finally a cup of tea. Only then is she sufficiently revived for what has to come next.

The bathroom. Specifically, the bathroom mirror.

Her reflection initially provokes a splutter of laughter, so perhaps it could be worse. There are tears running down her cheeks as well, but that's more because she's remembering the tickle of the falling strands as they drifted down over her face; the smell of Nathan's breath and the pressure of his body against hers. The way he so casually slapped her face whenever she tried to twist or pull away.

She stares at the mirror and whispers, 'This is who I am now.'

She isn't really referring to her physical appearance, so much as the change in her character. He's hurt her more severely in the past, and yet this feels different. A step further, somehow – although there is still a long, long way he could go. Providing he stops short of her death... well, then she'll always be around for more. There could be no end to the punishment.

This is who I am now.

* * *

His calls are infrequent but as a mother she forgives him. She's keen to discuss the good news, but Nathan hustles her past that. There's a problem, relating to the inquest.

'Misadventure,' Theresa says confidently. 'Done and dusted.'

'That's what I thought, so did the council. The coroner said her bit. The cops are happy. Well, not happy, but—'

'They don't have a choice. Misadventure seals the deal.'

'But if the dad won't accept that? I've got word he's sniffing around.'

'Word from who?'

'Doesn't matter. Fact is, he's talking to people.'

'Talking to who? Or does that not matter either?'

'Erin.'

Theresa sucks a breath between her teeth so forcefully that the crown on her right incisor shifts a fraction. Fucking dentists.

'You wanna take that woman in hand.'

'Oh, I have. Don't worry.'

'Good. And this bloke – what's his name?'

'Harry Manning.'

'That's it.' She remembers from the news reports. 'There's nothing he can prove – or is there?'

'No. But that won't stop him from making waves. And with the development about to start, bad PR could be fatal.'

'Bloody "PR"! Dunno what the world's coming to.'

'PR matters these days, Ma. Anyway, I've gotta decide what to do.'

'Listen to your mother, that's what you've got to do.' She considers. 'You have, what, ten million riding on this?'

'With the kickbacks, it should be at least that much.'

'So you'll wanna weigh up your options carefully. But worst-case scenario... I'd say you need to be ready to top him.'

A moment of stunned silence. Then Nathan says: 'You mean kill him?'

'Worst case, like I say.' A snort. 'Though not till your precious PR's in place, of course.'

23

Erin tours the upper rooms, checking the view from each window. Just as she expected, Nathan has put one of the wasps on guard duty. It's Louis, who favours a chunky mountain bike that looks far too big for him.

He's at the end of the street, intent on perfecting a manoeuvre that involves braking hard and slewing the rear wheel in a semicircle. She has no doubt that he'll spot her if she tries to leave the house.

This is who I am now. A prisoner.

Except it's Harry she sees in her mind's eye, shaking his head and saying, 'You're *not* a prisoner.'

Because this kind of thing just doesn't happen in Harry's world. No matter what their differences, people remain polite and respectful to one another. And as she knows from experience, someone who has only ever inhabited that genteel, vanilla environment finds it almost impossible to conceive of a life lived in savagery and abuse. Particularly when that abuse occurs behind a front door in one of the town's most desirable postcodes.

Louis is small and grubby, with unruly blond hair and poorly fitting clothes: a Dickensian urchin whose quick darting eyes seem to be continually on the lookout for predators. That he appears to be no older than thirteen or fourteen has given him a favoured status. The boy insists he's nineteen, and Nathan has assured her that he possesses ID to support that claim. What

Nathan doesn't realise is that Erin overheard him on the phone, sourcing the fake ID from one of his dubious associates in London.

Every week or so Louis comes to the house and collects a suspicious looking package, about the size of two 500-gram bags of sugar, wrapped in plain brown paper. In fact, these packages *do* contain bags of sugar, destined for a local food bank, and their suspicious appearance is deliberate. Nathan does this to ascertain whether his activities are being monitored by the authorities.

The real handovers are far more discreet, with no direct involvement on Nathan's part.

Erin spends some time on her make-up, and carefully wraps a silk scarf around her head. Then she opens the front door and marches up to the gates, waits until Louis turns in her direction and motions him forward.

She's wearing a cropped top and cut down denim shorts. It's brazen but effective; his eyes seem to drag the rest of his body in her direction, and he rolls to a halt at the kerb.

'Hey, Louis. You here for any reason?'

'Not really.' He won't look her in the eye.

'Would you like a drink, if you're staying around?'

'I'm okay. Not sure how long.' His body is strangely twisted, one arm hanging diagonally, and she realises it might be to conceal an erection.

'Well, if you do want anything, just ring the bell.' Smiling, she traps his gaze and holds it by sheer force of will. 'What're you up to tonight?'

'Going to Brighton, a whole load of us. Nathan's paying.'

'I think he mentioned that,' she lies. 'Hope you have a great time.'

'Cheers. Are you gonna have a good time in London?'

'I'm sure I will.' Somehow she's able to sound like she knows what he's talking about. London?

She turns away, then glances back; Louis has one hand on his groin. He knows he's been caught but just grins as he slowly lifts his arm. Erin makes a determined effort to ignore it, and says brightly, 'The code for the Tannery gate, it's not 7-1-7-2-7-3 any more, is it?'

'Nah. 7-2-7-4-7-6.'

''Course it is. Bye, Louis.'

* * *

It was around four in the afternoon when I noticed the status of my messages to Erin had changed. At twenty to five, an actual text materialised on my screen:

It's safe if you call me now. Erin x

I stepped outside, glad of some fresh air. Erin answered at once, and I didn't try to disguise my relief. 'I've been really worried about you.'

'So I saw. And last night, I take it you didn't try to climb over the fence?'

'No.' The question made me feel slightly inadequate. Why hadn't I tried to climb over the fence?

'Look, Harry, I'm not sure why I'm doing this – except that I don't think you'll be deterred, whether I help you or not – but the code is 7-2-7-4-7-6.'

'Fantastic. Thank you.'

'It's a bad idea, and I'm still urging you to forget all about this. But if you insist on going ahead, it'll probably be deserted tonight. The wasps are partying in Brighton. Nathan's treat.'

'Are you going to be there?'

From the noise she made, I guessed she had recoiled. 'Not really my scene, Harry.'

'I don't suppose you know your way round the Tannery?' I asked in a jokey tone. 'I'm not sure if I want to be exploring an abandoned building on my own.'

'Then don't. Stay home and enjoy your life as best you can.'

'Like you are?' I posed the question to invite a kind of sombre reflection, but I suspect it just sounded cruel.

'And on that note…' she said crisply. 'Goodbye, Harry. I don't think you'll be seeing me again.'

'Why not? Has something happened?'

'Let's just say that if you do care about me, you'll leave me alone.'

'But I'm worried *because* I care. Has Nathan threatened you?'

I waited, but she was silent.

'Or hurt you?'

Still nothing, though I caught a tiny sound. A whimper, maybe.

'Erin, please. I want to help you.'

Now came a slightly hollow laugh. 'And I wish you could. But you're a good man, remember? Much too good.'

Then she was gone, and it felt as though her final words hung in the air like a banner formed of smoke, the letters slowly dissolving as I grappled with her meaning.

I was *too good* for murder, that was her point.

And the only way I could really help her was to kill Nathan Webb.

* * *

Erin struggles to admit it to herself, but she has an ulterior motive in continuing to assist Harry. Nathan's death would release her in a way that nothing else could. So even if there's only the slimmest chance that Harry will actually go through with it (and even less likelihood that he'll succeed) it's not something she can turn away from completely.

That calculation surely labels her as devious, if not outright evil. After all, Nathan is now aware that Harry is trying to bring him down, and he'll be guarding against that eventuality. Supplying Harry with the entry code is tantamount to laying a trap and inviting him to walk into it.

Buried deeper still is the knowledge that if Nathan were to lash out against Harry, a long prison sentence would provide Erin with at least a degree of liberation. But is she really willing to put Harry's life at risk for that objective?

It plays on her mind for the rest of the day. Nathan doesn't message, so she has to be prepared for him to return at any moment. But by six o'clock, after another spell in front of the bathroom mirror, she reaches a decision about her own status.

'Hey, hun!' Stella greets her on the phone. 'How was Chris effing Hemsworth?'

'Took me to Hollywood and back. Now I need another favour.'

'Oh God, what is it this time?'

'Do you know a good mobile hairdresser? Someone discreet, and preferably not from round here.'

24

It was coming up to six o'clock when Gareth and I loaded our work into the van that the production company had sent for an urgent collection. After completing such a profoundly satisfying project, it was impossible to refuse Gareth's suggestion that we go for a celebratory beer.

Such decisions have sometimes resulted in long drunken evenings, from which I'd eventually stagger home after closing time, but this evening Gareth was keen to restrict it to a single pint. Anita was cooking something special, and woe betide Gareth if he wasn't back in time.

'You're welcome to join us,' he added, as something of an afterthought. I declined, with the excuse that I'd already prepared a meal for tonight. Gareth looked sceptical, as well he might.

'Okay, there's a pizza in the fridge,' I conceded. 'But I intend to have an early night. I'm knackered.'

At home I showered and dressed all in black: jeans, T-shirt, bomber jacket and shoes; I even fetched gloves and an old balaclava, just in case. It was a terrible cliché: cat burglar chic. But then I'd never intruded on to someone else's property before; I had only films and TV to guide me.

It wasn't fully dark when I set off for Barkers Way. I'd decided not to wait any longer, for fear that my nerve might fail me. I'd brought a small torch, and for protection I had a Swiss army knife – though frankly I'd be no more proficient warding off an assailant than I would be trying to get a stone out of a horse's hoof.

I walked slowly, conscious of my reluctance to go through with it. But Erin had put herself at risk by contacting me, and despite her insistence that I should abandon my quest, I had the feeling she wanted me to continue.

The street was quiet. Reaching the gate, my fingers trembled as I entered the code. The lock released with a click. I rocked back on my heels, slightly stunned that it had worked, then pushed the gate open and ventured on to Nathan Webb's territory.

I studied the waste land around the building. There was no one in sight, though that didn't mean a lot given all the places someone could hide. I shut the gate behind me and threaded my way across the uneven ground: a mix of earth and broken concrete and even some ancient flagstones. Weeds grew three or four feet high in places, and along with several partially demolished outbuildings I spotted the remains of two burnt-out cars and a dismantled motorbike.

I was perhaps fifty feet from the Tannery when I registered the sleek modern shape of a security camera. In a panic I donned the balaclava, hoping I hadn't already strayed into the camera's range. In my head I could hear Anita gently scoffing: 'Oh Harry, you really aren't cut out for this...'

* * *

I appreciated the importance of the perimeter fence when I drew closer and saw the main entrance had no door. Anyone who got through the gate had the run of the place.

The opening was like a black gaping mouth, and about as unwelcoming. Steeling myself, I stepped inside and paused to let my eyes adjust to the gloom.

The ground floor seemed to be one vast room, the far end lost in darkness. The ceiling was supported by brick pillars, and most of the floor space was occupied by ancient rusting machinery, piles of rubble and broken glass and lots of more recent waste: filthy bedding, piles of sodden cardboard and decaying garbage bags. Around half of the windows were broken, which ought to have meant the place was well ventilated, at least, yet it stank of rotting food, stale urine and faeces.

I removed the balaclava. As well as being hot and prickly, it blocked my peripheral vision and meant someone could easily sneak up on me. I knew I had to stiffen my resolve, and not be spooked by shadows or noise. It was already clear that even a light breeze caused the structure to rattle and groan. I could also hear the occasional skittering that suggested the Tannery was home to a thriving community of rats.

The building had a long and varied history. Just in the past century it had been an engineering workshop and a textiles factory; during World War Two it was commandeered as a storage depot for military supplies, and in the early seventies squatters had established a short-lived commune. There were still faded peace symbols and anti-Vietnam war messages among the other, newer graffiti on the walls.

I picked my way carefully to a staircase, the darkness seeming to intensify with each step. The ceiling sagged low over my head, cables hanging loose like arteries stripped from a corpse. The claustrophobia threatened to rob me of breath, and I made a conscious effort to inhale and exhale more slowly.

I used the torch to examine the stairs. They were simple wooden treads, but only about half were completely intact; the rest were broken or missing entirely, and the handrails were little better. The noise as I climbed made me cringe, the timber screeching out a warning that I was on my way up.

I didn't linger on the first or second floors. From what I could see they seemed to be more of the same: rusted machinery, rotting cardboard and other waste. The windows up here were thick with a century of grime, and even with my torch it was impossible to see more than a few yards.

Then I heard it: a sound from up above. Not a squeak or a rattle that could be explained by the breeze. Not the scratching of rodents or birds.

It was a cough.

* * *

I didn't have to continue. I could abandon this fool's errand right now. But if I did, I would only ever regard myself as a coward. And my boy deserved better than a coward as his father.

I ascended slowly, the hairs on my neck prickling with fear. If somebody was lying in wait, the bobbing light of my torch would offer them a perfect target. But neither could I risk trying to take these stairs in darkness.

As I reached the top and the thud of my footsteps died away, I had the sense that some other sound had ceased in the same instant. Now I could switch off the torch. I was already telling myself I'd imagined the cough, though I also had the unwelcome memory of the spectral figure who had been filming me on Sunday afternoon.

'Hello?' I called out, my voice almost cracking. 'Is someone there?'

No reply, just a silence that vibrated with menace. I considered drawing the penknife but decided I would rather have one hand free. I put the torch back on and shone it all around me, then directed it up at the roof. A large opening revealed the evening sky in a beautiful shade of indigo, no stars yet visible. The cool air wafting in meant the smell up here was a good deal more palatable than in the rest of the building.

The floor was littered with glow sticks, cigarette butts, fast-food containers and empty drink cans. I imagined the place humming with warm bodies, bright lights and laughter, the thud of drum and bass. It might feel special, up here in the early hours on a pristine winter's night, partying with like-minded people safely away from the disapproving older generation.

Using the void in the roof to orient myself, I advanced some fifteen or twenty feet, and then I saw it. There were actually four holes in the floor at this end, but a couple were only small – several inches in diameter – and one was a narrow *L* shape. The remaining hole was large and unmistakably lethal.

I slowed as I drew near. The hole was roughly circular, measuring about three feet in diameter. Just beyond it I saw a pile of timber planks, crudely broken into a variety of lengths. Some were possibly old floorboards, others were thinner and looked more like cladding. Most had jagged, splintered ends where they'd been broken with blunt force.

I knelt for a closer look. The edges of the hole were rougher than I'd thought at first, but they still troubled me in some way I couldn't clarify. I leaned a little further, trying to make out the floor below, but it was lost in darkness.

A tiny creak caught my attention; I held my breath, then realised I could still hear breathing. There was somebody close by.

Possibly right behind me.

In a panic I tried to twist round, lost my balance and toppled to one side, my hand flying out and meeting only air. My elbow hit the floor a moment later, and I saw how close I'd come to toppling through the hole myself.

Gasping with relief, I pointed the torch in the direction of the sounds, but I could see only meaningless shadows. As if to increase my torment, a sudden gust caused the scrape of metal on metal.

I climbed to my feet and edged towards the stairs. Somebody was up here with me. They might have a weapon.

They might have orders from Nathan Webb to deal with intruders like me.

I was undeniably afraid, but knowing how carefully the stairs had to be negotiated, I couldn't bolt if I wanted to.

I cleared my throat, and tried to project some confidence when I declared: 'Why don't you show yourself? I'm no threat to you.'

I listened, holding my breath again, but the silence was absolute.

'I'm here because my son, Freddie, died in this building. I need to know why.'

A sudden swooping – I looked up to see a gull zipping over the holes in the roof; a moment later its cawing echoed back at me.

'Were you there the night my son died? If there's anything you can tell me... I'm not too proud to beg, you see.' I wiped my eyes, and only then discovered that I was crying. 'I never intended this to be a... what do you call it? Soliloquy. But you can still speak. Please...'

No response. I waited forty, fifty seconds... and I might have waited longer still if a rat hadn't scampered across the floor in front of me.

Freaked out, and barely in control of my limbs, I descended as quickly as I dared. There was a scuffling noise above me, perhaps more rats, but as I reached the floor below I sensed rapid motion and heard a loud crash.

Something had just landed on the floor I was on.

I shone the torch upwards, first locating the hole in the ceiling. As I advanced, cautiously checking the floor before every step, I found a hole of exactly the same size and shape, directly below the opening in the top floor. This one had a motley collection of wooden planks across it. Lying in the centre was a chunk of masonry.

I knelt down, removed a couple of the planks and examined the hole. The sides were clean and smooth, with plenty of saw marks visible. Looking up from here, the opening was centred precisely in line with the one above. Which was, I reflected, the key reason that Freddie had died.

The explanation in the post mortem report hadn't made much sense at the time. Now I understood it a lot more clearly. After the boards on the top floor had given way, Freddie had fallen with such momentum that he'd smashed through the timber on the second floor and come to land on some of the old machinery on the first floor. This was where, in the pathologist's view, he'd sustained the injuries that had proved fatal.

When there was no other movement above me, I stood up and ventured a little further. About ten feet from the hole I found a pile of four single mattresses and another stack of timber.

I pondered for a moment, but this wasn't a sensible place to loiter. I returned to the stairs and descended another flight. On this floor I went just far enough to ascertain the position of the machinery beneath the hole. It was possibly some kind of lathe, a huge mass of metal with various protuberances that would cause devastating harm to human flesh. I immediately tried to clamp down on my imagination before it could get to work, but already my head was swimming, the nausea swirling in my gut. *Don't think about how he died...*

It was only once I'd made it outside, and taken a minute to bring my breathing under control, that I realised the one thing I *hadn't* seen or felt in there was Freddie. That seemed like something for which I should be profoundly grateful: to know that nothing of my son's essence – his spirit, if you believed in that kind of thing (and I had to confess that in recent months I'd been trying to believe it) – was trapped in that foul place.

Instead, I preferred to think that we, everyone who loved him, carried Freddie around with us wherever *we* went, and in us he would live for as long as we did.

25

Erin sleeps in the spare room on Friday night. This time it's her choice. Nathan arrives home at ten and immediately demands her phone for inspection. She has anticipated this and blocked Harry's number again, even though she's anxious to know whether he went to the Tannery – and if he did, whether he got out safely.

Nathan is steaming drunk, and for a moment looks bewildered when he sees the state of her hair. Then, remembering what he did, he bursts out laughing. Without a word, Erin walks out of the room. Nathan doesn't stop her.

The next morning is different. She's woken at six by the sound of her door being forced. 'Locked me out?' Nathan growls. 'You don't fucking lock me out!'

She's reaching for the handle when the door bursts open; she isn't sure how she reacts fast enough to avoid a broken wrist. Then he's in the room, shoving her on to the bed, and suddenly a broken wrist is the least of her worries.

'On your front,' he orders. 'I don't wanna look at your lying, cheating face.'

Afterwards he's no less disgusted; the way he sees it, she's brought this upon herself. He returns to his own room and within minutes she can hear him snoring. She thinks again of the sleeping pills, and whether she can abandon Milly. She maybe dozes a little, though it doesn't seem like it until a slamming door jerks her awake and somehow it's gone nine.

Nathan appears, in slacks and a T-shirt, looking fresh and alert, and tells her about London. 'Big party to celebrate the go-ahead.'

'I thought that was last night, in Brighton?'

'That was for the mugwumps. Tonight's the proper celebration.'

'Why didn't you warn me?' she asks, recalling that even Louis seemed to know about it.

'No need.'

'You don't want me to come?'

''Course I don't! Look at the state of you.' He waits a couple of seconds, savouring the impact of his message. 'I asked Keira. She's a classy girl, and it means we can discuss our plans for the show home. A working dinner,' he says, and adds, with a snigger, 'Maybe a working breakfast too.'

He's made his point, hurt her both physically and emotionally, and ten minutes later he's out of the house. Erin is now alone, potentially for twenty-four hours or more.

But a prisoner. Outside there's a tall, burly looking kid on duty. No one she knows, and she doesn't like the look of him.

She unblocks Harry's number and receives a message, sent at ten-twenty last night.

> I had a look round. Someone was there, though I didn't see them. The whole thing looks wrong in a way I can't explain. Don't suppose we can meet to talk about it?

She ponders a reply, and finally decides, as before, not to send one. Not yet, at least.

Instead she texts the number that Stella gave her:

> We're good to go!

* * *

On Saturday the seagulls woke me around 4 a.m., stamping over the roof and squawking at the top of their lungs. It sounded as though they'd assembled for a conference, and in my sleep-deprived, half-delirious state I felt I could translate their angry conversation.

This is the geezer that attacked us on the beach.

Let's wake him up and keep him awake.

He'll never have a good night's sleep again.

And that curry was disgusting. Didn't even have chips.

At six I got up and made tea, only to realise, as I sat drinking it in the kitchen, that the gulls had fallen silent. I returned to bed and slept soundly until ten, then woke feeling annoyed that I'd lost a big chunk of the morning.

No reply from Erin, though I hadn't really expected one. It had been a misjudgement to message her, but when I got home I was so disturbed by my experience at the Tannery that I had weakened and sent her a text.

I contemplated it again as I headed to the beach, too preoccupied even to appreciate the beauty of the summer morning. By now there was no prospect of any peace and quiet – not on a Saturday in July, with twenty-five degrees forecast – so I settled for a single swim and briskly completed my usual routine: exercise, relax, reflect, sob, submerge...

There was one odd moment. As I swam back towards the shore, I thought I glimpsed a figure on the promenade, partially obscured by the crowds strolling back and forth. I was about 60 per cent certain it was the pale, dark-haired youth from the Tannery – the same young man I suspect was hiding on the top floor last night. But he'd vanished by the time I got out of the water, and I didn't see him again.

It was nearly midday when I bought a sausage and onion sandwich from The Broad Beam Cafe and headed up to Melgar to do a few hours' work. I was looking forward to getting my head down with no distractions, and so the next couple of hours were a marvellous release. I barely thought about the Tannery, Erin, my broken marriage – though once or twice I wandered out to the lobby and surveyed the car park, just in case the dark-haired youth had followed me here.

Then Gareth turned up, and let out a laugh when he saw me. 'Great minds think alike, eh?'

In that we both fell for the same woman? The retort was there on my lips, but I had the good sense to jettison it. 'Are you and Anita not doing anything today?'

'No. We, er... we've had a bit of a bust-up.' He scrubbed at his head, sheepishly. 'Finding her some room to work at my place is getting to be a headache.

Files everywhere. Confidential papers. I had it all so neat and tidy, and now there's so much... *clutter*.'

I wanted to laugh, given the mayhem around us in the office, but I managed to tut in sympathy. 'Just teething troubles. I'm sure you'll soon work through them.'

'I hope so. Guess I'm out of practice at living with someone.'

'You aren't regretting it?'

'Not a bit – and thank Christ, eh? It'd be a bloody disaster if me and Neet couldn't make it work, now we've gone and screwed up your life!'

'I don't see it in those terms,' I said, though that was perhaps only a partial truth. 'We're all adjusting to a new routine. Probably not a bad thing for any of us.'

'Good point. Keeps us on our toes as we get older.' Gareth offered to make coffee, but I said I'd be heading off soon. 'Signed up to any of those dating sites yet?' he asked with a grin.

'On my to-do list,' I replied, matching his jocular tone, and there was a moment when I might have admitted where I'd been last night. But whilst I would undoubtedly value Gareth's opinion on what I'd seen – the indefinable sense that something wasn't right – I had to set that against what I knew would be his outright disapproval.

Not to mention that he would invariably report back to Anita.

So I said nothing, and I had no idea then just how much I would come to rue that decision.

26

It's around four in the afternoon when the burly, unpleasant-looking boy disappears and Louis rolls into view.

The woman recommended by Stella did a pretty good job, considering what she had to work with, but Erin still opts for the headscarf. She's wearing a summer dress in a shade of lime green that accentuates her tan, bare feet in a pair of Birkenstock sliders, and newly painted toenails.

None of it is for Louis – this is purely to make herself feel better, but if it helps to charm him into giving up some information, she won't argue with that.

As before, she wanders out to the gates and beckons him over. This time she brings a can of Pepsi, the aluminium glistening with condensation like something from a TV ad.

Louis seems more reluctant to approach today. He's twitchy, morose, his scowl so fierce that the lines on his brow look like charcoal stripes. His attitude prompts her to ask, 'Do you know why you're keeping a watch on me?'

''Cause Nathan's paying.'

'Yes, but why?'

'Who cares? It's twenty quid an hour.'

'Then you'd be mad to turn it down,' she says sardonically. 'You can sit in the garden if you want. Nathan's in London—'

'Ain't worried about him.' He rolls forward and almost snatches the Pepsi from her grasp. His gaze lingers on her headscarf. 'Bet he's with Keira.'

He puts a bit of weight into the woman's name, studying Erin carefully as he says it. She tries to hide her shock but probably doesn't succeed. 'You've met Keira?'

'She was there last night. Didn't stay long.' There's a deft pause, punctuated by the pop and fizz of the can opening. 'Neither did Nathan.'

'Oh.' Erin resolutely ignores the inference. 'Did you have a good time?'

'It was all right.' His tone is flat. 'Reckon he's done with us now. Millions coming from that site, he ain't gonna risk it all just to deal a bit of weed or coke.'

'You may have a point.'

'Guaranteed. Rest of 'em are too dumb to see it.'

She adopts a sympathetic pose. 'I'm afraid Nathan tends to act in his own best interests—'

'Don't blame him.' Louis takes a swig of Pepsi. 'I'm the same. Look after number one. Set a goal and fucking well achieve it.'

The change in him today is making her uncomfortable, but Erin has a game plan and needs to press on. 'So that party where the boy died. Freddie something. Were you there?'

Louis seems to draw strength from her discomfort. 'For some of it,' he says, then sneers. 'Kid was a dick.'

'Was he? Why?'

'Just was. And he fought with a girl.'

'He hit her?'

'Nah, an argument. I reckon she blew him off.' A snigger ends with a sniff. 'Indian or Paki, she looked like, but really fit. Then she left, and he got even more pissed.' Louis drinks again, staring at Erin's chest as if the ferocity of his gaze might be enough to dissolve the fabric.

'Did Nathan talk to Freddie that night?'

'A bit.'

'What about?'

'What do you think?' Louis mimes snorting coke from the back of his hand.

'Even though you said he has no more time for dealing?'

'That was, when, February? Lot can happen in a few months.'

'And were you there when Freddie died? Did you see him fall?'

'I'd gone by then.'

'You didn't talk to the police?'

He reacts as if stung. 'No way!'

'So what do you think happened to Freddie?'

'Just what I heard. He was off his head, jumped on the boards and fell through.'

'And you've never caught a whisper of anything different?'

'Why're you so interested?'

'No reason. I just wondered—'

'Nah. You want any more, you ought to be willing to pay.'

She laughs, incredulously. 'You're getting twenty pounds an hour and you're asking me for more?'

'Not money, then. Show us your tits and I'll answer your questions.'

For a second she can only stare at him, seeing not the weaselly little urchin in need of a bath, but a devious chancer who flourishes in his role of courier, precisely because of the assumptions that his appearance invites.

'I'm not going to do that, Louis. And if you ever suggest it again, Nathan will hear about it.'

'I ain't scared of Nathan.' He taps the side of his head. 'Remember what I know about him.'

'That goes both ways,' Erin reminds him. 'Make an enemy of Nathan and you'll learn just how far out of your depth you are.'

'What, like you?' he snaps back.

She gulps, but quickly recovers. 'Exactly like me.'

Louis's not expecting this, and it seems to subdue him a little. Erin is halfway back to the house when he calls out: 'The stupid twat got pissed and fell through a hole. That's all there is.'

* * *

I finished around half four, cautioned Gareth about working too late and set off for home. There was one occasion when I turned and thought I saw movement behind a parked van, as though someone had ducked out of sight. I stood and watched for far too long but nobody appeared.

I was about fifty yards from the house when I spotted the Mazda on the driveway. My first thought – which hit with the force of a thunderbolt – was that Anita had walked out on Gareth and come back to me.

Almost as shocking was the uncertainty it provoked. *Was that what I wanted?*

I unlocked the door and called her name. Anita replied from the box room that had been her office. I found her sitting on the floor, surrounded by stacks of paper.

'You all right?' I asked.

'So, so.'

'Gareth said you've fallen out.'

'It's ridiculous. I mean, he knows how I earn my living. I've got to have space for my paperwork.'

Yawning, she straightened her spine, then started to rise. I offered my hand and she let me help her up, and suddenly we were just inches apart. I could smell the fragrances of her hair product, her perfume. I noticed a few little lines and wrinkles that seemed unfamiliar, and I thought her face looked slightly thinner, though she was still beautiful. I felt blessed to have had all those years with her.

I stepped back, gesturing at the files. 'There's got to be a solution, surely?'

'Oh, Gareth's latest suggestion is that I rent a small office.'

'Won't that be expensive?'

'Yes. And a wholly unnecessary expense. But his initial idea – are you ready for this? – was that I use the spare desk at Melgar.'

I laughed for the second or so that it took to understand she wasn't joking.

She added, 'I told him it wouldn't work. Let's face it, we're probably skating on thin ice as it is.'

Shrugging, I said, 'Didn't that idea come up years ago?'

'Yes. Mel shot it down in flames – perhaps worried that I'd be trying to get my claws into her man.'

I winced. 'I don't think Melanie was like that. Anyway, you weren't interested in Gareth at that stage... were you?'

'No. But we women take care when we're on to a good thing.'

'Right.' I elected not to dwell on the obvious comparison there. 'So isn't the best option to go on using this room?'

'Come and work *here*?'

'Why not? It won't cost anything, and if it avoids tension between you and Gareth...'

'What about you?'

'I'll be at work most of the time you're here.'

Anita rested her knuckles against her hips while she pondered. 'I suppose it makes sense – although not if you start seeing someone. Imagine trying to explain that your ex-wife spends half the day at your home!'

'No harder than explaining that she now lives with my boss.' I shrugged. 'Might as well give it a try.'

'All right. Thank you. But we may have to reconsider if your situation changes. Whatever you think now, it's not impossible that you'll meet someone.'

She cocked her head as she said it, and my automatic response was to scoff at the idea. 'Honestly, it's the *last* thing on my mind at the moment.'

This, I realised too late, was an unwise thing to say. Now wary, she said, 'I hope that doesn't mean Nathan Webb is still on your agenda?'

'No.'

'Are you sure?'

'Anita, I'm not looking for revenge—' I was interrupted by a knock at the door, which startled us both.

27

It's still Louis on duty when she's ready to leave. Erin no longer cares how miserable or deprived an upbringing he must have fled: he's a slimy, dangerous little creep who is standing in the way of her objective.

As the gates open and she noses the Renault forward, there's a temptation to clip the wheel of his bike and send him flying. She pauses in her turn and allows him to draw alongside. Lowers her window to deliver an icy smile.

'I'm off to visit my sister in Seaford,' she lies. 'Pedal fast enough and you can follow me!'

Louis says nothing; he just lets her roll away and then slowly raises a middle finger to her rear-view mirror, turns it horizontal and inserts it between the circle he's made with his other hand.

It seems unlikely that he'll try to pursue her, but to be sure she takes a complicated route out of town, weaving her way through a couple of villages on the other side of the South Downs before returning, some thirty minutes later, through the dense, unlovely housing estates of the town's north east quadrant.

Erin doesn't give much thought to the Mazda on the drive until she's walking along the front path, and by then it's too late to turn back. After knocking, the door opens almost immediately and Harry is there – but then she spots the woman just behind him. His wife – *ex*-wife? – she guesses.

Harry goes white. 'Like chalk,' Erin will tell him later. Because of the woman, she assumes, but it's probably also the shock as he registers the change in her appearance.

He offers an awkward smile. 'Erin, hi! Come in.'

'I don't want to intrude.'

'No, no. You won't.'

The woman says, 'I'm just leaving.'

'There's no need,' Erin says. 'I was only—'

'It's fine.' The woman moves alongside Harry, one hand easy on his shoulder, and gives him a peck on the cheek. 'I'll see you soon, Harry. Thanks.'

'Okay.' He seems embarrassed. 'This is Anita.'

'Hello, I'm Erin.'

'Erin...?'

'A friend of Harry's.'

Anita eases past her and says, with only a hint of acidity, 'Have fun, "Erin, friend of Harry's".'

Erin catches Harry looking peevish at that, but just as quickly he's sombre again, and it's the scarf he is studying.

The scarf, and what's missing beneath it.

* * *

I didn't appreciate Anita's parting comment, or the manner in which she flounced away. Was she assuming a romantic connection between Erin and me, and if so, why on earth would she do that?

Erin, fortunately, seemed more amused than put out. And I suppose it was a trivial matter compared to whatever had brought her here. She was wearing a green dress and sandals and looked as extraordinary as ever, though there were a couple of bruises faintly visible beneath her make-up.

And then there was the headscarf.

I could tell at once that most of her hair was gone. I wanted to know the reason, but for a second or two we were distracted as Anita shut the car door with rather more force than was necessary.

'I feel I may have caused a problem,' Erin said.

I shook my head. I was immensely grateful that Erin hadn't taken the bait when Anita was fishing for a surname. I didn't want to contemplate what sort of scene might have ensued if she'd learned that this was Nathan Webb's wife on the doorstep.

'I suppose she must think you're... well, my girlfriend.'

Erin snorted, in a way that I naturally interpreted as a scornful reaction.

'Oh I know, it's ludicrous. But I'd just been insisting that I had no intention of dating any time soon.'

'In that case, she probably thought I was an escort you'd hired for the evening.'

'Good God!' The idea hadn't crossed my mind, but to Anita that might have been a more plausible explanation for such a beautiful woman turning up at my door.

I dismissed the subject, and felt a tremor of apprehension as I gestured at her head. 'What's the... why do you—?'

As if to spare me, Erin simply whipped the scarf away.

I gasped. Her hair had been cut mercilessly short, shaved on a grade two or three at the sides, and no more than half an inch on top. In places it looked to have been styled, and sat neatly against her head, but there were also patches that were almost bald, with the odd tuft that refused to lie flat.

When I thought of how long and lavish her hair had been – the very epitome of a fairy-tale princess with those complex braids; all the glorious shades of blonde – it brought me close to tears. This seemed to me such a brutal act that it could never have been voluntary.

'Nathan?' I asked.

'Nathan,' she confirmed. 'Rescued, to a degree, by the valiant efforts of a hairdresser from Polegate.'

I let out a sigh. 'Why did he...?'

'Punishment. Don't ask what for.'

'Was it me? Does he know we've been talking?'

She didn't answer, but I could see the truth in her face. I pictured my texts, pestering and pleading – all with barely a thought of the consequences for her.

'I'm so sorry. Could I—?' I choked up. 'Could I hug you?'

After a hesitation, she nodded. We embraced without inhibitions, albeit in a way that had no romantic or erotic components whatsoever. I held her tightly and for a few long seconds she was clinging to me, her face buried in my shoulder.

'I'm very sorry,' I said again.

'No.' We separated, and Erin wiped her eyes. 'I made choices, and they led to this. But with Nathan, lots of things would lead to this.'

'Then you have to get away from him. You can't risk more abuse.'

She was tight-lipped for a moment. 'That's a discussion for another time.'

I nodded, but I was already thinking of the other possibility. The other solution.

Kill him.

* * *

Erin accepts a coffee, and they drink it in the kitchen without saying too much. She's explained that Nathan is in London until tomorrow, so for now, at least, she can relax.

It amuses her that Harry keeps furtively studying her hair, and finally he says, 'You know, I hate how it came about, but that style really suits you.'

'Yeah, right.'

'It does. It was a shock at first, but actually you look amazing with short hair.'

Erin smiles, hyping her gratitude a little because he means well. It's a thing with men, she understands, to assume that physical appearance is always uppermost in a woman's mind.

But then he asks why she's here, and it's harder to explain the sequence of events that compelled her to leave the house. How, after talking to Louis, she felt unclean, and scared, but also bolder and perhaps even reckless.

'I've spoken to a boy called Louis, who says he was there that night but left before...'

'Before Freddie fell?'

'Yes. Though Louis isn't necessarily someone whose word you would trust. Which is important to bear in mind, given what else he said.'

His brow creases. 'Why's that?'

'Two things. At one point Freddie was talking to Nathan, and he claims it was about drugs.'

Harry pulls a face. 'Freddie wouldn't have anything to do with drugs.'

'Okay.'

'I mean it. He was vehemently anti-drugs. What was the second thing?'

'Louis says Freddie argued with a girl. Afterwards he got more drunk and maybe a bit... careless.' She makes eye contact with Harry, who looks forlorn. 'Does that tie in with anything you've heard before?'

'Some of it,' he admits, reluctantly. 'The girl is called Maya.'

28

I was beset by a sudden weariness at the prospect of having to explain. On impulse I checked the time – twenty past five – and said, 'I know it's early, but do you fancy getting something to eat?'

'In town?'

'Well, I'd cook for you, only I haven't got much to hand.' I realised why she was asking. 'You don't want anyone seeing us?'

'We could go somewhere else. I've got my car.'

'How about Rye? Lots of nice pubs there.'

She beamed. 'I love Rye!'

I excused myself to take the quickest shower in history, dressed in Levi's and a pale pink Ralph Lauren shirt, and was ready to go within fifteen minutes.

'So, this Maya...?' Erin said as we ascended the steep hill on the north eastern route out of town.

'Freddie got chatting to her in a bar, along with another guy, I think. One of them – Maya, possibly – knew about the parties at the Tannery and suggested they go along.'

'You got this from the police?'

'Yes. We were assigned a family liaison officer. I'm afraid I badgered the poor woman to the point where I managed to identify Maya, and find out where she worked.'

The tone of my voice caused Erin to glance my way. 'What happened?'

'I'm not proud of this. Please bear in mind I was half-crazed with grief, not sleeping or eating, unable to work. Maya had a weekend job at a garden centre. I approached her – well, confronted her, I suppose – because what she'd told the police didn't quite ring true. Of course, all I did was upset her. Their security guard threw me out.'

'Ah.' Erin didn't express any disapproval, but I could see she wanted a moment to digest what she'd heard.

We crested the hill and were momentarily dazzled by the splendour of the landscape that fell away to the east: the rolling acres of gold and green, a patchwork of wheat and barley fields, rich pastures and dark copses; here and there a human settlement revealed by the russet and terracotta of the ancient clay-tiled roofs.

'Stunning,' I murmured, and heard Erin exhale beside me, sharing my reaction.

'So maybe Louis was telling it straight?' she suggested. 'He seemed to think Freddie might have been coming on to Maya, and got rejected.'

'I suppose it's possible. Perhaps I should talk to her again.' I caught another glance, and nodded to acknowledge the foolishness of the idea. 'Or to this Louis – so long as it doesn't put you at risk?'

'I'd say that ship has sailed, Harry.'

'What about the others? Anyone who might be willing to talk to me – or you?'

'It's tricky. I have to assume their loyalty is to Nathan, which puts a limit on what they'll tell me.'

'And they might report back to him.' I sighed. 'Will Louis have done that?'

'Maybe, though he's not as well-disposed to Nathan right now. He thinks they're on the way out. As he said, why risk prison to deal drugs when you stand to make millions from your legitimate business?'

'True. That means we don't have much time, if we want to get him done for the drugs—'

Erin interrupted with a slightly bitter laugh. 'Whoa! That's news to me.'

'Sorry. It's been on my mind since Wednesday. If you were able to get some solid evidence, you wouldn't even have to go to the police. Give it to me and I'll take it.'

'That wouldn't work, Harry. He's far too careful. And even if I managed to find something, he'd know at once that it came from me.'

'Yeah, but by then he'd be sitting in a police cell—'

'Only until his solicitor arrived. Remember, he's very well-connected in this town.'

'Okay. But if these young people are disenchanted with Nathan, some of them might be willing to break their silence and tell us what really happened.'

'Didn't you hear what I just said? Nathan is like Teflon. The wasps know that.'

I nodded gloomily, and spared myself the indignity of a petulant response when I noticed Erin rubbing at one of the bare patches above her ear.

It was an important reminder of what was at stake.

* * *

Erin can hear how disconsolate he sounds. There's a natural instinct to respond with affection, but this is already dangerous enough, the game she's playing, so she keeps her hands on the wheel and her eyes on the road.

'How did you get on at the Tannery?'

'It was strange. I haven't really been able to work it out...' He tails off, then says, 'This boy Louis, what does he look like?'

'Louis? He's small, thin, with scruffy blond hair. Very young looking, but sly. A little street urchin.'

'Do you know anything about his family?'

'Doubt if he has one. Probably booted out years ago – or else did a runner from local authority care.'

'Would that mean he'd consider hiding out at the Tannery?'

'I think he sofa surfs. I mean, you'd have to be truly desperate to sleep in the Tannery.'

'I agree, though someone was in there last night.'

'Did you get a look at them?'

'No. But the other day I saw someone at the window when I walked past. A young man, tall and very pale with dark hair. Does that sound like anyone you know?'

'I don't think so. I can ask around.'

They're not far from Rye now, and Erin thoroughly enjoys putting on some speed for the final couple of miles along the twisting country road. Then, from Harry, comes an acknowledgement of what she's been thinking.

'I shouldn't be asking you to do more for me, should I? Not after what's happened.'

'Probably not. But I won't do anything I don't want to do.'

'Thank you. After last night I'm even more convinced it wasn't a straight-forward accident, which makes it very hard not to ask for your help, knowing you have access, contacts, that I don't have.'

'I realise that, Harry,' she says with a sigh. 'In your position I'd no doubt be the same.'

There's a car park close to the river which usually has spaces. This evening it's almost full, but Erin reverses skilfully into a tight gap. When they get out, Harry persuades her to dispense with the scarf. He's brought a baseball cap, which she's welcome to use if she wants?

'I do,' she says, and jams it down on her head.

It's now just after six. They take a stroll along the Strand and get lucky with the second pub they try: there's a table free in a discreet corner.

As they take their seats, Erin catches Harry's expression. 'What?'

'You genuinely don't notice it?' He sounds incredulous. 'In the restaurant the other night, when you walked in, everyone turned to look at you.'

'No they didn't!'

'They did. And it's just happened again. You must have seen the reaction?'

Erin is cold inside, though her face feels like it's glowing with heat. She wishes he'd drop the subject, but of course he doesn't understand. 'What reaction?'

'Like... well, like the most beautiful woman they've ever seen has just strolled past.'

'I think that's just your vivid imagination, Harry.' She touches the baseball cap, still unsure whether to remove it. 'I'm sure I probably get leered at, like most women, but I've learned to ignore it.'

Finally he reads her tone and looks sheepish. 'Sorry. I guess it's not always welcome.'

'It's almost *never* welcome. Especially when I'm with Nathan. If he catches the merest glance he'll call them out. "Yeah, that's my wife, mate. Better looking than yours, isn't she?"'

'He really says that?'

'Oh, yeah. And to women, it's: "Wanna shag her, darling? You'll have to let me watch."'

Harry, now thoroughly subdued, checks to see if they can be overheard before he asks, 'How often is he violent towards you?'

Her reflex is to dodge the question, but that doesn't feel right. 'The low-level stuff is so frequent, I don't really think about it any more. Actually it's the verbal and emotional abuse that affects me the most. The way I'm belittled. Controlled.' She feels the prickle of tears and quickly flaps the menu in the air between them. 'Let's order food and try to forget Nathan for half an hour, can we?'

29

Erin was right: we needed a break from it all. She insisted that I should have beer, and she had a single one herself, clinking her bottle against my pint glass. We ordered pizza and a couple of side dishes, and by the time my second pint arrived I was feeling more relaxed than I had in weeks. The same seemed to be true of Erin; without any fanfare she removed the baseball cap and play-fully twirled her fingers in her hair, *a la* Stan Laurel.

'See? The world hasn't ended,' I said, and when she grudgingly agreed, I added, 'It really does suit you.'

'Good job, seeing as it'll take months to grow back.'

Leaving the subject there, I asked if she'd swum lately, and from that we got on to sport in general. She was a big fan of Brighton & Hove Albion, and had seen them play at the Amex on many occasions. She also loved netball, and as a child had probably been good enough to play at county level, if her domestic life had allowed it. She told me about her mother's illness, her desperation to find Milly a loving home, and I was equally struck by the sacri-fices Erin had made, the selflessness with which she had supported her mum and sister.

We chatted about films and TV shows, and I managed to amuse her with a few more anecdotes about my experiences on location. It was an unremark-able comment about set dressing that led to a sudden moment of clarity, causing me to break off mid-sentence.

'What's wrong?' Erin asked.

'The Tannery. It's just struck me that the top two floors are like a stage set. An area that's been prepared for a specific purpose, and dressed with props. The piles of timber. A stack of mattresses.'

'But what for? The parties?'

'I suppose so. The other thing is the damage to the building. With parts of the roof missing there's been years of water getting in, so you'd expect to see holes in the top floor. But the main one – the one Freddie fell through – looks to have been enlarged, deliberately.'

'Remember that a lot of people have got inside over the years. They're often driven to smash things up, or start fires...'

'Could be. But on the floor below there's another large hole, positioned exactly in line with the one above. And I spotted the saw marks, where it had been cut and shaped.'

Erin looked taken aback. 'You mean like in a fire station, where they slide down the pole?'

'Exactly.' I tried to visualise a party in full flow: moonlight and glow sticks, a thumping beat, a dancing crowd getting drunk, high, playful. Maybe, the first time, something got kicked and fell through the hole: a beer can, an empty bottle.

Youthful high spirits. That was how one of the detectives had summed up the events of that night, based on what he'd been told by the attendees.

'At the inquest, the witnesses maintained that the hole on the top floor was kept covered up, and Nathan had apparently warned people about it. Neither we nor the police could dispute that. And Freddie, as a first-timer there, perhaps hadn't paid attention; he'd had a few drinks and was standing on the planks, maybe dancing a bit, when they gave way...'

Erin put her hands on her cheeks, her gaze filled with sympathetic pain. 'You don't think it's that straightforward?'

'What's preying on my mind is that a lot of the planks had these jagged ends, as though they'd been broken in half by jumping on them. So perhaps they didn't *avoid* the holes at all? Perhaps they walked or ran across them on purpose?'

'Why would they do that?'

'I don't know. They wouldn't be thinking rationally, remember. Has Nathan ever mentioned anything like that?'

'No. But then he wouldn't have told me, especially if it was something dangerous.'

'How about the wasps? Could you ask any of them?'

'Maybe. I can't guarantee...'

'No, no.' I knew I had to leave it there. We'd finished eating, and neither of us wanted a dessert. As we paid – this time Erin insisted on getting the bill, and handed over cash – I started to ponder the wisdom of asking her to come back to mine for a coffee. Best not to push it, I thought.

But when we stepped into the golden sunlight of late evening, Erin said, 'I'm not ready to go home yet. Can we take a walk around Rye?'

'Of course.' I tried to sound nonchalant, but my heart was thudding and a second voice in my head grew confident enough to shout down the first.

She's the wife of Nathan Webb.

And right now, I don't care.

* * *

When Erin looks back on it later, she will realise it was the walk that changed things. It shouldn't have – and that certainly wasn't her intention when she proposed it. But the connections people make, the way a friendship can ignite is a complex, mysterious thing.

And this place, the town of Rye, is magical to her: an almost sacred refuge. It might be only ten miles from home, but it isn't natural territory for the wasps, and she remembers that Nathan, on their one visit together, saw zero appeal in the cobbled streets and ancient buildings.

Harry is a far more amenable companion as they wander up to the grand church of St Mary in the heart of the old citadel. They enthuse over the views from the Ypres Tower, and talk vaguely of walking or cycling from Rye to Camber Sands, passing the majestic turbines of the wind farm on Romney Marsh. They weave through the lanes to the high street, pausing to admire the window displays in shops and galleries, then make another ascent to find the legendary Mermaid Inn is thrumming with life.

Erin suggests going in, and presses another beer on Harry. 'Trying to get me drunk,' he jokes. She denies the accusation with laughter, and could never convey how happy she feels, how gloriously, abnormally *normal* an evening this is for her.

Occasionally the real world intrudes; a shudder of recollection that compels Erin to check her phone. There hasn't been a single message from Nathan all day. The silence is unprecedented, and since she isn't sure whether this should bring terror or relief, it ends up producing a peculiar mix of both.

By the time they return to the car, it's past ten o'clock and fully dark. Harry seems more at ease than he's ever been in her company; several times they've bumped arms companionably as they walk.

After pulling on to the main road, she asks if he minds having the front windows open. Harry is resting back, eyes shut, a somewhat goofy smile on his face.

'Too much garlic on our food?'

'That, plus I like to feel the fresh air blowing in. It's a lovely evening.'

'It is. Hey!' He sits up so forcefully that the whole car rocks. 'How about a swim?'

'A swim?'

'Let's stop on the way back.' He chuckles to himself. 'Night swimming.'

'We don't have costumes.'

He sings something about being naked, then registers her confusion. 'It's from "Nightswimming", by REM.'

'REM? I know "Losing My Religion", that's all.'

'An alarming gap in your musical knowledge!' he declares. 'It's such a beautiful song. Are you sure you don't want to try it?'

'Skinny dipping? Not a chance, matey.'

'Well, we'll improvise. Anita's left quite a lot of stuff at the house. You could borrow something...'

'I'll see.' It's a bonkers idea, but quite appealing nevertheless. It isn't just that his enthusiasm is infectious, or that she's in no hurry to return home; she likes it that Harry is a mellow, cheerful drunk. He's fun to be with, and best of all she feels safe in his company.

They talk about music for the rest of the journey. Harry admits to being ignorant of most modern R&B, dance and rap music. He's an unashamed fan of dad rock, and promises he can convert her to the delights of his hero, Bruce Springsteen. '"Drive All Night" should do it – and if not, I can find a hundred more classics.'

This is all wrong, she thinks. They're acting like teenagers, giddily sharing enthusiasms, and it will fall to her, as the one with most to lose, to tamp it down.

So why, then, does she agree to go inside his house and wait while he searches for suitable swimwear? She takes a selection into the bathroom to try on, and settles on a black sports bra and shorts that he's picked up by mistake: they do a better job of preserving her modesty. She puts them on beneath her dress and comes out to find Harry holding a backpack with a couple of towels. They're both nervous and excited, though not necessarily in the same proportions – or for the same reasons.

'Which beach?' she asks. 'I can't go anywhere I might be seen.'

'Near the cliffs, maybe? It's a fair distance from any nightlife.'

That sounds okay, but Erin still pulls the baseball cap down tightly on her head. They're back in enemy territory now; she mustn't forget that.

But then she pictures Nathan and Keira together in a bar or a club. It's too early for them to be in bed – though maybe that's already happened, and will again – so with the reckless side of her character holding sway, there's a little *Que sera, sera* and a big *Fuck you, Nathan!* but mostly Erin is thinking: *I'm alive, alive, alive...*

And the night is young.

30

Not a good idea, Harry! The beers in Rye had gone to my head and I wondered whether now, as I began to sober up, I was suffering a commensurate loss of nerve.

We didn't talk much on the way down the hill. I suppose we were both aware of just how audacious this felt, given that even a basic friendship between us was unfeasible, not to mention foolhardy in the extreme.

And yet still our legs propelled us forward. Soon we were crossing the coast road and heading for one of the neglected beaches on the eastern side of the harbour, where the chalk cliffs rose out of the plateau on which the town had been built.

Erin used the torch on her phone to navigate our path. 'Hope this beach doesn't need cleaning, or else you'll be down here in the morning.'

'Ha ha,' I said, deadpan, though her teasing prompted an urge to confess. 'I was only cleaning up because the night before I'd tried to kill a seagull.'

'Why would you...?'

'To test my capacity for violence. A practice run.'

'Practice?' Erin halted, shining the torch in my face. 'Not for murdering Nathan?' she whispered.

'I'm afraid so.'

I tensed, anticipating a burst of laughter, but she merely switched the torchlight back to the stones and we continued to walk. If anything, her silence proved more unsettling.

It was about an hour from high tide, and the beach here shelved quite steeply. A good time to swim, providing you were comfortable with deep water.

'I'm fine,' Erin said when I warned her, 'and anyway, you're with me.'

I set the rucksack down ten feet from the water's edge and checked again in both directions. I felt certain we were alone, but still I spoke in a hushed voice, as though in a cathedral.

'You're not tempted to chicken out?'

'Not now. I mean, look at it.'

She gestured towards the sea. On calm nights I considered it to be a hidden thing, glossy black and motionless. Tonight the rising moon had cast a silver path across the surface: all we had to do was follow it.

'Beautiful,' I agreed, though when I said it I was staring at Erin, not at the sea.

* * *

Erin knows she will treasure this experience. The darkness, the solitude, the peace. For the first time in years she feels utterly protected. As she shrugs off her dress, the night is so deliciously warm and still that the air has no cooling effect whatsoever.

Harry has discreetly turned away. His body is a little paunchy, but more muscular than it looked from a distance when she watched him swim last week. Good shoulders, she can't help noticing. Good shoulders, strong arms... and beautiful hands.

'All set?' he asks, then takes a portable speaker from the backpack. He places it on a towel, taps at his phone, and she hears strings and then piano, a few heavy notes that settle into a compelling circular melody.

'This is "Nightswimming".'

The addition of music feels far too much like a romantic gesture. As such, Erin shouldn't even consider holding hands with him, and yet here she is, waggling her fingers by way of invitation, and Harry accepts, so that together they can totter and slide down the bank of stones and into the water up to their knees.

Harry, she can tell, is focused on the song. The singer's voice is rich and raw and wistful, the addition of strings conferring an extra layer of poignancy to his words.

'It's perfect,' she murmurs.

Harry nods, and now they are both solemn for a moment, as the lyrics of the second verse seem to caution against the risks they're taking.

Then Erin cries, 'Come on, Harry!'

After tugging on his hand she breaks free and dives under in one smooth motion. There's a glorious skin-tingling chill to the sea, a sensation Erin relishes as she kicks and swims a dozen strokes or more, chasing the moon across the water to an accompaniment of piano and strings and finally an oboe, the saddest instrument of all, and so apt for her present existence that when she stops and turns, with Harry surfacing only a foot or two away, there isn't a threat on earth that could prevent her from inviting him closer.

Harry obeys but doesn't read her intention, so there's a certain degree of surprise when she throws her arms around his neck and places her lips against his and kisses him with a hunger she had forgotten she could possess.

* * *

For a moment I thought my imagination had hijacked my conscious mind. That, to me, seemed a likelier explanation than that this incredible woman had elected to kiss me. It was barely a step down from actually being able to fly...

I could only just touch the bottom on tiptoe, and when the gentle swell of a wave lifted us into deeper water, neither of us realised until suddenly our heads went under and we couldn't breathe. We floundered, breaking apart, then kicked upwards and surfaced, spluttering and laughing.

We swam in. Erin stopped as soon as she could stand, the water lapping over her shoulders. She grabbed my hands and pulled me closer, our bodies touching for the first time, then not merely touching but pressing, and the intensity of that contact made the kissing yet more hungry, more frantic.

Sheer insanity! an unwanted voice was yelling in my head. *This will get you both killed!*

Despite that, I couldn't stop until she wanted to stop. Minute after minute of the most extraordinary passion, at a level I probably hadn't experienced since I was a teenager. The world closed in until it was only Erin's mouth, Erin's hands, Erin's body against mine. A bomb could have detonated on the beach and I wouldn't have noticed or cared.

We were shivering when finally we emerged from the water, hand in hand but both, abruptly, a bit subdued. Perhaps she was regretful; for my part I was simply reeling.

I grabbed the towels and handed one to Erin. She wrapped it around herself in a smooth motion that also, coincidentally or not, left her facing away from me. I was struck by a sudden conviction that I'd done something wrong.

'You okay?'

'Just cold.'

I retreated a little and also kept my back to her as I quickly dressed. I was staring across the harbour, and at one point thought I made out the distinctive silhouette of a solitary fisherman: Len Bowden at his usual station.

When I judged it to be safe I turned and found Erin slipping on her shoes. Her head was bowed, revealing the lacerations on her scalp where Nathan had scraped at her hair. It provoked a surge of fury.

'Seeing what he did to you, I want to kill him.'

She looked up. 'Don't say that. It wouldn't work.'

'Okay. But it's not as though...' My frustration was getting the better of me. 'I mean, you gave me the code. You've talked to the wasps. Why do that if you don't want me to bring him down?'

'Because...' Erin faltered, blinking rapidly. 'Maybe I do want you to find a way out for me. But it's a fantasy. I'm not thinking straight.'

'I guess tonight's the proof of that?'

'Perhaps it is,' she agreed sadly, and we stared at one another for a few seconds before Erin brushed her knuckle against her eye.

'Sorry,' I said.

'It's fine. We're both a bit...'

She didn't complete the sentence, but after I'd shoved the swimming gear into the rucksack, Erin crooked her elbow, inviting me to link arms, and in this courtly old-fashioned manner we strolled back across the beach.

The mournful cry of a seagull made us look up; we could see half a dozen of them floating above us, pure white wings against the velvet dark of the sky.

'Practice run!' Affectionately Erin butted her head against my shoulder. 'Good grief.'

Before she could quite straighten up, I planted a kiss on her head. 'I'm a useless idiot, I'm afraid.'

'No. I truly wish someone could get rid of him, but there's no way on earth I want you to try. I forbid you from even thinking about it, understand?'

'All right. But why?'

'God, Harry. I *care* about you. I don't want to see you – at best – in prison for the rest of your life.'

'At best?'

'Yes. Because at worst you'll be dead. Either way, Nathan will almost certainly survive – and then he'll take it out on me. So for that reason alone...'

'I get it. I promise.'

We hugged, and then kissed, rather demurely. We were approaching the broad path that ran along the base of the cliffs. There were several benches on this section, and on one of them I could just make out a young couple, their bodies entwined. The girl was unhappy, her knees drawn up over the boy's legs, her hands covering her face. The boy was leaning in, perhaps whispering in her ear or just waiting impotently for the weeping to cease.

And then, as we drew nearer, the boy looked round and somehow it was Freddie, staring at me with such raw agony that for a second I thought my heart would stop.

You didn't die. It was all a terrible mistake.

A choking cry emerged from my throat. Erin turned to see what was wrong, and in the same moment the girl poked her elbow into the boy's ribs and he fell back, wounded but laughing with it, and of course it wasn't Freddie. This young man was harder faced, and he didn't appreciate the way I was gaping at him.

Nodding an apology, I took Erin's arm as we sped up to pass them. She seemed tense, and I had another thought. 'He's not a wasp?'

'Don't think so. Are you all right?'

'Yeah. Just my mind playing tricks.'

I was grateful that she didn't push for an explanation. I knew I would long remember the expression I had pictured on my son's face, the sense that I had betrayed him – or *was* betraying him – and really, I thought, what more appropriate way to end this otherworldly evening than for Freddie to send a message that I was singularly incapable of deciphering?

31

The hotel is breathtaking. The hotel, the terrace on the fourteenth floor, the view of the Thames: all the lights of the city sparkling on the water.

Nothing but the best for her boy.

Theresa has thoroughly enjoyed the six-course meal, the champagne and cocktails. Now the coffees have been served, and soon the music will start: a live band renowned for their take on classic sixties songs.

Needing some air, she retreats to a quiet spot on the terrace. When Nathan joins her, she's idly watching the river traffic from a height that renders the boats as little more than bath toys.

'All right?' He's sipping from a tumbler of Scotch, and has brought a second glass for her.

'Marvellous.' She accepts the drink. 'Couldn't have gone better, if you ask me.'

'Cheers.' He's gazing down at the river when she hears a sigh. 'Just thinking, if Dad could see me now...'

Automatically she says what Nathan expects to hear: 'He'd be proud as punch, son' – rather than what she's thinking: *Your dad would be jealous, and finding fault, because Pierson Webb was a mean-spirited cunt, and he probably wasn't even—*

'You all right, Ma?'

'Fine.' She blinks out of it. 'Just know that *I'm* fit to burst with fucking pride, never mind what he might have thought.'

'Yeah, 'course. Didn't mean to upset you.'

'You haven't. But I'm sensing there's something on your mind? Not still this Harry bloody Manning?'

'Not just him.'

'What, Erin? If you can't trust her, that's serious, boy.'

He drains the Scotch and issues a burping laugh. 'So I kill *her* as well, do I?'

Theresa's brows knit together; she has never taken kindly to mockery. 'Well, you sure as hell can't divorce her, with what she knows.'

'Don't remind me. And don't say "I told you so".'

'It was understandable – the blue eyes, blonde hair, those bloody tits...' She nudges him, then gives a sly nod towards the function room. 'Hit on that interior designer yet?'

'Keira?' He tips his glass back and forth, and for a moment seems about to lob it into the air. 'Turns out she's gay.'

'*What*? She don't look like any kind of dyke to me.'

'Well, she is. I've seen pictures of her girlfriend. They're getting married in September.'

'And you couldn't change her mind?' Tutting, she takes his empty glass in exchange for hers. 'I don't care what people say these days, it's downright unnatural.'

'Fucking disappointing, is what it is. I'm gonna think about getting someone else in.'

'You do that.' She watches him drink again. 'But Harry Manning – you've got to deal with him, at least.'

'Actually, I've been thinking about that.' He describes what he has in mind, and to the surprise of them both, Theresa can't fault his plan at all.

'Not a bad little problem solver. Almost in your mother's league.'

The conversation is interrupted by the band tuning up, then Nathan says, 'I'll get things underway in the morning.'

Theresa opens her arms; he steps into the embrace and turns his head to one side, inviting a kiss on the cheek. The first song begins, and it's only 'Waterloo Sunset': her all time fave.

'For me?' she gasps, delighted.

He nods. 'Wanna get a cocktail?'

'Why the hell not? As the saying goes: you only live once.'

32

On Sunday I was startled awake at around eight o'clock. As I lay there, heart thumping, I picked up the vibration from outside that meant someone was walking along the path.

I raced to the front door and spotted a sheet of paper, badly folded, resting on the mat. Conscious that I was naked, I grabbed a long coat from the hook and unlocked the door. I ran barefoot along the path and glimpsed a tall, thin figure vanishing around a bend in the road.

The boy from the Tannery.

I hesitated, unsure whether to pursue him, then registered that the front door was slowly swinging shut... and my keys were in the house.

I'm not quite sure how I made it, but once inside I sank to the floor, panting and groaning. Finally I was able to snatch up the sheet of paper. The message was scrawled in biro, the handwriting large and uneven.

StAy AwAy froM the tAnnery.
FreDDie DieD HAppy. U wont.
A wArning Not A threAt

I read it several times, at first disbelieving, then shocked, then furious.

Eventually I was able to stand up. I got dressed, and over a mug of tea I studied the note and decided that, contrary to what it said, it was intended as both a warning *and* a threat.

I had a twinge of panic, recalling that I'd possibly sensed someone behind me yesterday morning. If Tannery Boy had followed me all day, he knew not only where I lived but also where I worked – and what else had he seen?

Had he been spying on me when I got back here with Erin last night?

The thought made me nauseous. I'd checked my phone but there were no messages from Erin. I decided it was probably safe to contact her, since Nathan was staying over in London.

I took a picture of the note and sent it via WhatsApp. My accompanying message said:

> Just had this through the door, from the boy I saw in the Tannery. Can we talk?

The instant I sent it, I realised I should have mentioned last night, but a follow-up message would just look tawdry. I'd have to hope she understood that my anxiety about the note was uppermost in my mind.

Then I wondered if I should be reporting it to the police. But if I gave a statement, I'd have to explain why the note told me to stay away from the Tannery. I'd be admitting to trespass, at the very least.

I was briefly elated when the WhatsApp ticks turned blue, but there was no reply. I sat and waited, fretting over Erin and the crazy, unexpected passion we'd shared the night before. In the sobering light of day, our behaviour seemed even more reckless.

And yet I had rarely felt so alive. Hadn't it been worth the risk?

When my mind went too far in that direction, I fretted over the note instead. One line kept catching my eye, causing my heart to contract. *Freddie died happy*. That struck me as a disgusting thing to say. Not content with threats, Tannery Boy was taunting me as well.

When ten o'clock came and there was still no response from Erin, I knew I had to focus on something else.

The garden centre would be open by now.

* * *

Erin enjoys a rare night of blissful sleep and wakes refreshed. The events of the previous evening, when reviewed in the cool, calm light of morning, seem best regarded as a fantasy.

She doesn't feel much remorse about kissing another man – Nathan has long since relinquished the right to her loyalty – but she does feel bad about the way she's treated Harry. As unhappy as she is in her marriage, there can never realistically be a relationship with another man, Harry or anyone else.

She's eating a yoghurt when Nathan texts.

> Got some business in town. May have to stay another
> night.

It's a worry that yet again he isn't asking where she's been or what she's doing. Too much on his mind, perhaps. But the sheer relief enables her to send an upbeat reply.

> Okay, hun. Hope it goes well!

Stay in London for days, weeks, years *if you like. Stay away from me for ever.*

Minutes later the good mood is dented by Harry's message, complete with a picture he's taken of an anonymous note. The words send a tickle of dread along her spine: this means Harry is being watched. The note doesn't read like something Nathan would send, but that isn't to say he's not behind it.

Erin can't face discussing it right now. Only on the second read does she notice that there's no mention of last night. Maybe Harry feels as awkward as she does?

It's another dry sunny day, but not as warm. She adds a cardigan to her shorts and T-shirt then wanders out to the gates. She's decided to try and get some more information, though if it's Louis here today she'll go straight back inside.

But it's a boy called Jax. She doesn't know much about him. He's medium height, tanned, with short brown hair and glasses that give him an owlish look. He has an e-scooter but it's propped against someone's fence while he sits on the kerb drinking a McDonald's milkshake through a straw.

He looks startled when she summons him over. She notices he walks with a slight limp, and has a vague recollection that he broke his ankle last year, which took him out of action as a courier for a while.

'Jax, isn't it?'

He nods warily, his gaze lingering on her new hairstyle. She wonders if the wasps have debated the reason for it – or perhaps Nathan has openly bragged about what he did.

'You're on my husband's payroll.' It isn't a question. 'Do you know why you're here?'

He shakes his head. 'No.'

'I'm not cheating on Nathan.'

'Okay.'

He's blushing. Erin smiles to signal a change of subject. 'Good news about the Tannery development – though I suppose you'll miss the parties!'

'A bit.' He sucks on the straw like a toddler; she swears he goes cross-eyed for a second. 'There's talk of one more, before they knock it down.'

'I've never been, but I love the idea of dancing under the stars.' When he looks mystified, she adds, 'Beneath the holes in the roof.'

'Yeah, sure.' He seems to be relaxing into the conversation. 'One time, in this *massive* thunderstorm, it was like a waterfall coming in. We got soaked and, like, didn't even notice.'

'Wonderful to be so absorbed in the moment. So what else makes them special? What do you do there?'

'Usual stuff. Drink. Talk. Dance. Smash things up if we're in that kind of mood.'

'Nathan doesn't mind?'

'Nah, it's all junk. Anyway, he gets his own back with his games and shit.'

'What kind of games?'

'He dares us to do stuff. It's a laugh,' he adds, and then snorts, a little ruefully.

'Dares you? How do you mean...?'

'We have to dance,' Jax says. 'Over the hole.'

33

The garden centre was a vast emporium that sold everything from sheds and garages to scented candles and cut-price paperbacks. Business was as brisk as you'd expect on a Sunday morning, and I was glad of that. I kept my sunglasses on inside, hoping I wouldn't be recognised by the security staff.

It took about ten minutes before I spotted Maya in one of the outdoor sections, arranging a display of pots. She didn't look up until I cleared my throat. 'Maya?'

I stepped back as she jumped, putting a hand to her chest and casting around as if in need of rescue. She was a tall, slender girl with delicate features and an expression that seemed – in my presence, at least – permanently anxious.

'I'm really sorry about last time,' I said.

She eyed me for a moment, before nodding cautiously. 'What do you want?'

'Just a few questions.'

'I have to work.'

'Absolutely. You carry on, and we can talk at the same time.'

With a huffing sigh, she nodded and turned her back on me.

'May I just check – and I don't mean to offend you – but are you certain you left before Freddie... had his accident?'

There was a half glance in my direction, and a curt, 'Yes.'

'And this was with... Ben, who you'd met at the same time as Freddie?'

'Yeah.'

I waited, and when she didn't elaborate, I moved to the far side of the display so I was facing her. 'Could you describe how that came about?'

'It's in my statement.' She kept her head down, positioning the pots with exaggerated care.

'I know. But... please.'

Another sigh. 'I was in the Hope & Anchor with Ella and Phoebe, who I'm at college with. Ella got talking to Ben, and then I think he, like, challenged Freddie to a game of pool. We kind of formed a group, then the guy Freddie was with left – I think he'd been invited somewhere and Freddie wasn't up for it – and then Ella and Phoeb left as well.'

'So it was just the three of you?'

She nodded. 'Ben was hungry so we went for burgers. We didn't want the evening to end, but the clubs here are scummy. I'd been to the Tannery once before, and I knew there was something happening that night, so we headed over. Me, Ben and Freddie.'

'But once you were there, you three didn't stay together?'

'No. I mean, like, you don't, do you? I knew some people. I think Ben knew someone—'

'And Freddie?'

'Yeah, no, maybe. I don't know.'

I was familiar with the way teenagers conversed, so I didn't think this confusion was suspicious in and of itself. After my next question, however – 'So what happened then?' – Maya looked not just uncomfortable, but slightly evasive.

'It was a party, so we, like... drank. Talked. Danced. But I had a shift here the next day, so around one, one-thirty, I decided to go.'

'On your own, or with Ben?'

'With Ben. That's in my statement.'

'Yes, sorry. Any, uh, reason why it was just you two...?'

She hesitated. A customer was approaching: a woman of about sixty who virtually shoved Maya aside to snatch up one of the pots, then marched away without a word.

'"Thanks, Madam!"' Maya muttered sarcastically. Then, in a shy voice, she said, 'I guess because me and Ben... we'd kind of realised we liked each other.'

'I see. So if Freddie had wanted to leave with you, that wouldn't have been welcome?'

"Course it would. We weren't, like, *doing* anything.'

'But Freddie didn't want to leave? It was his choice to stay.'

'I suppose.'

'You don't know for sure?'

'I didn't really see him. Me and Ben had been talking, quite... intensely. It's not one of those things where you, like, go round shaking hands and saying goodbye.'

I managed a grin. 'I suppose not.'

'That's all I can tell you. I don't, like, watch the news, and I didn't see anyone else from the party, so it was ages before I heard...'

This was what had enraged me last time: the fact that Maya had been blithely unaware of Freddie's death for nearly a week. But I couldn't afford to let it upset me again.

'Right.' I made as if to turn away, and for a moment I wasn't sure if my desire to remain civil would prevail over my desperate need for the truth.

Then I blurted out: 'Someone said you had a fight with Freddie. An argument.'

* * *

Erin knows she mustn't acknowledge the significance of what she's just heard. It takes quite an effort to scrub off any hint of shock and replace it with a snort of laughter.

'You dance over the hole? You mean, like, jumping over it?'

Jax shakes his head. 'It's covered with boards. We dance on them.'

'But isn't that dangerous?'

'Can be. Especially if you're stoned.' He grins, ruefully. 'Though if you're stoned, you don't think about the danger.'

'So the boy who died... is that what happened to him? A dare?'

Jax's whole body stiffens. 'Think that was just an accident.'

'Did you see it happen?'

'Nah. Only heard about it later.'

'But you were there?'

He nods, reluctantly. 'Had to talk to the cops.'

'Well, that's never fun. Did Nathan ask you to provide a statement?'

Jax narrows his eyes, unhappy with where she's taking the conversation. 'A few of us had to. Otherwise we might've got accused of stuff.'

He finishes the milkshake with a noisy slurp. 'I'll take the cup for you,' Erin says, and when he hands it over another question springs to mind seemingly from nowhere. 'Is that how you broke your ankle?'

Maya was staring at me, dumbfounded. 'L-look,' I stammered, 'I'm not saying it had anything to do with... But please tell me if it's true.'

Her lower lip wobbled and suddenly she burst into tears, covering her hands with her face.

'Oh, Maya. I'm sorry. I didn't mean—'

Recovering, she hissed, 'Be a customer.'

I looked round. A prissy looking man with a centre parting was advancing on us, quite clearly monitoring our interaction.

I gestured at a collection of pond bases. 'Maybe one of these?'

'Good choice. And perhaps think about a pump, if you're intending to keep fish in a pond of this size.'

'I certainly will. This is excellent advice, thank you.' I timed my response so that the man would hear it; after a brisk nod at Maya, he moved on.

'My supervisor,' she whispered. Then, without further prompting, she said, 'It's true. We did argue.'

'Badly?'

A shrug. 'He saw us kissing. Then, when Ben went off to pee, Freddie came over and, like, demanded to know what I was doing.'

'Why would he do that?'

'Because of earlier. In the pub, he'd kind of... not hit on me, exactly, but made it obvious he liked me. And I liked him,' she added. 'Just not... not in that way.'

'Whereas Ben...?'

'Yeah. I fancied him. We're still together.'

'And Freddie was upset about that? Jealous?'

Maya nodded, before staring at the ground. 'He said stuff. It upset me, even though I knew it was really just the drink. The disappointment.'

She sniffed, harshly rubbing her nose with the back of her hand, then looked me in the eye.

'When I found out he'd died... it broke my heart, you know? And then, with the police, I left out the argument because I couldn't face having to repeat what he'd said. I didn't want his family – you – seeing those words and having it change the way you remembered him. Because I'm sure he was a nice guy, really. Just a bit cut up that I'd gone with Ben and not him.'

'That's—' I broke off, on the verge of bursting into tears myself. 'That was considerate of you. The only thing is, if we *had* known, it might have offered us a better insight into Freddie's state of mind.'

Maya looked horrified. 'I'm so sorry. But after we'd had our... discussion, he seemed fine. It wasn't like a horrible atmosphere or anything.'

'I thought you'd left?'

'Not straight away. It was... half an hour, maybe? And Freddie didn't seem upset. I saw him talking to people—'

'Was Nathan Webb one of them?' I interrupted.

She thought about it. 'Not sure.'

'Okay. But Freddie... could he have been putting on a brave face?'

'I suppose.' She wore a haunted expression. 'Does this mean you think he might have... done it deliberately?'

She had every right to ask, but it was an almost unbearable thing to contemplate. All I could say was, 'I have no idea. It's why I'm here now, trying to find answers.'

She nodded. 'I'm very sorry. I really am.'

As I thanked her, I was conscious of a sudden bone deep exhaustion that made me want to sneak into one of the nearby garden sheds and curl up and sleep for hours. But I had something else to ask her.

'Do you know a small kid with scruffy blond hair, young looking for his age—?'

'That's Louis. He gives me the creeps.'

'Was he there that night?'

She nodded without hesitation. 'I mean, I don't know how long he stayed after I left, but yeah. Definitely.'

'What about a thin, pale young man with dark hair?'

'I think so. He wasn't really taking part.' A shiver ran through her. 'You'd just turn and find him watching from the shadows.'

'And Nathan Webb?'

'I hardly saw him. I've never said more than hello to the guy.'

'And you didn't feel threatened there? Unsafe?'

'Not really. Though I maybe wouldn't go there on my own – I only went because Ben was with me. And Freddie.'

And Freddie only went because *you* were going, I thought sadly. I couldn't say it out loud – and I certainly couldn't blame her for it – but after thanking Maya again, I had to make a swift exit. I didn't want her seeing how devastated I felt, knowing it had all come down to this young woman's preference.

If Freddie had appealed to Maya just a little bit more than Ben, my son might still be alive today.

* * *

Jax's instinct is to lie, Erin can tell, but it's already too late and the boy appears to recognise that.

'Boards gave way. There's mattresses on the floor below but I landed badly. Gave everyone a laugh.' He chuckles. 'I was so arseholed, it didn't even hurt that much.'

'You were dared to do it, though? By Nathan?'

'I didn't mind. He wasn't angry with me.'

Erin ponders for a moment. 'So what happens if you refuse to get on the boards?'

'Don't think anyone has.'

'No one's ever said they won't do it?'

The boy shrugs, unconvincingly. 'Dunno.'

'Did they call an ambulance for you?'

'Taxi. Buddy of Nathan's. And later he gave me money for the injury.'

'Nathan did? How much?'

Jax looks torn between pride and shame. 'Two grand.'

'Wow. So how often do people fall through?'

'Dunno.'

'But it does happen sometimes?'

A nod. He starts backing away.

'When you spoke to the police, did you tell them about these dares? Or your accident?'

He regards her with scorn. ''Course not.'

'No. Sorry.' She's happy for him to think she's being dim. 'What about these mattresses? Where do they go?'

'Over the other hole. On the floor below.'

'Ri-ight. But that boy who died, I think he fell through *two* floors. How come the mattresses didn't break his fall?'

'Dunno.' Jax continues his retreat. Erin tries to match his pace, without it looking like she's chasing him.

'Could someone have removed them?'

'Maybe. Or forgot to put them there. Just bad luck, you know?'

'Louis told me the boy had been arguing with a girl.'

The change of subject provokes a physical jolt. Jax, with panic in his eyes, says, 'I dunno why you wanna know all this stuff. You're hassling me a bit here.'

'Sorry. I didn't intend that.'

'You gotta keep this to yourself, yeah?'

'I will.' Erin smiles, as fondly as she can manage. 'Who's the thin boy with very pale skin and dark hair?'

'That's Ash. He's kind of weird. Keeps to himself.'

'Does he work for Nathan?'

'Not really.' Jax shakes his head. 'Look, any more questions, I think you should ask your husband.'

He crosses the road to his scooter, his discomfort only serving to emphasise the value of the information he's just supplied.

The question now: how to tell Harry what she's learned?

35

I felt disorientated when I blundered out of the garden centre. I had no reason to doubt what Maya had told me, but the thought of having to share this information with Anita, with Jody and Adam and others, was so dreadful that I wondered if it would be preferable to say nothing. Seal it up like toxic waste, no matter how corrosive the effect might be in the long term.

I was on the bus when I received Erin's text. To my surprise, she wanted to know if I was home.

> I'll be there within twenty minutes.

Soon after, she texted:

> I need to come and see you. It won't take long.

Once I got in, I dashed from room to room, gathering up clothes, stacking paperwork and magazines, shoving cups and plates into the dishwasher. When the doorbell rang I was relieved that the tidying up had kept me too busy to fret about how it might feel to see her again.

As ever, the first sight of her made me catch my breath. She was wearing denim shorts and a white cardigan. No make-up, as far as I could tell. The new hairstyle appeared more natural somehow, or perhaps she was just becoming more at ease with it. But Erin seemed apprehensive.

'I parked round the corner. Didn't want to risk the car being seen.' She told me how the wasps were still being stationed at the house.

'Do they follow you?'

'I don't think so. They're mostly on bicycles.'

'Then why bother to keep watch, if you can give them the slip?'

'Intimidation. That's the only reason I can think of.'

I nodded glumly. She was probably right.

'So, I spoke to the one on duty this morning,' she said. 'A boy called Jax.'

'I've just been to see Maya. And I found out something as well.' I paused, unsure which of us should go first, but we ended up speaking simultaneously:

'There was an *argument*.'

'They played a *game*.'

Hers was the more simple message, which cut through my own sentence.

'A game?' I echoed.

* * *

Erin's heart is thumping. On the way over, she decided to be as direct as possible. Now it's almost a relief to say it:

'Nathan dares them to jump on the boards.'

Harry is floored by this revelation. He virtually staggers to the kitchen and collapses on to a chair.

'He *dares* them?'

'It's a sort of challenge.' Erin takes it upon herself to fill the kettle. 'Jumping and dancing on the planks, to see if they give way. That's according to Jax. One time he fell through and broke his ankle.'

'Jesus Christ! Doesn't he hold Nathan responsible?'

'He views it as an accident.' She relays what she was told about the taxi ride to hospital, the compensation payment, and then parries an inevitable question about taking this information to the police. 'Jax will never admit it. Neither will the others.'

'So I was right about their statements being a cover-up? Nathan told them what to say.'

'We don't know for sure, but I think it's likely.'

Harry shakes his head. 'Why the hell do they accept the dare?'

'You know what teenagers are like. Then add booze, drugs, the desire to impress each other – and Nathan.' She sighs. 'Plus they're scared of him. That may be the key factor.'

'You don't think any of them could be persuaded to speak up?'

'I doubt it. Louis, maybe, is the most rebellious.'

Harry fetches the note. Erin studies it while they drink coffee. '"Freddie died hap—"' she begins to quote.

'Don't. I can't bear that line.'

'Sorry. What about this last sentence?'

'Pure bullshit. Of course it's a threat. If I don't do as I'm told, there'll be consequences.'

'It could also read as an afterthought. As if he realised the rest of the note was *too* threatening.'

Harry's scowl of disagreement triggers an automatic frisson; Erin is conditioned to expect a violent response for speaking out of turn. But he only releases a sigh. 'Either way, I intend to find out when I get my hands on him.'

'Ash,' Erin says. 'That's the name of the pale boy. Jax told me.'

'Has Nathan ever mentioned him? Because surely Ash delivered it on Nathan's behalf?'

Erin studies the message again. 'I don't think Nathan wrote this.'

Harry only grunts. 'When Jax broke his ankle, did he fall down two floors?'

'Just one. He said they stacked mattresses over the hole below.'

'I saw the mattresses. So why weren't they there when Freddie fell?'

'I don't know. Jax couldn't explain that, either.'

'Another question for Ash. I'm starting to think he could have a special status – especially if he's still living in the Tannery.'

'From what Jax said, he's a loner.'

'That was Maya's assessment, too. A skulker in the shadows.'

Erin feels the tension rise as Maya's name is mentioned. 'Was she happy to talk to you?'

'Far from "happy", but she was a lot more forthcoming this time.' Harry's face grows sad. 'It seems that Louis told the truth. Maya and Freddie *did* argue – and it was because Freddie had been rejected, or passed over in favour of the other boy they'd gone with. Ben.'

'I'm sorry to hear that. But how would there be a connection between

Maya's choice and Freddie being dared to jump on the boards? Is there even a connection at all?'

'That's still a mystery,' Harry admits. 'Maya is adamant she and Ben left before it happened. She claims Freddie was fine, apparently chatting to other people after the argument – including Nathan, if Louis is to be believed.' He stares pensively at his coffee mug. 'This boy Jax, and the others who gave statements, they almost certainly know more than they're letting on. They're the key to this.'

'Only if you can persuade them to talk. And I'm just really doubtful...'

'We can try, can't we? Maybe if I speak to Jax, or Louis?'

Erin finds herself nodding, without much enthusiasm. Harry is suddenly remorseful.

'I'm sorry. I can't expect you to take these risks. I've probably lost any sense of perspective.' With tears in his eyes, he looks up at her. 'It isn't just that Freddie apparently said some horrible things to Maya. His pride had been wounded and he lashed out – which I think anyone might do in that situation.'

'Of course they would,' Erin agrees.

'So maybe there is no connection, or not one we'll ever find. But what really tortures me is the knowledge that, if only Maya had chosen differently, my boy would still be alive.'

* * *

I was a mess. Vowing that I wouldn't lose control, and then I did.

Erin, thankfully, wasn't repelled by my grief. She came towards me and I stood up and gratefully received her embrace. We hugged each other but I was first to break away.

'Thank you. And sorry.'

'Don't apologise. It's bound to come as a shock.' She gave me a slightly curious look as I retreated to the other side of the kitchen, stopping only when I bumped against the fridge. 'I'd better be going,' she said.

'Is Nathan still...?'

'In London? Yes. He might be staying over tonight.' With a twitchy smile, she added, 'Thank God.'

I thought about suggesting dinner, but something in her body language dissuaded me. It felt like we were going backwards, and I wondered if this was to be my fate if I continued to pursue my obsession: alienating everyone who cared about me.

'Last night – the swim, and the other stuff... Did it actually happen?'

Erin looked confused. 'Of course. Why?'

'Just beginning to wonder if I'd had a very vivid dream!' I tried to sound jocular, which Erin acknowledged with a wry smile.

'Might have been better if you had.'

'You do regret it, then?'

'Not nearly as much as I should.' She opened her hands. 'Just the fact I'm here right now, that I'm asking questions on your behalf – it's complete insanity.'

'Then why are you doing it?'

At first she looked exasperated, but then she regarded me with a certain shrewdness. 'I haven't ruled out that I'm helping you because maybe – just maybe – the by-product of getting the truth about your son's death could also mean liberation for me.'

'I appreciate your honesty. So where does this leave—?'

'Hold on, I need to say something else.' Her hands fluttered like tethered birds, until she pressed them to her belly. 'Another reason, maybe, is that last night was the purest, sweetest experience I've had in years, and it felt so good that I'm risking everything to come to your house because I want to do it again.'

'You—' I couldn't believe my ears. 'Did you just say...?'

'No more questions, Harry. And spare the modesty, false or otherwise.'

'It's not false—'

'I know that, dimwit. For God's sake, just kiss me.'

I was flabbergasted. Unable to speak.

So I did as she asked.

werk's minat. It who is *watering nerods of this ober* other. she's dudse- and the rest her or "*wak is* the *basant* bewas sea'ffer o'iam there and this aquin ihe aresuse as we some 'heny theymehe' calha a ling

I was rest of *tu'* yarut okuh *K'lit to Kitty in Lfactme hander* e was the smharate *an*
her byt come her mat met as 'an is *na*   'bhawa'' and *willfidaline* 'mule
shortliy I'd kidhe 'Hiy soh and of *Harsar* and *enaughte ahs* of *no*plana
Rith *rece a*sriumag of *a knus Hepin us *ben*
nc *te o're e ro* all
its 'Hst **geshie *
Whath y ou're alwhys *yon* e *hne*
we **hinf *l' * ho ats *at oi* nay and now sbumed ber yhad *by*
that bes **al ffcoth
I *can* *pfs on ** * hnt *ass oa i*

36

This will end in disaster, a shrill voice is warning as they stumble, locked together, along the corridor to the bedroom. But that voice is so familiar these days, it's easy to ignore.

Because this is what Erin wants. What she needs.

She's aware that Harry is nervous. So is she. The key is to focus on the moment-by-moment sensations, the way he kisses, the soft touch of his hands on her back, her neck, the warmth and pressure of his body against hers; the desire in him meeting the desire in her and finding a perfect match.

While kissing they pull and claw at one another, and most of their clothes are off or partially removed when they spill on to the bed. Harry is on top of her briefly until Erin signals that she needs to be in control; it's a matter of feeling safe, which instinctively he seems to understand.

'Oh my God.' He looks ecstatic as he gazes up at her. 'You're so beautiful—'

'Don't, Harry. There's no need.'

They kiss again, and if it weren't for the fact that they're both still wearing a single item of clothing, he would already be inside her. He breaks off the kiss to take a nipple in his mouth and it feels sublime: the touch of his lips, his tongue so gentle, so utterly different from what she's used to enduring. A shimmering wave runs through her entire body, an effect that's both physical and emotional; suddenly she's desperate for more, feels like she'll explode if he doesn't fuck her *right now*, but then her phone emits an angry buzz, and by a terrible quirk of fate it's resting screen up, the caller's identity clearly visible, and all her desire is gone in an instant when she sees Nathan's name and feels certain that somehow he will know where she is and what she's doing.

* * *

I was only dimly aware of the phone ringing; far more noticeable was the change in Erin.

Then came her muttered exclamation – 'Nathan!' – and with that I understood why I'd lost her. Why she slid off the bed and crouched over the phone with the concentration of a bomb disposal officer.

'Let it go to voicemail.'

'He'll keep calling.'

'What if you're driving somewhere?'

'Ever heard of "hands free"?' She looked up, and now seemed horrified by the fact that I was almost naked.

I turned away while we both hurriedly dressed. Her phone cut out, only to start buzzing again.

'I can give you some privacy if you want to call him?'

'I need to go.'

'But if Nathan's in London, surely you could speak to him, and then... maybe stay?'

'I can't risk it. I have to get home.' Erin sounded so decisive, it was difficult not to translate this as: *I've changed my mind. I don't want to sleep with you.*

I felt physically sick as I followed her along the hall. Erin grabbed her bag before confirming my worst fears.

'You know, this might be for the best.' She attempted a smile. 'We both got carried away, didn't we?'

I nodded mutely. Erin opened the front door and peered out as tentatively as a civilian under sniper fire. Her phone started buzzing again, just as I said, 'Contact me later if you can. I need to know you're all right.'

'Don't worry about me. And let's forget about this, shall we?'

'But that's not what—' I began, only for her to pull the front door shut.

* * *

'Where are you?' Nathan growls, and Erin only just remembers in time: he might ask Jax to corroborate her story.

'I went to Battle. I'm heading back soon.'

'Why didn't you answer before?'

'I-I was in a shop.'

'Well get yourself home pronto. I'll be there in twenty minutes and I'm horny.'

He rings off. Erin starts the car and pulls away before spotting the problem. Twenty minutes is about how long it would take her to drive from the town of Battle, meaning she and Nathan ought to reach home at around the same time. But Erin wants to shower before she greets him; she's terrified that he'll know she's been with someone else.

Forced to choose, she decides she can always fudge the journey time; claim she drove like a demon in her eagerness to see him.

She's back within ten minutes and races upstairs and into the shower. His car pulls on to the drive when she's in the bedroom, frantically putting on clean underwear. She hears his key in the door, his footsteps on the stone floor; she adds shorts and a T-shirt while rehearsing what to say and how to be.

Her phone is on the bed. Suddenly she realises she hasn't re-blocked Harry's number.

'Babe!' Nathan yells. Stomping up the stairs like an ogre in a fairy tale. The fear is so intense that Erin retches, tasting bile. Can she erase the knowledge that she's falling in love with another man?

If she can't, Nathan will almost certainly see it.

If he sees it, he will kill her.

* * *

The rest of my day was thoroughly miserable. For hours I struggled to process how, in an instant, we had gone from the most incredible passion to a kind of brutal indifference.

When my phone rang at ten to four I was briefly overjoyed – Erin had found an opportunity to call and reassure me – but in fact it was my son, Adam. He meant well, checking up on his poor old dad, but I'm afraid I was slightly brusque. Afterwards I vowed to make it up to him as soon as I could, and fought the impulse to get in touch with Erin. Give it another hour, I thought.

Those sixty minutes were spent drifting from room to room, reviewing the whole event so frequently that it began to seem unreal, a product of my over-active imagination.

At five o'clock I texted:

> Let me know if you're all right, please. I know it's not my place to say, but I don't think you should go on like this. Make the move and I will help in any way I can. All my love H x

Then I reproached myself. The entire message was unwise, and that sign-off was an unspeakably selfish indulgence.

The lack of a reply only ramped up my anxiety. I spent the evening slumped in front of the TV, a chocolate bar and a couple of beers taking the place of a meal. By ten-thirty I was in bed, with no real expectations of a restful night.

But I must have drifted off, for I jerked awake to find it was a little after 2 a.m. and something had disturbed me. My phone was on vibrate; perhaps Erin had messaged?

I checked but there was nothing. As I settled back I heard a tiny thud, followed by the raucous caw of a seagull. Of course. This was earlier than usual, and no doubt the noisy buggers would see to it that I remained awake for hours.

I was debating whether to get up when I heard a creak that sounded horribly like the gate at the side of the house. Was that boy Ash prowling around outside?

I froze, straining to hear more, but there was only the damn seagull clumping across the roof.

So maybe I *had* got it wrong. Certainly my heart rate was settling as I rose from the bed, pulled on a pair of shorts and trotted out to the hall. There was nothing by the front door – I was half expecting to find another note – so I headed for the kitchen, peered out of the window into the darkness, then unlocked the back door and stepped outside.

The night was still, and pleasantly cool. The seagull cawed again, seem-ingly only a few feet above me. I turned and craned my neck to look, just as it

made a sudden panicky attempt at flight. I must have startled it, I thought –
until something dark came down over my head. Robbed of sight, I felt the jab
of a needle in my arm, and although I went on struggling for a few more
seconds my limbs were turning to jelly and there wasn't a thing I could do to
stave off oblivion.

37

Erin wakes at seven on Monday and finds herself alone in the vast double bed. It's practically the first time she's been on her own since Nathan returned yesterday afternoon; for hours she felt as helpless as an insect pinned beneath glass, so this brings a welcome sense of relief.

But the anxiety doesn't abate entirely. She can't make sense of the change in Nathan.

The previous afternoon, as he thudded upstairs, she braced herself for fury and violence. He was in the room before she could delete Harry's last couple of texts, and she couldn't risk being distracted. But Nathan wasn't just thrumming with energy and good humour; he seemed genuinely pleased to see her.

True to his message, he took her straight to bed, but what transpired is still messing with Erin's head when she considers it again this morning.

They made love. There really isn't any other way to describe it.

At first Erin was tense, partly from the fear that her own arousal owed more to what had happened with Harry – and surely Nathan would somehow divine the truth? But he hadn't. And as Erin willed herself to relax, she gradually found herself responding to his attention. He was remarkably slow and gentle, apparently intent on her pleasure rather than his own.

Finally, after almost an hour, she experienced a genuine orgasm – and for once she only had to exaggerate the intensity of her reaction (because Nathan's expectations, needless to say, came from noisy, aggressive porn). Afterwards they dozed in one another's arms, just as they had in the long-ago months before they married.

Waking at five in the afternoon, feeling groggy and disbelieving, she crept to the en suite and was sitting on the toilet when she remembered her phone. She washed as quickly as she could and opened the door. Her phone was on the bedside table. Nathan remained asleep. She was safe.

She crept around the bed and was climbing in when the phone buzzed. Nathan stirred but didn't wake. Erin retracted her leg and turned to sit on the bed, picked up her phone and opened the message.

> Let me know if you're all right, please. I know it's not my place to say, but I don't think you should go on like this. Make the move and I will help in any way I can. All my love H x

She only skimmed the words, the danger coursing through her like poison in her veins. When Nathan's fingertips brushed against her spine, she almost screamed.

'All right?'

She faked a yawn to release the tension, deleted the text and said, 'Bloody spam messages.'

Nathan didn't question it. He didn't snatch the phone from her hand, or slap her and demand the truth. He sat up, stroked a hand through her hair, nuzzled the back of her neck, and murmured, 'You smell nice.'

'Do I? Thank you.'

'And I like your hair. Have you done something to it?'

Erin stifled the urge to cry. Something very pure inside her was shrivelling at the hypocrisy, the shame. Not just that he could be so admiring of his own brutality, but that Erin didn't dare challenge it.

'I just... tidied it up a bit.'

'Well, it's looking good. Maybe you should have tried that style years ago?'

And he chuckled, as though it were one of life's funny little discoveries, and coaxed her back into bed for another round. Afterwards he went for a shower, giving Erin an opportunity to block Harry's number. It felt cruel not to reply, but he surely understood the situation she was in.

For safety she took her phone when she went for a shower herself, and emerged to find Nathan unpacking. An odd expression formed as he noticed something in his case. He drew out a small package, clearly a jewellery box in an exquisitely decorated gift bag, and said, 'Got you this.'

'Oh?' She hoped Nathan didn't catch the note of scepticism. Something about his demeanour suggested this was an afterthought, and she wasn't dissuaded of that notion when she opened the box to find a pair of ruby drop earrings. They were beautiful, but their colour and style would be far better suited to someone with dark hair and pale skin.

Someone like Keira, for instance.

Despite that, Erin couldn't entirely dismiss the tender way Nathan kissed her after she'd displayed them for him. This was a reminder that he had always been capable of great charm and generosity.

It was only later that night, once he was asleep beside her, that she could admit to her self-loathing. *Is this how easily you can be softened up – with a pair of earrings he probably bought for his lover?* A few hours of laughter and pleasant conversation, and never mind that three days ago he held you down and hacked off your hair.

She reflects on it now, and decides that the gratitude was in part the product of guilt. Yesterday she had cheated on her husband, but had done so in the certain knowledge that he despised her. With that certainty challenged, it feels natural that she should be eager to dismiss the past and consider a fresh start.

She hears the front door, and frowns. It's unusual for him to have gone out so early. He bounds up the stairs and comes in beaming with good cheer. He took the car for a spin, he says. 'Blew away the cobwebs.'

He showers while she gets breakfast started and comes down in a suit, clean shaven, his hair damp, and kisses her on the cheek when she hands him a coffee. *We're characters in a sitcom,* she thinks.

A phone call interrupts their chit chat. She moves away to give him space but he gestures: no need. It's a pretty one-sided conversation, Nathan mainly grinning and saying, 'Uh huh.' It's more good news.

'Demolition's on for next week!'

'Of the Tannery? Wow.' *Keep smiling don't think of Harry don't think of his poor boy it's good news keep smiling—*

'Will you do me a favour? I wanna get some cameras set up to record the moment. Covering all four sides, and at least one drone overhead. But they've got to be able to do that ultra-slow-motion thing, like you see on nature documentaries. I need you to find me some specialist companies, get a couple of quotes. You up for that?'

Erin nods, trying not to gape at him. This is unprecedented, and frankly terrifying. What if she screws it up?

He moves in fast. Erin cringes ahead of the first punch – only to be enveloped in his arms.

'Don't look so worried, babe. The cost is irrelevant. Gonna be rolling in money soon!'

This seals it, she thinks. Nathan must have been taken in the night and replaced with an android. It's a mark of her rapid adjustment that she isn't afraid to ask, as he grabs his briefcase, where he's going.

'Brighton. Meeting a couple of new interior designers.'

'What about Keira?'

'Not sure if she's right for this project, to be honest.' His eyes widen with affection. 'Good luck with those quotes.'

After he's gone she creeps upstairs and watches his car disappear from sight. She feels energised by the task he's entrusted to her, and it's ridiculously satisfying.

Before getting to work, she unblocks Harry's number, intending to send a final text making it clear that they mustn't speak again.

But there's a new message from him, sent at six-thirty this morning. Short but far from sweet:

Get out of my life, skank.

38

Erin, perhaps, should be glad that Harry has turned against her. But the message is so hurtful, it makes her feel sick. That hideous word, *skank*, was her stepdad's favourite insult for a woman.

It doesn't seem in character for Harry to be so crude – and in any case, what would have prompted him to turn on her like this? Could it be her sudden departure yesterday?

The text continues to chafe as she sets to work on the task Nathan has assigned her. After identifying several candidates, speaking to one on the phone and emailing two others, she breaks off for a cold drink and on impulse decides to phone Harry and ask him outright.

But the call goes straight to voicemail, and she can't bring herself to leave a message. Forget Harry, she tells herself. It's for the best.

Around eleven, Nathan texts to say his first meeting went well.

> Guy's bent as a 9 bob note but seems to know his
> stuff. (Bit unPC there, whoops!) Next one's delayed,
> so I'm gonna grab lunch at the Ivy.

Translation: *I won't be back any time soon.* Erin checks the road and for once there are no wasps in sight. Has Nathan stood down the guard?

She decides not to drive, and instead retrieves her bicycle from the garage. No one follows her to Harry's, she's fairly certain about that. But the sight of the Mazda parked on the drive is a problem she hasn't anticipated. This is not a conversation to be had in the presence of his ex-wife.

And *is* she his ex-wife? For the first time it strikes her that perhaps Harry hasn't been entirely honest about his marital status. And if this morning's text didn't sound like Harry, could it be because Anita got hold of his phone and sent it herself?

Erin glides on to the pavement, unsure at this stage whether she'll just carry on past. There's movement in a front window; Erin looks away but feels the gravitational pull of someone's attention. Glancing back, she finds Anita beckoning to her.

Erin sets the bike down on the lawn as the front door opens. Anita is wearing a pale pink belted shirt dress that accentuates her figure, along with leather sandals and a hint of make-up. A picture of respectability, which prompts Erin to recall that Anita might still believe she's an escort.

'You're... Erin, isn't it?'

'Yes. Is Harry here?'

'No. He's not.'

'Oh.' Erin offers a tentative smile. 'I thought I'd try here first, but I assume he's at work?'

The smile has no effect; Anita only crosses her arms and says, 'He's not there either. Can I ask why you want him?'

'Just to talk to him about something. He texted me earlier.'

'Saying what?'

'Nothing, really.' Erin becomes aware of her hands twisting together and shoves them behind her back. 'I'm not his girlfriend, or anything—'

'None of my business if you are.' Anita's tone has been curt, but now a little more warmth comes into her eyes. 'I could do with knowing what he said to you. He's got me a bit puzzled.'

'Why's that?' Erin asks, as she reaches, reluctantly, for her phone.

Anita gestures behind her. 'You might as well come in.'

* * *

Erin follows her to the kitchen, passing a room she didn't notice the day before, a converted office where a radio is playing quietly.

Anita must pick up on her curiosity, for she says, 'Where I'm living now isn't quite suitable for my work. Harry said I was welcome to use my old office for the time being.' She stops abruptly and turns. 'But that's all it is. The marriage is over, I can assure you of that.'

'I-I don't need to be assured.'

There's another moment of appraisal, then a shrug. 'Tea? Coffee? Juice?'

'A coffee would be nice. Thank you.'

Anita grabs the kettle, empties the dregs and refills it. 'What time did he message you?'

'Uh... it came through at half six. It's quite... well, embarrassing. And strange.' Erin holds out her phone for the other woman to read. 'I've no idea what prompted this, which is why I came to see him.'

Anita studies the message intently before finally looking up at Erin. 'Are you sure there's nothing he might have misinterpreted?'

'No. Well...' Erin feels horribly close to tears. 'I'm married. But Harry knows that.'

'Married?' Anita repeats. But she doesn't ask to whom, and Erin is in no hurry to volunteer the information. 'So how did your "friendship" come about?'

'It's a long story, not important. What did you mean about being puzzled?'

'Because I received a text from him this morning. So did Gareth, his boss.' She clears her throat. 'Gareth is also now my partner.'

'Harry told me. What did he say?'

'That he needed to get away for a few days. "Time to think," is how he put it. Gareth had virtually the same message. Harry also warned us that he wouldn't be replying if we tried to contact him.'

'Is that something he'd normally do?'

'Not at all. Particularly when it comes to work – he's leaving Gareth in the lurch, and normally he's very dedicated.' Anita heaves a sigh, which coincides with the kettle boiling. 'But he's also under a lot of strain, with our marriage ending, and some other personal issues to deal with...'

'Losing your son,' Erin says quietly.

'You know about that?'

She nods. 'I'm very sorry. So did Harry say where he was going?'

'No. Which isn't like him, either. And despite his warning, I did try phoning. It went straight to voicemail.'

'I know. I've tried calling him, too.' Erin watches Anita fussing over a cafetière, and says, 'What about your other children? Have you checked with them?'

Anita looks at her sharply, as if surprised by how well-informed Erin appears to be. 'Not yet,' she says. 'But that's a good idea.'

'And has he packed a bag? Is his passport missing?'

'He's taken a small suitcase, and a peculiar assortment of clothes... Hold on.'

Anita hurries away and returns within half a minute, brandishing a passport. Erin says, 'So maybe he just wanted a getaway in the countryside somewhere?'

'But why this insistence on not communicating? It's very odd, although, as I say, he hasn't been himself since the inquest...' Anita blows on the surface of her coffee, still holding Erin's gaze through the steam. 'How much do you know about our son's death? The Tannery? Nathan Webb?'

Erin's shudder is so violent, there's no possibility of Anita missing it.

'I know more than I want to, I'm afraid,' she says. 'Nathan Webb is my husband.'

39

Theresa Webb hasn't been this busy for years, and certainly not with such interesting work. Unlike most folk her age, she's pretty good with technology. She took pictures of the messages and now both she and Nathan have had a chance to consider them.

'It's got me steaming, Ma,' he says. He's busy with meetings today, but naturally he's made time for this.

'You and me both, son. You holding it together?'

'Oh, you wouldn't believe how well.'

'Performance of a lifetime?'

'Gotta be, for this to work. But it's gonna taste so sweet, when I can finally let go.'

'And you'll deserve it, son, after what they've put you through.' Theresa sighs. 'Then there's the rest of them.'

'Manageable, I reckon, except for the little runt. He's seriously out of line.'

'In that case, dealing with him could be just what you need.' Theresa smiles to herself. 'I'll get my thinking cap on.'

* * *

After admitting who she is, Erin has no choice but to tell Anita the whole story, more or less. She omits the physical attraction between herself and

Harry, and says nothing of Nathan's treatment of her. But Anita is shocked enough by the extent of Harry's quest for the truth, as well as by what that quest has uncovered. She seems stunned when Erin describes how Maya apparently rejected Freddie; then her sorrow turns to anger as she learns of the dares, and how at least one other young man had fallen through the hole.

'Why won't they go to the police and tell the truth?'

'Most of them don't have the kind of relationship with the authorities that you or I might have. And there's other reasons. Things they'd want to hide.'

'Drugs?' Anita asks, before muttering, angrily, 'You know, I warned Harry not to pursue this. Forget it and move on, I said. Otherwise you're just prolonging the pain.'

'I think Harry does see that, though if you consider what he's managed to find...'

'But what has it achieved? Nothing we do will bring Freddie back, and if you're right that no one will admit to the truth, we'll never have the satisfaction of seeing justice done.'

They both lift their coffees and drink. Anita's rage seems to subside as she checks her phone. She tries Harry's number once more and says, 'Still nothing.'

'I suppose he could be travelling. Or he's somewhere with no signal?'

'I hope that's all it is.' For a moment Anita closes her eyes, pinching the bridge of her nose, then throws out a question, almost harshly: 'You don't have children, do you?'

'No.' Unconsciously, Erin wraps her arms around herself.

'Then let me tell you, from the instant you become a parent, losing your child is the very worst thing you can imagine. You live in terror of it, especially when they're babies, and again when they first gain some independence. And if you hear about it happening to someone else – usually only on the news, thankfully – you immediately think, it must feel like their world has ended. How could any parent want to go on living after the loss of a child?'

She is weeping now, but Erin is too transfixed by the woman's pain to say anything.

'And then it happens to you,' Anita goes on, 'and it *does* feel like the world has ended. But the horrible truth is, it *hasn't*. And even though you don't really want to carry on... well, somehow you just do. Day by day, week by week. Thinking about him, grieving for him, almost every single second—'

She stops, clamping a hand over her mouth. Erin now reaches for her, but Anita flaps her free hand: *Don't comfort me.*

'But that's not the worst bit. The worst bit is that, somehow, there's suddenly a day when the pain isn't quite as unrelenting. A day when something makes you smile – or even laugh, God forbid!' A burst of laughter now, at the recollection, while the tears still stream from her eyes. 'It was something on TV, just one of those silly panel shows – and my word, I felt like some kind of monster. I remember thinking, thank heaven there was only Harry to witness it – because anyone else, and especially another parent, would be so disapproving. *You shouldn't want to go on living,* they'd be thinking, *never mind finding something to laugh about!*'

Erin is nodding sadly. 'I've only lost a parent, not a child. But I can understand that.'

Anita regards her carefully, almost tenderly. 'So many people don't, you see? You learn that very fast, and then it becomes easier, simpler, just never to mention your loss. Never discuss it with anyone outside the family. I know Harry found that *incredibly* difficult to bear. And if I'm honest, in the days and weeks after Freddie's death, I think Harry came closer than I did to...' She gulps. 'To *not* carrying on.'

Anita fetches a box of tissues and blows her nose. Erin is glad of a few extra seconds to process her own shock.

Finally she says, 'Are you saying Harry would be capable of taking his own life?'

'I don't think it can be ruled out.' There's a long pause before Anita adds, 'But equally, I'm wondering now, could your husband have had something to do with this? Maybe threatened Harry, scared him to the point that he felt compelled to flee?'

'I'm not sure. But I do know Harry received an anonymous note, warning him to stay away from the Tannery.'

'He's been to the Tannery? You mean, actually *inside*?'

Erin nods. 'He sneaked in last Friday. He thinks there was someone in there – possibly the same young man he saw running away after delivering the note.'

Anita covers her face with her hands, and growls, 'Why does he have to be so bloody stubborn? Gareth and I warned him.'

Erin, nodding sympathetically, says, 'I don't suppose you've seen the note anywhere?'

'No. And I had a good look round this morning.' Anita meets her eye. 'Would the note have come from Nathan?'

'It's possible,' Erin admits. 'And I'm not going to lie, I've even wondered if he's behind Harry's disappearance in another way.'

Anita gasps. 'You mean hurt him, or...'

'But I don't think he did. He was in London overnight Saturday and only got back yesterday afternoon. I was with him all evening. He didn't make any phone calls or do anything suspicious.'

Anita lifts her coffee to drink, then changes her mind. 'What about my son's death?' she asks. 'Do you think your husband had some involvement? Or that he's hiding something?'

'I've no idea. Genuinely.'

'But he did encourage some degree of collusion with these other partygoers?'

'It looks that way. To what extent, I don't—'

'You know, it amazes me you're still married to the man. You seem far too nice.'

Erin flinches. 'That's maybe a conversation for another time.'

From the way she nods, Anita has perhaps glimpsed a hint of Erin's inner torment. 'Yes. I'm sorry.'

'So what do you want to do?' Erin asks. 'Call the police and report him missing?'

'I don't know. I imagine they'll say he isn't *actually* missing, given that he texted this morning to say he was going away.'

'If you need me to back you up, in terms of explaining why we have concerns about him...'

'You'll do that?' Anita looks surprised. 'Won't it get you in trouble?'

Erin tries to shrug, but ends up saying, 'Probably, yes.'

'My bet is they won't want to know, not at this stage. But I'll think about it. Thank you.'

They swap numbers and Anita shows her out. As she wheels her bike along the path, Erin checks the surrounding properties for security cameras. Footage of Harry's departure, perhaps on foot or in a taxi, would put their minds at rest.

But with no obvious cameras in sight, she has little choice but to set off for home and accept the possibility that she may not discover Harry's fate for a long time – if at all.

That grim thought sparks an even grimmer question. It's accompanied by an image of the two of them, kissing in the sea on Saturday night, then rolling half naked on his bed yesterday afternoon.

Did I sign Harry's death warrant?

40

There was a loud clunk, my whole body jolted and suddenly I was conscious again. My head was pounding and I could barely breathe. The air around me felt hot and thick with moisture, and I opened my eyes to utter darkness. All I could smell was my own breath and maybe a hint of oil or grease. The only sounds were the roar and rumble of a diesel vehicle on a fast road.

My terror was overwhelming. My stomach cramped and roiled. There was a hood or a sack over my head, and it seemed to be tied around my neck. If I vomited, I'd be in danger of suffocating.

I tried to suppress the panic and assess my circumstances. I was lying on my back on a cold metal surface, naked except for my boxer shorts. My limbs responded normally when I tried flexing them, though I discovered that my hands and feet were bound together with what felt like rope.

Another clunk sent a wave of pain along my spine. My best guess was that I had been placed in the back of a van, and the driver wasn't too fussed about avoiding potholes.

But who was the driver? Why had I been kidnapped, and what were they going to do with me?

Faced with such questions, staying calm became more difficult by the second. I tried to recall how this had happened. I'd been woken by a noise and had gone outside to investigate. The hood came down over me – and hadn't I been jabbed with a needle?

Drugged.

As for the who and the why, there could be only one answer: Nathan Webb. I reflected on my bravado of the night before, how my desire for Erin had overridden all my instincts for self-preservation. I thought about the way we'd kissed during our swim. In the heat of passion I might have been able to argue it was worth the risk, but of course that was absurd.

My actions this weekend might well result in my death. *That* was where my bravado had taken me.

And I wasn't ready to die. I understood this with a clarity that was truly illuminating. Since Freddie's death I'd often adopted a nonchalant attitude to my own mortality. I'd lost my youngest son: what did it matter if I died too?

Well it would matter to my two other children, for a start. It felt unbearable to think I might never see them again. Adam and Jay were mulling over adoption, and last year Jody had talked of getting married, teasing Freddie that she'd insist on making him a pageboy. He'd countered by saying that, if she did, he would turn up dressed as a bridesmaid.

I knew Jody's tentative plans had been shelved as a result of her brother's death, but I still hoped one day to be present to give her away in the time-honoured fashion. And I had a keen desire to become a grandfather; Anita and I had several friends who'd commenced that stage of life, and they were unanimous that it was infinitely more enjoyable than being a parent.

I also wanted to take on more challenges at work for another decade or so, and then enjoy a decent spell of comfortable retirement. A chance to improve my golf; maybe trek the South Downs Way. And I'd never learnt to ski...

All of it, lost. Lost because you went poking into the activities of a vicious criminal, then compounded it by falling in love with his wife.

My insides turned to ice at the thought of how Nathan would respond to Erin's behaviour. Here I was wallowing in my own self-pity, when God only knew how he had vented his fury on her.

The realisation that Erin could already be dead was truly debilitating. I tried to keep my senses sharp enough to consider the next steps.

Could I fight back? Could I escape? If I had any chance at all, it had to be when we arrived at our destination.

As I attempted to sit up, a sudden left turn pitched me on to my front. Then the van braked sharply and I slid forward, bumping my head. We appeared to have switched to a minor road, where every manoeuvre sent me rolling helplessly from side to side.

After perhaps ten minutes of this, the van halted. I froze, listening hard, and thought I heard two doors open at the front of the vehicle. A few seconds later there was a heavy sliding noise and I felt a rush of cooler air.

'Stay still and be quiet,' a male voice growled. Next came a tapping of metal on metal. 'Hear that?' Something hard was jammed into my stomach. 'This is a gun. Give us any reason, and we'll use it.'

All thoughts of resistance were immediately jettisoned. I allowed myself to be lifted under the arms and dragged from the vehicle. Once on my feet, I discovered there was enough play in the rope for me to take small, waddling footsteps. I shuffled forward, guided by someone each side of me, their hands like pincers on my upper arms. The second man, whose voice had more of a reedy quality, repeated the warning that I was to stay quiet. 'A bullet through the kneecap is painful as fuck.'

I registered damp grass beneath my bare feet, the chill of night air on my skin. Apart from the distant drone of traffic, there was the kind of deep silence that indicated a rural location.

The surface soon changed to concrete, and I was bundled through a doorway. The one with the reedy voice ordered me to get down, and at the same time he karate-chopped my shoulder. I fell to my knees, wondering if I would even register the gunshot that ended my life.

I felt hands working at my wrists and feet, then the ropes were yanked away, burning the skin as they went. The man stood and kicked me, half-heartedly, in the thigh.

'Sweet dreams,' he said, both men chuckling as they strode out and shut the door. I heard the clunk of a bolt sliding home, then silence.

Once it had sunk in that I was alone, I sat up and rubbed at the skin on my arms and legs, then ran my fingers over the hood. A cord or drawstring held it tight around my neck, but I managed to widen it and then, with a mixture of trepidation and relief, I took it off.

I was in a cell. It measured about ten feet square, and contained only a mattress and a bucket. The floor was dusty cement, while the walls and ceilings were formed from panels of chipboard, painted grey. A single dim lightbulb had been fixed to the ceiling, but there was no switch in the room.

I stood up and examined the ceiling, which was about ten feet high. Something dark and glossy was embedded in the corner: a CCTV camera.

The knowledge that I was under observation filled me with dread. It wasn't the lack of privacy so much as the likelihood that they intended to keep me here for an extended period. But why? And what would they do to me during that time?

My imagination was only too well equipped to come up with some truly gruesome scenarios. I tried not to speculate, and focused on the door. It was solid timber: no window, and no handle on the inside.

The bucket was empty except for a roll of toilet paper, which left no doubt as to the bucket's purpose. In despair, I sat down on the mattress. It was thin and discoloured with years of use. There were no sheets, just a rough woollen blanket that smelt like it had come from a stable. When I lifted the blanket I discovered a cheap pair of grey jogging pants and a white T-shirt, both of which looked brand new.

The cell wasn't freezing cold, but it wasn't particularly warm either, so I put the clothes on, even though it served as a bitter acknowledgement of my status.

I was an inmate. Nathan Webb's prisoner.

When the light snapped off, I let out a cry of alarm. I was back in total darkness. Presumably it meant I was to sleep. I couldn't imagine anything less likely, but after sitting hunched over in defiance for a few minutes, I rested back and tried to cover myself with the blanket.

The mattress was vaguely damp and stank of mildew. I shut my eyes and vowed to stay strong, even as a solitary tear trickled down my cheek. I had never felt as scared or vulnerable as I did now; not even as a child, woken in the midst of a nightmare.

Guiltily – because I'd had no firm religious beliefs since the age of eight or nine – I resorted to prayer. I prayed that I would be found and rescued unharmed. I prayed that Nathan and his thugs would be brought to justice. But mostly I prayed for Erin to be alive, and safely beyond her husband's reach.

I gave it my best shot, but deep down I didn't expect a single one of those prayers to be answered.

41

I must have managed to sleep, because a sudden noise jerked me awake. The door opened, revealing a glimpse of pale light filtering into a space with a concrete block wall. Two men hurried in, dressed in black, with ski masks hiding their faces. One carried a torch, which he switched on just as the door shut behind them.

'Lie on your front.' This was Gruff-voice.

'What are y—?'

'Do it!'

I had no choice but to obey. That was what I told myself, though it didn't assuage the shame. I'd always felt I was a physical coward, but it had only been something to joke about in a self-deprecating fashion. Now it was viscerally relevant.

I felt them move in, one of them pressing down on my lower legs, the other shining the torch in my face. He had something in his other hand, which he brought into view. It was a sex toy. A dildo.

I tried to say something but produced only an incoherent noise. The other man grabbed my waistband and pulled my joggers and boxer shorts down to my ankles.

My bladder nearly failed me. I tried to speak again but even breathing was impossible. My chest was too constricted, my lungs no match for a heart beating fit to explode.

'Arse in the air,' Reedy told me.

'And open your mouth.'

When I didn't immediately comply, Gruff hit me in the face. Reedy took my legs and hoisted me on to my knees. Both men stank of sweat, nicotine, the greasy odour of fast food. They were going to rape me and there wasn't anything I could do to prevent it.

'Reckon he's a virgin,' Reedy muttered.

'Virgin to this. He'll learn.'

'We'll turn him into a pro.'

'Fucking ruin him.' Gruff cackled, and hit me again.

Blood streamed from my nose. I had to open my mouth to breathe, and he shoved the dildo inside. I felt a convulsion in my throat as my airway was blocked. The obstruction made me gag; then, from behind me, came the sound of Reedy unzipping his trousers.

'Here we go,' he crooned.

In desperation I arched my spine, kicking backwards with one foot while trying to swing at the man in front of me. It was clumsy and amateurish and destined to fail. Both men drew back, easily avoiding my blows. The sex toy dropped to the floor, followed by a spray of vomit. My body sagged as I coughed and spat and gratefully heaved in a breath.

I was braced for severe punishment but all I could hear was sniggering. The torch beam had been swooping across the walls like a rogue searchlight; now it picked out the mess on the floor, then swivelled towards the door. Gruff opened it, and as the two men filed out I heard Reedy say, 'Good first lesson, that.'

'Plenty more to come.'

I listened to the bolt sliding home, then rearranged my clothes and sank on to the mattress. I had never felt so degraded. The knowledge that I couldn't have stopped them going through with it was almost as dreadful as if they *had* gone through with it. And I was certain that had been part of the plan.

This was psychological torture, as much as physical. I pictured Nathan Webb roaring with laughter as he was told of my reaction – or perhaps he'd been watching on the security camera? Once again it sickened me to think what Erin might have suffered – or was still suffering – at his hand.

And it was my fault. All my fault.

* * *

What followed was a long restless period where I was plagued by waking nightmares. At one point I had terrible stomach cramps, and only just groped my way to the bucket before my bowels emptied. Trying to clean up in total darkness, the stench and squalor made me vomit again.

After that I slept heavily. When I woke it was to the sound of the bolt drawing back. I instinctively cowered, trying to shrink beneath the blanket.

The light snapped on and the two men entered the room, their faces hidden once again. I registered that they were both over six foot tall, with the hulking demeanour of nightclub bouncers.

'Rise and shine, darlin',' said Gruff. He had a noticeable beer gut straining against his black sweater, whereas Reedy was trimmer. My guess was that both were heading for middle age, which meant they weren't any of Nathan's 'wasps'.

Reluctantly, I straightened up. Reedy stayed by the door while Gruff loomed over me. He was holding a banana and a plastic beaker full of liquid, which he set down on the floor.

I thanked him, in a timid begrudging voice that I scarcely recognised as my own. As he made to turn away, I added, 'W-would it be possible to empty the bucket?'

'Over your head?'

'No, I mean—'

'Your choice. It's that or leave it the fuck alone.'

Snickering, Reedy pointed at something on the floor. Gruff bent over and scooped up the sex toy. As he hefted it thoughtfully in his hand, I felt my guts turning to water again.

'There's been a mistake. I shouldn't be here.'

The two men exchanged a glance, before Reedy said, 'Harry Manning, yeah?'

'Yes, but—'

'Then it ain't a mistake.'

He opened the door. Despite my fear of a further assault, I felt childishly bereft at the idea of being left alone again.

'Is someone paying you to do this?'

Reedy was already out of the room, Gruff a couple of steps behind him, half backing away so he could keep his eye on me. In desperation I pointed to the patch of vomit on the floor.

'Let me have a cloth or something, so I can clean up.'

'What do you think this is, the fucking Hilton?'

He strode out and the door slammed shut.

Slumping on the mattress, I tried to look on the positive side. They hadn't hurt me – plus they'd brought food and drink.

My stomach grumbled at the very concept, and I remembered how, in the funk that descended after Erin's sudden departure yesterday afternoon, I had eaten no more than a few biscuits.

I peeled the banana and devoured it in three bites. Then I picked up the beaker of water and immediately saw a gel-like substance floating on the surface. My stomach flipped as I worked out that it was phlegm.

I put the beaker down, now regretting that I'd consumed the banana so quickly. My mouth felt furry, painfully dry. I had no idea when – or if – they would bring me more provisions.

Succumbing to depression, I lay on my back and stared at the ceiling and felt thoroughly sorry for myself for what felt like hours. Without a phone or a watch, without regular input from the world around me, it was impossible to gauge the passing minutes.

This was prison, and eventually I thought to apply an inmate's perspective. How to fend off the boredom? The madness?

I pictured the films I'd seen and came up with an answer: exercise. What movie about incarceration didn't include an exercise montage? Some tough-guy actor performing press-ups and sit-ups and squats, pecs and biceps gleaming with sweat.

'Huh,' I said aloud. 'Maybe a couple of star jumps before bed.'

My voice sounded croaky and weak. I realised the camera might also be picking up sound. Was it better, in that case, to stay silent, or should I give them a piece of my mind?

I was still brooding on that when somehow I drifted off to sleep. I woke disorientated and a lot thirstier. But I still couldn't bring myself to drink the water, even after I'd tried stirring it with my finger.

A spell of pointless anger followed. I thumped on the door, shouting and raging, which resulted in nothing more than bruised hands and a throat so raw it brought on a coughing fit.

Then I sat and moped some more. I stood and waved and pulled funny faces at the camera. I tried addressing it, calmly: 'Are you watching me? Christ, you must be nearly as bored as I am. Can you bring me more food and something to drink? You have no right to do this to me.'

Sometime later the door opened. Reedy came in, this time alone. I caught a clearer view of the building beyond the cell: blockwork walls and a hint of corrugated iron.

Reedy shut the door and leaned back against it. His eyes were small and mean, and the skin around them looked puffy.

'What's your problem?' he demanded.

'I'm so thirsty. May I have some clean water?'

'You've got water.'

'Someone spat in it.'

'So?'

'I can't drink it. I'll be sick, and then even more dehydrated.'

'Life's a bitch, eh?'

My shoulders slumped. 'At least tell me why I'm here.'

'You know why.'

'I don't. I haven't done anything to deserve this, I swear to you.'

There was a change in Reedy's eyes, a sheen of what I first thought was humour, but turned out to be scorn.

'Sure about that, are you?'

42

Erin receives the text at just after nine on Tuesday morning. A little earlier and it could have been tricky; Nathan is still a changed man, but he might reasonably have asked who it was, and lying to him is a much tougher challenge at the moment.

It isn't Harry – which is what she hopes – but his ex-wife, Anita.

> Any chance you can pop round at midday?

Perhaps she's being deliberately vague, now she appreciates the perilous game Erin has been playing. Fortunately Nathan is visiting kitchen suppliers today, so she's able to accept the invitation with relatively few qualms.

She has tried Harry's number a few times and got nothing. Concealing her anxiety about him hasn't been easy. With Nathan in such solicitous form, she has to maintain absolute concentration when she's in his presence.

Last night he was effusive in his compliments for the work she'd done. Dining at her favourite Chinese restaurant, they reviewed the best candidates for filming the demolition, huddling together to watch chimneys and tower blocks being reduced to rubble.

Back home they made love – yet again it couldn't be called anything else – and slept entwined. *Too good to be true*, Erin knows in her heart. But what can she do?

There are no wasps on duty. Erin drives to Harry's and makes only a few cursory checks in the mirror. Along with Anita's Mazda, there's a Ford Focus parked outside. Erin experiences a flutter of unease.

Anita, in jeans and a T-shirt, greets her warmly. 'Nothing from Harry,' she says, then explains that someone else wants to hear what they have to say.

Erin is introduced to a plump, dark-haired woman with heavy-rimmed glasses that add a sternness to features which are actually quite soft and appealing. This turns out to be Detective Constable Jessica Leung, who'd acted as family liaison officer after Freddie's death.

Erin tries to shake off the tension that seizes her when she learns this woman is a cop. And of course Leung's interest in her is evident from the moment Anita says the dreaded surname, 'Webb'. Her gaze, while friendly enough, runs over her like a scanner.

'Nathan's wife. I've seen you once or twice, I think.' The woman rubs her lips together, as if she's just applied lipstick. 'Didn't you used to have long hair?'

'I decided on a change.'

'A dramatic change.' Leung's half smile signals that she knows bullshit when she smells it.

Erin declines refreshments and takes a seat. DC Leung sits opposite, nursing a glass of water, while Anita perches on the arm of the sofa, next to Erin.

'Mrs Manning has given me the background,' the detective says. 'I've seen Harry's message about wanting to get away, but I gather you both have your doubts?'

Erin shares a glance with Anita, and says, 'That's correct.'

Leung considers. 'Harry isn't picking up his phone or responding to texts, but his farewell message indicated he wouldn't. Why do you believe he's come to harm?'

'"Believe" is maybe too strong a word,' Anita says. 'We're worried he may have... done something to himself, or that someone else has hurt him.'

'"Someone else" being Nathan Webb,' Erin adds.

DC Leung looks at her in surprise. 'Why do you say that? Because of Freddie's death?'

It's Anita who explains: 'Harry, I'm afraid, has been trying to find out what "really" happened in the Tannery. He's gone as far as enlisting poor

Erin, who has spoken to a couple of the young people who were there that night.'

Leung does the lip rubbing thing again; it's a kind of tic, which perhaps helps her to think. 'Is Mr Webb aware of this?' she asks Erin.

'I want to say no. But I'm not entirely sure.'

'And if he were to find out, are you suggesting he'd take action against Harry?'

Erin hesitates. She's being asked to place her husband's neck on the block, an invitation that isn't nearly as appealing as it might have been even a couple of days ago.

'I don't know. I haven't picked up any hint that he's done anything. But Harry was warned off, with a note.' She explains about Ash. 'It feels like a huge coincidence, if his disappearance isn't connected to that.'

'Coincidences happen, to be fair.' Leung turns solemn as she addresses Anita. 'Just suppose Harry was intent on self-harm. Would he send the type of message you received, or would he just get on and do it?'

Anita gives it some thought. 'I suppose he might send a text, to put my mind at rest.'

'Except it hasn't. Telling you to leave him alone only prompted you to call and text him, and now his lack of a reply has worried you more than ever.'

Erin can see where she's going. 'You think he'd have known that?'

As Leung nods, Anita goes from confused to relieved. 'So self-harm is less likely?'

'Let's hope so. At the same time, there's very little to support the theory of foul play.' Leung glances at each of them in turn. 'This certainly wouldn't meet the usual threshold for a missing persons enquiry. I accept there may be some extenuating circumstances, but I don't see any grounds to track his phone, or monitor the use of his bank cards.'

'You're saying that reporting him missing won't achieve anything?'

'I'm afraid not. If a recently separated man, sound in mind and body, has decided to go away for a few days and ignore his phone, that's his business, not ours.'

Anita looks glum, perhaps taking this as a gentle rebuke. 'It's not like I have any interest in harassing him. If he's chosen to seek a bit of peace and quiet, good luck to him.'

Erin, nodding, says to DC Leung, 'But if it's *not* that, what then?'

'I'd suggest leaving it until he's been gone two days. If you still haven't heard anything, let me know and I'll get things moving. And I will make sure it's taken seriously.'

Anita thanks her, and then Leung turns her probing gaze upon Erin once more. 'I imagine you're in an unusual position with this? Divided loyalties and so on.'

Erin shrugs. 'Harry's a nice man. I want to help him if I can.'

'Is that at any personal risk to you?'

The question makes her so uncomfortable, it takes Erin a second to work out the subtext. 'Are you suspicious of Freddie's death? Do you think Harry's on to something?'

Leung stays poker faced; she doesn't even roll her lips. 'There was a thorough investigation, led by Detective Inspector Hawkins. At its conclusion the CPS felt there was no prospect of criminal charges, and that concurred with DI Hawkins's judgement.' She catches their scepticism, and says, 'Ultimately, I'm afraid, it's irrelevant what we as individuals may think. Our gut instincts – or prejudices, sometimes – can't and shouldn't play any part. It's purely about evidence that will stand up in court.'

'So Harry's been wasting his time?' Anita asks, with a slightly bitter chuckle.

'I didn't say that. If he or anyone else unearths new evidence, then of course we'll take a fresh look.' DC Leung seems to give Erin a loaded glance. 'I take it you don't know anything that differs from the official account?'

'Nothing substantial,' Erin says. 'But if I hear something, I'll tell you.'

'Even at the cost of making an enemy of your husband?'

'Yes. The truth is important.'

'A very admirable stance,' Leung says, breaking eye contact to study Erin's hair.

With the detective about to leave, Erin says her farewells at the same time and accompanies the woman to her car. As they part, Leung says, 'Just be careful, Mrs Webb. I'm aware of the rumours that surround your husband...'

'Rumours?'

'That he operates on the wrong side of the law. Though it's more the domestic sphere that concerns me.'

It's an invitation to say more. An invitation that, right now, Erin has to decline.

'Please remember, you can get in touch any time. At the very least I could give you the numbers of some organisations that offer help.'

Erin isn't sure whether she should even nod her head, knowing it will acknowledge the validity of Leung's suspicions.

'I'll bear it in mind,' she says at last. 'Thank you.'

43

After the visit by Reedy, I sat slumped in despair for a long time. Eventually I roused myself, and tried to do some jogging on the spot, only for the light to go out.

I felt my way back to bed, abandoning the plan I'd just formed to drink the water through my T-shirt. I thought the material might filter the worst of whatever had been deposited in it, but in total darkness it would be asking for trouble.

I dozed off quite quickly, and didn't feel I'd slept for long when the light snapped on and there was a pounding on the door, followed by a barrage of threats from my jailors. Any second now they were going to come in and kick the crap out of me, stamp on my balls, shove my head into the bucket of shit...

On and on it went as I lay there, braced for violence, but the door didn't actually open. After perhaps ten or fifteen minutes the barrage ceased. The light went out again.

When it happened the next time, probably less than an hour later, I finally got it. More psychological torture.

The pattern was repeated three or four times. There was also an instance where they entered the cell, stripped me naked and held me down, then just waited, staring at the open door. When I asked what they were doing, Gruff slapped my face and said, 'You'll see.'

'He'll be here soon,' Reedy added.

I wondered if they meant Nathan, but didn't dare ask. The next few minutes were an agony of dread. Their weight on me, the foul smell of these men, nearly made me sick. There were tears streaming down my face, and I was on the brink of pleading with them, offering them anything they wanted, when they abruptly stood up and walked out.

Another bluff. And it had almost destroyed me.

By now my throat was as raw as sandpaper, my lips so dry I probably could have peeled them off my face. The light was still on, so I picked up the beaker and tried to scoop out the upper layer, then used two fingers to stir the liquid before taking several rapid sips.

It was warm, stale, gluey. Like drinking slime. I swallowed, then retched, but held it down. I tried to drink some more but had to stop when I felt my stomach turning over. Furiously I hurled the beaker at the wall and watched the liquid splatter over the floor. My satisfaction at this small act of rebellion lasted about a millisecond; it was replaced by horror and regret and pure self-loathing. I was so weak, so stupid, so fucking useless.

* * *

At some point I must have dropped on to my side and fallen asleep. What followed was a long period of confused, delirious slumber. I seemed to run a fever, sometimes waking drenched in sweat; at other times my very core felt frozen, my body shivering frantically to keep me alive.

I had no idea if the light stayed on or off, no idea if my jailors came to visit; my dreams were such a vivid jumble of real life and fantasy that I couldn't hope to tell them apart.

Then I must have slept more soundly. I woke feeling marginally better, lay on my back in the darkness and tried to reassemble some of my fragmented thoughts.

More than once I despaired at my missed opportunities on Saturday. I could have told Anita and Gareth that I'd ventured into the Tannery, and befriended Nathan's wife. If I had, my disappearance now would have far more significance, and they would know where to direct the police.

I thought about my children, whom I might never see again. I already knew I loved them, but it had taken this period of isolation to understand just how much I *liked* them. And why hadn't I made it clear how proud I was of them as adults? If I ever got out of here, I resolved to be a better, more thoughtful person in all manner of ways...

I had to smile. Didn't I resemble a little boy at bedtime, dutifully saying his prayers because he wants Santa to know he's been good when Christmas comes around?

Then there was Freddie. In his case I reproved myself. Because he was our youngest we had no doubt been guilty of indulging him, as had his older siblings. With tighter boundaries, maybe he wouldn't have ended up somewhere like the Tannery, reacting with petulance because a girl had rejected him.

I reflected on my marriage, and Anita's terrible observation that I was never fully present. And what was my facetious response: *Then where am I?*

The emotional and psychological distance between us might have spurred the break-up, even if Anita hadn't fallen in love with someone else. But I did feel increasingly sure that I should have fought harder to save our marriage.

When the light came on, I covered my eyes and felt the usual churning in my guts as the door opened. Both men came in, Gruff in the doorway while Reedy regarded me with disdain.

Then something materialised in his hand. A small carton of orange juice. He held it over my belly and let go; I fumbled my attempt to grasp it, nearly bursting the carton, but finally I cradled it in both hands.

For a second I couldn't speak. The carton was intact, and even felt quite cool. I looked up at Reedy; as usual all I could see were his eyes, shining with malicious humour.

'Thank you. Thank you so much.'

I gave no thought to how demeaning it was to express such gratitude. When Reedy grabbed the bucket, I felt horror at the thought of it being emptied over me. Instead he carried it out, with Gruff remaining at the door. I caught a vague odour of dung. We were in a barn, I thought – for all the good it did me to know.

Still holding the juice like something you'd have to prise from my cold dead hands, I asked Gruff, 'Do you know how long I'm being kept here?'

He held my gaze, but said nothing.

'Are you going to kill me?'

An audible snort. But still no answer.

Then Reedy returned with the bucket, now empty, and both men left. The door shut and I immediately examined the carton to be sure it was real, and not a prop.

My hands trembled so much that I had to abandon the first attempt to open it, afraid I might spill the precious liquid. This was what I'd been reduced to, I realised as I sat cross-legged, trying to breathe slowly to bring my nerves under control. Unable to trust myself to open a carton of orange juice, and so pathetically grateful that even the anticipation of drinking it was enough to move me to tears.

44

When the idea strikes her, Erin can't believe she didn't think of it before. There's one obvious place to look for Harry.

But the search has to wait, because Nathan is back home by early afternoon. 'Cameras will be in place first thing next Wednesday,' he tells her. 'The building comes down at eleven.'

He's giddy at the thought of it, so Erin has to be the same, even though she's now picturing Harry's body crushed among the wreckage.

Around four o'clock Nathan says he's off to check a complaint about damp in a property he owns in Hailsham. Erin gives him ten minutes, then hurries on foot to the Tannery. The afternoon is warm but dull. The low cloud lends a brooding aspect to the building, a malevolent presence squatting amid rubble and weeds.

She carries a shoulder bag large enough to accommodate a flashlight and a can of self-defence spray. At the entrance she listens hard before switching on the flashlight and venturing inside.

The ground floor smells so hideous it makes her gag. She conducts a cursory search, then picks her way up the stairs. That's when she hears a scrabbling from above.

Rather than flee, something makes her switch off the torch and continue up, treading so lightly that she won't be heard. Her heart is thudding from excitement as much as fear. Could Harry have chosen to hide out in here, perhaps lying in wait for Ash?

As she ascends, there's a little more silvery light, filtering in through the holes in the roof. She reaches the top floor and stops. Hearing nothing, she moves a few paces into the shadows just as footsteps start up, hurrying towards her.

'Harry?' she calls, his name catching in her throat. 'Ash?'

But the figure who emerges from the gloom is small and blond and scruffy. Erin hurriedly switches on the flashlight, thrusting it out as if the beam might hold him at bay.

'What're you doing here?' Louis demands.

Staggered by his arrogance, she summons her most haughty voice. 'My husband and I *own* this site.'

Louis merely shrugs. 'Why did you think I was Ash?'

'I... I'd heard he stays here.'

'Who told you that?'

'One of your friends.'

His eyes narrow; he doesn't believe her, or maybe he doesn't recognise the concept of friendship.

'Ain't seen him in ages,' he mutters. 'Must've found somewhere else.'

Wandering over to a pile of timber, Louis studies it before selecting a few of the planks. He carries them to the hole which Harry told her about, directly below the largest opening in the roof.

'Here for the loser's dad, are you?'

Erin is sickened by the casual cruelty of his remark. She directs the light on to the hole and understands what Harry means. It's been shaped, enlarged, for a specific purpose.

'Wanna see how it looks?' Louis wears a cheeky grin.

As he starts arranging the timber over the hole, Erin backs away, simultaneously horrified and fascinated by what he proposes to do. But Louis appears perfectly relaxed as he steps on to the planks. Bending his knees causes the wood to flex; the groaning noise pierces Erin's stomach.

'Is that a good idea?'

'Why not?' He jumps a few inches. Erin gasps.

'Are there mattresses below?'

'Dunno.' He stands on one leg for a second. 'Wanna try?'

'No.' She's trying to remember if she saw the mattresses on her way up. 'You've shown me. Come off now.'

He chuckles, flexing the boards harder. Erin can't tear her gaze away from his feet.

'You think Ash had something to do with the kid's death?' he asks.

'I don't know. What do *you* think?'

'Already told you. It was an accident.'

'But what do you know about Ash? Is he dangerous?'

Louis seems to give the question some consideration. 'Tell you what,' he says, sliding carefully along the timber. 'You find out where he is, and I'll get you the answer.'

She experiences a surge of relief when he steps back on to the solid floor. Now she can think clearly about his offer. 'Why would you do that?'

''Cause I'm a helpful sort of person.' A leer at her chest. 'Don't even want anything in return.'

Erin finds that hard to believe but decides that, right now, the prudent thing is to nod.

'I'll think about it,' she says.

* * *

The orange juice was a lifesaver, but it was gone within seconds. I was still desperately thirsty, as well as ravenous. But to my astonishment, the guards were soon back again, bringing me two packets of petrol station sandwiches and a bottle of water.

The light stayed on for a long time – several hours? – which gave me an opportunity to do some stretches and run on the spot. Then I lay down and had the pleasure of dozing without quite such an aching hunger.

When I woke, the door was being unlocked. More food? I wondered hopefully.

Both men strode in, and I was ordered to my feet. As I stood up, Gruff punched me in the stomach, the blow so unexpected that I crumpled to my knees.

Reedy lifted the mattress and flipped it over. 'Where is it?'

'What?'

'You know what. Where're you hiding it?'

'I-I'm not hiding anyth—'

'Lie to us and we'll fucking kill you!' Gruff yelled.

'Y-you put me in here virtually naked. How could I h-hide—'

A snigger from Gruff, who cuffed me lightly on the head before following Reedy out of the cell.

After that, I was furious with myself for believing their attitude had changed. I stayed on edge for a long time, and couldn't sleep even when I felt exhausted.

Eventually I did succumb, so heavily that the next time I woke the men were already in the cell. One knelt on my lower back, the other clamped a hand over my mouth and pinched my nostrils together. I writhed and bucked but couldn't break free.

It was Gruff's voice who counted the seconds. Slowly, endlessly. My chest was being crushed. I tried to pretend I was swimming; I remembered the day I met Erin, how I'd swum out for as long as I could bear in a childish attempt to impress her.

'...forty-five... forty-six... forty-seven...'

But now I was fading. The pain in my lungs was unbearable. Lightning flashed in front of my eyes.

'...sixty-two... sixty-three...'

I was going to faint. Pass out and then die. Erin, Anita, Adam, Jody...

Freddie—

They released me at the point where I was losing consciousness. After the door slammed I buried my face in my hands and wept. As I did, it was the question prompted by Anita's despairing comment that tormented me the most. It was specific and general and existential all at once, and in the asking, it caused me to regress.

Where are you, Harry?

I don't know.

Where are you, Harry?

Lost. I'm lost.

Where are you, Harry?

I just want to go home. Please. Let me go home.

45

Thump-thump-slap.

I woke to a sound like a slowed down heartbeat.

Thump-thump-slap.

The light was still on, so I'd slept with my face buried in my forearm. I lifted my head slightly, wincing at the pins and needles when I tried to move my arm.

Thump-thump-slap.

I glanced to my left and there he was, sitting in the corner with his knees drawn up, head resting back against the wall, one arm raised to shoulder height and holding a small white ball.

My son Freddie.

He tossed the ball against the adjoining wall – *thump* – and watched it bounce once on the floor – *thump* – before he caught it neatly at shoulder height – *slap.*

Then he turned his head and gave me that familiar, slightly crooked grin. *He's so handsome*, I thought. How could Maya have turned him down?

Her choice, Dad.

I nodded, unsurprised that he could read my mind. 'How... how have you been?'

Oh, you know... He gave a shrug, and threw the ball again. *So what game are we playing here?*

I blinked a few times, and slowly dragged my legs into a sitting position. 'Not superheroes, that's for sure.'

Is it an escape movie? Alcatraz or something?

'Perhaps.' I had a spasm of fear; what if the guards came in and found Freddie? I knew I would gladly die in order to protect him, but I also knew it wouldn't be enough.

I watched him throw and catch again. 'Colditz, maybe. Was it Colditz?' I enquired.

Never heard of it.

'Maybe it's not that. But there's one with an American actor – Steve McQueen!' I exclaimed 'And how did you know about...?' I indicated the ball.

I didn't. This is from your memory, Pops. Not mine.

He tossed the ball in my direction; only gently, but still I jerked and flapped my hands and missed it completely. It struck my elbow, bounced on the floor and rolled behind the bucket.

'Sorry.'

Freddie stretched out an arm and retrieved the ball, grinning wryly at my lack of coordination. *No worries, Dad. I was getting bored.*

'Tell me about it. I've been in here hours. Days? Fuck knows how long, in fact.'

He snorted. If he was surprised by my use of the *F* word, he didn't let on. But in many ways he was a man of the world now, if not the entire universe. He'd had experiences that I could barely imagine.

My breath caught in my throat at the realisation that this was my opportunity. I could learn the truth, at last.

'Will you... will you tell me what really happened that night?'

He gazed at me with huge, sad eyes. *Oh, Dad*, he sighed. *Don't you see that's the one question you can't ask?*

'Please, Freddie. I have to know. Was it Nathan Webb?'

He shook his head. *Why can't you recognise that this is only making things worse?*

He sounded so disappointed in me that I dropped my head in shame; when I looked up, Freddie had gone. Without thinking, I slammed my head against the wall, possessed by a sudden impulse to crack my skull open and go with him. I didn't quite knock myself out but it left me reeling... and holy Christ did it hurt!

Served me right, of course.

I buried my face in my arm and eventually fell asleep. I think I woke briefly to find the guards in my room, but it was dark and I couldn't work out if I was dreaming. I was far more concerned that Freddie might still be nearby, knowing I lacked the wherewithal to keep him safe.

In that context I barely noticed the tiny stabbing pain in my arm. Then I was out of it – until I awoke in the midst of a nuclear explosion.

* * *

Well, not quite. I was lying face down, and when I shifted in my sleep the brilliance of the sunshine blasted me awake. I had to put my hands over my eyes and wait before allowing the tiniest amount of light to penetrate. Just enough to peep out at the world around me.

The outside world.

Impatient for my vision to adjust, I sat up and examined my surroundings. I was on heathland, among patches of bracken and gorse and dry summer grass. The ground sloped away towards woods and farmland. There was no one in sight, perhaps because it was early in the morning; from the position of the sun I guessed around 5 or 6 a.m.

I was still dressed in my prison garb, and barefoot. But a few yards away there was a flight case which I recognised as my own. I crawled over and opened it up. Inside I found a bundle of assorted clothing, taken from my wardrobe, along with a pair of trainers.

My house keys were at the bottom of the case, and so was my phone. I grabbed it in excitement, only to find it was completely dead.

Bewildered, I pulled on the trainers and stood up, then carried out a brief physical assessment. My head hurt, my whole body ached and throbbed; I was anxious, confused – maybe even traumatised – and yet I felt exultant.

I was alive. I was out of the cell.

On the other hand, I cautioned myself, was it too soon to believe I was safe?

The answer came a few seconds later, after I'd picked up the case and set off along a grassy track leading up the hill. I passed a large clump of gorse and found a clearing in which a wooden bench had been thoughtfully provided.

Sitting on the bench, relaxed and trim in a designer tracksuit, was Nathan Webb.

46

Erin wakes on Wednesday with the sense of a connection she's failed to make. She feels confused, unsettled, and puts it down to a dream she can no longer remember.

She is alone in bed, although it's only ten past six. Another unusually early start for Nathan.

She spends a while thinking about yesterday's discussion with Anita and Detective Constable Leung. Then about Louis, and his dubious offer to help her get answers. The back of her neck had prickled as she left the Tannery but Louis hadn't tried to pursue her.

Eventually she opens the curtains and instantly spots a sinister figure in a dark hoodie, lurking on the corner of the street. Pulling on shorts and a T-shirt, she hurries downstairs and slips out of the back door, through the garden gate and into the side road. This way she can walk up behind him and take the initiative.

'You're Ash, yes?'

He jumps so dramatically, it's almost comical, spinning round to gape at her. Up close he's incredibly pale and gaunt, and yet he doesn't look as unhealthy as he ought to, as though, in his case, an aversion to sunlight and a near-starvation diet are appropriate lifestyle choices.

She says, 'I thought Nathan had called you off.'

Ash seems baffled. When he speaks, his voice is unexpectedly deep and rich. 'Why are you talking to Louis?'

'Because of Freddie. The boy who died in the Tannery.'

'You should stay away from all that,' he says.

'Harry – Freddie's dad – knows you put that note through his door. He could go to the police.'

'Maybe he should.'

He sounds casual enough but Erin reads it as a bluff. 'Look, if you know anything—'

'Just wanna forget it. Nothing will bring the kid back.' He grows agitated, swallowing heavily; on such a scrawny neck his Adam's apple looks like a ping pong ball lodged in his throat.

'Are you still living in the Tannery?'

'Not any more.'

'You know it's being demolished, next Wednesday?'

He nods sadly. 'Nathan is "moving up in the world". And he sure as shit isn't taking us with him.'

'Us?'

'Jax. Louis. Tam. The whole crew.'

'Nathan would argue that he doesn't have a responsibility to any of you.'

'Maybe.'

'So you're not bothered about it? Not like Louis?'

He flinches. 'Don't go near Louis. He's trouble.'

And you're not? Erin thinks. 'Have you talked to him recently?'

'No.'

'So how do you know I've been speaking to him?'

'Got it from Jax.'

She frowns. It's not good news if Jax is spreading gossip.

'Why are you here?' she asks.

'Just looking at this place.' Ash nods at the house, then studies her again. 'Did Nathan cut off your hair?'

The question is so unexpected that Erin can't reply; what makes it worse, somehow, is his sympathetic tone. Flustered, she retreats. It's a relief when he too starts to wander off, though his parting comment, muttered quietly, could be interpreted in a number of ways.

'Please be careful, Mrs Webb.'

* * *

I was debating whether I could creep past without being noticed when Nathan turned in my direction. There was little option but to approach him.

As I drew closer he shifted position, allowing his tracksuit top to fall open and reveal the butt of a handgun protruding from his waistband. Presumably this was in anticipation of a violent reprisal, though right now I barely had the energy to stay on my feet, let alone launch an attack.

'So it *was* you,' I muttered.

'Got a bunch of candidates, then?'

'Not really.' I was struck by how isolated it was here: how easily I could picture my body being deposited in a freshly dug grave. 'What are you going to do to me?'

'I've done it. You've had your lesson.'

'Lesson?' I repeated. 'They tortured me. Threatened to rape me.'

'*Threatened* is right. In prison it would have *happened*. All you got was a tiny taste of how it feels to be on edge, every second of every day, surrounded by people who hate your guts.'

I stared at him, trying to contain my emotions enough to speak coherently. 'That wasn't a lesson: it was punishment. For daring to investigate my son's death. And why would you do that, if you weren't hiding something?'

'Because you're a royal pain in the arse, Harry. The Tannery development is all set to begin, and I don't need a lot of bad publicity blowing up in my face. Your son's death was an accident, yeah? But if you can't accept that, you're gonna end up doing something stupid. You'll take a pop at me, and end up in prison. And you won't survive prison.'

When I didn't try to deny it, Nathan smiled, though his eyes remained cold. 'What I figured out is that you're probably not scared of dying – at your age, with fuck all left to live for. But twenty years in a tiny little cell... day after day, month after month, coping with all the scary shit you just experienced. I don't think you could handle it, do you?'

I was so livid that, perhaps foolishly, I took a couple of steps towards him. 'It won't be me behind bars. I could have you put away for this.'

'Not a chance,' Nathan sneered. 'You don't know where you were held, and the cell is already being dismantled. As for this, you and me – it never happened. I'm somewhere else right now, and I've got people who will back me up on that.'

I hated his smug certainty. I hated the nonchalant way in which he'd effectively dismissed my very existence. I knew I had been comprehensively outplayed, and yet I couldn't back down.

'That night, at the party, you were talking to Freddie.'

'Who told you that?'

'Doesn't matter.'

He squinted at me. 'The girl he came with?'

'No. It was a boy called Louis.'

Now there was a hint of concern in his eyes. 'You've talked to Louis?'

I gulped, aware of the trouble I could be causing – especially as it was actually Erin who had spoken to Louis on my behalf. 'Yes.'

Nonchalant again, he said, 'We may have had a chat. Don't remember what about.'

'Was it drugs?'

'Don't push your luck, Harry.' Then he blindsided me with a question of his own: 'You got sent an anonymous note, is that right?'

'Didn't it come from you?'

'Nope. Who's the boy from the Tannery?'

'I'm not sure. But he was the one who put the note through my door.'

'Describe him.'

'Dark hair. Thin. I didn't see him clearly.' I was vaguer than I could have been. If Nathan wasn't behind the note, I didn't necessarily want to implicate Ash at this stage.

Again he took a few seconds to chew over what I'd told him, and when he next looked up he seemed irritated to find I was still there. 'Off you trot.'

'How do I get home?'

Nathan delved into his pocket and produced a fiver. 'Catch a bus from the main road, couple of minutes up that way. First one's at seven.'

'What time is it now?'

'About half six. Oh, and it's Wednesday.'

My captivity had lasted just over two days, and yet it had felt like a week or more. I reached for the banknote, only for him to flick it out of reach.

'One more thing.'

'What?' I knew only too well, of course. My insides were watery with dread as I waited.

'You and Erin. I guess you thought I was clueless?'

'There isn't—'

'Don't bullshit me. I know you encouraged her to leave me.'

On this last sentence he bared his teeth at me. I had been so stupid, forgetting he'd had my phone. *Of course* he knew.

He observed my thought process and grinned. 'Once you were in the van, they held your thumb to the phone and unlocked it. I've read your messages, Harry. Now I'm giving you a very generous final warning.'

'You haven't hurt Erin?' I shouted. 'Because if you have, I'll—'

'You'll what, Harry?' He reached inside his jacket, tapping a finger against the gun.

Meekly, I dipped my head. My humiliation was complete. He thrust the money out, glaring at me until I took it.

'Go near my wife again and I will make you suffer so much, you'll end up begging to be put out of your misery.' Nathan paused, licking his lips as if savouring the message. 'And however much *you* suffer, it'll be nothing compared to what I'll do to Erin. You get that?'

Reluctantly, shamefully, I nodded.

'Good. Now piss off, and don't ever come near me or my property again.'

47

Erin drinks some cranberry juice while reviewing her conversation with Ash. It's troubling, on a number of levels. She regrets not asking more about Harry. Even if Ash wasn't involved in the disappearance, it's possible he was watching the house when Harry left.

The young man presented as an enigmatic, troubled figure, but nowhere near as frightening as she'd come to believe. If he and Louis were to face off, she suspects Louis would be the one to prevail.

It's twenty to eight when her phone buzzes. *Got to be Nathan*, she thinks as she reaches for it. But there's a tiny spark of hope that it will be Harry, or at least Anita with news of Harry.

She's wrong on all counts: it's Gordon Ryan, who blurts out, 'Barb just went into Milly's room and it was empty!'

'What?'

'We'd assumed she was just sleeping in for a bit. But she's not here.'

'You've looked round the house?'

'All her usual hiding places. Except the front door's only on the latch.'

'She's gone out!' Erin is so intent on what this means that the noise outside doesn't immediately register.

'Anyway, Barb said not to worry you – we know how Milly likes her walks, and we're just off to check her favourite routes right now...' Gordon's voice wobbles, and Erin struggles to hear what he says next: '...so if you have any idea where—'

'*Who the FUCK is that?*' Nathan roars.

Erin turns to find him storming towards her. Before she can say a word he snatches the phone from her hand and shouts, 'ARE YOU TAKING THE PISS, AFTER WHAT I JUST—'

Erin staggers, making a helpless clawing motion for the phone. *You've got it all wrong*, she wants to say, watching Nathan's expression change as he registers who is speaking. But it's a reluctant transition: the wild beast forced back into its cage.

'Yeah, yeah, total mix-up. I'll put you back to...'

He thrusts the phone at Erin without a word of apology. Gordon starts to ask what's wrong but she cuts in: 'I'm coming over. You two head out. Text me if you find her.'

She ends the call. Nathan glowers at the coffee machine before saying, 'What's up?'

Her concern for Milly makes her brave, snapping back: 'I feel like I could ask you the same thing.'

He only shrugs, calmly, and says, 'What did the Ryans want?'

'Milly's gone out somewhere on her own, without telling them.'

'Well, it's a nice morning. I just got a bit of fresh air myself.'

His tone is casual but there's a teasing glint in his eye, a sense that he has a secret. Could he have done something to Milly?

'She isn't safe on her own. I need to help search for her.'

From the way he purses his lips, she's certain he will forbid it. But then he says, 'Quick coffee and I'll come with you.'

'There's no need. You've probably got work to do.'

'I can spare an hour or two. The more hands on deck, the better.'

It's a reasonable point, though generally his concern for Milly is non-existent. But when she stresses the urgency, it becomes clear that she won't be permitted to go to Seaford on her own.

After a sip of coffee, he says, 'Aren't you gonna ask who I thought it was on the phone?'

Erin can only manage a pantomime frown. 'I don't get you.'

'Yes you do. Your mate, Harry Manning.'

'Harry? I haven't spoken to him—'

'Lie to me now, Erin, and I'm gonna get *really* fucking angry.'

'I wasn't going to lie. I haven't.'

'I hope not, babe. For your sake.' Another mouthful of coffee, which he swallows with relish before he looks her in the eye. 'Because I know all about you and Harry.'

* * *

I might have been relieved to get away from Nathan, but that wasn't to say I felt remotely happy about the conversation we'd just had. I trudged up the hill, suitcase in hand, vibrating with impotent rage.

The footpath ended at a small layby on a country road that I vaguely recognised. There were no parked cars in sight, so I had to assume Nathan's vehicle was secreted elsewhere. The sign for the bus stop was about fifty yards away. I walked along to it and then sat on the suitcase and waited.

It was perhaps twenty minutes before a bus rumbled into view from the north. By then the traffic was building a little, mostly trucks and vans, and I was aware that I must have represented a somewhat unusual sight.

The driver scowled when I offered him cash and reminded me that the company had a ticketing app. The bus was quiet but it wasn't empty; all eyes were upon me as I made my way to a seat at the rear. I imagined this was exactly how a newly released convict would be regarded when travelling home from prison.

Within a few minutes we'd crested a steep hill and I had a better idea of where I was: some ten or twelve miles from the coast. I rested my head against the window and tried to zone out. I was too drained to think clearly, so it was better not to think at all.

The bus deposited me at a stop near the town centre. With dark clouds stealing overhead, the air had become very humid. I was sweating profusely as I lugged the case uphill, and it was with an incredible surge of relief that I unlocked my front door and stepped inside.

The first thing I did was put my phone on charge. Then I took some painkillers, drank copiously and wolfed down a couple of cereal bars before stepping into the shower.

By the time I'd dressed and made tea, the phone had sufficient power for me to check it for messages. There was a deluge of missed calls, along with worried texts from Anita and Gareth. Their texts were rather odd, phrased as if in response to communications from me, but if any messages had been sent on my behalf, they were no longer present.

And nothing from Erin. They'd deleted her from my contacts, along with all of our conversations.

I sat down heavily on a kitchen chair. Only now was I able to contemplate the scale of what I'd done. The selfish stupidity of it.

Nathan Webb had seen the contents of my phone. He'd know that Erin and I were conspiring against him, and no doubt he had picked up on the mutual attraction between us. I could hardly dare to contemplate the price that Erin might have paid for my recklessness, but calling her now was out of the question.

It was almost eight-thirty. I ought to be letting Anita and Gareth know I was all right – and what about the police? I could dial 999, but the idea of a long morning in an interview room, describing everything I'd endured, was almost as unbearable as the captivity itself.

I couldn't do it; not now, at least. I was too bruised, a wounded creature that craved only solitude and a safe place to hide.

I staggered along the hall, undressed and climbed into bed. The cool sheet felt delicious against my skin; I buried my face between two pillows and shut my eyes and slept like a child—

To wake, after only an hour, my body bathed in a cold sweat. I'd heard a noise at the front door. Someone was intent on getting inside.

As I sat up, praying I'd imagined it, there were footsteps in the hall and then a tiny exclamation.

'Harry?' my ex-wife called out. 'Are you here?'

48

I know all about you and Harry.

Even her sister's disappearance struggles to compete with the shock of Nathan's declaration. Erin is quiet as they drive along the coast road towards Seaford, but she's frantically thinking: What does he know? *How* does he know?

And the other, more serious question is creating a physical pressure, like a balloon expanding in her chest, until it cannot be contained any longer.

'Have you done something to Harry?'

'Like what?' Nathan sounds surprised.

Her hands curl into fists and she presses them down on her legs. 'Have you... had him killed?'

There's a burst of laughter. The Jaguar veers a little towards the centre line as he turns to look at her.

'Why would you say that?'

'Because he's missing. I spoke to his wife, Anita. He went somewhere on Sunday and he's not answering his phone.'

'Doesn't mean he's dead. Maybe just wanted some peace and quiet.' Nathan waits a second or two. 'Is he still with his wife? I heard they'd split up.'

'I think they recently separated.'

'Schmoozing with the ex. You're not planning to take her place, are you?'

'No. I'm married to you—'

'I warned you, remember?' he growls. 'I thought cutting your hair was the lesson you needed, but all you did was turn it into a sexy new style. I should have cut you somewhere that leaves a scar.'

As usual, the fear has enveloped her like a thick black cloth, robbing her of light and air. To throw it off, Erin has to be bold.

She takes a deep breath. 'If you know about me and Harry, you must have spoken to him. So where is he?'

'I've got ways of finding out stuff,' he says, casually. 'And you don't get to interrogate me. Not when you're undermining the project that was meant to set us up for life – and making me look a prick in the process.'

'I haven't. Anyway, it's hypocritical to accuse me of being unfaithful when you were taunting me about "working breakfasts" with Keira.'

'Christ, that was a joke! Plus it's different with men, you know that.' He sniffs, saying prissily, 'I haven't shagged Keira. You can ask her yourself.'

'I don't want to ask her,' Erin responds, nearly adding, *I don't care who you've shagged*.

But that would be like declaring the marriage is over, something which, in Nathan's view, will never be Erin's decision to make.

* * *

'Why'd you get involved with Harry?' Nathan asks. 'Tell me that.'

The mildness of his tone is disconcerting, particularly as her own attitude has become more confrontational than she would normally dare. It heightens Erin's suspicion that he is toying with her.

'It was a chance meeting,' she says. 'At first I had no idea who he was. Then he asked for my help. He won't accept Freddie's death was an accident.'

'Even though there's not a scrap of proof it was anything else.' Nathan sighs. 'Have you been feeding his conspiracy theories?'

'I've never tried to suggest anything. Because I don't know anything.'

'But you've talked to the mugwumps – and don't lie about that.' A little more of a snarl in his voice. Erin flinches, in case he's about to lash out.

'I've spoken to Jax. He told me about going on the boards as a dare. Said he broke his ankle.'

'Silly twat.' Nathan snorts with laughter. Before Erin can point out that this information was kept away from the police, he says, 'And Louis?'

'He insisted it was an accident, then suggested he could tell me more if I showed him my tits.'

'*What*?' Nathan's vehemence makes her shudder. 'Are you serious?'

'I don't know if he was joking or not, but I told him where to go.'

'You better have. Who else?'

'No one – oh, a boy called Ash. Harry thinks Ash put a note through his door, warning him off.'

'Ash,' Nathan murmurs to himself. But the existence of the note doesn't seem to come as a surprise.

'Wasn't it done on your instructions?' she asks.

'Of course it bloody wasn't! When were you talking to Ash?'

'This morning. I noticed him over the road and assumed he was on guard duty like the others.'

'Huh. I wouldn't rely on Ash to take the fucking bins out.'

Nathan lapses into a moody silence as they cross the bridge at Exceat and climb the final steep hill into Seaford. They rendezvous at about ten to nine on the coast road, not far from the recreation ground. As he slews across two parking bays, Nathan mutters, 'Bloody weird town. Miles of seafront and not a single frigging pub, hotel, restaurant...'

Erin has heard this before, and would agree it's unusual. The kind of place that, in both their minds, is permanently a Sunday afternoon in March. Where they differ is that Erin rather likes that.

The Ryans are surprised to see Nathan, Gordon in particular frowning when they shake hands. But Milly's welfare is the priority; Erin quickly asks if they've contacted the police.

'Not yet,' Barbara says. 'I suppose we'll have to, soon.'

'We can't have flashing lights and sirens,' Gordon points out. 'It'll scare the poor soul half to—'

He breaks off, reddening. Erin establishes that they've covered most of the town centre. It's really only the coast that remains.

'I hate to think of her on the beach.' Barbara is grey-faced, haggard, and somehow looks years older than when Erin last saw her.

'She won't go near the water,' Gordon says, though he doesn't sound completely convinced.

As one they turn and gaze at the sea, which is pea green and flat as a pond beneath a leaden sky. Milly's never been a swimmer, though she can be persuaded to paddle if Erin's alongside her. But accidents are always possible: the beaches here shelve steeply, and there's a powerful current.

With that comes a flashback to Saturday night, and Erin's swim with Harry. *Harry, who might also be dead—*

'Love, it's all right.' Gordon gently grasps her arm. 'We'll find her safe and sound, don't you worry.'

'That's what I've been telling her. Isn't it, babe?' Nathan gives Erin the wolfish grin of a born mind reader. 'You think someone's missing and then' – he snaps his fingers – 'hey presto, there they are!'

49

At the sound of Anita's voice, I was overcome with emotion. She had to call my name again before I could respond, and even then it was more of a cry than anything verbal.

She came into the room and exclaimed, 'Harry! Where have you been?'

I opened my mouth but nothing emerged. Anita rolled on: 'It's fine that you wanted to get away, but to break off all communication – what were we to think? Especially when you've... well, not been yourself lately. That's why I kept trying your phone, even though you'd told me not to—'

'I didn't,' I managed to blurt out.

'Didn't what?'

'Tell you not to. If you got a message, I didn't send it.'

She squinted, as if seeing me properly for the first time. 'Harry? What happened to you?'

'I was abducted, Sunday night.' I paused to swallow. 'I heard a noise in the garden, went outside. Two men grabbed me, kept me in a cell.'

Recounting it caused my heart rate to shoot up, so the words emerged in gasps. Anita finally grasped the state I was in and came to sit beside me. 'This isn't just a nightmare...?'

'It was a nightmare all right – but I'm not making it up.'

'No, no. I believe you.' She reached out and tenderly stroked the back of my neck. 'But who—?'

'Nathan Webb.'

I saw her flinch. 'Are you sure?'

'A couple of hours ago I regained consciousness in some countryside north of here. Webb was sitting nearby. He did it to teach me a lesson, he said. To stop me from investigating Freddie's death.'

'Then you need to tell the police.' Anita took my hand. 'Call them right now.'

'I'm not ready for that. In any case, Webb's confident that I can't prove a thing – and he's probably right.'

Anita was shaking her head, as if wishing to deny what she'd heard, but then she said, 'We had a horrible feeling it could be something like this.'

'What, you and Gareth?'

'No. Your friend Erin.'

'You've spoken to Erin?' I yelped. 'Is she all right? Are you sure—?'

'Yes, yes. Stay calm. She came here Monday to find you, after getting a nasty text.'

'From my phone?' This caused a bolt of panic. 'Are you sure she's okay?'

'I saw her again yesterday, and she was fine.'

'And what did it say, this message?'

Anita grimaced. 'It told her to stay away from you, and called her a "skank".'

'Oh my God!'

Anita, just as disgusted, said, 'Presumably it was written by Webb?'

'I think so.' I frowned; my brain still wasn't firing on all cylinders. 'I can't believe Erin was able to come here. I was convinced he'd do something to her.'

'According to Erin, he's been nice as pie – which she did say was out of character.' Anita made sure she had my attention, and asked, 'Are you sleeping with her?'

'No.' I felt blood rushing to my face. 'Though we have, er... kissed, once or twice.'

'And is Nathan aware of that?'

'If he read what was on my phone, he'd be able to infer...' I put a hand over my eyes. 'It's possible he's just biding his time. I ought to warn her.'

'Nothing hasty,' Anita cautioned, and I knew she was right. 'Why don't I let her know you're back?'

I could only stare, dumbly, as she fetched her bag. When she returned, I registered that she was in a skirt and blouse. 'You came round to work?'

'I didn't know what else to do. You weren't officially missing, because of those texts.'

'No, of course.' I indicated her phone. 'But you have Erin's number?'

'We thought it was a good idea to keep in touch.' She looked up. 'We also spoke to DC Leung.'

'About me?'

'We were worried, Harry. And with good reason, it turns out. At that point we had nothing concrete, and on the face of it those texts made it clear you wanted to be left alone.'

'So Leung didn't pursue it?'

'No. But I think you should consider speaking to her.'

I nodded. 'Perhaps if she'll talk to me unofficially?'

'I'm sure she will.' Anita was studying her phone. 'Gareth's texted again, asking if there's any news.'

'Tell him I'm sorry. I'm not sure if I'm fit to work today...'

'Oh, Harry.' At Anita's behest I opened my arms and we embraced. She held me tightly and I heard a sob burst from her throat. 'For goodness' sake, we could have lost you!'

This was a comment that should have invited bravado on my part. Some flippant remark that would have had Anita chuckling and disapproving at the same time. But drained of energy as I was – drained of hope as well, I suspect – I heard myself saying, 'I should have listened to you, shouldn't I? I was never cut out to be a superhero.'

* * *

It's Erin's suggestion that they split up. Nathan isn't happy with that idea, but the Ryans immediately agree.

Since he has the car, Nathan is dispatched to the old ruins at Tidemills before joining up with Barbara, who will check the beaches near the yacht club. Gordon and Erin will go east, in the direction of Seaford Head.

'If there's still no joy, I'll trek along the base of the cliffs while you head upwards. But stay well away from the edge,' Gordon adds grimly. 'There have been a lot of falls in the past few years.'

Erin agrees to be careful, but she knows what is really on his mind. If there's a body to be found on the beach, he wants to spare her the pain of discovery.

Despite the warmth, the threat of rain has kept people away. There's a sprinkling of beachgoers, but when Erin shows them a picture of Milly on her phone, she gets only shaking heads and expressions of sympathy.

Along with the concern for Milly, she can't stop thinking about Nathan's cryptic comments. He's withholding what he knows about Harry's fate, and relishing every moment of the torment it's causing her.

They stop briefly to rest at the base of the cliffs. Thankfully the tide is low enough for Gordon to safely continue along the beach.

'Nothing from Barb,' he reports. 'Has Nathan updated yet?'

'No. But I'm sure he'll message if he finds her.'

'She wouldn't like that. Milly's never warmed to him – and I can't say I blame her.' Staring at Erin, Gordon looks as craggy and worn down as these ancient cliffs. 'That business this morning, on the phone...'

'I'm so sorry, Gordon. But I'd rather not—'

'Are you safe? That's all I want to know.' He eyes her hairstyle, which neither he nor Barbara has commented on. 'Is he hurting you?'

Erin summons an unconvincing smile. 'I'm gonna start moving up. See you in a bit.'

There are several footpaths on the steep grassy slope towards Seaford Head. The hillside is dotted with walkers, and Erin, panting with exertion as she ascends, speaks to three different groups on their way down before one elderly man says he believes there was a young woman sitting alone just over the brow of the hill.

'Was she near the edge?' Erin asks in a panic.

'Not too close, dear. She was drinking a can of cola.' The man smiles. 'And singing to herself, I think.'

Thanking him, Erin starts to run. She tries to stay hopeful, despite how much is riding on a stranger's definition of *Not too close*. After cresting the hill, she has to bend double for a moment; that's when she hears Milly's voice drifting from beyond a clump of bushes.

Erin hurries forward, silent on the springy grass. She discovers Milly some fifteen or twenty feet from the cliff edge, sitting with her legs straight out in front of her. She's in black joggers and a navy blue sweatshirt, and cradling a can of Coke in her lap. Her head bobs rhythmically in time to the sound – 'singing' is perhaps a generous description. It's more a kind of chanting, Milly's personal take on eastern meditation.

Erin draws near before she speaks, wanting to be within reach if her sister is startled. 'Hey there, beautiful.'

Milly glances round, her face transformed by a gleeful smile. Erin drops beside her and they embrace, Milly smacking kisses against Big Sister's cheek: Mwah! Mwah! Mwah!

'You know you're not supposed to come up here. The cliffs are dangerous.'

Milly nods gravely, and stares down at the drink nestled in her lap.

'You shouldn't go out on your own, either. Mum and Dad were worried about you.'

'Mummy Sonia?'

'Mummy Barbara. She and Gordon have been searching all round town for you.'

Milly nods again, a single tear rolling down her cheek. She offers Erin the Coke.

'Thanks.' Erin takes a sip. 'Where did you get this?'

'The man buyed it for me.'

'What man?'

'Nice man. In the park. I said I was thirsty and he buyed it for me.'

Erin feels her stomach lurch as her imagination swoops in on the worst possible scenario. 'Was the man on his own?'

'He had two boys. One of them did this.' She sticks her tongue out. 'It looked funny.'

'Talking to people we don't know, Milly, that's not a good idea. Why did you come out on your own?'

The girl wriggles on her buttocks until her body is pressed against Erin's. 'Bad dream,' she says.

'Oh, honey. You know dreams are only pretend. Nothing to worry about.'

Milly studies her carefully, alert to any sign of dishonesty. She reaches up, tentatively strokes the side of Erin's head, and says, 'You had long hair in heaven.'

'In...?' Erin feels a lump in her throat. She realises belatedly that she needs to let the others know Milly is safe, but for a moment she can only stare at her sister. 'I'm not in heaven, sweetheart.'

'In the dream you were.' Milly's bottom lip firms up, as it's wont to do in the face of a challenge. 'No-than put you in heaven. It was you and Mummy Sonia. You left me behind.'

50

Together, Anita and I drafted a text to Erin:

> He's home, all well. But call me if you get a chance.

'It'll take her, what, half a second to read and delete?' Anita said. 'And if her situation is that bad, then frankly she ought to leave him.'

'Easier said than done,' I pointed out, half expecting her to disagree. Anita could sometimes take a harsh line with people who, as she saw it, had a tendency to bring misfortune upon themselves. But on this occasion she only nodded, ruefully.

After messaging Gareth, she offered to make tea. I accompanied her to the kitchen and started to tell her about my confinement, though I was sparing in my description of exactly what I'd experienced. I suspected I would need time to process it myself before I could go into detail.

An urgent knocking at the door almost stopped my heart. Anita opened it and Gareth bowled inside, took in the sight of me and seemed overcome with emotion. I was pulled into a fierce bearhug, and could have sworn he muffled a sob as he held me.

'Nathan Webb kidnapped you, is that right?'

We moved to the living room, where I went through it again. I told them exactly how I'd gone about investigating Freddie's death, and I didn't shy away from recounting Erin's part in it. Anita remained preternaturally still, whereas Gareth was continually stretching and lunging and crossing his legs, as if barely able to contain his desire for action.

They posed a number of astute questions, and before I knew it we'd reached the crux of the matter: What was I going to do now?

'Go to the cops, surely?' Gareth turned to Anita. 'I take it you've already said this?'

Anita nodded, but not wholeheartedly, and left me to elaborate on what I'd told her.

Gareth, to his credit, remained open minded as I pointed out how difficult it would be to pin anything on Webb. 'Sneaky bastard, isn't he?'

I nodded. 'And frankly, I'm worried about future reprisals. Who's to say he won't bide his time and one day go after you two, for instance?'

'Like to see him try,' Gareth retorted, all chin-thrusting machismo; then he seemed to appreciate how absurd he sounded, and sheepishly said, 'Nah. You're right.'

We broke off around eleven, in part because Anita could hear my stomach rumbling. Gareth had driven here, and it was his idea to pop into town and fetch us pizza.

Shortly after that, Anita looked up from her phone. 'Erin says she's glad to hear you're back. She can't talk now but will try to call me later.'

I was filled with relief that Erin was apparently unharmed, though I remained desperate to confirm it for myself. *Out of the question*, as Anita reminded me.

When Gareth returned with the pizza, the smell alone nearly drove me into a frenzy. I ate ravenously, and ended up being told not to keep apologising for my lack of manners.

'We get it, bro,' Gareth said. 'You're starving.'

Then it was back to the discussion. We concluded that I had three basic options. The first was that I go to the police and tell them everything, in the hope that it would spur them to conduct a thorough enquiry. And then – in the very best-case scenario – they would bring charges against Nathan both for my abduction and for Freddie's death.

It didn't take long to agree that this was the least likely outcome. There simply wasn't enough evidence, and whilst I'd anticipated that Anita would be hardest to persuade of this, it was she who told us that DC Leung had said much the same thing.

In addition – and this was something I kept to myself – it was clear that if I took this route, my own enquiries would have to cease.

Which led us to option two: I wouldn't involve the police, but instead I'd continue, in one way or another, to search for answers. This one received short shrift from them both.

'You shouldn't even consider it,' Anita maintained.

'A step too far, even for a stubborn old sod like you,' Gareth added.

'In which case,' I said, 'the third and final option is to forget all about it.'

Anita nodded firmly, and Gareth said, 'Yep.'

'I forget what Nathan's done, I accept he's got away with it – and, of course, I abandon any hope of finding out why Freddie died.'

'Can you truly do that, Harry?' Anita asked.

'Guess I'll have to. It's both the easiest option, and the most sensible.'

'Not just sensible. Pragmatic.' She looked at me askance, as if doubtful whether to take my assurances at face value. 'But I do realise how much it will hurt to let it go.'

'The fact is,' Gareth said, 'you got way out of your depth and only just made it ashore. You'd have to be a lunatic to plunge back in and hope to survive.'

Anita, nodding, said, 'Exactly. You could have died.'

'I know I could have died. But Freddie *did* die.' I couldn't help throwing up my hands in frustration. 'And the man responsible on both counts has got away with it. How do you measure "pragmatism" against an injustice on that scale?'

I saw them both readying another protest and quickly turned my gesture into one of surrender. 'But it doesn't mean I'm going to "plunge back in". Because even I'm not that stupid.'

* * *

It takes Erin about half an hour to soothe Milly enough that she'll come home. By then she's fired off texts to Gordon and Barbara and had a brief conversation with Nathan.

They're descending the hill when she receives a message from Anita: Harry is back home. It's such wonderful news that at first Erin is slightly incredulous. But there's no opportunity to reply. The Jaguar is waiting in the parking area at the end of the promenade, Nathan scowling at the wheel.

The Ryans spot Milly and rush over to take her in their arms. Gordon hugs Erin as well, and over his shoulder Erin sees Milly flinching in her stepmother's embrace. Something not quite right there.

Then Milly spots Nathan and for a moment looks like she might bolt. She refuses point blank to get in his car, so the Ryans say they're fine to walk with her. Then Milly insists that Erin has to come with them, leaving Nathan to drive back on his own.

No one says much on the slow walk home. Milly is tired and tearful, Gordon and Barbara uncharacteristically subdued. Nathan has parked outside the house, and even from a distance Erin can tell he's in a foul mood. When she declines an offer of refreshments, the Ryans look relieved.

'Two minutes to get her settled, and I just need the loo,' Erin tells Nathan, who has deigned to lower the car window.

'Fucking hurry,' he grumbles.

From the privacy of the toilet Erin dashes off a reply to Anita:

> Great news! Can't speak now but will try to call you later.

She's desperate to know more, but from outside comes the blarp of a car horn. Subtle, Nathan ain't.

Erin kisses her sister and promises she'll visit again tomorrow. Gordon accompanies Erin to the front door, and she gives him a brief account of the dream that upset Milly. Gordon doesn't seem unduly surprised.

'She's been very withdrawn the past few days. I think she tends to pick up on any kind of atmosphere.'

A shadow in the doorway; Barbara leans round to say, indignantly, 'There hasn't been an "atmosphere".'

Gordon jumps. 'Well, not with us arguing or anything, no.'

Barbara is glaring at him, and after Erin has looked from her to Gordon and back, she merely says, 'It's something and nothing.' They hear the car horn again; if anything, Barbara looks grateful for the intervention. 'You'd better get gone, or that husband of yours will be breaking the door down.'

Gordon dredges up a sad smile. 'You take care, all right?'

Erin nods. 'I'll see you tomorrow.' *If I get permission*, she adds to herself.

Nathan barely speaks on the drive back, except to remind her of the sacrifice he's made in coming over here.

'Milly's definitely not herself,' she tells him. 'I may need to visit her tomorrow.'

'Depends if you've learned your lesson.'

It's such a demeaning comment, Erin can't bring herself to do anything more than nod. After a second he punches her thigh. 'Well?'

'Yes. I have.' Blinking away tears, she tries to remind herself that it's all good news today. Milly is safe and sound and so, apparently, is Harry.

Then why does she still feel uneasy?

51

It was around one o'clock when Gareth departed, after insisting I shouldn't hurry back to work. I agreed to see how I felt in the morning.

Anita was ready to go soon after; she had client meetings this afternoon. Before she left, I extracted a pledge that she would tell me as soon as she heard from Erin.

'Whatever you do, don't try to contact her yourself,' she warned.

'I won't. Promise.' We hugged, and then she was gone and I was alone.

I'd never before had any difficulty with solitude, but after two days locked in a cell this felt like a very different proposition. I was aware of a craving for more conversation, more smiles and laughter and physical affection.

I pottered around the house, fighting a constant urge to make sure the doors and windows were locked. My mind kept returning not to the prison cell, but to the lonely hillside where Nathan Webb had set out the brutal logic that lay behind his actions.

You'll take a pop at me, and end up in prison. And you won't survive prison.

Much as I despised him for it, I understood that the lesson he'd given me wasn't without merit. After all, I *had* given serious thought to killing him – and I almost certainly would have made a mess of it.

Talking through my options with Anita and Gareth had felt strangely hypothetical. Now I had to confront the truth: I had reached the end of the road with my vendetta, with my attempt to get the facts about Freddie's death. With my foolish, unrealistic desire to be with Erin. All of it had to be forgotten.

* * *

When they get home, Nathan expects lunch to be made for him. They eat together in a strained silence; afterwards he heads for his study but emerges frequently, often with no apparent purpose beyond keeping an eye on her.

Then there's a knock at the door. Nathan gets there first, and from the kitchen doorway Erin sees Jax, cowering on the threshold. He nods at Erin without meeting her eye, and is ushered into the study.

Erin is now a ball of molten worry. In all the drama over Milly, she'd forgotten Nathan's vow to speak to the wasps. They're going to be asked precisely what was discussed, and the more perceptive ones will spot an opportunity to ingratiate themselves with him.

It might not be Jax, but one of them will rat her out.

And the irony, Erin thinks, is that she was beginning to wonder if Nathan's denials about Harry were genuine. He seems to be playing a game on so many levels that she no longer knows what to believe.

With the study door shut, Erin hurries upstairs and calls Anita. 'I can't speak for long,' she says. 'Harry's home, yes? And he's all right?'

'It was a horrific experience, by the sound of it.' Anita's tone is heavy. 'He was abducted. By Nathan.'

'What? He can't—'

'Two other men took him. They held him somewhere, in a kind of replica of a prison cell. But this morning, when they released him, Nathan was there. He did it to teach Harry a lesson.'

This has sucked the air from Erin's lungs. 'When this morning? Nathan was here overnight.'

'It was early, around six, in the countryside north of here.'

Now Erin remembers waking to find him absent. He'd come in at, what, about seven-thirty? *Blew away the cobwebs*, he'd told her.

She hears a noise downstairs, and says, 'I wish I could talk to Harry, but from now on I can't risk any more contact. I've deleted his number. Please tell him how sorry I am.'

'It's not your fault. And Harry's very worried about you. We both are.'

'Thank you. And I'll—' Erin breaks off, hearing urgent footsteps on the stairs. 'I'll try and call you tomorrow.'

She stabs at the screen, tosses the phone on to the bed and snatches up a bottle of nail varnish, then reacts with mock surprise as Nathan storms into the room.

'Were you on the phone?'

'No.'

'Screen's still lit up.'

'I was online. Did you get what you wanted from Jax?'

He isn't letting it go. 'I heard your voice.'

'Just singing.' She's suddenly giddy with defiance, and the playful tone throws him off balance.

'Singing?'

'That's right. From the sheer joy of being alive.'

He registers the sarcasm but doesn't know how to respond. Erin takes advantage by grabbing her phone and shoving it in her pocket. She veers round Nathan, and only then does he recover.

'You spoke to Harry?'

'Of course not.'

She's at the door when he snarls, 'Where're you going?'

'Downstairs.'

'I haven't finished—'

He's fooled her by starting to speak; Erin can't help glancing back while also reaching for the door. She stumbles as Nathan lunges in her direction and kicks out, not at her but at the door, and as it swings and slams she realises too late what he's doing.

She feels a terrible crushing pain in her left hand: two of her fingertips are trapped between door and frame, and combined with her scream there's a kind of primitive animalistic howl; black flashes in front of her eyes, her vision fading as Nathan wrenches the door open and her arm flops at her side, stomach churning, her legs giving way and the world dissolving to nothing...

52

I was considering an afternoon nap when I received an update from Anita. She'd heard from Erin, who was delighted to know I was safe, but shocked and confused that Nathan was responsible.

Sounding a little dubious, Anita said, 'It seems crazy he can do all this without her knowing.'

'Oh, I don't doubt his ability to keep secrets from her. How did she seem?'

'I wish I didn't have to say this, but I thought she sounded scared.'

'Scared? Should we be going up there?'

'I don't mean quaking with fear. "Nervy" might be a better word. I'll maybe text her tomorrow. But you *have* to leave her alone, Harry.'

'I know, I know.' Irritably, I ended the call and took my melancholy mood off to bed. I woke after three hours with none of the usual grogginess that I associated with daytime naps, made a sandwich and ate it while standing at the living room window. I felt energised, restless, and knew I had to get out.

I fetched my swimming gear and headed for the seafront. It was seven o'clock, and the air was thick with humidity. The beach where I'd tussled with the seagulls was all but deserted.

In a light south-easterly breeze the sea had a pleasurable swell, the waves powerful but somehow languorous. It enabled me to swim and then drift, allowing my body to be carried through the water: a physical surrender that was immensely calming. For perhaps the first time since I'd been abducted, there were positive thoughts in amongst the negative.

I could come back from this.

I was not entirely defeated.

Anita had mentioned speaking to DC Leung. It reminded me of a brief conversation I'd had with the young detective, a couple of weeks after her senior officer had confirmed there was no hope of bringing charges against Nathan Webb. I'd encountered her by chance in a supermarket, and after an exchange of pleasantries I had expressed my dismay at that decision. Not only had Leung sympathised, she'd also said, 'Webb's hiding something. I suspect they all are.'

Encouraged by her candour, I had said, 'I know you can't prove it, but do you think they killed him?'

Leung had thought carefully before responding. 'I'm not sure I'd go that far. I certainly feel there was more to Freddie's death than meets the eye. But, as you say, we just can't prove it.'

Reflecting on it now, I felt comforted by the reminder that at least one police officer shared my suspicions. It might be worthwhile speaking to her again, I thought, though maybe not for a day or two. A decision of that magnitude shouldn't be made impulsively.

Along the horizon there was a yellowish tint to the sky. Once or twice I caught the flicker of distant lightning. After changing, I picked up my bag and walked across the beach. I felt lighter, unburdened, and when I trotted up the steps and saw Len Bowden heading towards the breakwater, I was glad to alter my course and say hello to a familiar face.

'Off for an evening shift?' I called.

He turned, looking startled, then appraised me with a slightly disturbing intensity.

'That's it,' he said. 'And you, Harry? You look a bit under the weather.'

Shrugging, I indicated the sky. 'Talking of weather, it looks like a storm's coming in.'

'Conditions are heavy, but I don't think it'll make landfall just yet.'

Even as he spoke, there was a flash on the horizon. 'Want to reconsider?' I joked, but he didn't look amused.

'Dry lightning. Won't amount to anything.'

'No, well... I'm sure you're a better judge of these things than I am.'

'I see a lot out here, that's for certain.' He sounded so emphatic that it triggered a tiny alarm, but I was no less blindsided when he added, 'Messing with another man's wife, Harry. It never ends well.'

* * *

When Erin regains consciousness there's no confusion, no loss of memory and, worst of all, no respite. The pain in her fingers is an unending scream.

It doesn't help that Nathan's face is swimming in and out of focus before her. He looks horrified. His voice when he speaks is dripping with sympathy.

'Erin, I'm so sorry. My foot hit the door by accident.'

This is a lie. She knows it's a lie but she will almost come to believe it over the next few hours, not least because Nathan has bought into the fabrication with the commitment of a method actor. In the world he creates it is believed by everyone who is required to believe it: the doctor, the nurses, the X-ray technician, all of them charmed by Perfect Husband.

She doesn't want to go to the hospital but weakly succumbs to Nathan's insistence. Before that, she is copiously sick, screaming between each heave because the spasms are causing her fingers to throb even harder. The pain barely recedes in the car, despite the ice pack Nathan makes up before they leave. She weeps in a hopeless, pathetic fashion for the entire journey, and then for much of the interminable wait in A&E.

The time given to assessment and treatment of the injury is a mere five or six minutes – which would be fine, if those few minutes weren't plucked at random from more than five hours in the over-lit, soulless waiting area, surrounded by her fellow wretches.

In the company of the medical professionals, Nathan can't do enough for her. He helps her walk along the corridor, an arm around her waist as though it's her foot that's injured rather than her hand. He fetches drinks and snacks, and buys her a couple of glossy magazines from the hospital's shop.

The prognosis: there are no bones broken; it's only the tips of the two middle fingers that were partially crushed. Treatment is simple, and it's essentially more of what she's already been doing: ice packs, elevation and ibuprofen. There's a chance she'll lose one or both of the nails, but aside from that the doctor thinks she's been lucky.

Lucky.

'I didn't need to come,' she moans, bitterly, as they head out of the building.

Perhaps because there are people within earshot, Nathan says, 'You had to get them X-rayed, at least.' When they reach the car, he opens the door and guides her into the passenger seat. 'Better safe than sorry,' is his last cheerful observation.

The battle to endure the pain has left her exhausted. All she can think about is climbing into bed and sleeping for as long as her body will accept – which seems like a perfectly natural reaction, until they're home and she makes for the stairs.

'Where're you going?' he demands, in a tone that belongs firmly to Bad Old Nathan.

'Bed.'

'It's not even nine o'clock.'

'I'm shattered. I need to sleep.'

'We haven't had dinner.'

'I don't want dinner. I feel dreadful.'

He seizes her gaze, his eyes a furnace. 'I'll allow that... *when* I know you've accepted your punishment.'

The words are like a steel cable around her chest, yanking her back to reality.

'Punishment?'

He nods disdainfully. 'Cutting your hair didn't work. Maybe this will.'

53

On Thursday, woken early by the seagulls stomping on the roof, my automatic irritation was superseded by pure relief. What a privilege that I could be disturbed by the gulls, while safe and comfortable in my own bed.

I drifted back off and slept until seven, and realised I felt pretty good, relishing the prospect of fresh coffee and hot buttered toast.

After breakfast, I decided to go in to work. We'd agreed that Gareth would tell the staff I'd gone down with a stomach bug, so nobody would be asking about my ordeal.

The morning was cool and overcast, but it didn't seem to have rained overnight, meaning Len Bowden had been correct. I reflected on his comment about messing with another man's wife. Immediately after that bombshell he had walked away, and frankly I had been too stunned to call after him and ask what he meant – or how he knew.

I guessed he must have seen us together on the beach on Saturday night. I'd known Len for many years, albeit on a superficial level, but now I had to trust that he wouldn't be trumpeting that knowledge to all and sundry.

I texted Anita, letting her know the house was free if she needed to work there. Afterwards my fingers hovered over the screen; I was aching to message Erin. Last night I'd found her in my blocked numbers, and for better or worse she was now back in my contacts. But so far, common sense had prevailed.

Gareth was thrilled to see me, but after settling down to work I soon became aware that all was not well. His movements were loud and aggressive: stabbing at his keyboard, thumping files down on his desk. When I asked if he was okay, he nodded. 'Yeah, yeah.'

'I mean it, mate. Because I don't think you are.'

'No, all right.' He picked up his coffee mug, found it empty and managed to set it down without smashing it into pieces. 'Actually, I'm steaming with rage.'

'Why?'

'Because of what happened to you! Nathan bloody Webb. I had to hide it from Neet – and she'd have my guts for garters if she heard me saying this – but it must have left you wanting revenge?'

'Er... that's what landed me in such a mess in the first place.'

'Fair point. But jeez, Harry. He can't be allowed to get away with this.'

'There's no evidence, remember? He's been careful.'

Gareth was silent for a few seconds, but clearly readying himself for a confession of some kind.

'This is just between us, but soon after me and Mel got together, there was a guy from work sniffing round her. She thought it was harmless, said she knew how to keep him at bay, but one night I saw him at it, in the pub. Hands everywhere, even though she was slapping him away.'

He paused. I could tell from the look on his face that I wasn't going to like this.

'A few days later I followed him home and confronted him. Things got heated, and I laid him out. Could even have killed him, if he'd hit his head when he fell.' He rubbed his jaw. 'In truth it haunted me afterwards, thinking about that possibility.'

'So violence isn't the answer, then,' I pointed out.

'Well, no. But also yes. Because he never went near Mel again.'

It made me wince, having to point out that in this scenario I was basically Melanie's colleague. 'From Nathan's perspective, I've been trying it on with Erin.'

'Totally different,' Gareth asserted. 'The way he's treating her, what does he expect?'

This wasn't a conversation I wanted to have, especially given our own complicated situation. I sat back in my chair and said, 'You can't really be suggesting I try anything?'

'I dunno. Can we really let it lie? I mean, how about the two of us get him in a dark alley one night. You, me and a couple of baseball bats.'

'Gareth.' I tutted. 'Imagine what Anita would say if she could hear this.'

For a moment I thought he might explode. Then, looking slightly dazed, he pushed a hand through his hair and said, 'Yeah, no, you're right. Forget I said it. A moment of madness.'

I nodded in agreement, even as I was thinking: *That's all it would need.*

* * *

Erin elects to use a spare bedroom. It's not a pleasant night, partly because her hand can't be accommodated in a posture that's conducive to sleep. But mostly it's the thoughts that swirl around her head.

It wasn't an accident, it was another punishment.

You can't leave Nathan. But if you stay, the next time he will probably kill you.

Either you find a way to escape, or you'll end up dead.

A third option creeps up on her, a siren voice in the hours before dawn: *You could kill him.*

It isn't completely unfeasible. She might be able to catch him asleep, or hit him from behind when he's on his laptop. But in that scenario she can't see a way of avoiding prison, which effectively means abandoning Milly.

She surfaces late, around ten, and finds Nathan in the kitchen. He's on the phone, and when the call ends he doesn't ask how she is. From the way he's dressed, it looks like he intends to go out: a huge relief.

'You seeing Milly?' he asks suddenly.

'I'd like to.'

'Keep me updated.' She takes that as permission, but he's still gazing at her like a butcher preparing to skin a carcass. 'If you see Ash anywhere, I wanna know at once. Same with that scrote, Louis. Call me straight away.'

She nods, but doesn't dare ask why he's so eager to locate them. Ash, she feels, would probably be discreet about the conversation they had the previous morning – depending on what kind of pressure is brought to bear. But with Louis, all bets are off.

Nathan leaves without a word about his plans for the day. Erin calls Gordon and learns that Milly is 'still not herself' and agrees to be there by midday.

She's carefully wrapped the injured fingers in a bandage, purely to make it harder to forget the injury and accidentally touch something. Driving is fine, she explains to Gordon; she uses her palm for steering and changing gear.

She tells them it was an accident, of course. 'I shut the door on my hand – what an idiot!'

Milly is impressed with the bandage, and insists on playing nurse. After lunch Erin takes her for a walk and tries to get to the root of what's bothering her. Once again Milly talks of various frightening dreams that involve heaven – that mystical abode where Mummy Sonia resides – and being abandoned.

Back at the house, they cuddle up on the sofa and watch a *Toy Story* movie. Milly dozes off halfway through. 'She's not sleeping well,' Gordon whispers.

Barbara is in the kitchen, absorbed in an unnecessary chore. She's been making herself scarce at every opportunity and Erin decides to confront the issue head on.

'I feel like there's something wrong,' she says to Gordon. 'What is it?'

To his credit, he doesn't try to fob her off. Tapping his chest, he says, 'Barb's found a lump.' He's welling up, which gives the lie to the reassurance he tries to provide: 'Might not be anything... nasty. But they're arranging a scan.'

Erin checks that Milly is still asleep. 'I assume you haven't discussed this...'

'No. But she's picked up on the mood. She knows we're worried about something.'

Erin expresses her sympathy, eases free of Milly and then joins Barbara in the kitchen. There isn't time to beat around the bush.

'Gordon's just told me. When is the scan?'

Barbara's expression is severe. 'End of next week.'

'Okay. Well, if you need anything, just ask. And obviously I can stay with Milly that day.'

Barbara seems set to refuse, but nods instead. 'That's probably a good idea.'

'And let's hope it's nothing serious. Most of the time it isn't.'

'I hope so, too.' She forces a cheery tone into her voice. 'Anyway, we've been wondering if you'll put in a good word for us, with Nathan.'

Erin is thrown. 'What do you mean?'

'I thought maybe an apartment in his posh new development. Doesn't have to be a penthouse!' She issues a fake, fluttering laugh. 'Must be some bargains going for friends and family?'

Erin knows she should play along, treat it as banter, but she doesn't have the strength.

'Nathan has no friends. And apart from his mother he doesn't have any family, either.'

Barbara looks confused. 'There's you, though.'

'No, there isn't,' Erin says. 'Not any more.'

54

I left work at six, after a thoroughly enjoyable day where I focused almost entirely on the business of prop making, rather than on my myriad worries. The sky had cleared and the air was less humid than before, so I decided to take a stroll around town before going home. There were no ulterior motives whatsoever, not even when my route took me into Barkers Way.

I walked briskly, head down, and genuinely wasn't conscious of my proximity to the Tannery until I heard a rattle, and saw the gate open slightly just as I drew alongside it. The figure who peeped out had unkempt blond hair.

My reaction took *me* unawares, so Louis didn't stand a chance. Acting on the most primitive of instincts, I shouldered the gate open and shoved him to the ground. He landed heavily on dirt and broken concrete, but his angry cry wasn't loud enough to bring anyone running.

He seemed to be alone. I shut the gate behind me, so we couldn't be seen from the street.

'Hello, Louis,' I said with sarcastic good cheer. 'How's your buddy, Ash?'

'Ash ain't my buddy.'

He made to get up but I kicked him in the leg. 'Stay there.'

He winced, grasping his calf in both hands. 'What do you want?'

'I want you and the others to stop pissing around and tell the truth.'

'You're wasting—'

I kicked him again. I can't say I was proud of my actions, but nor did I feel overly ashamed. I had been treated despicably by Nathan, and since Louis was one of his willing accomplices, I felt he was due a bit of rough treatment himself.

'You haven't even asked who I am. That means you must know.'

'You're the dad,' he muttered. 'Of the kid that died.'

'That's right.' I glanced at the building. 'Is Ash there now?'

'Ain't seen him for ages. How do you even know—?' A sly smile crept over his face. 'Erin told you?'

I ignored the question. 'Ash has been threatening me. I think he was involved in my son's death.'

'Then sort it out with Ash. If I knew where he was, I'd tell you.'

'Nathan dares people to jump on the boards, doesn't he?'

Louis said nothing. I feigned another kick and he scrabbled backwards.

'Did he challenge Freddie to stand over the hole?'

'Dunno. I'd left before then.'

'So you didn't give a statement to the police?'

He shook his head, and when he registered that I believed him, there was a barely perceptible change in his expression. A hint of gloating.

'You must have heard what went on,' I said. 'There's no way you didn't discuss it in the days that followed.'

Now a tiny concession, in the form of a shrug. 'Nathan was taking the piss a bit. Just having a laugh.'

'At Freddie's expense?'

Louis nodded. 'Calling him posh boy, stuff like that. Said he was a pussy if he wouldn't try it.'

'But why? What had Freddie done to deserve being singled out?'

''Cause he was new. Nathan thought he'd be useful, selling weed at the sixth form. But your kid didn't want to know.' Louis gave a contemptuous snort. 'I could've told Nathan that, the second I saw him. Totally straight.'

The disparaging tone made me want to throttle him. 'So being opposed to drugs is a crime in your world?'

'Nice to have the choice,' Louis snapped back. 'Soft boys like him, they make me wanna...' His mouth turned down in disgust, then he seemed to remember who he was talking to. 'Freddie was chasing some girl. When she blew him off he went mental on the boards. Trying to act brave in front of Nathan.'

A distant look had come into his eyes. I realised he was visiting a memory. 'You lied to me,' I growled. 'You were there.'

* * *

Everything's in place and ready to go. A show of strength, that's how Theresa has described it to her boy. If it goes to plan, it will deliver the perfect message to the entire crew. And to that cheating hussy of a daughter-in-law.

There's only one small hitch so far: the damn kid is lying low. Not responding to messages.

'Could he have run off already?' she asks Nathan.

'Doubt it. He wouldn't have the cash.'

'If he's hiding from you, then either he's got wind of what we're planning—'

'Not a chance.'

'*Or* he's planning something of his own. I'll put a few feelers out.'

'Really?'

'Hey, I still have a useful contact or two in this town,' Theresa reminds him. 'And I hope you of all people wouldn't make the mistake of underestimating me?'

''Course not, Ma. Though anyone you talk to has gotta be discreet.'

'They will be.' She tuts, a little wounded by his attitude. 'I'll make a call right now. Work my magic.'

* * *

'Were you there?' I shouted at Louis. 'I want the truth.'

Spotting a brick in the weeds, I snatched it up. In that moment I felt capable of slamming it down on his head, and that reality wasn't lost on Louis. It came as quite a shock to appreciate that I could instil such fear in another human being.

'Yeah, yeah, I was,' he admitted. 'A few of us left before the police showed up.'

'Why?'

'Why d'you think?'

'Drugs, I suppose?'

'It was only weed, a bit of coke. But we had to clear out anything the cops could use to stitch us up.'

'What about the security camera on the door?'

Louis snorted. 'There's twenty other ways of getting in and out.'

I took a breath. Here, at last, was the information I'd been striving to find. Not 'misadventure' at all, but a cover up. A conspiracy.

'What about the mattresses on the floor below?'

He looked confused, or maybe surprised that I knew about them.

'Why weren't they in place?' I pressed him. 'Did Nathan get them removed? Did anyone check the lower floor before Freddie went on the boards?'

'I dunno. Couple of other people were dancing on them earlier.'

'Okay. So who made sure—?'

'No one! We're all off our heads, remember? Including your kid.'

'But didn't anyone check? It should have been Nathan's responsibility—'

'Don't work like that. We're chilling out, someone dances on the boards... it just happens.'

'Did you see Ash that night? Could he have removed the mattresses?'

'I dunno. I've told you everything I can.'

He eyed the brick. Suddenly I felt slightly ridiculous, and tossed it into the weeds. 'I need you to come forward, Louis, you and your friends, and tell the police.'

'No way.'

'You have to. Can't you see how important this is?'

Louis remained impassive as he sat up. He couldn't care less about Freddie's death, about my grief or the need to get justice. There was only one thing he cared about, I realised, so with a heavy heart, I said, 'What if I pay you?'

That got his attention. 'You serious?'

'The way I see it, you and your friends have just become surplus to requirements, while Nathan stands to rake in a fortune from the development. Isn't that right?'

He nodded, grudgingly. 'How much?'

'First I want to know if you agree in principle?'

'What would I have to do?'

'Make a statement, saying what you've just told me.'

'I'll get in trouble.'

'I'm sure you won't. You can explain that Nathan pressured you into lying.'

A sneer. 'I mean, I'll get in trouble *with Nathan*.'

'So what? Once the police have your evidence, he'll be going to prison for a long time. And if you can persuade some of the others to come forward, that's even better.'

'Do I get paid more if I persuade anyone else?'

'We'll see.' Working hard to conceal my loathing, I gestured at him to stand, and suggested we discuss the details.

'Okay, but not here.' Louis got to his feet, brushing dust and debris from his oversized cargo shorts. 'I'm starving.'

55

By Friday morning Erin's hand is feeling better, but it's been another bad night. This time she was plagued by dreams of death and loss; in one she murdered Nathan and was led to the gallows while Milly watched on, sobbing.

She carries a matcha latte down to the basement gym, where she works hard on the stationary bike and considers each of her worries in turn.

Milly, right now, is her primary concern. The poor girl has already lost one mother; Erin can't imagine how it might affect her to lose another. And if the worst does happen – or even if Barbara is laid low by a long period of treatment – is it fair to expect Gordon to take on full responsibility for parenting?

Not really. But if Erin offers to have her instead, she'll be overruled by Nathan. There's no way he'd allow Milly to come and live here.

She thinks about Harry, and whether he's finally let go of his obsession. Better for him if he has, but is that truly what she wants?

She's noticed that he comes to mind far more than he should. *What would Harry say about this? How would Harry react to that?* Questions that point to an infatuation which could get them both killed.

After almost an hour she hears Nathan moving around upstairs, but he doesn't come down to check on her. When she reaches the kitchen he's eating cereal and staring at his iPad. Through a sloshing mouthful of Frosties he says something like, '...doing today?'

'Nothing much.'

'Not going to your sister's?'

'I hadn't planned to. Why?'

'Got tonnes on. Might need help, so I want you here.'

That's the last they speak until almost eleven, when he finds her in the utility room, ironing his shirts. He's changed from this morning's jeans into a suit. Behind him on the kitchen floor, waiting like an obedient pet, is a small suitcase.

'Got a call from Rafe.' Rafe is one of the architects. 'There's a site near Birmingham that's putting in a heat recovery ventilation system and rainwater harvesting. He's gonna be there today and he's offered to show me around.'

'Birmingham?' Erin repeats, thinking: he won't want to drive there and back in a day.

'Bastard of a journey, but I've booked a decent hotel for tonight. Back tomorrow afternoon, I expect.' His eyes narrow. 'Can I trust you?'

'Yes.'

'Sure?'

'Yes.'

'Spoken to Harry?'

'*No.*'

'Correct answer.' His phone buzzes; he swipes away a message and slips it back into his pocket. 'Oh, and Ma needs a favour. Something in the garden. Pop over and help, will you?'

Erin barely tries to disguise her displeasure. She loathes Theresa Webb, and the feeling is mutual. 'When?'

'Dunno. Best call her first, yeah?'

The relief when Nathan drives away is delicious. She can surely bear a short time in Theresa's company, knowing she has more than twenty-four hours to herself.

How sweet is the freedom to check her phone and not go weak with fear when she discovers a message from Anita, asking how she is. As sweet as the freedom to reply:

I'm fine, hope you are too?

And adding:

> Can you let me have Harry's number?

* * *

I was in a meeting at work when I received Erin's text. Gareth was sitting opposite, along with the workshop manager, a carpenter and a designer, so there was no way I could read the message properly. We were discussing a commission to build a working replica of a medieval trebuchet for a castle in County Durham, a subject that instantly became of zero interest to me.

It would be foolish to claim I had no reservations about the deal I'd made with Louis, but they were eclipsed by the thrill of what I'd learned, and the prospect of being able to use that information to bring Nathan to justice. Now I was eager for an opportunity to discuss it with Erin.

Last night, Louis had insisted on us walking independently to the seafront, where he wanted to eat at the town's 'posh' – in his words – fish and chip restaurant. I'd sipped at a mediocre coffee while he consumed a gigantic haddock and chips plus a meat pie, bread and butter and three large glasses of Fanta.

The waiting staff had regarded us with a mixture of curiosity and contempt. 'They'll think I'm your rent boy,' Louis drawled, a comment which had a depressing similarity to Erin's observation that Anita might have assumed she was an escort.

Is that how I now appeared? The kind of man who had no option but to purchase companionship, affection, sex?

Questions about Louis's background and upbringing were casually deflected, but whatever he may have lacked in formal education he more than made up for in sheer nerve. He was a tough negotiator, and I ended up agreeing a far higher sum than I'd first envisaged.

Fifteen thousand pounds, in cash.

We shook hands on it, and at his suggestion we departed separately. I was first to make my exit, and was aware of Len Bowden on the breakwater, though I purposely avoided looking in his direction. At some point I would have to query what he'd said on Wednesday night, but this wasn't the time.

I'd spent the remainder of the evening fretting over ways in which I might source the money. This morning's trebuchet meeting had first come as a welcome diversion, but it dragged on for another fifty minutes. Finally, a little after midday, I slipped outside to make the call.

Erin picked up at once. Upon hearing her voice I felt my mouth go dry. 'Are you okay?' I croaked. 'I've been so worried—'

'Never mind me. Anita said you were kidnapped. Did you see who took you?'

'No. Two burly men with London accents. They kept their faces covered the whole time. I was thrown into a van and taken to a replica of a prison cell, possibly built inside an old barn.'

'And what... what did they do?'

I cleared my throat, conscious that any attempt to describe it would bring me perilously close to tears. 'Gave me a taste of incarceration, to put it bluntly. There was a bit of violence, and some other... mistreatment. More psychological than physical.' I tried a light-hearted snort. 'At the time it was bloody terrible, but I don't feel too bad now.'

'You're sure?'

'I think so. Anyway, when I was released, I'm afraid to say... Nathan was there.'

'Anita told me,' she said softly.

'I imagine it came as quite a shock?'

'Nothing shocks me any more, Harry. Not where Nathan's concerned.'

I didn't like the way she said that. 'Has something else happened?'

'Doesn't matter now. What did Nathan say?'

I briefly explained the warning I'd been given. 'He acted like he's fireproof, which meant I came away thinking I had to give it up. But not any more. I've convinced one of them to come forward.'

'One of who? The wasps?' Erin sounded completely thrown. 'Which one?'

Now came the tough part. I could feel the tension in my gut when I said the name.

'Louis.'

56

Even as they talk, Erin is aware of how much she wants to see Harry in person. She suspects he's downplaying what they did to him, and she needs to witness the truth in his face. But it's too risky, much too risky, after what Nathan has done this week.

And the wasps are back. The burly, unpleasant-looking one is sitting on a neighbour's garden wall, smoking what appears to be a joint. She's puzzled that no one in the street has called the police, until she realises that the other residents here will know of Nathan's reputation and won't dare make a fuss. And now Harry is bubbling over with the news that one of the wasps is prepared to betray Nathan...

'*Louis*?' she echoes. 'When did you speak to him?'

'Last night. I happened to walk past the Tannery when he was coming out.'

'He's in the Tannery? I thought Ash was there?'

'Apparently not. Though there are lots of hiding places, by the sound of it.'

'Nathan's desperate to find them both. I hope they're good at lying low.'

'They seem to be. I got the impression that Louis is trying to find Ash.'

'I had that impression, too. What did Louis tell you?'

'That he was there when... when Freddie died. Afterwards he and some of the others sneaked out, taking the drugs with them. And Nathan...' Harry's voice catches. 'Nathan was teasing Freddie. Not just daring him to go on the boards, but mocking him.'

Sensing Harry's fragility, Erin says, 'Please bear in mind that Louis can't be trusted.'

'I know. But I trust him on this. And he's prepared to make a statement to the police.'

'Seriously? How did you get him to...' She falters. 'Oh, Harry. How much?'

She can hear the embarrassment in his cough. 'Fifteen grand – and yes, I know it's a ridiculous sum. But if it gets us justice—'

'It won't. Think how a payment will look in court. Any evidence he gives is tainted.'

'But he's also going to speak to the others, and if they back him up...' Harry sounds despairing, as if her failure to embrace the idea has let him down. 'This is a great chance to put Nathan away.'

'If it was anyone but Louis, then maybe. But he's a nasty little creep. Give him that money and you'll never see him again.'

'I'm not a complete idiot,' he huffs. 'He's agreed to write a statement telling me everything he knows. I'll then give him three thousand, but he won't get the rest until he's gone to the police and they've accepted that evidence.'

'Harry, please think about this. Talk to the police first – DC Leung, maybe, and get her advice.' A ringing sound makes her jump: it's the landline, and there's only one person who calls them on the landline. 'I need to go. Sorry.'

'Can we talk later? Is it safe?'

'I'll see.'

Erin cuts the call, asking herself whether he's truly lost his sanity. After the warnings, after being abducted and tortured and left in no doubt as to what could happen to him, still Harry won't give up. For a man who comes across as gentle and law-abiding, it astonishes her that he'll risk so much in order to find out the truth.

This is what she's thinking as she hurries to answer the phone. The display reveals that it is, as she feared, Nathan's mother. But there's another idea, another question floating in her mind as she reflects on Harry's fervour and what it might mean if he succeeds – or if he doesn't.

Is he trying to save me?

* * *

I was used to our conversations being curtailed in this abrupt manner, but that didn't make it any easier to deal with. Especially not after Erin, quite frankly, had left me feeling like a sap.

Of course I understood that Louis was devious and untrustworthy. There was no way I'd be handing over a penny until I had something of value from him.

Louis hadn't wanted to take my phone number; instead he'd supplied me with a number and instructed me to text him when I had the initial payment. I knew that would give me a day or two to contemplate whether this was the right thing to do – and even to seek advice from elsewhere. Erin's suggestion that I consult DC Leung made a lot of sense. It might even be possible for the detective to compel Louis to talk without any financial inducement.

I turned as the main doors clattered open and Gareth emerged. 'Got a snag with regard to ammunition.'

For a moment, dumbfounded, I could only picture a gun like the one I'd spotted beneath Nathan's jacket. 'Ammunition?'

He made an overarm bowling action and whistled. 'For the trebu-thingy. Can you and Mark brainstorm it?'

'Sure,' I agreed, then saw how he was staring at the phone in my hand.

'You aren't still talking to her, are you? That Erin?'

'Definitely not.' I pocketed my phone. 'Let's get back to work.'

* * *

'Can you be here for half one?' This is Theresa Webb's opening comment on the phone. 'Got some stuff to shift in the garden.'

'Don't you have a gardener?'

'He's off with his sciatica.' She clicks her tongue. 'Won't take more than five minutes.'

Erin glances at her fingers, still bruised and tender. 'How heavy is it, because—'

'It'll be fine between the two of us. Just can't do it on my own, that's all.'

As ever, Nathan's mother sounds cranky and impatient. There's zero gratitude when Erin agrees to be there.

Her next call is to Gordon, who tells her that both Barbara and Milly are in better spirits today. When Erin apologises for being unable to visit, Gordon says, 'Don't be silly. Lord knows, you've got your own problems.' He sounds far too heartfelt for her liking.

For lunch she nibbles at a sandwich, and at ten past one she leaves the house, sparing a sardonic wave for the thug on duty. Theresa Webb resides in a coastal village a couple of miles to the east. Her home is at the end of a private lane, a 1930s bungalow compromised by several ill-advised extensions. It wouldn't be considered anything special if not for its location: perched right on the clifftop, with an expanse of lawn that terminates in a two hundred foot drop to the sea.

To preserve the view, Theresa has never bothered with a fence at the end of the garden. 'If I have a grandchild I daresay I'll have to put one up,' she once remarked, with a scornful glance at Erin's belly. 'Till then I don't see the need.'

Erin is still thinking about Harry, and what she feels sure is his misplaced faith in Louis. It strikes her that she didn't have a chance to mention her conversation with Ash. It's also playing on her mind that Nathan would want to know of Louis's whereabouts the night before, though Erin has no intention of telling him.

Theresa opens the front door and offers her usual twisted smile. She's a tall, heavy woman in her mid-seventies who still dresses like the 1970s starlet she once was. Today that means a low-cut summer frock in a shade of pink that clashes with her skin tone, which isn't tanned so much as deep-fried. Her hair is currently dark blonde, and she's gone heavy on the mascara as usual. Bright peach lipstick, with a smear of it on her teeth.

Theresa scrutinises her carefully, paying particular attention to the short hair. No questions about when or why it was cut, which means she knows the truth.

'Was this something you arranged with Nathan?' Erin's nostrils twitch as she follows Theresa through the house, passing a succession of expensive reed diffusers. 'He only mentioned it to me this morning.'

'I only asked him this morning,' Theresa snaps. 'I didn't want to. Poor man is rushed off his feet.'

Whereas you aren't. That's the inference, and Erin directs a sarcastic *fuck you* smile to the old woman's back.

* * *

Stepping into the garden brings a momentary pleasure. There are low hedges on either side, but the only neighbour is to the right. To the left, looking east, the clifftop meadow dips and then rises to the next peak, clad in heather and gorse, about two hundred yards away.

Looking straight ahead, there's just miles of pale blue sea and a slightly darker blue sky, bubbles of cloud drifting up high, seagulls gliding on the thermals. 'A million-dollar view,' Nathan has said before. 'At least till the fucking place drops into the water.'

Today's task is simple enough. Theresa has half a dozen large pot plants that she wants to re-position. Erin is able to help, though only by gripping the pots with her right hand and just the little finger and thumb of her left hand.

When she notices, Theresa sneers, 'What's up?'

Erin displays her injured fingers. 'Nathan closed a door on them.'

The woman only shrugs. 'Accidents will happen.' She indicates the pot: back to work.

The final couple of plants are almost too heavy for them. By now Theresa's face looks dangerously flushed. At her urging they take it slowly, dragging the pots across the lawn and resting every few feet. When it's done Theresa actually says thank you, and indicates the cane furniture at the end of the garden.

'Have a sit down. I've got fruit cocktails in the fridge.'

'I'm driving.'

'Non-alcoholic.' Her smile is determined, brooking no dissent. 'Very refreshing.'

Erin just wants to get away, but she supposes a few more minutes won't hurt. She walks over to the chairs, which are some eight or ten feet from the cliff edge.

Too far for the old witch to push me over, Erin thinks, and of course that's only a joke.

Ninety-five per cent a joke.

She rests back and shuts her eyes. The breeze up here takes the edge off the heat. She'll have her drink, try to stay civil in the face of Theresa's provocation, and then get going.

Until now the only sound she's registered is birdsong, but something else captures her attention: the distant growl of a diesel engine accelerating over bumpy ground. The engine noise steadies, and there's the clunk of doors opening and closing. As Erin sits forward and opens her eyes, she can just make out the top of a dark blue van on the next peak along, barely visible above the gorse.

It all happens so quickly – two or three seconds at most – that Erin struggles to make sense of what she witnesses. The three figures that emerge from behind the bushes are all male: two are large and clad all in black, their faces covered, while the one between them, struggling in their grasp, is more of a boy than a man. He's trying to cry out but one of his captors has something clamped over his mouth. The other man grabs his legs and hoists them up, while the first man, releasing the gag, takes him by the underarms. In unison they swing their prisoner back and up, the boy a writhing mass of limbs, and it does no good that he issues an incoherent cry of desperation as they swing him forward and hurl him off the cliff.

Erin isn't certain whether she hears the impact when he lands. There's a buzzing in her ears, caused by the pounding of her blood. She blinks a couple of times, but the two assailants have already vanished behind the gorse. She struggles to restore that first image of the three of them, knowing it could be important – for the police, for the prosecution – and that's when it hits home, just who it is she has seen.

Small and blond and scruffy.

57

A louder noise grabs her attention: here comes Theresa, marching cheerfully across the lawn with a tall glass in each hand.

Erin looks back at the clifftop. Nobody in sight.

Maybe she imagined it?

That's what she wants to think, because to be hallucinating in that sort of detail would still be preferable to the alternative. That she has just seen Louis murdered.

She puts her hands over her face for a second. Theresa bustles up, breathing hard. 'Here you go.'

Erin turns. God only knows how shocked she must look, and yet her mother-in-law's expression never falters. If anything, her inane smile broadens slightly, which is when the truth hits home.

I was meant to see it. This was arranged, deliberately, so that I would be here to witness it.

'Your drink.' Theresa shoves the glass at her. Erin is trembling and has to grasp it carefully in both hands. Theresa moves past and sits down, the seat groaning beneath her weight. She takes a gulp and smacks her lips with pleasure. 'Just what the doctor ordered.'

Erin is staring at the clifftop again, too numb to speak. The body won't be visible from here, but either it's smashed on the rocks or lying in the sea. The men who did it have driven away. It's quite likely that Erin is the only person who saw what happened.

She jumps at a nudge from Theresa's elbow. 'Go on, try it!'

Obediently, Erin takes a sip. Even these drinks must have been part of the plan: Theresa's excuse to go inside and leave Erin alone for a minute.

And Theresa isn't at all discomfited by the stricken silence. She rests back, gazing in the same direction as Erin. 'Never get tired of a view like this. So peaceful.' She chuckles. 'Little corner of paradise, that's what I have here.'

It isn't until later, when she's home, that Erin decides she should have confronted Theresa. Challenged her to admit to her involvement in what she's just seen. But right now it's far beyond her capability. The trembling is getting worse; surely Theresa must be aware of it?

You're laughing at me, she thinks. *You and Nathan.*

She pushes herself upwards, tossing the glass on to the lawn; there's a protest from Theresa but Erin ignores her, breaking into a staggering run across the garden, through the house and out to the car. She resolves not to look back, but in manoeuvring the car she catches a glimpse of Theresa in the doorway, and sure enough Nathan's mother is wearing a broad smirk, as though she's just been told an off-colour joke – the kind of thing decent people would find offensive – and thoroughly enjoyed it.

At home there's another shock in store. The idea has bubbled up on the journey, and by the time Erin parks the Renault there are tears streaming down her face; the world around her is blurred and so is the world inside her head. No place for logic or reason. No place for Milly, or anyone else.

One thought: oblivion. She hauls herself up the stairs and kneels at her bedside drawer, rooting through stockings and tights for the box of zopiclone.

But it's not there. She pulls out the drawer and tips everything out. Gone.

After emptying the other drawers she has to accept the truth. Nathan knew where they were hidden and he's removed them, precisely because he anticipated that this might drive her to take an overdose.

She checks the bathroom cabinet, and finds that even their normal painkillers are missing. Somewhere, in Birmingham or wherever he might be, she pictures Nathan smugly congratulating himself.

I've thought of everything, babe.

You'll never escape.

* * *

After an intense day's work I found myself wilting a little around four o'clock. When Gareth suggested I get off home, I didn't offer much resistance. As well as feeling exhausted, I'd also found it difficult to focus after speaking to Erin at lunchtime.

I felt slightly guilty that I hadn't owned up to Gareth about the conversation with Erin, or told him of the deal I'd made with Louis. I'd promised myself I would seek advice, and yet I had declined a good opportunity.

Another presented itself sooner than I expected. Anita's car was on the drive. I felt a tickle of apprehension: suddenly my justification seemed rather flimsy, whereas Erin's warnings carried far more weight.

I let myself in. Anita emerged from her office and frowned. 'You look shattered. Have you been pushing yourself too hard?'

'Maybe. At least it's the weekend now.' I gestured towards the kitchen. 'Shall I put the kettle on?'

'Lovely.' But she wasn't to be deflected. 'How's Erin?'

'Erin?'

'She messaged me for your number. I take it you've spoken to her?'

'Oh. Yes. She sounded okay, actually, considering...'

Anita gave me a sceptical look; she knew I was keeping something back. 'Has she said anything to Nathan, about what he did to you?'

'I hope not. Confronting a man like that...' I shuddered, and was uncomfortably aware of Anita's scrutiny as I made us tea.

'According to Gareth, you seemed very chirpy this morning but downbeat this afternoon. I was worried that meant you'd had bad news. From Erin, perhaps?'

'It's more that I was excited about something. And Erin... not exactly burst my balloon, but let some of the air out.'

Anita scowled. 'You're making no sense, Harry.'

I took a deep breath. 'Last night, I bumped into one of the kids from the party. Louis, his name is. A conniving little runt, in many ways – and Erin has made it clear he's not to be trusted. But even allowing for that, I may have persuaded him to come clean about that night.'

Anita did a kind of double-take, as though what I'd said was so preposterous she must have misheard. I ran through the details of my conversation, omitting the violence I'd inflicted on Louis, and tentatively mentioned that the deal involved money changing hands.

Anita, naturally, insisted on knowing the exact amount. When I told her, she clapped her hands to her cheeks. 'You can't be giving him *fifteen thousand pounds*! He'll just do a runner, or tell the police he was coerced into providing a new statement.'

'This will be his first statement,' I corrected her. 'Louis scarpered from the Tannery precisely to avoid—'

'You know what I mean. His evidence won't have any value whatsoever. Nathan's defence will go to town on the fact that you paid for it.'

'That's what Erin said – and I know you both have a point. But what else can I do?'

'Forget it. Move on with your life, just like you pledged to do yesterday.'

I nodded despondently, and we lapsed into silence. After glancing at her phone, Anita seemed distracted by something, so I drank my tea and reflected on the likelihood that I was back at square one.

'Breaking news on the *Argus* website,' Anita murmured. 'Someone went off the cliffs near Fairlight Glen. They found the body on the beach this afternoon.'

My heart started thumping; quite irrationally, since I'd spoken to Erin and she'd sounded fine. 'Do they know who it is?'

'All they're saying is a young man.' Her voice wavered, and I knew she would be remembering the way Freddie's death had been reported – and sometimes callously commented upon – in the media. 'A teenager, maybe. Poor lad.'

* * *

Theresa phones him at ten. She spent the evening drinking with some girlfriends, following a posh afternoon tea that became progressively lighter on cucumber fucking sandwiches and heavier on the Veuve Clicquot.

Now, nicely sozzled, she starts with: 'How's Brum?'

'Shithole.' Nathan chuckles. 'Nah. Some of it's all right – for the North.'

'Birmingham's not the North.'

'Yeah it is. Two hundred miles north.'

'It's the Midlands, boy.' She exaggerates her disgust, muttering, 'All that money we spent on your education.'

'I never used to go.'

'Don't remind me. But, moving on...'

'All done,' he says happily. 'Went like a dream, didn't it?'

'You tell me, son. I didn't see a thing.'

'Perfect. Happened right on cue. The local media have already picked it up.'

'I've not seen any news,' she says. 'I was out painting the town red.'

'While that little scrote was painting the *beach* red.' He guffaws at his own joke. 'How did she react?'

'Thought she was gonna keel over. If she had, maybe I could've rolled her off the edge an' all!'

Nathan snorts, but sounds vaguely regretful when he says, 'Shouldn't be any need for that.'

'Maybe not. Now, let's get the damn Tannery wiped off the map!'

'Amen to that,' he says with a yawn, then claims to need an early night.

'Tell me you're having some fun while you're there?'

'Kind of.'

'Good lad. What's she like?'

'Oh, not that. I'm playing *Fortnite*.'

'Jesus H!' Theresa exclaims. 'Never thought I'd raise a fucking lightweight.'

58

Erin is up by six on Saturday morning. What sleep she had was plagued by nightmares; now another day stretches ahead, with nowhere she can go, nothing she can do to escape the reality of her predicament.

Last night Nathan texted to say he was impressed by the eco build and eager to incorporate some of the ideas in the Tannery development. He didn't ask how she was, but he did want to know if everything had 'gone well' at his mum's.

She settled for a single word: *Yes.* It won't ever be a subject she can raise. Having put himself far away from the scene of the crime, with a rock-solid alibi, Nathan would be crazy to acknowledge knowing anything about it.

This action had a dual purpose, she realises: to silence Louis, who may or may not have been willing to betray Nathan, and to send yet another warning to Erin about the consequences of disloyalty.

But how did Nathan find out what Louis was doing? And what will it mean for Harry, that he's still working to bring Nathan down?

After hours of brooding, she concludes that Nathan might not be aware that Harry and Louis were talking. Louis's prior actions could have been enough to condemn him, including the way he'd tried to extort sex from her.

In which case I'm partly to blame, she thinks. *I didn't have to tell Nathan about that.*

At eight o'clock he messages to let her know he'll be home mid-afternoon. And there's more bad news: they're going out to dinner tonight. A table has been reserved at the town's most-overrated gastropub. There'll be three other couples present; Erin isn't told who, but she is expected to look magnificent.

Despite combing through the local news sites, she hasn't found any detailed reports. The body recovered from the base of the cliffs is described only as 'a young man', as yet unidentified. There's a heavy implication of suicide. No suggestion of foul play.

Of course not, she thinks. *Because nobody saw him thrown off the cliff.*

Except me.

Ironically, this latest display of Nathan's power has a counterproductive effect. Erin can't fight Nathan and win. She can't kill him. She can't run away. It feels as though her downfall – maybe even her death – is already priced in, so she might as well do whatever the hell she wants.

She leaves the house at eight-forty, carrying a bag that contains her swimsuit and a drink. It's the burly, menacing-looking kid outside. From the car, she beckons him over. 'What's your name?'

'Uh, Dane.'

'Morning, Dane. I'm heading out for a few hours. Is that a problem for you?'

He considers the question, blinking slowly. 'Where you going?'

'The beach. See?' She hoists her bag so the towel is visible. He's staring at it when she asks, in a conversational tone, 'Did you hear about Louis?'

He frowns. 'Who's Louis?'

Erin regards him with disbelief, though all she can really do is laugh. 'Oh Dane, mate, you stick with that line if you want.'

* * *

When the doorbell rang, my first instinct was to ignore it. I was in a particularly low mood on Saturday morning, still smarting from the message I'd had from Erin. I'd finally weakened and sent her a text at about nine o'clock last night, asking whether she'd heard this news of an apparent suicide. Her response:

I can't talk. Please leave me alone.

I'd gone to bed wracked with guilt. I was continually pledging not to put her in danger, but each time my resolve seemed to count for nothing.

Much of the evening had been devoted to finding out more about the young man who'd died. Despite a growing body of speculation online, there were still no clues as to his identity, although a few disparaging comments suggested he was involved in drugs.

The doorbell rang again. Ten to nine seemed early for a cold caller, and a friend would probably text first, so I pulled on a pair of joggers and mooched along the hall. Still in a cautious frame of mind after my abduction, I first checked from a window at the side...

And couldn't quite believe my eyes.

Hurriedly I unlocked the door and stepped back to let her in. Erin was dressed in brown tailored shorts and a white knitted top. She wore sunglasses, which she now removed, and I saw she looked just as exhausted as I did.

'I thought we couldn't risk any more contact?'

'I've stopped caring about that.'

'Why? What's happened?'

'Later.' She folded the sunglasses and placed them on the windowsill. I noticed that a couple of fingers on her left hand were curled up, as if she couldn't use them.

'Is something wrong with your hand?'

'Shut it in a door.'

'An accident?'

'No.'

I stared at her, shocked anew by Nathan's brutality but aware that my sympathy for Erin meant little. In the silence she dropped her bag and slipped off her shoes. The front door was shut but she flipped the lock, then turned and met my eye again.

'They're still a bit tender. Bear that in mind when you get close.' She smiled, almost shyly. 'Because right now I could use a hug.'

I opened my arms and she clung to me as though I were a life raft in a stormy ocean. Speaking into my shoulder, she said, 'I'm sorry about that message last night. I hope I'm forgiven?'

'There's nothing to forgive.'

When she grasped my hand and drew me into motion, even I – slow on the uptake as I was – could tell she had come here with a purpose.

'Don't say how crazy this is, Harry. And don't be grateful. Or embarrass me with compliments.'

'I can't help it, I genuinely—'

'Yeah, yeah. But if I kept saying you were "beautiful", wouldn't it make you a bit uncomfortable? Because I do think you're a beautiful person.'

In my bedroom, after a wry smile at the unmade bed, Erin removed her top in such a matter-of-fact way that I couldn't help laughing in sheer disbelief.

She looked puzzled. 'What?'

'This. Tell me I'm not dreaming?'

'Would you prefer me to be a figment of your overactive imagination?'

'God, no. What I mean is... why me? Why now?'

'Because life is shit, Harry. My husband is a psychopath, a sadist, a torturer, and I don't think I'll ever get away from him. My sister's mum may well have cancer, and if it turns out to be serious I have no idea where Milly will live or who'll look after her, because Nathan sure as hell won't want to accommodate her. I'm finally waking up to all the terrible choices I've made throughout my life. The fact that I found the courage to stop my stepfather from abusing my sister, but when it was my turn, a few years before that, I didn't fight, and after that I couldn't—'

'*What*?' I broke in, almost winded with shock. But Erin was too far gone to stop now.

'After that I couldn't enjoy... intimacy. Sex. Not unless the guy was really gentle, and Nathan was never gentle, even in the early days. After it was done I used to crawl away and cry. Tell myself it was *me*, my dysfunctional brain and body at fault, and that Nathan deserved someone better...'

'Erin—'

'Harry, shush! This is my one last chance, okay? One final experience that I want to be slow and sweet and special, because after this...' She issued a terrible, cracked laugh that nearly broke my heart. 'After this, the world might just as well explode for all that I know what to do.'

59

It all comes spilling out, revealing far more than Erin intended. Harry, of course, has questions galore, but Erin won't consider them.

'This is about *need*, Harry. What I need right now. So, please...'

In bed he's slightly nervous, which is understandable: so is she. But where she was prepared for him to be endearingly inept, on that count he surprises her. Once he relaxes, he plays to perfection the role she had hoped he would play. He is a tender, considerate, skilful lover.

Afterwards they lie together in silence for what seems like an age, but it still isn't long enough for Erin. Harry signals its end by slowly exhaling.

'So... your stepfather?'

'A piece of shit, but he's ancient history.'

'So you'd rather not talk about it?'

'Correct.'

'Okay. But I'm glad you felt able to confide in me. You really don't deserve to have gone through that.'

'Who does? Countless women and girls have to deal with abuse from men.' She tuts. 'For years I told myself it didn't have any lasting effects, but then, when you look at the situation I'm in with Nathan...'

'But Nathan's obviously very good at hiding his true nature. Devious, manipulative, cruel.'

'I still should have spotted it. I'm constantly asking myself, why didn't I run a mile the first time he mistreated me?'

Harry caresses her cheek. 'Don't berate yourself over the past. It's the future that matters.'

'The future,' she echoes, with such a bitter laugh that it can't fail to alert him.

'There's something else. What is it?'

'Harry...' She steels herself. 'The body they found yesterday afternoon. It was Louis.'

'Louis?' Harry gapes at her. 'Oh my God! Whatever he was up to, he didn't deserve that.' Then he frowns. 'Who told you it was Louis?'

'No one. I saw it happen.'

'*What*? How?'

'Nathan's mum lives on the clifftop. They cooked up some story about her needing help in the garden, while Nathan was in Birmingham—'

'Giving himself an alibi?'

'Exactly. After we'd moved some pot plants, Theresa went to get us drinks. Further along the cliffs these two guys suddenly appeared, holding Louis between them, and they just... threw him off the edge.'

'Can you describe the men?'

'Both large. Strong. All in black, with their faces covered.' She nods at the look on Harry's face. 'So maybe the same ones who kept you prisoner.'

'Do you have any idea who Nathan would employ for this?'

'I know he has connections in London, some of them from his old man's days, but nobody I could name.'

Harry's shoulders have slumped. He stares at the bedclothes, and she can almost feel the churning of his thoughts.

'This has to mean his mum is implicated,' he says. 'Along with Nathan. Could that be possible?'

'Oh, yes. That woman has scared the crap out of me from day one.'

Erin recounts what she knows of Theresa's background: her mother was a South African beauty queen, her father a serial fraudster. In the 1970s Theresa was the classic actress-slash-model, but her career was washed up by the time she met Pierson Webb.

'Her last role was in a soft porn film. "Confessions of..." something or other.' Erin grimaces. 'Nathan delighted in telling me that. He wanted me to watch her in action.'

Harry recoils. 'What about his dad? I mean, I've heard various rumours he was in the drugs trade himself.'

'Oh, he had fingers in a lot of pies. A nasty piece of work, I suspect. To Nathan, his dad is still some sort of hero, but I've seen the way Theresa looks whenever Pierson gets mentioned. I suspect she was relieved when he died.'

'Does that mean she could have arranged his death?'

It's a spontaneous question, and seems to startle them both.

'I don't know why that never occurred to me.' Then she sighs. 'I suppose you could say Nathan never had a chance of turning out well.'

'Isn't that letting him off the hook? Lots of people overcome shitty parents or a lousy childhood.'

'But plenty don't – like Louis, and half the other wasps.'

They are both sombre. Harry clearly has his own son on his mind when he says, 'Somewhere out there are parents who don't know Louis is dead.'

'And might not even care,' Erin adds sadly.

* * *

That was a dreadful thought, but I suspected she could be right. At Erin's suggestion, I went online to see if there had been any developments.

'Seems not,' I told her. 'The police are appealing for witnesses who were in the area between midday and 4 p.m.'

'That's me,' she pointed out. 'For what little it's worth.'

I said nothing, not wanting to load more pressure on her. In her position, I had absolutely no idea what I would do.

Then she said, 'If they can't identify him, I'll have to tell them, won't I?'

'I don't know. Coming forward a day or more after the event might attract suspicion.' We discussed that aspect, and agreed that she'd have to emphasise just how scared she was. 'I'll back you up,' I said. 'And remember we could speak to DC Leung, if that's easier.'

'It'll never be easy,' Erin countered. 'But it might be necessary.'

She went on to tell me about a conversation she'd had with Ash on Wednesday morning. 'I assumed he was outside on Nathan's orders, but he didn't know anything about that.'

I recalled how Nathan had seemed genuinely baffled about the note. 'You think Ash has an agenda of his own?'

'Possibly. He didn't really come across as intimidating. And I'm still not convinced his message was intended as a threat.'

'Well, I'd certainly like a chance to ask him. How do you think he and the others will react to Nathan having Louis killed?'

'Who's to say they'll ever know it was him? Anyway, it's probably irrelevant now he doesn't need them any more. He's letting them have one final party – tonight – before the Tannery gets demolished.'

I gasped as something else occurred to me. 'Could Nathan have found out about my deal with Louis? Is that why he was killed?'

'Unlikely. What they did to him would have taken some planning. Nathan's been trying to locate him for a while.' She paused. 'I suppose it's possible someone spotted him in town on Thursday evening.'

'He did seem anxious to keep a low profile. And if Louis was seen with me, that could mean I'll be in Nathan's sights again.'

Erin gave a sombre nod. 'You need to be very careful.'

'So what chance do we have of pinning any of this on Nathan? Zero, I suppose.'

'Practically zero. Perhaps if the police found the two men and put pressure on them, but it'll take a miracle for that to happen.' As if she was reading my mind, Erin added, 'Supposing I do go to the police and tell them what I saw, there'll be absolutely nothing to corroborate it. And when Nathan hears what I'd done...' She raised her injured hand and let it flop back at her side, a lifeless thing.

'You can't carry on like this. You've got to leave him.'

'Not that simple, Harry.'

'I know. But when the alternative is so horrific...'

'This isn't just about me. It's Milly. Milly's parents.'

'So you'll stay until—' I stopped, needing to clear my throat. 'Until he kills you?'

Erin stared at me for a second, then murmured, 'Or I kill him.' I wasn't sure if I'd heard her correctly, and only became certain when she backtracked: 'Forget I said that.'

'You've thought about it, though?'

'Yes. Until I realised I'd only be exchanging one prison for another.'

60

It's a big mistake to admit to something so personal. Erin has urged him to forget it but she knows he won't be able to do that.

She asks if she can use the shower. Harry tells her to go ahead. By the time she returns to the bedroom, he's made coffee and put together an idiosyncratic selection of snacks: cheese and crackers, olives and peanuts and a packet of chocolate digestives.

'Got this bachelor lifestyle nailed down, then?'

Harry grins, sheepishly. 'Just missing a Pot Noodle.'

They sit cross-legged on the bed, like teenagers at a sleepover. A couple of times Erin catches him staring at her. When she reacts, he says, 'What?'

'Your expression. Like a cat that fell asleep and woke up inside a dairy.'

'Sorry. I'm still just... kind of gobsmacked.'

She shrugs. 'Don't you think we both knew this would happen, sooner or later?'

'I didn't. Well, only in my wildest dreams.'

'Saturday night, I wanted to,' Erin admits. 'And again on Sunday.'

Harry's blushing fiercely. 'I'm very flattered.'

'You shouldn't be. You're attractive, funny, kind. You're smart – though maybe your judgement can be a bit faulty at times – but you also seem at ease with yourself. A man who knows his own mind.'

'Good grief, I'm anything but.'

'Well, compared to me...'

'Erin, no. We're all screw-ups at heart. What I've found is that maturity isn't about learning to cope with the chaos of existence. It's about learning how to *look* as though you're coping with the chaos.'

'Something for me to work on, then.' Erin eats an olive, then shifts closer to him. 'You know, when you first told me about the arrangement with Anita and Gareth, I thought it was ridiculous. There was no way anyone could be so *thoroughly* sensible, practical, generous...'

'Funnily enough, during my imprisonment I started to view it as a weakness, the way I'd let them—' He breaks off, shrugging. 'Though it's a bit more complicated than I told you before.'

'Really? Do you wish you were still with Anita?'

'No, no. Certainly not in the context of... us. Not at all.' Flustered, he snatches a handful of peanuts and weighs them in his palm. 'Confinement made me mean-spirited, eager to lash out. And that's really not in my character.'

'Except for wanting to kill Nathan.'

He winces, drops the peanuts back on his plate and brushes his hands together. 'I don't really know what I want any more. Other than...'

'Yes?'

He looks at her, very intently. 'You say it's impossible to get away from him. Don't you think there's any chance he'd ever let you go?'

'Absolutely not. Why?'

'I'd hope it was obvious.' His face reddens again. 'What's happening here – is it a kind of friendship? Is it comfort, a brief diversion from all the stress and pain? Or is it something more?'

'I'd like it to be more. But it's impossible—'

'No. We have to *believe* it can be possible.'

'Harry, please. Let's not spoil this.'

* * *

She dipped her head and slowly pitched forward, into my arms, and a hug became a kiss. I felt our passion reignite and pulled her closer, and the second time we made love was, if anything, even better than the first.

The aftermath felt different, though: a few subtle changes that signalled how much better we knew each other, but also how grave were the risks we'd taken. Without prompting, I decided to tell her what I had kept to myself for the past four years.

Gareth and Melanie had been our closest friends for most of our adult lives, so naturally Anita and I had sought to do all we could to help them through Mel's long, tenacious battle with ovarian cancer. When it became evident that the fight could not be won, Melanie had asked us to pledge that we would look after Gareth once she was gone. Naturally, we were only too happy to agree.

During her final spell in the hospice, a routine began that saw Gareth eating at our house several nights a week; it continued after her death, and occasionally, when we'd all drunk too much, he would stay over in the spare room. Because the four of us had regularly attended the theatre, the cinema and live concerts together, this practice also resumed now we were down to three, and it was over a period of about two years of socialising in this way that I watched Anita and Gareth gradually fall in love with one another.

And then, one morning, as I was due to fly off to a festival in Italy where a movie we'd worked on was nominated for its production design, I took Anita aside and said, 'If you want to sleep with Gareth while I'm away, I don't have a problem with that.'

Anita seemed utterly aghast: either because of the suggestion, or because only now did she appreciate that it was as obvious to me as it was to the two of them.

'I'm not *asking* you to go ahead, obviously,' I added. 'Just... I think you should do what feels right.'

'But why?' she asked.

'Because I can sense how much you want to. Both of you. It's getting closer to happening, whether I approve or not, and I'd just... the two of you mean so much to me, I'd hate to think of you going behind my back. This way, instead of a betrayal, it can be something positive.'

Then I kissed her on the cheek and headed out to my taxi.

'All that, and we didn't even win the award,' I said drily.

Erin looked almost as gobsmacked now as Anita had done then. 'And did they?'

'I never asked. If I had to guess, I'd say yes.' I cleared my throat. 'I should also say, I'm not squeaky clean in that respect.'

'What do you mean?'

'About ten years ago, there was a New Year's Eve party where Melanie and I kissed... well, a little too enthusiastically.'

'A kiss? And that was all?'

'Absolutely.'

'And were you and she attracted to each other?'

'Not particularly. Drink played a part, for sure.'

'And that was on your mind when you saw how Anita and Gareth felt about each other?'

'Not as much as I'd like to say. But it meant I understood that these things are rarely straightforward. That's really the point I'm trying to make. And I know this doesn't compare to the position you're in with Nathan, but I refuse to accept that there isn't an answer. Between us, there must be a way we can bring Nathan down.'

'Like how, exactly?'

'Louis admitted there were drugs in the Tannery. Nathan made sure they vanished before the police arrived. What if I can get one of the other wasps to talk about Nathan's role in the drug trade?'

Erin shook her head. 'The police already know about Nathan and drugs. They can't prove it – that's what I told you before, but actually, I suspect it's worse than that. They don't *want* to prove it.'

'Why not?'

'Because drugs are, like it or not, part of everyday life. Sure, the police and politicians have to pretend it's a "scourge" that can be eradicated, but they know it's bullshit. In reality, they prefer a situation where the flow of drugs is controlled by somebody they know. Somebody who'll keep it within certain limits. That could be why they've never moved against Nathan. Because he might be replaced by someone worse.'

'If you're saying the local police are corrupt, then we'll go further afield. I mean, we know he's committed another murder—'

'We don't know for sure.' Erin cut me off. 'Yes, it's likely he had Louis killed, but we can't prove it. And Freddie's death wasn't necessarily murder, Harry.'

She tensed as she said it, as if fearing my reaction. For that reason, I turned away, scraping a hand through my hair.

'Now I'm back to wondering why you ever helped me, if this is what you think.'

I didn't deserve the affection with which she grasped my arm. 'I'm sorry. I realise I'm guilty of... feeding your obsession, I suppose. Because I hoped that might help *me*.'

'To get rid of Nathan?'

'Essentially, yes. It was wrong of me. It gave you a false sense of what we can do about this mess we're in.'

Now thoroughly deflated, I lay back on the bed. Seconds later I heard her phone vibrate. Erin sighed, leaning over to read the message that awaited her.

'I need to get going.'

I nodded, but said nothing. I didn't think there was much hope of Erin wanting to see me again after this.

61

Nathan has said he expects to be back around two, but instead of returning home Erin drives a couple of miles east, towards Bexhill, and finds a place to park on the coast.

She told the oafish wasp, Dane, she was going to the beach, so now she must have salt in her hair, a damp towel and swimsuit for when Nathan returns. More than that, she needs to reflect on what she has done, and what she yet may do.

The afternoon air has a sultry haze. The sea is pea green and sluggish. Erin dives beneath the surface and wishes she and Harry were swimming together, with nothing more taxing to contemplate than where to eat this evening.

Making love with him felt like something from a dream, and that sense of unreality is vital to her state of mind. She can keep the panic at bay by convincing herself it was merely a fantasy. By the time she reaches home it won't have happened, and there will be no consequences to fear.

Harry, she knows, wants today to be the beginning of something. Impossible, but he refuses to see it. She's thought for a while that his stubborn nature is likely to get him in trouble, and now – after Louis's murder – there's a very real possibility that he'll end up dead.

That, too, has to be forgotten when she returns home. Dane is still loitering, and mouths an obscenity in response to her sarcastic wave. She enters the house, relieved that Nathan isn't here yet, and trudges upstairs to take a shower.

The noise of the water pummelling her skin obscures all other sound, so there's a terrible jolt when she steps out of the cubicle, wraps herself in a towel and turns to find Nathan in the doorway. She reels back, almost slipping on the stone floor.

'Well that's a nice greeting,' he says sourly.

'It was the shock. I didn't hear you come in.'

He's already undoing his belt when he nods at the towel. 'Drop it.'

'How was your trip?'

'Tell you later. This first.'

The sex is as fast and brutal as it has ever been. She's face down on the bed, and when he's done Nathan rests his full weight on her, nuzzling his chin against the back of her head. His left hand fumbles its way down her arm and encloses her hand, gently at first, but she's hyper-aware of the sensations from her injured fingers as they are gathered in and pressed together.

'Still painful?'

'Not too bad.'

He increases the pressure, laughing at her squeal of pain. 'Hurts now, yeah?'

'Yes,' she gasps.

'Worth knowing.' He rolls off, retrieves his phone and examines the screen. 'We're meeting the others at the Wheatsheaf for seven.'

When Nathan goes to shower, Erin slips beneath the duvet and cradles her throbbing fingers and doesn't think about Harry, and how safe she felt with him.

Nathan snorts when he finds her back in bed. 'Tired out, are you?'

'I might have a nap. I assume it'll be a late night?'

'Dunno yet.'

He's still more interested in his phone; a twitch of a grin as he reads something. After a few seconds, she says, 'Why was Dane outside today?'

'I like to keep them busy.'

'You still don't trust me?'

'Nope.'

He is mulling over his suit selection, and has his back to her when she decides there's nothing to lose by testing him.

'And what about Louis?'

He goes very still. 'What about him?'

'Well, I've not seen him out there for a while. Is he still on the team?'

'Still on the...?' he echoes, mystified, slowly turning to stare at her. 'Nah, Louis's history.' His eyes glitter with malicious delight. 'I slung him out.'

* * *

Erin's departure left me feeling thoroughly dejected. I made a less than valiant effort at combating the depression by drinking a couple of beers and watching some tennis on TV. But my mind kept straying back to this morning, and the intimacy we'd enjoyed.

I wanted us to go on seeing each other. Erin didn't. I thought we should work together to bring Nathan to justice. Erin regarded that as an impossible ambition.

I was falling in love with her. Erin, it seemed, didn't feel the same.

Eventually I made myself get on with some chores. The bungalow's garden had been woefully neglected in recent months. After a couple of hours weeding and cutting back the overgrown bushes, I was glad to be interrupted by a phone call from my daughter.

Jody sounded anxious, though she denied having been primed by her mother to check up on me. In fact she was still rather belligerent on the subject of Anita and Gareth. When I urged her once again not to be too judgemental, I was reminded of what Erin had said.

Did I wish I was still with my ex-wife?

I was careful to end the conversation on good terms. Then I rang Adam, who was with Jay at a friend's barbecue, and we shared several minutes of slightly awkward small talk. I was conscious that there was no real purpose to the call, and while a father doesn't need a purpose to phone his son, in our case it occurred so seldomly that it felt slightly unnatural. Afterwards, what unsettled me most about both calls was that they had the air of a farewell.

As the evening came in I decided to take a walk, and perhaps even go for a meal. While away on business I'd think nothing of dining alone in a restaurant: why should it be any different in my home town?

When I left the house it was just after seven-thirty; the air was warm and thick, with a layer of gauzy cloud that obscured the setting sun. I realised it was exactly a week since I'd swum with Erin. A week since we'd eaten out together in Rye.

You can't be with her, the voice of brutal reason told me. *Nathan will make your lives a misery – if he permits you to live at all. And you can forget vengeance. Forget justice. Forget Erin...*

'But I won't forget my son,' I whispered aloud. 'I'll never forget you, Freddie. I tried—'

I heard a tiny exclamation, looked up and saw a couple of young women staring at me. I hurried past them and continued, this time only mouthing the words: 'I tried to get answers. I had a crazy idea about avenging your death, but I have to accept it won't happen. I'm so sorry.'

Tears distorted my vision. My body was coated with sweat. When I reached the pedestrian precinct I made for the nearest seat and took a few minutes to compose myself.

Once I felt slightly better, I wandered through the centre and into Robeson Street, where most of the town's best eateries were located. Up ahead was the Star Inn, which had long been one of my favourite pubs for food. I wasn't completely sure I wanted to dine alone in a place that had been the venue for so many happy family gatherings, but I stopped and peered through the window, just to see how busy it was.

Then I spotted them, and froze.

62

An hour or so in, and Erin would class the evening as 'bearable'. Which is a significant improvement on her expectations.

Most of the guests are familiar faces, but nobody she knows well. The main contractor and his wife. One of the architects and his wife. An important councillor and her husband. And a late addition, which Nathan only revealed, with a smirk, when the cab dropped them off: Trevor McPherson, the slimy 'roads' guy who wants to get her into bed.

The more perceptive of them – the women, invariably – have picked up on the vibe between her and Nathan, and what began as friendly conversation has become significantly more guarded. Any attempts on Erin's part to engage with them quickly fizzle out.

Nathan organised a seating plan. McPherson has been placed directly opposite her. When someone enquires after his wife, he says, 'No longer on the scene, I'm glad to say!' – and delivers a pantomime wink in Erin's direction.

More than once she's caught a significant look passing between him and Nathan. A deal has been made, she thinks. Nathan intends to farm her out like a whore, and if she objects he'll point to her behaviour with Harry and say she's brought this upon herself.

She opted for the lightest meal available: smoked salmon salad followed by a risotto. She's still worried about keeping it down, and has calculated how quickly she can reach the ladies. It's when she glances towards the toilets that she catches movement through the main window and her heart nearly stops.

It's Harry.

She sees him pause, then stare into the window of another pub across the street. If Nathan looks round and sees him, it'll be a disaster. Fortunately, Nathan is deep in conversation with the female councillor.

Instead, it's slimeball Trevor McPherson who registers her anxiety and sends her a teasing, quizzical look. Erin bares her teeth before mouthing a single word at him.

'Never.'

* * *

They were at a table near the back: Gareth and Anita, hunched together, talking in what I imagined to be seductive whispers. A bottle of wine rested in a cooler beside the table.

I was still frozen, convinced that the slightest movement would catch their attention. If I was spotted, they would invariably coax me inside, whereupon I'd be cajoled into joining them for a meal. Right now I couldn't bear that.

When a diner at a neighbouring table got up and walked past them, it gave me the split second I needed to dart out of sight. I hurried away, feeling vaguely ashamed. There was another gastropub just across the road, but I couldn't face sitting there alone while Gareth and Anita enjoyed their romantic dinner a few yards away.

I wandered aimlessly until I ended up on the seafront, where the aromas of a fast-food takeaway caused my stomach to rumble. I bought a double cheeseburger and devoured it with unseemly haste, keeping a wary eye on the gulls that prowled nearby. The sun had set and the cloud layer was lower than before, hastening the transition from dusk to darkness. Most of the beaches were deserted, but as I dumped the packaging in the nearest bin I spotted a tiny flare of light at the end of the breakwater.

I recalled Len Bowden's warning, and thought maybe now would be a good time to find out what he meant.

* * *

Erin feels a yearning to be with Harry, but that doesn't mean it's not a relief to check the window again and find he has gone. Nathan didn't see him, which means on that count at least she's not in further danger of punishment.

The main course is complete. Amid the usual comments about 'finding room' for dessert, McPherson spots his opportunity to lob a compliment across the table: 'I'm betting you're not one for puddings, Erin. You wanna keep that trim little figure of yours.'

Erin swallows an urge to plunge a fork into his hand. She senses Nathan's keen interest in the exchange, and in that instant the decision is made.

She is doomed, in all the ways that matter. And if that's the case, there is one thing she wants to do for Harry before it ends.

Get him the answers he needs.

Picking up her phone, she reacts to a non-existent message, fakes typing a reply, then gives a resigned sigh. It's aimed at Nathan, but he is still deep in conversation with the councillor, whose husband is pissed off and trying not to show it. Only when Erin slides her chair back does Nathan turn sharply.

'I'm sorry,' she says. 'I need to go.'

'What?' Although he scowls, his eyes aren't properly focused; he's been throwing back a lot of champagne.

'It's Milly. I don't want to explain it now—'

'What're you on about?' The question comes out slurred, and far too loud. Most of the conversation around the table has ceased.

'Nathan, please. She's my sister. I won't be late back.'

'Nah.' He shakes his head in irritation, but now the councillor has tuned in.

'Your sister, did you say?' she asks Erin. 'What's wrong?'

'Ha!' Nathan exclaims. 'Easier to ask what *isn't* wrong with Milly.'

* * *

The breakwater had attracted a number of anglers, including a father and daughter and a couple of teenage boys. But Len Bowden was, as ever, sitting alone at the very end. Perhaps I should ask his advice on coping with solitude, I thought.

At a distance of about twenty feet I felt my nostrils twitching at the distinctive tang of marijuana. Len had been gazing out to sea but he must have sensed my approach. He turned and looked at me for a moment, then switched the rod to his left hand, took the joint from his mouth and blew out a long stream of smoke.

'Harry,' he murmured.

'All right, Len. I didn't realise you, er...'

'Only weekends and special occasions.' He offered it to me, but I shook my head. 'I did way too much dope in my twenties,' he admitted. 'Broke the habit for decades. Now I'm at an age where I reckon it's more beneficial than harmful, so why not partake?'

'Why not, indeed?' I said, not wanting him to think I disapproved. 'Is it easy to get hold of?'

He gave me a quizzical look. 'Looking to score?'

'No, no. Just asking out of interest.'

He shrugged. 'There's a few scallywags that sell it round here. Though the lad I bought it from went over the bloody cliff, didn't he?'

I felt my legs go weak. 'Do they know what happened?'

'Probably jumped. Don't suppose the little tyke had much to live for.'

'In the article I saw, he hadn't been identified.'

'Oh, I heard through the grapevine. Kid called Louis.' He tutted. 'A cheeky sod, but I sort of liked him.'

'Louis was your supplier?'

Len put the fishing rod aside and studied my face. 'Sounds like you know the lad?'

'I know *of* him, that's all.' I took a deep breath, aware that I was in danger of getting too emotional. 'You realise who's ultimately supplying that cannabis?'

'Go on.'

'Nathan Webb.' I paused, but Len didn't react. 'It's Webb who controls the supply of drugs in this town.'

'If you believe the rumours.' Easing himself off his folding chair, Len joined me at the railings. He took a last drag on the joint and tossed it into the sea.

'Don't you believe them?'

'Haven't given it much thought.'

Something in his manner had changed. He wasn't hostile, exactly, but nor did I feel my presence was entirely welcome. It reminded me of the tone he'd taken when we last spoke.

'"Messing with another man's wife",' I quoted. 'What were you getting at there?'

He gave a gentle snort. 'Out here, I see and hear a fair bit. And I saw you and Nathan's missus getting friendly. It's a mighty dangerous game you're playing, believe me.'

'If you're warning me off, join the queue.'

'But will you heed the warning, Harry? You've already lost a son.'

I turned on him sharply. 'What do you mean by that?'

'Hey, hey.' His face remained stern, even as he raised his palms to placate me. 'I feel for you, Harry, I really do. Lord knows, I've made some mistakes in my time.'

I nodded, not yet sure whether to trust him. 'How about telling me exactly what you know and who you've been talking to? Is it Nathan?'

Len looked aggrieved. 'I have very little to do with the man.'

'Then who?'

'His mum. Theresa is... someone I know from years back.'

Catching the rueful note, I said, 'How well did you know her?'

'As youngsters we dated a bit, before Pierson came on the scene.'

'Right. But what you said the other day...'

'Pierson Webb was a grade A tool,' he growled. 'Screwed everything that moved while he was off on his dodgy business trips. When Theresa cottoned on, she decided that what's good for the goose...'

I gasped. 'You had an affair with Nathan's mother?'

'Nothing as grand as an affair. Just a bit of fun when it suited.'

Reeling at this information, I was initially struck by the parallels with Erin and myself – and then a new and quite horrifying possibility came to me.

'Was this after Nathan was born? Or before?'

Len broke eye contact to cough, then wiped clumsily at his mouth. His mumbled reply was something like: 'I don't have to tell you that.'

Which told me all I needed to know.

63

To Erin, it's obvious that Nathan is lashing out because he's embarrassed, and as such Erin should simply offer another gushing apology and get the hell out of there.

But she doesn't. The mocking contempt in her husband's voice can't go unanswered.

The councillor, diplomatically, has ignored Nathan's intervention and continues to wait for Erin's reply.

'My sister has some, uh, quite complex special needs,' Erin tells her.

'I see. Does she live independently, or...?'

'With adoptive parents. Our own parents are no longer with us.'

The councillor winces. 'I'm so sorry.'

'Shit happens in any family,' Nathan cuts in. 'But this lot drew the short straw. Milly's an adult but has a mental age of... what, three or four?'

'About that,' Erin agrees. She can tell that Nathan, angered and perhaps humiliated by her decision to leave, means to have some fun at her expense.

'Nothing really "special" about it,' he drawls, 'but that's the *woke* thing to say. Can't call her "simple", or "backward".' After an incredulous eye roll, he adds, 'Still, it's a damn good reason not to have kids, eh, babe? Who knows what might be lurking in that DNA of yours?'

He's sniggering as he speaks, and Erin's impression is that those who stand to gain most from his patronage are grinning along with him. The others wear less certain smiles, registering that his gaze is loaded with malice for the woman he introduced earlier as 'my gorgeous wife'.

'I'll let you know how I get on,' Erin tells him, then forces a smile for the other guests. 'Enjoy the rest of your evening.'

'We will,' Nathan answers for them. 'The real fun starts here, don't you worry.'

It's a petulant response from a man who insists on having the last word. Erin manages to get out of the pub before the tears begin to flow. She checks her phone: no messages. She's tempted to call Harry, but knows it's not a good idea.

None of this is a good idea, she reminds herself as she hurries along the street. But if she speaks to Harry now, there's a chance he will dissuade her from what she intends to do.

Or worse still, go in her place.

* * *

I held back from voicing my suspicion. I recalled that Len had been out here when I'd had my clandestine meeting with Louis, and it seemed more important to ask him about that.

'Louis didn't jump off the cliff,' I said. 'He was thrown. Probably by the same couple of thugs that went for me last week. They work for Nathan Webb.'

Looking troubled, Len asked, 'Where are you getting all this?'

'In my case, from Nathan himself.' I briefly described what had happened to me, and felt that Len was less sceptical than he wanted to appear. 'Did you know that Nathan was looking for Louis?'

'Why would I?'

'Thursday night, you were out here. I was talking to Louis, trying to get him to help me.'

'I didn't see you,' he snapped.

'But you saw Louis?'

Len opened his mouth, perhaps to deny it. Then he sighed. 'Theresa had mentioned that they were worried about Louis, and asked me to keep an eye out for him. I just sent her a quick text.'

And signed Louis's death warrant. My eyes must have conveyed that message, for Len's posture changed. He suddenly seemed older, less confident.

'The impression I got was that they valued Louis. And Nathan... okay, he sails close to the wind, but he wouldn't *murder* anyone.'

'You can't say that for sure. How well do you know him, really?'

'I know—' When Len broke off, I looked into his eyes and knew I had to say it.

'Is Nathan your son?'

★ ★ ★

It's a quarter to ten when Erin reaches the gate. She can hear the muffled thump of a bassline, though it's not as loud as she was expecting.

She called in at an off licence in the town centre, and now tucks the bag containing her purchase under her arm. She enters the code and opens the gate, while the voice of reason says, *You can still change your mind...*

But she doesn't. The Tannery building is straight ahead, with a vague impression of multicoloured lights flashing on the top floor. In the gathering gloom the waste ground is a landscape of mysterious, sinister objects. Erin takes careful steps through the weeds, her senses on high alert.

As she nears the building there's a scuffling noise and a tiny crack, which might have been a fragment of concrete breaking under foot. She freezes, but nothing reveals itself.

If you're this jumpy, turn round and go home...

Again she ignores the inner voice and enters the building. She's braced for the stench, but still it makes her gag. The music is only slightly louder but she can feel the vibrations through the floors and walls; the ancient fittings tinkling like wind chimes, or a tolling bell.

On the second floor the stack of mattresses is over the hole. They must have been rejected as too filthy by the couple having sex against one of the building's pillars, who are too engrossed even to notice Erin moving past.

The final flight is like a walk to the gallows. She can hear laughter, the buzz of conversation: warm, inviting sounds that ought to be drawing her in. Instead she is fighting an impulse to turn and flee.

A group of people are clustered at the top of the stairs, cans of WKD and

Absolut in hand. A girl looks her over, then nudges the boy next to her. Erin pretends she doesn't notice their open-mouthed surprise.

She's not overdressed, particularly; Nathan wanted her done up like a tart as usual, but she managed to get away with a sleeveless blouse and a short skirt, along with low-heeled sandals. It's a starkly different look to most of the people here – they're in T-shirts and leggings or shorts – and it's also a pointer to the one glaring contrast: she's probably ten or fifteen years older than anyone else.

The first familiar face is Dane, the burly and not-too-bright wasp. He's engaged in some kind of drinking game, kneeling on the floor and throwing back a line of shot glasses arranged in a circle on top of an old oil drum. Then a figure emerges from a larger group who are dancing and drinking in the middle of the room. Jax offers a shy smile, though he also looks concerned. To reach her he has to skirt round the largest hole in the floor, which is covered with planks.

'ERIN! IS EVERYTHing okay?' Just as he yells the question, the volume of the music is abruptly reduced.

'Fine. Why?'

'Well...' Jax is twitchy, self-conscious, as he realises that practically everyone is watching them. 'What are you doing here?'

'Just wanted to check it out, before it's too late.'

'Is Nathan with you?'

'No.' She opens her bag and produces a litre of Grey Goose. 'I brought this.'

'Oh. Cheers.'

'So how many are here?' Erin asks.

'Thirty, forty, maybe? More than usual, because it's the last one.' He hefts the bottle. 'Want a drink?'

'Just a beer for me, thanks.'

He moves across to a group clustered at a makeshift bar: an old door laid over two piles of bricks. There are several buckets filled with water and ice, and from one of these Jax fishes out two bottles of Bud. Erin can see him fielding questions, and when he shows them the vodka and nods in her direction, she senses the mood shifting a little in her favour.

He returns, looking more relaxed. They clink bottles and he asks what she thinks.

'There's a nice vibe.' She means it. Up here there's a sense of space, of freedom, that you wouldn't get in a nightclub. And the LED lights strung haphaz-ardly from the ceiling leave large patches of darkness, concealing much of the damage and decay to the building.

'We can party all night and no one bothers us.' Jaz sounds wistful; she assumes the upcoming demolition is on his mind, but then he says, 'Did you hear about Louis?'

64

'The honest answer, Harry, is that I don't know if Nathan is my son.'

'But it's a possibility?'

'In terms of the timescale... yes. Theresa claimed her sex life with Pierson was practically non-existent in the eighties, but I don't know if that's true. Dunno how many other lovers she might've had, either.'

'Would she really do that, with a husband as dangerous as Pierson?' Even as the words emerged, I appreciated the irony that I would ask such a question.

'Looking back on it, we took some crazy risks. But there's a certain kind of passion that overrides common sense.' Len eyed me with a slightly bitter smile. 'I reckon you'd know about that yourself.'

'There's no relationship between Erin and me,' I said, somewhat disingenuously.

'Fine. Whether there is or not, I haven't said a word to Theresa – or anyone else. After what you've suffered, I'm hardly gonna add—'

'What I've *suffered*,' I reminded him through gritted teeth, 'is completely down to Nathan Webb. And did you know that he abuses Erin? Physically, mentally, emotionally...'

'No!' Len slapped a hand on the railing and a metallic clang reverberated along the breakwater, causing several of the anglers to peer in our direction.

'You may have your issues with Nathan, but I won't be dragged into it, you hear?'

'I wouldn't lie to you, Len. Is Nathan aware you might be—'

'Doesn't have a clue. And that's how it needs to stay.' He spoke with such force that I couldn't help glancing at his tackle box, aware that it probably contained a knife.

'You've never wanted to know for sure?'

'Nope. A few months after he was born, I decided it was all too messy. Too volatile. I buggered off abroad and didn't come back for more than twenty years.' He spread his hands. 'With that decision, I relinquished any right to claim parentage, or mess around with all that DNA nonsense.'

'It's a shame. You could have been a steadying influence on him.'

'Who says he needs it? Nathan Webb is about to create something magnificent for this town. You don't get to do that by tiptoeing around, trying not to offend anyone.'

Len's eyes were alight with enthusiasm, and perhaps something akin to fatherly pride. It was evident that nothing I said would convince him of Nathan's true nature.

'One question,' I said. 'Did you ever hear any whispers about how my son died?'

'In an accident,' Len answered firmly. 'A lot of kids messing around, late at night. I know from Theresa that Nathan was as shocked as anyone. The last thing he wanted was a tragedy like that – from a selfish point of view, I mean. A tonne of bad publicity just when he was trying to get the plans approved.'

Almost exactly what Nathan told me on Wednesday morning, and it chimed with Erin's own instincts. So was there a chance it could be the truth?

'I'll leave you to your fishing.' As I started to back away there was a low rumbling sound. We both turned and gazed out to sea, the horizon now blurred by low cloud. 'So,' I asked, 'is the storm coming in or not?'

Len clicked his tongue. 'If what you've said is legit, it's already here.'

* * *

Erin is struck by Jax's matter-of-fact tone; there's certainly no indication that he is grieving for Louis. 'What did you hear?' she asks.

'Most likely he fell. Dude was always really reckless. Some mad idea would get into his head and he'd just do it.'

'That isn't what happened, I'm afraid.' She checks that no one else is within earshot. 'He was thrown off the cliff. I saw it.'

Jax rears back. 'You actually *witnessed* it?' Then he squints at her. 'They're not talking about murder on the news. Have you been to the cops?'

'I can't. It was my husband who had him killed.'

'You're kidding? What did you see?'

'Two men in a dark blue van. It was over within seconds.'

'No way.' Jax sounds both shocked and excited. 'Couple of the others have mentioned seeing a blue van, two guys inside. It's been outside here a few times. But how do you know there's a link to Nathan?'

'They match the description of the men who abducted Harry Manning. Freddie's dad. When Harry was released, Nathan was there to greet him.'

'This is heavy stuff.' Jax takes a long drink. 'What're you gonna do?'

'The truth? I don't have a clue.' She sips her own beer, and finds the bottle almost empty. 'Is Ash here?'

'Think he was, earlier.' They both peer into the darker recesses. The music changes and it's louder again. 'Why do you want him?' Jax shouts.

'No real reason. Was he one of the people who saw the van?'

Jax frowns, as though she's just read his mind. 'Yeah, he was. Stuff like that freaks him out. He does way too much dope – makes him paranoid.'

'"Just because you're paranoid, it doesn't mean they're not out to get you."'

The frown deepens: he obviously isn't familiar with the quote. But Erin thinks she has edged a little closer to the truth.

She holds out the empty beer bottle. 'How about something stronger?'

* * *

I felt disconsolate as I walked back along the breakwater. It was like I'd been handed an unexploded bomb: I might be able to use it against my enemy, but at what risk of collateral damage?

I thought about stopping somewhere for a drink – really just to delay going home – but knew it wouldn't help. A few more rumbles of thunder followed me back, though there was no rain yet. The air held a syrupy warmth, and the humidity left me short of breath.

I'd forgotten to leave any lights on, so the house was dark and unwelcoming. For the first time it occurred to me that I should consider selling up. This had been the home we shared: Anita and Freddie and me. It wasn't right to live here alone.

After making tea, I drank only a couple of mouthfuls before pouring a large brandy instead. I sat in front of the TV, my mind still whirling from the conversation with Len. On several occasions I found myself bringing up Erin's number, desperate to talk to her, but each time I managed to resist.

Too restless to watch TV, I ended up online and found that Louis's identity had been released to the media. His full name was apparently Jordan Louis Smith and he was believed to be fifteen. He'd run away from a children's home in South London more than two years ago. There was no mention of his role as a drug courier; nor did Nathan Webb's name appear anywhere in the article.

I felt sick when I read that an inquest had been opened and adjourned, pending the outcome of the police investigation. It struck me that, unless Erin came forward – notwithstanding some kind of miraculous intervention – the eventual verdict might well be 'misadventure' for Louis.

Once again Nathan would get away with murder.

I closed my laptop and made a conscious effort to stop dwelling on it all. Scrolling through the TV channels, I found a Marvel Avengers movie with enough noisy, colourful action to keep me occupied for a while. Freddie had loved this franchise, and I too had always had a soft spot for superheroes.

By eleven o'clock I was ready for bed. My phone buzzed as I was trooping along the hall. When I saw Erin's name on the screen, I nearly cried out.

> I'm trying to find Ash. I think he'll have an interesting story to tell.

I typed a reply:

> Really? Can I call you?

> No point. Too noisy here!

I frowned as I typed:

> Where are you? Hope you're okay?

> Stop worrying about me, Harry. It's too late for that.

I read her message several times and didn't see how it could be interpreted in anything but an ominous light.

> I don't understand. Please tell me what you're doing.

> Partying! Spoke to Jax and he says it was LOUIS that Ash was scared of, not Nathan. Don't know if it'll help but try to use that info if anything happens to me.

> What do you mean? Are you in danger?

> Always Harry lol

Then nothing. In desperation I rang her, but the call diverted to voicemail. I cut the connection, just as another text glided on to the screen.

> I love you, Harry. Shouldn't really admit that, but for what it's worth, I really do.

I stared at the screen, my heart beating so fast I thought it might explode. I felt almost overwhelmed by my emotions, but what really hit home, as I read that message again, was that it sounded like a goodbye.

Late on a Saturday night, I'd assumed she would be with Nathan. Instead she was talking to Jax, and on the hunt for Ash. And she'd said she was partying, which could only mean one thing.

She was at the Tannery.

65

Erin's feeling good. Relaxed, confident, light on her feet and full of energy. After the beer she switched to vodka, and she's had three of those in quick succession. Or is it four?

Jax was sorting out her drinks, but then he slipped away, saying he needed to pee. In his absence, a few other partygoers started engaging her in conversation; maybe just taking pity on her, though they're perfectly friendly.

Everyone seems to know who she is. One or two are still scowling when she looks in their direction, but most seem pretty chilled out, and why not? There's music and booze and God knows what other stimulants, and the air wafting through the broken roof is fragrant and warm.

'Such a great venue!' she's said a few times, to nods of agreement. 'Shame it's coming down next week.' *Can you stop it?* one of them asked, and she shook her head gravely. 'Too much money involved.'

She didn't feel drunk as she tapped out the messages to Harry, though she's conscious that it probably isn't wise to be talking to him. But the last couple of drinks, brought to her by Dane and the moody-looking girl he's with, seem to have gone to her head a lot more.

She still hasn't spotted Ash, though she made Jax promise to keep an eye out for him. Earlier she'd raised the subject of Louis again, and the fact that both Louis and Ash seemed to be lying low. Jax was cagey at first, but did admit that Ash had been, in his words, 'shit scared' of Louis.

'Really? I thought he was worried about Nathan.'

Jax shrugged. 'Why would Ash be worried about Nathan?'

The question had her stumped. 'I dunno, actually. Why is he scared of Louis?'

'The guy was one sneaky little bastard. You couldn't trust Louis for a second. He'd trample on anyone to get ahead.'

'But *you* weren't hiding from him. So what was it that Ash, spefic... sepific...'

'Specifically?' Jax queried with a smile.

'Yeah. Why Ash?'

'Not sure, to be honest. Ash doesn't say much.'

Reflecting on it now, Erin considers whether Ash, perhaps needing to get Louis out of the way, might have engineered his murder. Could Nathan have acted against Louis on the basis of something he was told by Ash?

Her train of thought is interrupted by Dane, who is suddenly in her face, holding a couple of shot glasses.

'Down in one,' he orders, his voice even more slurred than hers. She does as she's asked, and screws up her face at the taste of aniseed. It's either ouzo or sambuca, and she isn't fond of either.

Dane bares his teeth at her. 'You didn't ought to be here.'

'Why not?'

'You know why. Your husband wouldn't like it.'

'Well, my husband doesn't get to decide where I go – and neither do you, Dane.'

A low rumbling noise distracts them for a second; it makes Erin think of the upcoming demolition, but of course it's distant thunder.

She thrusts the glass back at Dane. 'Get me another and then we'll start the games.'

He looks at her in confusion. 'Games?'

'Yeah. Like you normally play.' She swivels, stumbles, regains her balance with a giggle and indicates the hole in the floor. 'Isn't someone gonna dare me to dance?'

* * *

It was almost eleven-thirty. The night was pitch black, though the town's streetlights, reflecting against the low cloud, created an eerie glow. I grabbed a jacket and wriggled into it as I hurried along the road. A low peal of thunder seemed to go on forever, and I caught a few distant flashes of lightning far out at sea.

It's already here, Len had said. Maybe he was right. A storm of one type or another was going to get a lot worse.

I was constantly checking my phone, willing there to be a message from Erin. After a couple of minutes I realised it was slowing me down.

I'd barely considered the situation I was about to face. I hadn't considered whether I'd be able to help Erin, or whether my presence would make things worse rather than better.

Nothing mattered except getting there.

* * *

Dane fetches her another drink. Erin is tipping it down her throat when she spots Jax in the crowd that is starting to drift in her direction.

'Hey, Jax. You're just in time.' She points at the hole. 'We're gonna dance. Play some games.'

Jax squirms. 'You don't want to be doing that.'

'I do – it'll be fun.'

He frowns a warning, as though that could have an effect on her now. 'Anyway, I saw Ash downstairs.'

'Is he coming up?'

'He might. He knows you want to talk to him.'

Erin nods happily. 'So come on then. Let's do it.'

'Please don't—'

'It's a laugh, Jax.' She gestures at their fascinated audience. 'The night Freddie was here, who dared him?'

No one answers for a long time. After sending her another imploring look, Jax turns away in exasperation. A rumble of thunder shudders over the roof. As it fades, Dane says, 'Who'd you think? It was your husband.'

'Right. Nathan set the challenge.' Erin claps her hands a couple of times. Her plan was to lull them into cooperation by pretending to be drunk, but in fact she doesn't have to fake it. *All good then*, she tells herself. 'So how does it start?'

Another silence. Well, not quite: they're muttering or whispering; a lot of smirks and sidelong glances. She turns to see what Dane has to say, but he's no longer in sight.

Then a couple of them shift aside, and Erin realises it's to make way for a newcomer, tall and thin and deathly pale.

'Hey.' She nods a greeting but for some reason she doesn't want to say his name out loud; perhaps fearing he will vanish in a puff of smoke.

Ash looks even more worried than Jax. 'You shouldn't do this,' he says.

'I wanna know. I want to experience it for myself.'

Ash purses his lips, then automatically rears back as Jax sidles closer to him.

'It's a stupid game,' Jax says. 'Somebody has to stand on the planks and jump around. Everyone counts along: ten, fifteen, twenty seconds—'

'What's the time to beat?' To her own ears Erin sounds giddy with enthusiasm; to them she might just sound deranged.

Ash says, 'Twenty is long enough,' and Jax quickly nods.

'Now, now boys.' Erin wags a finger at them. 'I don't think you're being straight with me.'

'Twenty seconds is good,' Jax insists. 'But you have to move the whole time.'

'Got it.' She takes a step towards the planks. 'How long did Freddie last?'

66

I reached the Tannery in record time, breathless and bathed in sweat. The thunder continued, still miles out at sea. From inside the Tannery came the low-pitched thrum of dance music.

My hand trembled as I entered the code. I put it down to an excess of adrenalin. I was far more determined than nervous. Far more anxious for Erin than afraid for myself.

I must have hit the wrong digit because the gate refused to open. A moment of pure panic until I re-entered the code and heard the lock release. I took in the lights on the top floor but had to focus on making my way across the waste ground.

The interior of the building was as fetid as ever, but at least I knew a safe route, and by now my eyes had adjusted to the darkness.

I climbed the first two flights of stairs with a little less caution than was sensible. On the second floor I was vaguely aware of the hole, covered in boards, and the stack of mattresses beyond it. Something caught my attention to the right of the mattresses; possibly someone moving into the shadows, though when I paused to look there was nobody visible.

I made my way up the final flight of stairs, slowing as I sensed some kind of drama unfolding on the top floor. Aside from the music I could hear very little: no laughter or jeering, no singing or celebration. Instead I sensed a kind of solemnity, a stillness that was borne out when I saw a huddle of young people standing with their backs to the stairs.

I crept up behind them and went on tiptoe to see what they were staring at. There were a lot of bodies clustered together, so I actually heard Erin's voice before I saw her. It was phrased as a question, and although I didn't catch exactly what she said, one word jumped out at me.

Freddie.

* * *

'He did about twenty-five seconds.' Jax glances at Ash, who after a moment's awkward hesitation gives a nod and says, 'But he had more boards than that.'

They're conspiring in order to protect her, Erin understands. It's kind of sweet. Giggling, she narrows her eyes. 'Are you telling me fibs?'

'Nope.' Jax quickly fetches half a dozen planks and adds them to the boards already over the hole. These are about a quarter of an inch thick, stained with paint or creosote, but not as obviously cracked or rotten as some of the boards beneath them. They might help to bear her weight, and Erin isn't so far gone that she doesn't appreciate the gesture.

But to get answers, she will need to take a genuine risk.

'Let's have that music up!' It's David Guetta's 'I'm Good': a nice heavy beat as she ignores a final plea from the sensible, sober portion of her brain and leaps towards the middle of the hole, landing with enough force to give the timber a stern test. She feels the boards flexing beneath her, dipping an inch or two then propelling her upwards. It's an exhilarating sensation, enhanced by the awareness of danger. 'Like a trampoline!' she cries, though Jax and Ash look far from thrilled.

She scans the crowd and notices Dane, shouldering his way past a couple of kids near the stairs, and wonders where he's been.

Dane spiked my drinks. It's a revelation that comes from nowhere but immediately feels plausible. She normally has a much better tolerance for alcohol than this.

'Was Freddie dancing on the planks, or jumping?'

Ash only shrugs. Jax shakes his head, regretfully. A lot of her audience, all in their teens or early twenties, look as though they can't believe that someone of her age would behave so recklessly.

Erin bends her knees and jumps, just a couple of inches, then does it again and finds a rhythm that matches the beat. With each landing she feels multiple layers of timber give and resist, give and resist.

'Freddie was dared, right? What kind of things was Nathan saying?'

Now it's Jax who shrugs. Erin can tell he doesn't want anything to do with this. She switches her focus to Ash, who stares back like a deer in headlights.

'Nathan challenged him to stay on for twenty seconds or more. He said Freddie wouldn't manage it, because he was a pussy. A gay boy student.'

'And that made Freddie more determined?'

'Maybe.' Ash winces at a slightly different sound from the boards; one of them may have cracked, but Erin can't afford to let it worry her.

'Did Nathan try to keep him on here for longer than he wanted?'

Before Ash can reply, Jax cries out, 'Erin, don't do this.'

She shakes her head at him – *I'm not listening* – then notices how Dane seems to be gloating. Her vision distorts for a second; she doesn't know what he slipped into her drink, but whatever it is, it's filled her with pure energy. Makes her feel fantastic, even if she'll pay for it later, during the comedown, and she knows for sure that she's losing the plot when she glimpses a face in the crowd and would swear it's dear old Harry...

* * *

At first I was too shocked to react.

Erin, for some reason, was jumping up and down on the planks.

I craned my neck to see if Nathan was anywhere in sight, in case this was some twisted form of punishment, but he didn't appear to be present.

This was solely Erin's doing. And when I finally recovered enough to grasp what she was saying, I understood her motive.

She was trying to help me. Risking her life, on my behalf, to get the truth.

I couldn't allow that. I tried to ease my way through the partygoers, some of whom were filming her on their phones. Others were expressing their derision at Erin's behaviour. I got a little more forceful, pushing past them. One of the boys was trying to persuade Erin to get off the planks, but she wasn't having any of it. I could see she was quite seriously inebriated.

I moved closer, debating whether I could haul her to safety without adding more weight to the planks. But as I reached the front of the crowd she met my gaze and broke into an irrepressible smile.

'Hey Harry! Am I hallucinating, or are you really here?'

I couldn't help but grin. 'No, I'm here. What are you doing?'

'Dancing, with my friends – like Jax.' She indicated the boy who looked horrified by the risk she was taking. 'It's such fun!'

I doubted that pleading with her would work, so I just nodded. Then I realised that the pale young man standing close to Jax was probably Ash. He too seemed appalled by what was happening.

'Maybe I'll have a go after you,' I said. 'But can we talk first?'

'Not yet, Harry.' She was getting out of breath, but seemed to leap even higher. Looking past me, she cried, 'Who's counting the seconds? Where am I at?'

'Twenty-eight,' a young man piped up, monitoring his phone as he spoke.

'I'm storming it!' Erin said. 'Twenty-nine – count with me! Thirty. Thirty-one.'

I wasn't sure if I heard one of the boards crack; something changed in Erin's face, and she almost stumbled. She faltered in the count but the crowd had taken it up – 'Thirty-two, thirty-three' – and suddenly I couldn't bear it any more.

'Erin, that's enough.'

'I'm winning this, Harry. I'm gonna find out what you need—'

The next splintering noise was unmistakable; everyone heard it, including Erin, but at that point her body was rising, floating free in the air for that perfect, priceless fraction of a second, utterly safe in her ascent. And so, in that fraction of a second, I put my imagination to work and pictured her suspended over the hole, suspended and safe for as long as she needed to be – and if she could levitate, I thought to myself, then why not Freddie as well? I could keep both of them right there, delirious with joy at their great good fortune—

Until reality stomped back.

Gravity reasserted itself.

Erin hit the boards and this time her weight and momentum were more powerful than the remaining strength in the planks that lay over the hole; a void opened up and in an instant the illusion of levitation – of safety – was gone, and Erin along with it.

67

Erin brushes off another plea to stop, though Harry just flinched and maybe she did too. One of the boards seemed to react differently when she landed on it, so maybe it's time to get off – she has a sudden certainty that on her next landing the boards will fracture and possibly give way, and there's a small but distinct part of her mind that *wants* this, and while she knows the mattresses on the floor below should protect her from serious injury, a tiny part of her mind is celebrating the possibility of dying in this manner.

What a glorious irony, Erin thinks as her feet make contact with the boards and the collapse begins – and what a relief to have escaped from Nathan at last...

Except she hasn't. Not quite.

There's a moment of eye contact with Harry as she falls, then her gaze flicks past him and her husband is there, regarding her with a kind of furious incomprehension that's so typically Nathan, she could almost laugh.

Then he's not there.

Nobody is there.

* * *

Just like Freddie.

Erin had fallen, just like Freddie. I'd tried to fix her in place, there in my imagination, but the simple fact was that she couldn't float in mid-air forever. She had to come down and she did.

As she vanished, there were gasps and cries and a single involuntary scream. Then a terrible crash from the floor below, followed by a second or two of the most chilling silence.

I think I was first to move, spinning on my toes to face the stairs. Around me some of the partygoers were exchanging looks, others tapping at their phones as if eager to review the footage they'd just captured. I was too stricken to be angry, but as I started towards the stairs I saw that someone else had joined us.

Nathan Webb.

He looked dazed, even a little frightened, but I didn't know if he'd actually witnessed Erin's fall. As I raced for the stairs, a burly young man started talking urgently into his ear.

The mattresses weren't over the hole below, I remembered that. But I couldn't recall how many boards had been in place.

I was almost at the bottom of the stairs when there was another splintering noise. I caught sight of Erin lying twisted on the timber before it gave way and she began to fall once again.

* * *

No mattresses.

In her shock, it doesn't quite compute. Erin lands with almost enough force to punch through the next hole, but the boards hold for now, even though many are cracked and will soon split completely.

She hasn't blacked out but her senses are scrambled; she feels groggy, confused, and most of all surprised by the absence of pain.

She hears the thump of footsteps and twists her head slightly to see who it is. Her heart melts a little at the sight of Harry, at the panic and desperation on his face. Then the boards come apart, and she recalls the one time that Nathan started describing the horrific injuries Freddie suffered. So horrific that she couldn't bear to listen.

She's never said a word of that to Harry, of course, and it's Harry she thinks about now. Poor Harry who will have to witness what's left of her—

* * *

I don't know how I reached her in time. Much later I would be told it must have taken a superhuman effort to cross the distance between us and grab Erin's hand before she fell.

I dived to the floor, my knee smashing against a lump of masonry. I was stretching out my right hand and just managed to snatch at Erin's right wrist as she scrabbled at the boards that were collapsing all around her. One of the planks sprung upwards as it snapped and caught her on the side of the head. She groaned, but I felt her fingers clutching at my arm and then our hands were locked together.

I heard the clatter of timber bouncing off the industrial machinery twenty feet below us. I knew that if I let go of Erin's hand, she would almost certainly die. At the same time I could feel her skin was damp with sweat, and difficult to grip. Her entire body weight was pulling against me. I needed to anchor myself and try to hold her with both hands: only then would I be able to lift her clear.

We were both gasping from the effort, the fear, and I didn't register anything else until someone came stomping past and knelt down next to me. It was Nathan. He didn't even glance in my direction as he took hold of Erin's left hand. Whatever my feelings for the man, in that moment I was jubilant.

Together we would save her.

Then I registered that Erin looked more terrified than ever; her face contorted, her body bucking and writhing, and I felt her hand slipping from my grasp...

* * *

He's done it on purpose: grabbed her left hand in both of his, and while he appears to be trying to pull her to safety, Nathan is actually putting more effort into squeezing her injured fingers. It's just like it was at the hospital. On the surface he oozes concern, but there's a nasty glint in his eyes that only Erin can see.

This searing agony is even more urgent than the mortal danger she's in. But rather than scream, Erin clenches her teeth and lets out a growl that expresses not just her pain but her fury. Her determination.

She can't break free of Nathan, so she has no choice but to endure it. Her other hand is slipping, and with a terrible clarity she sees how this will play out.

Once it's only Nathan holding her, he'll be able to let go and claim he tried his best, but it wasn't enough to save her.

* * *

I'd nearly lost her when I realised what was going on. Nathan was crushing Erin's left hand – the one he'd shut in a door. Under the guise of coming to her aid, he had the perfect opportunity to finish her off. Punish her for daring to fall in love with me.

I grabbed the edge of the hole with my left hand and levered myself forward, got up on my knees and then clamped my left hand around her upper arm, taking her weight for a second while I got a better grip with my right hand. Now I was able to lift her slightly, whereupon she switched her attention to me, and with a tortured shriek she wrenched her left hand free of Nathan's grasp.

Now other people were rushing over, including Jax, who pushed Nathan aside and took Erin's left arm. Between us, we were able to drag her out, and she collapsed on the floor; still wracked with pain, but safe.

I suppose I felt relief, but it seemed a low priority. As I straightened up, I noticed a splash of blood where the masonry had cut my leg. It was a shard of brick, with one edge as sharp as a knife. I snatched it up.

Nathan was still kneeling, focused on Erin and gently calling her name. Surrounded by an audience, he had little choice but to play the role of caring husband.

I threw myself forward, butting him in the face and shoving him down on his back, then quickly sat astride him, pinning his arms with my knees.

'You did that on purpose. You knew she couldn't grip with her left hand.'

Nathan seemed too disorientated to speak. There was blood running from his nose. Around us, the crowd had pulled back in alarm, except for Jax, who was crouched beside Erin.

I looked over my shoulder and glared at those closest to me. 'If any of you want to film this, go ahead. We're gonna get some truth at last.'

'Fucking lunatic,' Nathan muttered, trying to wriggle free. 'Let me go.'

'Not till you admit what you've done.' I put the shard of masonry to his neck, and he lay still. 'We'll start with the thugs you hired to abduct me and hold me prisoner.' I made sure there were plenty of people listening before I added, 'And we'll come to what else those thugs did for you in a minute.'

Nathan glared at me but said nothing. I glanced round again. Jax was helping Erin to sit up. She gave me a weak smile, which vanished when she saw what I was doing.

'Harry...'

'It's okay,' I said. 'Did Nathan set this up to happen?'

'No. He...' She stared at the hole in confusion. 'When I came in, the mattresses were over the hole.'

There were gasps at that, and several people muttered in agreement.

'Did you have them moved?' I asked Nathan.

"Course I bloody didn't.'

I decided not to press it. I knew I might have only a limited opportunity to get answers, and there was a lot more to cover.

'What about when Freddie fell?'

'Oh, Christ, this again? You might as well just cut my throat.'

The fact that Nathan would goad me like this meant he didn't believe I was capable of carrying through on my threat. There was only one way to prove him wrong.

I lifted the shard of masonry and whipped it lightly across his brow. The skin opened like a zip, the blood flowing across his face as he cried out and twisted his head from side to side. A ripple of horror ran through the crowd, which I suppose was understandable. They didn't yet know what I knew about this man.

'Tell me,' I snarled, putting the shard back at his neck.

'I took the piss out of him, that's all. Cocky little student who'd come to my party chasing skirt, then acted like a brat when she wasn't interested. He had the cheek to turn me down when I offered him a chance to sell weed at his sixth form. All right, I thought, let's see how tough you look when you're crashing through the ceiling.'

'You *wanted* it to happen? You pressured him to go on the boards without knowing whether he could survive a fall?'

'I didn't think he'd get badly hurt. Maybe a busted ankle at worst.' His gaze shifted towards Jax. 'Other kids had gone through before. It's all part of the thrill.'

'Is it now?' I studied the faces around me. 'And none of you said a word to the police?'

There was a sombre, embarrassed silence. Then, from within the crowd, someone piped up: 'He told us not to.'

'Nathan?'

Several people nodded. I turned back to him. 'What about the mattresses? If they were there for this other kid, why not for Freddie?'

'I don't know, I swear.'

'But you didn't think to check?'

'It was a piss-up, remember? I had no reason to think they'd been moved.' Nathan tried to gesture towards the crowd, his hand flapping limply where it was pinned beneath my legs. 'They'll tell you, I was gutted when I came down and saw he'd fallen to the floor below.'

More nodding, including from Jax, who at this point I was inclined to trust.

'So who?' My question emerged as a cry. 'Who moved them?'

Nathan shook his head. He looked a dreadful sight, with trails of blood running across his face.

'I don't know. That's the God's honest truth.'

I looked around in despair, conscious that what I'd learned wasn't nearly enough to justify the ruptures in my private life, the pain I'd caused to others and brought upon myself. The consequences that would inevitably stem from my actions tonight.

'Anyone?' I asked, my voice gone shaky with desperation. 'Does anyone know?'

Erin was slowly shaking her head. From Jax, there was only a shrug, as with the other young people gathered here: shrugs and blank looks. It seemed utterly hopeless until the thin, pale figure of Ash emerged from the shadows and shyly took centre stage.

'It was Louis,' he said.

68

This is another Harry she's seeing. The one who evidently hadn't been joking when he talked about revenge. And even while Erin is aware that she owes him her life, she isn't sure she likes how he resorted to violence in his bid to force Nathan to talk.

Erin herself is dazed, hurt, scared, but grateful to be alive. The only serious injury seems to be to her right ankle, which produces a sickening sensation whenever she tries to move it. Given what she's just heard, even that now seems insignificant.

'Louis?' Harry repeats. He's staring at Ash, who looks intensely awkward at being the centre of attention.

'I saw him go downstairs when your boy went on the boards. Everyone else was watching Freddie. After he fell, we all ran down there. Louis just became part of the crowd.'

Harry is lost for words, his gaze full of wretched confusion. The fact that he still has Nathan pinned to the floor seems irrelevant. 'I don't understand.'

Neither does Erin. She rises slowly, teeth gritted, and crawls towards Ash, not wanting to spook him, but determined to grab him if his nerve fails. He can't be allowed to leave until this has played out.

'I know I should have said something.' Ash looks to be on the brink of tears. 'But if I had, he'd have killed me.'

Harry is sceptical. 'A little runt like Louis?'

'A little runt who ran away from a children's home because he'd stabbed another kid.' Ash gestures at the crowd. 'I'm not the only one who knew what Louis was like. I got word he was looking for me, because he thought I'd ratted him out.'

Many of the others are nodding, including a regretful-looking Jax. *It was our questions that had alerted Louis*, Erin thinks. *Our pressure that nearly got Ash killed.*

'All right.' Harry swallows heavily. 'But what would have prompted Louis to remove the mattresses?'

'You can't apply logic to Louis. He'd just get some crazy idea in his head, and see it through. Sometimes it was hilarious, other times it was...'

'Insane,' someone mutters, but then Jax speaks up.

'He was jealous of Freddie. On that night, I mean. He heard Nathan making the offer to supply the college, and it pissed him off.'

Harry returns his attention to Nathan. 'Did you know this?'

'Louis was... He'd been pushing for a larger role. I'd told him... all in good time.'

'Which was a lie,' Jax cut in. 'Because you didn't need him any more. Him, or any of us.'

'I didn't know that then,' Nathan snaps, peevishly.

'Bullshit!' Erin cries. She finds a new confidence as she absorbs his hate-filled glare and realises that their relationship, finally, is ended. She will not be spending another night with Nathan. 'Are you going to explain why you had Louis killed?'

There are gasps from the crowd. Nathan tries to look scathing. 'Total bollocks—'

'It's not.' Harry looks ready to cut him again. 'You used the same thugs that abducted me.'

'In a dark blue van?' This is from Ash. When Harry nods, the pale young man seems to grow in stature, regarding Nathan with undisguised contempt. 'I've got it on film,' he says. 'When it came past the Tannery.'

* * *

I felt Nathan flinch beneath me. He looked pathetically afraid, and that was because the entire crowd had picked up on his reaction.

'He deserves to die,' someone called out.

'No. He deserves to rot in prison.' I turned to Ash. 'Are you willing to supply this video to the police?'

After a heart-stopping moment, Ash nodded. Then Jax listened to someone muttering in his ear, and said, 'We've called 999. Police and ambulance.'

'There's no fucking need,' Nathan muttered, but his objection had a half-hearted quality.

A young woman I didn't know approached us and looked about to spit on Nathan. 'You're a bully, and you deserve everything you're gonna get.'

'That's right,' I agreed, raising my voice as I climbed off Nathan, confident now that he wouldn't be fighting back. 'But it'll require your help,' I told them all. 'This time round, you have to be willing to give the police the full story.'

The girl nodded solemnly. 'We will. And we're sorry.'

Jax echoed her statement. I asked him to keep an eye on Nathan, then moved across to Erin, who was trying to stand up. I gave her some support, and someone found a rusted section of pipe that she could use as a makeshift crutch.

'See?' she said. 'Probably just a sprain.'

'Look, Erin. I realise you did this for me, and without it we might not have got answers. But even so...'

'I saw it as a calc... a calculated risk.' Her voice was still slurred, but clearer than it had been. 'The mattresses were here when I came in, honestly.'

'Nathan denied moving them, so someone else—'

'I have my suspicions.' Her eyes flashed a warning. 'I think the same person got me drunk on purpose.' Then she pointed to a sorry-looking Nathan. 'Let's take this as a victory, eh?'

I started to agree but my words were drowned out by a rumble of thunder. It sounded close by, though I'd seen no lightning. As the sound faded, I heard sirens and couldn't help sighing at the thought of what was to come.

After embracing her, I returned my attention to Ash. He was scrolling and tapping on his phone. Footage of the van represented a vital step forward, but Ash, as he came to stand beside me, looked acutely uncomfortable.

'I-I'm s-so sorry...'

It was a mystifying way to start, but before I could query it there was a sudden commotion. Nathan had leapt up and was trying to barge his way through the crowd. A few people tried to grab him, but desperation made him quick and brutal. He pushed and punched and shoved; one girl went down heavily, with a piercing scream, and I felt a suffocating dread at the idea that he would get away...

Fortunately, Erin had other ideas.

69

The sight of Nathan lashing out is more than Erin can bear. It releases a fury that has been building up, both consciously and unconsciously, ever since that first night when he threatened her for supposedly flirting with a barman.

The ankle injury has robbed her of speed and agility. Her head is spinning; she still feels drunk, probably still sounds drunk, but that doesn't matter. What she has in her favour is determination.

'*You raped me.*'

The words come out loud and clear, despite the cries from the partygoers. Despite the music playing on the floor above. They all hear it, because Erin's is the voice of a woman who has had enough.

And Nathan responds. He can't help himself.

'That's a fucking lie!' he shouts. And with that, his fate is sealed.

Closest to him is a man Erin has never seen before. He's tall and wide and maybe a bit older than the others. He's in a steaming temper himself (as Erin will later discover) because the woman Nathan has just knocked to the ground is his girlfriend. That second when Nathan insists on getting the last word is used to draw back a huge fist and ram it into Nathan's stomach, felling him as effectively as a bullet.

By now Harry has reacted, too, taking Erin's arm as she stumbles towards Nathan. Not to restrain her, as she thinks at first, but to support her. Nathan has drawn up his knees and he's writhing in pain, his eyes shut. But that's fine; Erin doesn't need him to see her. He just has to listen.

'You raped me, Nathan. You know that's what it was. Time and time again. And just in the past week, you've pinned me down on the floor and cut off my hair. You've deliberately slammed a door on my hand. Those charges need to be added to all the others. And I intend to make sure that they are.'

* * *

I was so proud of her, I could have applauded. Nathan was whimpering and groaning from the blow he'd taken. He kept his eyes closed, which I took as a mark of the man's cowardice. Then another mighty crack of thunder rendered us all speechless. It was accompanied by an instant downpour, the rain rattling on the windows like handfuls of gravel.

Now Ash was back at my side, with Jax hovering anxiously behind him. I registered their expressions and felt a sudden chill along my spine.

'What?' I asked. Erin caught my tone and turned towards me.

'I made a mess of everything,' Ash said forlornly. 'That note – I genuinely meant it as a warning.'

I frowned, remembering the line that had so incensed me: *Freddie died happy.* Before I could respond, Ash continued: 'Y-you have to understand how scared I was. Of Louis, I mean. It's why I couldn't...'

As he tailed off, Jax said, 'Just show him.'

Nodding, Ash lifted the phone in one trembling hand and fumbled with the screen until a video began to play. The image was dark and blurred from rapid movement, the sound a tinny representation of the kind of music still playing on the floor above us.

'Is that—?' Erin asked, leaning in to look.

And then she recoiled, while I froze in place, unable to believe what I was seeing.

Freddie.

* * *

It was the night of the party, I knew that at once. So did Erin, who plucked at my sleeve. 'Harry, don't watch it.'

'I have to.' I could barely say the words, my throat was so constricted.

On screen, the picture juddered as the zoom function was deployed. Now Freddie was easier to see, out there on the planks, drunkenly cavorting while around him the revellers watched and chanted, counting the seconds clearly enough to be heard:

'Seventeen! Eighteen! Nineteen!'

Freddie's body jerked, and he peered down, slightly confused. I guessed that one of the planks had cracked. After a moment he dismissed it and looked up, grinning defiantly at someone off camera. He muttered something but I couldn't make it out. From his eyes I could tell he was quite drunk.

Then the camera swooped to Freddie's left, where it came to rest on Nathan Webb, his arm round a young woman's shoulders, both of them nodding vaguely in time to the count. Freddie's words had obviously been directed at Nathan, whose eyes narrowed in contemplation before he half turned to the girl and said, 'Maybe he's not a pussy.'

I wasn't sure that I heard the words so much as lipread them. When the camera returned to Freddie, the count had reached twenty-three... twenty-four... and there was a grisly splintering sound. Again Erin clutched at my arm. 'Harry, please. Don't do this to yourself.'

But to her credit, she seemed to recognise that I couldn't turn away. I owed this to Freddie, after everything I had done to get the truth.

On screen, some of the crowd were growing concerned. A young man I didn't recognise shouted, 'Gonna bust through.' The woman next to him called to Freddie: 'Come off now.'

But Freddie ignored them. The camera swung round to Nathan, whose gaze had a downward slant. Studying the boards.

He gave a couple of sardonic hand claps. 'Well done, kid. Off you get.'

'No, no,' I heard my son resist, and the camera swerved back in time to catch that quintessentially Freddie Manning smile.

'I'm gonna fly!' he declared – and I understood that for one fleeting instant it was true. Suspended in mid-air, Freddie would have experienced a sense of weightlessness and perhaps been able to believe that superheroes were real; that he had defied his father's wisdom and grown up to achieve what I had once assured him was impossible.

But of course he wasn't a superhero.

He didn't fly.

He fell.

* * *

There was a hideously loud crack, and the images on screen were reduced to a crazy swirl of party lights, the music drowned out by shouts and screams. Some drunken laughter ended abruptly when the terrible crash of the second impact cut through, and the partygoers understood that the mattresses hadn't broken his fall the way they must have expected.

Then darkness. Silence. Back here in the present, I looked up at Ash and saw a tear trickling down his cheek.

'I haven't edited it. I just couldn't... couldn't go on filming.'

'We're really sorry,' Jax said. 'I didn't even know this existed until tonight. But I told Ash he needed to show you. So it's my fault, if you...'

I shook my head. Despite the pain in my heart, I gave them what I hoped was a genuine smile.

'I'm glad you showed me. And it's nobody's fault.'

Erin's hand slipped around my waist, and in turning to her I saw the first police officers appear at the top of the stairs. I felt suddenly woozy, and wondered in a distracted way if I was about to faint.

'Nobody's fault,' I repeated, as the greater truth of that statement hit me like a sledgehammer.

Not even Nathan's.

EVER AFTER

70

When the day came, I was awake early but gave no thought to a morning swim. I was far too preoccupied by what lay ahead.

Besides, it was now late September and seemed to have been raining for weeks. The sea had become a baleful churning creature, best avoided.

I regarded today's event as quite a formal occasion, though I had no real idea what to expect. In the end I opted for jeans and a tailored jacket. I wasn't hungry, but I'd eaten toast and somehow managed to keep it down.

A sudden heavy shower ceased just as I was about to call a taxi, so I walked instead. It had become a familiar route, these past few weeks, from my home to Erin's, from hers to mine; and perhaps it wasn't too great an exaggeration to say that our lives had been transformed since the night of the final party.

At the time, the arrival of the police had been something of an anti-climax. A total of four uniformed officers had appeared, and initially they seemed bemused by the scale of the accusations being made against a prominent local businessman. Rather than the drunken dispute they might have expected to find at a late-night party, they were hearing allegations of murder and abduction, domestic abuse and torture, drug dealing and obstruction of justice.

As a result – and despite my best efforts at the time – Nathan Webb wasn't arrested and marched out of the Tannery in handcuffs. Far from it. Once they'd absorbed my passionate overview, the police officers split us up and spoke quietly to Nathan, Erin, Ash and others. While these discussions were in progress, the music was switched off and most of the partygoers, after giving their names and addresses to the police, were permitted to leave.

An ambulance arrived, and Erin, Nathan and I were all checked over. A paramedic determined that Erin's ankle was probably just a bad sprain, but should be X-rayed to make certain. I asked to accompany her to the hospital, and fortunately by then one of the officers had spoken to DC Leung and it was agreed that Erin and I could provide our statements on the following day.

The storm continued to rage overhead, but I was glad of the cold stinging rain as the paramedic and I helped Erin over the rough ground towards the ambulance. It made me feel more connected to the world, penetrating the numbness which had settled on me over the past hour or so.

For months I had been convinced that if I could get to the truth about what happened to Freddie, then justice would be done and seen to be done. With that, I would have the sense of closure, the peace of mind I so desperately needed. But of course the reality had turned out to be messy, complicated and confusing – as reality so often was.

* * *

At the hospital a minor miracle occurred: within little more than thirty minutes Erin had her ankle X-rayed and a fracture was ruled out. Before I knew it we were in a taxi back to my home, where we collapsed into bed and slept for six or seven hours.

I'll never forget that moment on Sunday morning when I snapped awake and saw Erin lying beside me, watching me with a wry smile. She reached out and caressed my cheek, and I had a sudden profound realisation that a new stage in my life was just beginning.

We held each other and talked and made love, an experience so sublime that we might have spent the entire day in bed – had I not received a call from DC Leung, asking to visit us later that morning. 'I think you're going to welcome what I have to say.'

I relayed this message to Erin, who earlier had chided me for being pessimistic when I predicted that Nathan would somehow talk himself out of trouble. She wasn't so sure he could call in favours or strongarm anyone in this instance, and so it proved. DC Leung, when she arrived, informed us that urgent enquiries had been made into the van which Ash had caught on camera.

'It had false plates, or rather the plate came from a different vehicle.' Raising a hand to forestall our obvious question – *Wasn't this a dead end?* – DC Leung said, 'These men assumed that using stolen plates would cover their tracks, but once we had the registration number, we were able to track back and locate the vehicle the plates were taken from. It was at the Lakeside shopping centre, in Thurrock – and CCTV in the area picked up their van *before* the plates were swapped.'

'Meaning you got the genuine registration number?' I asked.

'Correct.' Leung confided that the registered keeper of the vehicle was well known to the Metropolitan Police. 'He has an equally well-known associate, and both individuals are visible on camera in the car park, stealing the plate and fixing it to their van.'

She assured us that arrests were imminent. Better still, some background research had indicated that the father of the van's owner had been a close friend of Pierson Webb. 'A strong indication that we're on the right track,' as Leung put it.

The events of the following week made that comment seem like an understatement.

71

Erin is in her office when he arrives. It's not the room Nathan designated for that purpose: she didn't feel comfortable in there, so she set up her own work-space in one of the spare bedrooms. The single bed has become home to all the files and folders that have occupied so much of her time in recent weeks.

Harry lets himself in with the key she'd given him, and as they embrace, he says, 'I don't think I'll ever get used to just swanning in here.'

'Hopefully you won't have to for much longer.'

He looks slightly confused, before cracking a smile. 'You're gonna dump me?'

'As if.' She nudges him, playfully. 'Nathan's agreed to put this place on the market.'

'Wow, I like that explanation much better. I never thought he'd go for it.'

'He wants the best lawyers money can buy. Which is a waste of time, if what DC Leung tells us is true. But I'm not gonna stop him blowing his share of the equity, especially when it means I can move to a home of my own.'

She asks if he'll make coffee while she finishes up in the office. In truth there's no particular urgency, but she's immersed herself in paperwork to stave off the nerves. This is a big day, in all sorts of ways, and she wants to avoid dwelling on it until the last possible moment.

The aftermath of that Saturday night was even more dramatic for Erin than for Harry. While he was understandably floored by what Ash's video revealed, Erin had long feared that Harry wouldn't get the neat, clear-cut explanation he had been seeking. But if Nathan was no longer in the frame for Freddie's death, he was now exposed to a host of other charges.

As such, it came as a terrible shock to see her husband stride out of the Tannery without so much as a glance in her direction. Erin was receiving medical treatment at the time, with Harry by her side. Nathan looked pale and shaken, and Erin knew him well enough to see how much effort he was devoting to staying calm. He couldn't afford any kind of outburst in front of the police.

Harry had insisted she come back to his house, and in fact she ended up staying for the best part of a fortnight, by which time Nathan had been taken into custody, charged with multiple offences and denied bail on the grounds that he was both a flight risk and liable to intimidate witnesses.

It took Nathan slightly longer to appreciate just how dire a predicament he was in. His final few days of liberty were spent ensconced in meetings, trying to salvage the Tannery development. Erin later found out that Nathan had been told, unequivocally, that the project was doomed for as long as he was at the helm. Nobody would risk the bad publicity of a close association with a man accused of abduction and murder.

But at the same time, nobody wanted to see the project fall apart. It was up to Nathan to opt for the very obvious solution.

With one of his legal team acting as go-between, they thrashed out a deal that saw Erin become managing director of a brand-new company, Chyngton Estates, which would work with the local authority on the site development. Nathan was permitted to retain a small shareholding, albeit in the name of a shell company to better obscure his involvement.

It was agreed that he would be supplied with progress reports, but have no actual part in the decision-making. That meant he could only stew with frustration when Erin immediately set about making changes. Her main proposal was to reduce the scope of the build to allow more green space, while also altering the balance of accommodation to include far more genuinely affordable properties. This met with some resistance from Nathan's cronies, but it had the welcome effort of transforming the council's attitude towards what had become a political hot potato.

'At least this way it goes ahead,' she reminded her new colleagues during a tempestuous summit meeting. 'Would you prefer it to be delayed indefinitely, or cancelled altogether?'

With the support of Nathan's lawyer, who'd turned out to be a reasonably straight guy, a revised scheme was presented to the planners and promptly approved. 'Demolish the old building, get the diggers in, and everyone can forget about the unpleasantness,' the lawyer had said, adding with a snort: 'At least until the trial.'

That remains a long way off, given the parlous state of the justice system. She's been warned to expect a delay of at least a year, and possibly more. Perhaps before that, there will be a trial for Dane Marshall, the wasp who, it turned out, had sneaked downstairs and removed the mattresses when Erin began to dance.

Dane was implicated by his girlfriend, who claimed not to have realised in time what he was doing. Dane himself stuck to 'No comment' throughout his interview, and Erin suspects no one will ever know why he did it. She's also been warned that, in view of the complicated circumstances, he might not get more than a year in prison for an act that could have led to her death.

Now she checks the time. It's almost ten o'clock, and they have to be there for eleven. She joins Harry in the kitchen, accepts a coffee and slurps it, spilling a few drops. Harry takes the mug from her as she wipes her mouth.

'Nervous?' he asks.

'A bit jittery.'

'Me too. But it'll be fine.'

'Yeah, I know. Anyway, this is nothing compared to when I'll have to give evidence in court.'

Now she's made Harry look as grim as she feels. 'One day at a time,' he reminds her, mixing sternness with a smile.

'Absolutely. God, it'll be so nice when today is finally done with. I've been thinking, maybe we should try to go away somewhere?'

Harry nods. 'Funny you should say that. I have a little surprise for you.'

'Oh. I have a surprise for you, too.'

'Okay.' He's blushing, the first time she's seen that in a while. 'Would you like to go first?'

'Mine's for later,' Erin says. 'But tell me yours – anything to help distract me!'

Harry now looks slightly uncertain, making Erin regret having mentioned a surprise of her own.

'A holiday,' he says. 'Two weeks in South America. Machu Picchu included.'

72

Erin seemed genuinely thrilled by the idea of us going away together, though she still wouldn't reveal her own surprise. And she was worried about Anita and Gareth: 'Won't this be rubbing their noses in it, when they cancelled their own trip?'

'They've rescheduled for next year, and they're fine with us going. I checked with them before I booked it.'

We walked down to the site. The day was dull, cold and blustery, but the rain was holding off. In Barkers Way a large section of the boundary fence had been removed, making the whole area seem much more spacious. We had hired a security firm to work alongside the demolition crew, and a couple of them were stewarding the invited guests towards a large marquee on the westernmost point of the site.

Another half dozen personnel were busy with crowd control, marshalling what seemed like a couple of hundred local people to a safe vantage point on the far side of the road, behind a long stretch of plastic barriers. I scanned the crowd as we passed, idly wondering if I might spot Len Bowden. I hadn't seen him since the night of Erin's fall, and the word among local anglers was that he'd upped and left town without a word to anyone.

If I did set eyes on him, I wasn't sure what I would say. He was a man I'd previously looked up to, without ever quite analysing why. On reflection, I didn't think he'd wittingly played a part in Louis's capture – and his reluctance to pass judgement on Nathan was understandable, if not entirely forgivable. Just more of that messy, complicated reality.

The media were out in force: I counted three TV crews and perhaps a dozen photographers. In addition, we had the specialist drone operators who would capture aerial footage of the demolition.

In the marquee, catering staff were serving champagne and canapés. Erin was conducting a brief inspection when the first dignitaries began to arrive. She saw it as her role to greet each of them personally, so I stood just behind her like a monarch's rather hapless consort, exchanging my own slightly awkward greetings. It wasn't easy to bury my natural antipathy towards these local 'worthies' whose loyalty might still lie with Nathan Webb.

If I was gutted that, ultimately, Nathan would face no charges in connection with Freddie's death, there was the very significant consolation that his downfall had come about as a result of my abduction.

The two men with the van had been interviewed under caution and initially gave 'no comment' responses. But while they had tried to protect their identities by using burner phones, for some reason they had kept one of them. The phone records guided the police to a farm near Biggin Hill, where they found a barn in which a makeshift cell had recently been dismantled. The barn was full of the men's DNA, and they found tiny bloodstains on the floor that matched with my own DNA.

Then a forensic specialist managed to recover dozens of deleted texts from the phone, including many to another burner phone that seemed to reside in the same part of town as Nathan Webb. When presented with this evidence, one of the men instantly saw the benefit in being first to come clean. He went on record that Nathan had been the mastermind behind both my abduction and the murder of Louis Smith.

And with that, Nathan Webb was finished. A life sentence on those two charges, without a doubt, never mind the drug dealing or the violence he'd meted out to Erin. She'd been more than willing to testify to all of that, but both DC Leung and I had persuaded her that she shouldn't put herself through the ordeal of cross-examination on such personal matters. Her satisfaction would come from providing witness evidence of Louis's murder.

It was a severe disappointment that Theresa Webb would face no charges. There simply wasn't a viable case against her. But we took consolation from the knowledge that she was devastated by her son's arrest, and by her own loss of status in the town. She'd put her house on the market the day Nathan was charged, though a recent cliff fall had swallowed a large chunk of her garden, and to date nobody had shown any interest in buying a property that was destined to end up in the sea.

Good riddance if Theresa goes with it, I thought.

* * *

It's a strange feeling, Erin thinks, but nowhere near as nerve wracking as she anticipated. For the past few weeks she's become accustomed to thinking she was merely playing the role of a businesswoman, a developer. It isn't until she gets here, and finds the nerves dissipating as she smiles and shakes hands and checks on the current arrangements, that she understands that while this may indeed be a role, it certainly isn't playacting.

It doesn't even bother her when she notices how many of the VIP guests are checking out Harry. Nobody who saw them together could fail to spot that they were a couple – which, in Erin's opinion, is a good thing. She has no reason to conceal the truth; not when most of the people present know exactly how Nathan treated her.

All that's forgotten when the genuinely "Very Important" guests arrive, in the form of Milly and the Ryans. Erin's still worried about how her sister might react to the noise, but Gordon has assured her that he'll whisk Milly away at the first sign of agitation.

Erin receives a heartfelt embrace from Barbara. Three weeks into a course of chemotherapy, she's looking remarkably well. Erin has made it clear she'll fund private treatment, but Barbara says the NHS has been wonderful.

'So far, at least. Though perhaps if that ever changes... I'll take up your offer.'

Harry's children and their partners are absent today, but he doesn't seem overly concerned. Erin has already met them, and detected no overt hostility. In just over a week they're due to attend Jody's twenty-fifth birthday party and stay over in Devizes. That, she suspects, might be a slightly more daunting test of the new reality, but she is determined not to worry about it.

She thinks she has said hello to almost everyone, but there's a significant omission. Just as she nudges Harry to get his attention and ask where they are, she spots Anita hurrying towards them with Gareth in tow, his tie askew, jacket hanging unevenly on his shoulders. 'Mix-up over the time,' Anita says, with an expressive eye roll.

'Entirely my fault,' Gareth agrees. Erin catches him winking at Harry.

After the initial greetings, Erin has a brief whispered conversation with Anita that clearly gets Harry's radar twitching. It feels a little mean, so Erin beckons him over and together they withdraw to a quiet corner of the marquee.

'So,' she says. 'My surprise, in a sense, is right here.'

He looks around, frowning. 'I'm clueless.'

'The development. There's a whole load of details still to work out, but basically I've been talking to Anita about her idea for a way of commemorating Freddie.'

'Like a bursary or something?'

'Yeah. So basically we're gonna set up a charity, with the four of us as trustees.' She nods at Anita and Gareth, who are standing at a discreet distance, carefully observing Harry's reaction. 'A percentage of the profits from Tannery Heights will go into a fund, to use for helping young people in the town. I haven't fixed on an exact percentage yet, but I think it should be a minimum of four million, don't you?'

Harry only gulps, his eyes as wide as a character in a cartoon. Before he can respond, she spots someone trying to catch her attention.

'That's Brian. Looks like they're all set.'

Harry is still flabbergasted. 'Erin, I don't know what to say.'

They kiss, and then Harry turns, misty-eyed, and embraces his ex-wife, while Gareth slaps him on the back.

'Neet only told me this morning,' he says. 'Bloody brilliant idea they cooked up between 'em!'

'It is,' Harry agrees, turning back to Erin as Brian Sparrow approaches.

The demolition project manager is a tall man in his late thirties, his prematurely bald head encased in a protective helmet, walkie talkie gripped in one hand. Greeting Erin, he says, 'Final checks are done, so on your say-so...'

Erin glances at Harry. He takes her hand, squeezes it, and whispers, 'I love you.'

'I love you,' Erin replies, then nods at Brian. 'Let's do it.'

73

I was moved beyond words by Erin's proposal, as well as touched and frankly astonished that she and Anita had dreamt this up between them, and I hadn't had a clue. The knowledge of this endowment – the fact that the coming development would now do some good in the world – transformed my perspective on today's demolition.

Because although I hadn't said so, in truth I had been dreading it, for reasons I could never have expressed to Erin, and barely understood myself. Now, unashamed of my emotional reaction, I wiped my eyes and took my place beside Erin on the viewing platform in front of the marquee.

An expectant hush descended as Brian Sparrow strode up to the safety fence, the walkie talkie clamped to his ear. Erin seemed to give a little shudder, bumping her hip against mine. For a second I flashed back to her fall, and my breath caught in my throat, thinking about how narrowly she'd survived.

Everyone present had been supplied with safety goggles and FFP3 dust masks. After we'd put them on, the demolition manager made eye contact with Erin, then with me, and he nodded.

The actual detonation was surprisingly muted, a sound like distant fireworks, along with an eerie subterranean whump as the implosion was brought about by a simultaneous destruction of the building's foundations, designed to bring the structure down within its own footprint.

A tiny puff of smoke drifted languidly from a broken window on the ground floor. At the same time a kind of shiver passed through the Tannery, not unlike the one I'd caught from Erin a few moments ago. The bricks seemed to ripple, as if something behind them was probing for weak spots, in a bid to escape.

It was an extraordinary sight as the building folded in on itself, graciously, like some magnificent beast preparing for slumber. I could tell it was going to look even more spectacular in the ultra-slow-motion footage, where we would see how each individual brick, liberated from the whole, appeared to hang in the air for a moment before accepting its destiny and dropping to the pile below.

The final stage was the loudest: the tonnes of rubble landing with a terrific crash that shook the ground beneath us. A cloud of dust rose above it and began to spread in all directions; even before it reached us I realised my eyes were watering.

Erin leaned in to me, and I put my arm around her. Like me, she was in tears. So was Anita, while Gareth kept wiping his nose with the back of his hand. I daresay that we had all resolved not to get upset, but the parallels between Freddie's accident and the building's demolition were impossible to ignore.

Freddie's accident. That was how I had begun to think of it, now that we had a more complete picture.

I'd spoken to Ash a couple of times since then, and thanked him for his courage in making a statement to the police. I also asked about that day in the Tannery when he'd been hiding from me, and had dropped a piece of masonry through the hole. Had that been to alert me to what had gone on there?

Ash had looked embarrassed. 'I was just trying to get back to my hiding place when I accidentally kicked it.'

So it hadn't been a clue at all: a useful reminder that not everything in life was meaningful, or neatly signposted. If only I'd appreciated that fact a few weeks ago, instead of charging headlong into a quest to prove Nathan guilty of murder...

Then what? I wondered. Would Louis still be alive? Would Erin still be trapped in an abusive marriage? The only thing I could say for sure was that she and I probably would never have spoken – beyond that first chance encounter on the beach – and of course I wouldn't have known the truth.

Freddie wasn't a murder victim. The verdict of misadventure was, on balance, the correct one.

A welcome wind off the sea was rapidly dispersing the dust. The caterers were moving among us, bearing trays of champagne. I felt a sudden reluctance to participate, a familiar cussedness that both Erin and Anita would meet with short shrift, so I fought it off and accepted a glass and did my best to return Erin's smile.

'Okay?' she asked, and I nodded firmly. I could sense Anita listening for my answer, and she would immediately pick up on any false note.

'I'm okay.'

And I told myself: *I am okay*. With the Tannery gone forever, heralding the birth of a charity that would honour his memory, our beloved son Freddie, our superhero, had another chance. Another shot at immortality.

From today, the falling boy would fall no more, but only fly: here in my mind, in my heart; here in the hearts of everyone who loved him and everyone whose lives he had enriched.

'To the future,' I murmured, and we shared a gentle clink of glasses, a soft collision of souls: Anita, Gareth, Erin and Freddie and me.

* * *

MORE FROM TOM BALE

Sins of the Father, another brutal and breathtaking thriller from Tom Bale, is available to order now here:

https://mybook.to/SinsOfFatherBackAd

ACKNOWLEDGEMENTS

After a turbulent few years, it's an enormous pleasure to find a safe haven at Boldwood. As such, I'm very grateful to Victoria Britton for pouncing so quickly to acquire *Deadly Games* – and then for blowing my mind by wanting lots more books from me. Thanks also to Amanda Ridout and the whole team at Boldwood for making me so welcome.

Thanks as ever to my family and friends, including some valuable first readers – on this occasion a shout-out is due to Gary and Debbie, Steve and Sharon and Lou and Tricky. Thanks to Jackson Keeler, who kept my writing ambitions alive throughout a troubled project that might yet see the light of day. Much love and appreciation to Emily, James and Lizzie – and of course to Theo and Arthur, who fill my life with joy. Most of all, to Niki, my ever supportive co-pilot for whom the above-mentioned turbulence has become less an occasional hazard and more a way of life!

ABOUT THE AUTHOR

Tom Bale was born in Brighton in 1966. After working a variety of jobs, including a career in the insurance industry and as a househusband, his publishing breakthrough came in 2006. Tom has now been a full-time writer for more than fifteen years.

Download your exclusive bonus content from Tom Bale here:

Follow Tom Bale on social media here:

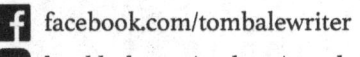

facebook.com/tombalewriter

bookbub.com/authors/tom-bale

ALSO BY TOM BALE

Deadly Games

Sins of the Father

THE *Murder* LIST

THE MURDER LIST IS A NEWSLETTER DEDICATED TO SPINE-CHILLING FICTION AND GRIPPING PAGE-TURNERS!

SIGN UP TO MAKE SURE YOU'RE ON OUR HIT LIST FOR EXCLUSIVE DEALS, AUTHOR CONTENT, AND COMPETITIONS.

SIGN UP TO OUR NEWSLETTER

BIT.LY/THEMURDERLISTNEWS

Boldwood

Boldwood Books is an award-winning fiction publishing company seeking out the best stories from around the world.

Find out more at www.boldwoodbooks.com

Join our reader community for brilliant books, competitions and offers!

Follow us
@BoldwoodBooks
@TheBoldBookClub

Sign up to our weekly deals newsletter

https://bit.ly/BoldwoodBNewsletter

www.ingramcontent.com/pod-product-compliance
Lightning Source LLC
Chambersburg PA
CBHW011759010726
47497CB00012B/3200